DARK CHILDREN

THE CHRONICLES OF FREYLAR

- VOLUME 6 -

by

Liam W H Young

First edition printing, 2023

ISBN 978-1-80352-554-9

A catalogue copy of this book is available from the
British Library.

Printed and bound in the United Kingdom by Biddles.

www.thechroniclesoffreylar.com

ACKNOWLEDGEMENTS

Foremost, I would like to thank the series' resident artist Hardy Fowler, as always, for the superb cover art illustration for this book. Hardy continues to be an absolute pleasure to work with, and really understands my vision for the world of Freylar.

I would like to thank Matthew Webster, once again, for his enormous contribution to this book and the series as a whole. Not only is Matt a long-standing friend and series editor, but also an amazing sounding board for this ongoing project. I am extremely fortunate to have him along for the ride.

Lastly, special thanks goes to Tibor Mórocz for proofreading this book. His keen perception continues to challenge me, giving me the impetus I need to complete my storytelling – the whetstone of my sword.

Throughout the entirety of this series – which I have now devoted over a decade of my life to writing – there has been one fan in particular who has fervently followed The Chronicles of Freylar like no other. This passionate individual has continuously motivated me, encouraging me to continue writing the chronicles through their own insatiable need to discover what happens next. Though my commitment to the series has never waned, this individual gave me the push I needed during those inevitable moments when a writer becomes mired or lost in their own work.

"Morning. Am shot to bits – finished reading your book at 2am this morning. It was absolutely brilliant, thank you." – My Dad, Number 1 fan.

TABLE OF CONTENTS

ONE
Disconnect

She was running, faster than she had ever known. Her inexplicably long stride carried her rapidly across the Kalak-ploughed field, the heavy fall of her large feet paying no heed to the virgin shoots reaching towards the Night's Lights, leaving them trampled in her wake. Flanking her, others desperately fled, as she did, racing towards the farmstead emerging from the distant gloom. From the corner of her eye, she caught a glimpse of the Freylarkin to her left, who tripped and fell. She gasped at the sight of their face grinding against the furrows, before the body buckled and bounced. As she focused on the farmstead ahead, ephemeral shapes formed on the dark horizon, blocking the path to her salvation. Without hesitation, she adjusted her bearing, veering left, causing those around her to follow suit. She glanced over her shoulder, briefly witnessing the horrible demise of another, consumed by dark shapes emerging from wisps of smoke that rose up from the ground. They ran, their numbers continuing to dwindle as they tried in vain to evade the invisible attackers who sought to surround them, picking them off one at a time. Yet there were no screams, no moans of pain as the shadows pursuing them preyed on her kin – there was no sound at all. Her mind wanted to call out to the others, eager learn of their plight, but her mouth remained closed, her body instinctively directing her every action. The farmstead became a blur in her periphery, no longer a concern, replaced by the promise of sanctuary amongst the trees rising to meet them. Faster she ran, causing those alongside her to fade from view as she sprinted ahead,

1

through the trees she darting left and right, narrowly avoiding several impacts, oblivious to the foliage slapping against her body. Despite the branches raking her face, she felt nothing. She was a mute spectator, impervious to touch, her actions like a marionette dancing to the whim of another – her other self. The sensation felt strange, as though she was floating. She was an autumnal leaf separated from its host, now carried upon a stream with no control over the current and its direction. The future was preordained, her desires counting for naught. All she could do was experience the silent ride, praying that the one in control would not usher in her release.

Reaching a clearing amidst the trees, she came rapidly to a halt. Bending over, she placed her hands on her knees. Was she gasping for air? She could not tell. There was no burning sensation in her lungs, nor the rush of air down her windpipe – she felt nothing. Someone else appeared alongside her, followed by several others. All seemed to be panting heavily, breathless from their ordeal. She straightened, regaining her composure, before issuing a series of rushed commands to the others, accompanied by rapid hand gestures. The group began to disperse, as wisps of grey smoke rose from the ground, hastening their departure. After running a short distance, she slowed her pace, allowing her to steal a glimpse of the ephemeral shapes manifesting at the centre of the recently abandoned clearing, slowly taking shape until each form resembled a large wolf. The silvery lupines sprinted towards them with preternatural speed. Chasing down their prey, the wolves mercilessly pounced on their victims, ripping apart their quarry with fanged jaws revealing blood-soaked gums and stained teeth. What she saw was ghastly to behold; the

2

images of torn flesh and severed tendons would forever plague her thoughts and dreams, denying her future solace. The butchery intensified, and with it, feeling slowly returned to her limbs, along with muffled screams that now rang in her ears. The cacophony of sensation and sound assaulting her increased, but despite the din, two words made themselves known to her.

'Wake up!'

She had burst into her daughter's room, almost knocking the wooden door from its hinges. Rarni was screaming loudly, the shrill sound splitting her ears. She had run to her daughter's side as soon as she heard the screams, desperate to wake her from the nightmare tormenting her.

'Rarni, wake up!' she cried again, this time gently shaking her daughter where she slept. 'Come on, wake up!'

Rarni's eyes flicked open, but her daughter's vacant stare suggested that the nightmare still had a hold on her.

'You have to wake up. Come on, Rarni, damn it, wake up!'

Shaking her daughter again, aggressively this time, Rarni suddenly came to. She scooped up her daughter who immediately clung to her, arms and legs wrapped tightly around her torso.

'There, there. You are safe – I have you now.'

Slowly, she paced around the room, gently bobbing her daughter up and down, tying hard to comfort her. Rarni sobbed intensely, tears streaming down her cheeks. It was then that she realised how much her daughter had grown, and, more importantly, how heavy she had become. Wandering slowly back to the bed, she gently laid Rarni

3

down before climbing in alongside her distressed daughter, still shaking. The sheets were damp and Rarni's skin was clammy to the touch.

'You had a nightmare – the dreams cannot get you now.' she said, gently stroking her daughter's dark hair.

It was normal for her daughter's blonde hair to darken a shade during winter. However, Rarni's had darkened considerably now, becoming more brown than blonde. The curious metamorphosis concerned her, as did the nightmares.

'It was real.'

'They often *feel* real, but it was just a dream.'

'No, I was there.'

'Where?'

'In the woods, with the spirit wolves.'

'Rarni, you were here, in your bed, tucked up safe and sound. Those creatures are folklore, tall tales meant to scare disobedient children.'

'But I was there – it was real!'

'It was just another nightmare – like the ones before.'

'No, you do not understand. I was there!' her daughter insisted vehemently, whilst blubbering through an endless stream of tears. 'They were all released!'

'There, there, please do not cry. You are perfectly safe here with me – they cannot harm you.'

'I think that they already did.'

She hated feeling so helpless, unable to console her terrified daughter. The nightmares were becoming darker, more violent and increasingly frequent. They had started during the tail end of winter, following her daughter's violent abduction. At first, she had believed the turbulent dreams to be a direct result of Rarni's recent trauma; the

4

vivid images were no doubt a means of processing the kidnapping. However, throughout spring, they had evolved into something far worse, becoming more sinister in nature. Lacking the necessary skill to diagnose and treat such a condition, all she could do was attempt to console her daughter, but it was clear now that Rarni required specialist help.

It took some time for her frightened daughter to settle down and eventually fall asleep, by which time dawn was breaking. The incessant chorus of Sky-Skitters denied her further sleep. Unable to drift off, she slid out of the bed, careful not to disturb Rarni, before quietly making her way downstairs. She grabbed a thick blanket from a small wooden chest and sat on the steps outside their tree, quietly reflecting on the sad events that had brought about her daughter's condition. Though she was grateful to have Rarni back, the sick ordeal suffered by her daughter had left its mark, perhaps even permanently. Realising her inability to remedy the situation, by undoing the mental damage caused by recent events, the hopelessness she felt intensified before suddenly overwhelming her. Burying her head in her hands, she began to sob quietly. As a parent, she had one job that was paramount above all others: to protect her daughter. Yet knowing one's purpose was very different to fulfilling it. She lacked the skill to protect her daughter from the encroaching darkness, yet, despite her pride, she was strong enough to recognise and accept the fact. Regardless of her inability, there had to be a way of saving her daughter from further torment – the strength of her conviction would not allow her to believe otherwise. There had to be others whose aid she could call upon. Her thoughts quickly turned to Nathanar, Captain of The Blades.

The dogged Paladin had rescued Rarni from the evil force responsible for both abducting and mentally traumatising her daughter. However, Nathanar was a soldier, skilled in combat. Rarni required help of a different sort. Furthermore, she was loath to request the Paladin's aid for a second time; there were limits to how much of a beating her pride could endure. Even so, as mother, she knew that her own self-esteem was not a priority – her daughter's wellbeing was the only thing that truly mattered to her. Rarni's ongoing battle had shifted to one of the mind; her daughter now required the support of a telepath, or perhaps a scrier. Yet, the most powerful scriers in the vale, the sisters Darlia and Kirika, were beyond her social reach – at least *directly*. Nathanar had been seen with Darlia numerous times in the forest, where the infamous claw-handed scrier had taken up residence. If she could swallow her pride again, perhaps Darlia would be willing to help her daughter for a second time – the renowned scrier had lent aid to the Captain of The Blades during his investigation into Rarni's abduction. Then there was Darlia's sister, Kirika, a former forest dweller, now a well-respected member of the ruling council and resident within the Tri-Spires. Although she had no dealings with Kirika, it was possible that she could ask The Guardian to raise the matter on her behalf. Rayna chose to live amongst the forest dwellers and had become a local hero. The Guardian had no seat on the ruling council, however, despite this fact, the commander of The Blades spent a lot of time with its members and her close relationship with Kirika was well known. Furthermore, Rayna was universally liked by the people and extremely approachable; The Guardian always took the time to listen to the concerns of others and her candid nature was refreshing. Still, the very notion that she could gain access to a member of the ruling council was one bred from pure hubris; would a member of the ruling council even entertain giving her a moment's notice, she wondered?

Pulling the blanket tightly around her, she stared into the depths of the gloomy forest, pondering the best course of action. The temperature had increased significantly since the arrival of spring in the vale. Her breath was no longer visible, yet there was still a crispness to the air. She continued to gaze into the forest, lost in thought, barely acknowledging the subtle movements of the surrounding flora as it was disturbed by local fauna. Of the two options available to her, seeking out Nathanar and Darlia directly was clearly the more sensible approach towards helping her daughter. Wrestling with her pride, trying to subdue its stubborn nature, a single thought took root in her mind, rapidly sprouting, eclipsing all others. With the advent of spring, maybe it was time to tread a different path and take a fresh approach. Although eternally indebted to the Paladin for rescuing Rarni, Nathanar had not returned her daughter entirely – but perhaps The Guardian could finish what the Paladin had started. Muffled screams from her tree shattered her reverie. Whichever path she followed, she needed to act quickly, for her daughter's sake.

'Do you remember when I first combed your hair?' asked Kirika softly, gently drawing the wooden comb down the length of her long red hair. 'Back then, you were plagued by memories of your former life, tormented constantly by impossible decisions.'

'I remember. So much has happened since then.'

7

'Yes, your hair has grown longer.' said Kirika, whose cool smile beamed at her in the mirror.

Ordinarily, she would have returned the scrier's affections, but her mind felt fuzzy.

'What is the matter?' asked Kirika, abruptly ceasing the ministrations to her hair. 'You seem conflicted.'

'I am.'

'What do you mean?' asked Kirika, 'I assume this is to do with our previous conversation, before you left to assist the outlying communities?'

'Yes.' she replied, followed by a weary sigh. 'I thought that time away from the vale would give me some breathing space, allowing me to make sense of everything that has happened to me since my arrival.'

'That is rather a lot to process in such a short period of time, or so I would imagine.'

'Yes, it is.' she replied, laughing awkwardly to herself.

'Rayna, you *can* talk to me.'

'I know. It's just…'

'Just what?'

'I feel awkward and confused.'

'Of course you do. You were born male. Recently, you became female, you are now attracted to someone of the opposite gender, formerly your own – an individual who once loathed you, may I add – and have been pulled into a completely different world, whose problems you have decided to shoulder. Furthermore, you believe that you are an agent of release, for some ancient, all-powerful, entity, within which you believe that our world resides.' explained Kirika in a tongue-in-cheek manner, defying her normally polite disposition.

8

Kirika's blunt and unexpected assessment left her dumbfounded. The compassionate, modest and politically astute scrier was typically reserved in her responses. However, she had noticed a growing confidence in Kirika's demeanour since the scrier's appointment to the newly reformed ruling council.

'In all seriousness, if you need to talk, I am always here for you.'

'I know...I appreciate it. If I'm being completely honest, I still haven't fully come to terms with this new facade of mine – I still feel like a lodger.'

'Based on what you told me, Alarielle gave up her claim to that body when she chose to move on to the Everlife – it is rightfully *yours* now. Nathaniel, her father, your adopted father, has accepted this. The Blades, Knights Thranis, your friends, all have accepted you for who you are. Indeed, the only person yet to fully embrace your altered form is yourself.'

'You're right, I know this, yet I still wrestle with this new guise of mine every cycle. I thought I had a handle on it, but Alarielle's parting gift, worsened by the lack of a good crisis to distract me, has knocked me back a few steps. All this time to think has only left me feeling more confused – I don't know how to move forward.'

'Rayna, it is time to let go of your past, indefinitely. The memories that you harbour tether you to a place of great darkness. The emotions that they foster, anger, hatred and revenge, served you well during times of war, but that time has ended. Freylar needs to heal, as do you. Let go and embrace the bright future that you have worked so hard to achieve – you deserve it.'

'But my grimy past has shaped who I am today.'

9

'Yes, who you *are*. There is no longer a need to dwell on who you *were*. You have reconciled your past demons – it is time to move on. Alarielle's gift is not a curse, nor was it ever intended to torment you – at least, that is my belief.'

'Then what is it?'

'Is it not plain to see? Alarielle removed the barriers in your mind, previously holding you back in this new form of yours. She gave you the gift of freedom, allowing you to move on.'

She stared vacantly into the mirror, considering Kirika's words carefully whilst absentmindedly observing her feminine visage. Kirika was right – as was typically the case. The barriers holding her back had been removed, with the exception of one: the barrier of her own making. She had reached a nexus in her new life. To progress any further, she needed to take a leap of faith into the unknown.

'That settles it.' she said, ardently. 'I'm going to talk to him!'

'You mean Lothnar?'

'Yes.'

'When?'

'I don't know. I have only just decided to--'

'How about this cycle?'

'What!'

'Are you scared?'

'No.'

'Then it is settled.'

'Kirika!'

'So then, how to wear your hair?'

'Is that really important?'

'Of course it is; you are good with your blades, but there are other weapons that you still need to master – I am

10

certain that Larissa and I have imparted this valuable lesson to you many times before.'

'I may have glossed over those particular sermons. I was never a typical student; speak to Nathaniel, he will attest to that fact.'

Kirika laughed, before sliding the comb down the length of her hair once more. Despite her head being jerked and wrenched by Kirika's ministrations, removing the knots from her hair was a therapeutic experience. Admittedly, she was lazy when it came to personal grooming – a failing that she needed to correct – and had done very little as Callum during her former life. Fortunately, Kirika was always more than happy to help. Since her arrival in Freylar, they had become like sisters, freely sharing their innermost thoughts with one another. Kirika was always very critical of her appearance, setting the bar high when it came to one's own presentation. Still, having a personal stylist was no bad thing; Kirika's keen sense of fashion plugged the gaps in her own skillset.

'You would be lost without me.' said Kirika, jovially.

'Certainly dishevelled!'

'That too.'

They laughed, like a pair of adolescent, giggling school girls, before a loud knock come from the door to their tree.

'I had better go and see who it is.' she said, quickly rising from her chair. 'Nathaniel left early for the arena – as he so often does.'

She stood up, oblivious to the comb still clinging to her hair, which Kirika quickly retrieved. She hurried down the curved wooden stairs leading to the main ground floor living space, hoping to catch their visitor in time. Pulling open the door, a slender female, accompanied by a young child – presumably the daughter – stood before her. She focused her attention on the mother, whose wide-eyed expression was one of both hope and sorrow, curious as to their sudden visit.

'Hello. Can I help you?'

'Not me.' replied the mother, directing her gaze towards the young child. 'This is my daughter, Rarni. She requires your assistance. Specifically, we need your help to contact Kirika, so that--'

'Rayna, who is it?' asked Kirika, who came bounding down the stairs, still clutching the comb in her hand.

'Kirika!' cried the mother, suddenly. 'It is you. Please, will you help my daughter? I do not know what to do.'

'Callum, to be completely frank, this is your last opportunity within the system. You have been bouncing around, in and out of different children's homes, for a while now, which has lead you to us – your final stop.'

The venerable man sitting opposite him leaned forwards, placing his elbows on the wooden desk between them, before slowly resting his head upon his interlocked fingers.

'Indeed, we have both come to the end of the line; I will be retiring soon and you are now seventeen, bordering on adulthood – you have less than a year.'

The man opposite him held his gaze with an unwavering stare. No doubt, the home's director of operations had hosted countless such meetings over the decades, inducting an endless stream of waifs sent to the facility for processing. He wondered if such a career path was fulfilling, or whether it slowly chipped away at one's soul, grinding away all vestiges of motivation and empathy, until only indifference remained.

'I am not here to judge you, Callum. Life is hard enough without the opinions of others weighing you down. Besides, everyone's story is a familiar one to me now. However, the sobering fact remains that the system will be closing its doors to you soon. How quickly that happens depends on your actions during your stay with us.'

The Director suddenly rose from his chair, before walking over to the dingy office's only window.

'If you adhere to this facility's rules, you could spend up to a year with us, giving you time to make arrangements for the future. However, should you choose to disregard them, your time with us will be cut short. In that scenario, you will not be considered for further placement. The system will conveniently delay your processing – I have seen it, many times before – until you turn eighteen. That is the grim truth of it, Callum. I am being completely transparent with you.' explained The Director, who was clearly disinterested whilst gazing out the window.

'I see.' he said, acknowledging The Director's cold words.

'I have done this job for as long as I can remember. I have seen countless boys like you, each come and go. There was a time when it broke my heart to see your ilk end up out there, on the streets. However, over the years, I have reluctantly become desensitised to it all.'

There was a pause in their one-sided conversation whilst something outside caught The Director's eye. He took the opportunity to glance around the office. Except for a clock and a couple of shelves, the walls were bare. There were no indications of any personal interests or photos of

13

family or friends dotted around, nor any sign of a wedding band on The Director's finger. From what he could ascertain, either The Director kept his personal life just that, or he simply did not have one. Whatever the cause of The Director's brief distraction, it did not last, and he soon sat back down, assuming his previous position.

'What do you hope to achieve here, Callum?' the man asked bluntly.

'In truth, I haven't really given it any thought.' he replied, concerned that his apathetic response would tarnish his initial standing. 'Sorry.'

'Well, at least your answer is genuine. I would appreciate it if we remained candid with one another during your time here.'

He nodded in response, signalling his agreement.

'Good.' replied The Director. 'As with any facility of our nature, we have our share of difficult residents. Do yourself a favour, Callum. Stay away from Sebastian and his merry little band of sheep. Any entanglement with them will not serve you well.'

'Thank you.'

'You owe me no thanks. The system placed you in my care – the same system responsible for the defamation of your social class. You have a hard road ahead of you, Callum. I suggest that you use what little time you have with us to plan your next move. The streets are harsh; most do not make it.'

'What do you mean?'

'I used to review the ongoing progress of the residents after leaving the care of this facility. Most disappeared, or were the subject of autopsy reports that I bore witness to. After a decade of it, I began sending others in my stead.'

14

'I understand.'

'Indeed, I am certain that you have witnessed such atrocities already, despite your youth. Even so, burn this lesson into your mind, Callum. It may be the only one that you need to stay alive.'

'I appreciate the forewarning. I am not looking for trouble.'

'I do not suppose for one moment that you are. However, some people attract the wrong sort of attention, regardless. Besides, you are Shadow class – trouble will come looking for you, whether you choose to seek it out or not. Even so, try not to hasten its arrival.'

Turning his head towards the dirty window, his gaze lingered on the polluted sky whilst he considered the bleak sermon he had received. Despite the blunt delivery, The Director's words rung true. From an early age, after the loss of his parents, he knew the time would eventually come when the system would close its doors to him. The thought of leaving the system was both terrifying and exhilarating. He had spent most of his adolescent life within the system, shunted between numerous children's homes, none of which had felt like home. Then again, what was home, he mused. The promise of something new was truly exciting, and yet equally frightening. Where would he go, how would he earn a living, how would he survive? All were questions for which he had no answers. During the few occasions that he had spoken about the matter with other members of the Shadow class already living off the streets, he had been met with disdainful looks or was shunned entirely. The hostile encounters left him wondering if his people simply did whatever was required to survive, regardless of ethics – that was the part that scared him the most. He was no saint and

15

had been in his fair share of scrapes over the years. However, despite these incidents, he still maintained a strong sense of what was right and wrong. He had never pushed his personal beliefs onto others, but had tried hard to adhere to his own code of morality.

The light in the room began to fade, waking him from his bleak reverie. He turned his attention back to The Director, who was now slumped back in his chair staring vacantly at an empty glass on his desk. He felt no hostility from the man, nor any empathy. The Director was in the twilight of his career. He sensed that the man had become hollow due to his experiences, his soul depleted by all that he had witnessed over the decades. He pitied The Director; it could not be easy realising that one's life work had been largely pointless. Still, regardless of the facility's post-care success rate, helping others in need was, in his mind at least, always a worthy cause.

'When I leave here, there will be no autopsy report with my name on it – I intend to survive.'

The Director fixed him with an intense stare, narrowing his eyes slightly. After a long pause, the man stood up, abruptly, before offering to shake his hand.

'Good, see that you do. I would like to retire on a high note.'

He rose from his chair and shook The Director's hand with a firm grip.

'Let us get you settled in.'

TWO
Visions

'Come inside.' said The Guardian, ushering them both in towards a small wooden table. 'Please, make yourselves comfortable.'

She looked to her daughter, who was clearly in awe of The Guardian's presence. Stories of Rayna's adventures were widely known amongst the forest dwellers and were a source of inspiration to her daughter prior to the incident, back when Rarni still possessed a blithe disposition.

'You mentioned that the name of your daughter is Rarni, am I correct?' asked Rayna, once all four were properly seated.

'Yes, that is correct.'

'Then, you must be Lyra.'

'You know of me?'

'Of course – we both do.' replied The Guardian, who turned her attention to Kirika. 'Nathanar told us about you in his report, he...'

The Guardian ceased talking mid-sentence, her attention now fixed on Kirika, who seemed intently focused on her daughter. There was a strange silence whilst Kirika studied Rarni. She wondered, indeed, she hoped, that the renowned scrier saw something the rest of them did not. Bringing Rarni to one of the vale's most powerful scriers had been her final throw of the dice – she prayed that her last hope of salvation for her daughter would not be in vain.

'Rarni,' said Kirika softly, before placing a small wooden comb upon the table. 'My name is Kirika. I am a scrier. Will you permit me to hold your hand?'

17

'I don't understand.' said Rayna, clearly confused. 'Kirika, what is going on?'

'I will let Lyra explain.'

'Lyra, is there something the matter with your daughter?' asked Rayna.

'She has been having nightmares.'

'I see.' said The Guardian. 'Forgive my seeming lack of empathy, but, are such things not common amongst young Freylarkin?'

'These are different. I am certain of it.' she replied, vehemently. 'The visions started after Rarni's abduction. They have been growing more intense since then, becoming increasingly frequent and darker in nature.'

'Darker?'

'When I hear Rarni's screams, I run to her. I find her lying in her bed, awake, but not awake. Like in some kind of trance, caught in the space between places – somewhere that I cannot reach. I try to console my daughter as best I can. However, it is not enough.' she said, wiping the tears collecting along her lower eyelids. 'I fear the damage these visions are causing to her soul; Rarni is no longer the carefree child that I raised. Though she will not recount all of the details to me, I can sense that the images she has borne witness to haunt her.'

'Could the Soulmancer have retuned?' asked The Guardian, turning her attention back to Kirika. 'If so, do you think that it is somehow responsible for Rarni's nightmares?'

'I do not believe that the Soulmancer has returned. Nathanar's report on Xenia's account suggested that the Soulmancer had an alternate agenda, one that lay beyond the vale. If Xenia's account is accurate – and I have no reason to doubt it – the Soulmancer would not concern itself with the vale. However...'

'What is it?' she asked, impatiently.

'The way you described Rarni's nightmares, or *visions*, as you put it, interests me. Your daughter's experiences sound more akin to scrying.'

'Kirika, how is that possible?' she asked, astonished by the renowned scrier's outlandish suggestion.

'Nightmares fade rapidly; they lose clarity the instant the sleeper awakens, leaving only a lingering fear that rapidly subsides. From what you have told us, your daughter's experiences sound different. Rarni,' said Kirika gently, now focusing her attention on her daughter. 'How much do you remember of your visions?'

Rarni said nothing, instead lowering her head, avoiding eye contact with their hosts.

'I realise that this is a difficult subject to talk about. Therefore, will you permit me to scry your past instead, so that I may see for myself that which torments you?'

Her daughter continued to remain silent.

'If you permit my scrying, I believe that I can help you.'

'Rarni, it breaks my heart that I am unable to help you with whatever it is that troubles you. However, it is possible that this kind Freylarkin *can* help you, where I cannot. Will you please allow her to at least try to help you?'

Again, Rarni remained silent, lowering her head even further. She turned to Kirika once more. The scrier continued to focus her attention on Rarni, looking for a sign, the consent needed to trawl through her daughter's troubled past. Without any warning, Rayna leaned across the table,

19

stretching her arms towards her daughter. The light bringer wiggled her fingertips, causing gentle sparkles of light to dance across the table towards Rarni. The soft twinkling lights cast ephemeral shapes across her daughter's face, quickly garnering Rarni's attention. Rarni tried to keep a straight face whilst more and more of the sparkles spilled from Rayna's fingertips. They bounced across the wooden surface towards her daughter, before tumbling over the table's edge into Rarni's lap, like the Eternal Falls crashing onto its rocks below. A thin smile formed on her daughter's face.

'They are beautiful.' said Rarni suddenly.

'So are you, when you're not being sad.' replied Rayna.

'I do not want to be sad.'

'Then allow my friend to help you. She's very good – but I don't tell her that, otherwise her head might grow too big.'

She smiled as her daughter laughed quietly, the first time since the abduction. The sparkles became more energetic, bouncing enthusiastically towards her daughter, lighting up Rarni's entire face before spilling onto the floor where they quickly faded into nothingness.

'It tickles.' said Rarni, now giggling quietly.

'I can do this all cycle.'

'OK, she can help.'

'Who can help?'

'Your friend.'

'Which friend is that?'

'Kirika.'

'Oh, you mean the one with the big head?'

'Yes!'

20

She laughed, watching as Kirika gave The Guardian a brief sidelong look of disapproval, which Rayna and her daughter found highly amusing. The forest dwellers often talked of Rayna's unusual dialogue and otherworldly ways, and now she was witnessing proof of the rumourmongering. The Freylarkai were typically a formal lot, rigid in their ways. Therefore, seeing her kin from a fresh perspective was a refreshing experience. She admired Rayna's unconventional approach. Notwithstanding repeatedly flouting the norm, The Guardian seemed to bring the best out of people, regardless of her strange demeanour. Now, she saw first-hand how The Guardian emboldened those around her. The once familiar warmth of Rarni's carefree disposition suddenly radiated through the cracks forming along the surface of the porcelain doll that had replaced her daughter, following the awful abduction. Despite the growing laughter around the table, she could not hold back her tears of joy that glistened in the light of Rayna's ability, sparkling as they fell upon the wooden table.

'I cannot…thank you both enough.' she stammered, struggling to clear the sudden lump in her throat. 'Until now, Rarni has not opened up once since the…abhorrent event. Finally, my daughter is…returned fully to me.'

'You do not need to thank us.' replied The Guardian, before showering her daughter with one final flurry of twinkling lights. 'I suspect that the difficult part is yet to come.'

As the last of Rayna's light dissipated, she slowly reached across the table.

'Rarni, will you hold my hands?' she asked softly, giving the child a warm smile.

Lyra's daughter tentatively placed her hands upon the table. She continued to reach forwards, slowly, until her fingertips touched those of the child. Turning her hands upside down, she pushed her fingers underneath Rarni's own, before clasping the child's hands firmly.

'You will not feel a thing – I promise!' she said, hoping to ease the child's fears. 'Oh, you should probably know something else before we start: my head is not that big.'

Rarni smiled, before releasing another weak laugh, no doubt caused by Rayna whom she sensed was playfully mocking her from the periphery of her physical vision.

Hundreds of images flooded her mind's eye the instant she engaged her second sight. She travelled backwards rapidly through time, disregarding the visions leading up to their encounter. She saw Lyra shaking her gently. Then afterwards, disturbing images of Freylarkin butchery as she ran, whilst desperately seeking to evade what appeared to be lupine attackers. The images were not akin to those plucked from one's dreams or dark fantasies – they were too lucid for that. The perspective was all wrong for someone of Rarni's height and the glimpses she caught of her hands suggested that they belonged to someone of working stock, as opposed to those of a child. It was clear, to her at least, that the images she bore witness to belonged to another and not Rarni. For someone of her ability and experience, it was easy to understand why Lyra's daughter felt so frightened by the images; they were not dreams, but instead, actual events that had transpired, witnessed from the perspective of another. She continued to sift through the galley of grim imagery, looking for clues that would reveal more of the child's story to her. The nature of the attackers, the attire of the victims and what appeared to be a distant

22

farmstead told her everything that she needed to understand the source of the imagery. Even so, how had Rarni made such a connection, she mused. The child was no scrier; at least, the typical signs were not present. Yet somehow, Rarni had acquired the visions of another, something that, to her knowledge at least, was only possible through scrying.

The familiar room, its occupants and the wooden table snapped into focus once more. The others were staring intently at her, no doubt seeking answers that only she could provide.

'Rarni, you have been scrying.'

'What!' Lyra blurted out abruptly.

The child's mother was clearly both confused and concerned by the frank diagnosis.

'How is that even possible? Rarni was not born early in the pass. The colour of her hair--'

'Has darkened.' said Rayna, quickly interjecting. 'Nathanar described your daughter's hair as being blonde in his report, her eyes a pale blue. Yet that is clearly no longer the case.'

'Her hair has darkened considerably. Although I must confess, I did not notice the alteration of Rarni's eyes.'

Lyra lowered her head suddenly, cupping her face with her hands, and began to sob.

'I am a terrible mother! How could I let this happen to my daughter?'

'This is not your fault!' she said, rising suddenly from her seat. 'From what I understand, this change in your daughter began *after* the abduction.'

She circled around the wooden table towards Lyra, before embracing the distraught mother, comforting her.

'You had no way of predicting the events that unfolded in the arena that cycle. If anyone *should* have known, that person was me.'

She continued to comfort Lyra, whilst Rayna saw to the child, giving Rarni an enormous hug.

'You're a brave young Freylarkin.' said Rayna, pulling Rarni up onto her toes in a tight embrace.

Rarni said nothing, but she could tell that the child was sad seeing her mother in distress.

'Scrying is a powerful ability, Rarni. It is fortunate that you are still young enough to be trained to wield your newfound power responsibly.' she said, earnestly, before returning to her seat. 'You have been given a gift. When used appropriately, scrying can help our people enormously. However, the images you saw concern me, as does the manner in which your ability has manifested. How you are able to trigger your ability without any apparent contact with the source of the visions is alarming.'

'They just happen.' said the child, meekly, as Rayna released her grasp.

'When you are sleeping?'

'Mostly. When I sleep, the images often come.'

'With time and training, you *should* be able to control your ability. As such, I would very much like for both you and your mother to take up residence within the Tri-Spires, so that I can train you personally.' she said, now shifting her focus back to Lyra. 'Regrettably, my duties tether me to the Tri-Spires, therefore I am unable to visit you both here, at least not frequently enough for adequate training purposes. Of course, this is not a summons. I only request this of you both so that I can maximise my time spent schooling your daughter. Assuming of course, that you wish to accept my offer – you are in no way obligated to do so.'

'Thank you.' said Lyra. 'I hope you will understand that I need to discuss this opportunity with Rarni first?'

'Of course. This is your home. Living in the Tri-Spires is very different and often scary at first.' she said, followed by another reassuring smile.

'Mummy, I would like to go.'

'Rarni, are you certain?' asked Lyra, whose voice was still broken with emotion.

'I do not want to feel this way.' explained Rarni, solemnly. 'If this lady can help, I would like to go with her.'

'Please, call me Kirika, or big head if you prefer.'

Rarni laughed again, the joyous sound of which prompted a weak smile from her mother, Lyra, who nodded in acceptance.

'We would like to accept your kind offer.'

'I am pleased.' she said. 'Make your way to the Tri-Spires in your own time. Ask for Kayla when you arrive. She is my administrative aide who will help to get you both settled in – I will inform her of the situation.'

'Thank you. Rarni, please thank Kirika for her kind offer.'

'Thank you, Kirika.' said the child, earnestly.

'You are most welcome. It will be an honour to instruct you. Once we begin your training, you will get to meet another young scrier, whom I also instruct. Her name is Keshar.'

'Mummy, can we go *now*?' asked Rarni, enthusiastically.

Lyra laughed gently.

'No, Rarni. We need to first pack our belongings, before we can make the journey to the Tri-Spires. I suggest that we start preparing for your grand adventure.'

'In which case, we had best let you both get on with your extensive preparations.' she said, rising from her seat, thus formally concluding their meeting.

'Thank you again, both of you.' said Lyra, before escorting her daughter to the door. 'I am indebted to you both.'

'You owe us nothing.' said Rayna, before politely bidding the mother and daughter farewell. 'See you both soon!'

After the pair had left, Rayna quickly closed the door, pressing her back firmly against it. She could see the look of concern on her ochre-coloured face.

'They're gone.' said Rayna. 'It's time to spill it!'

She had known Kirika long enough to know when the scrier was withholding information. Upon her arrival in Freylar, its former queen, Mirielle – now ensconced at Scrier's Post, following the end of her reign and subsequent self-imposed exile – had tasked Kirika with the responsibility of ensuring her integration into Freylarian society, specifically within the vale. However, since that time, she and Kirika had become like sisters, sharing their innermost thoughts with one another. As such, she knew her surrogate sister's mannerisms well, in particular, when there was more information to be gleaned.

'What did you see?'

'One of the farmsteads has, or will be, attacked.'

'What!'

'I cannot be specific. It is impossible to narrow down the timing of events, since I witnessed the images second-hand through another. Though Rarni's own visions took place in the past, I do not know if what she saw has yet to pass.'

'I have The Blades garrisoned out there to prevent such attacks.' she explained. 'I will send word to those commanding them and have them report back to me.'

'Leave that to me. I intend to call a council of war regarding the matter. As such, I need you to go and find Lothnar; despite agreeing to remain within the vale, I find it impossible to track his movements.'

'You realise the irony, being a scr--'

'Yes, yes – rub it in.'

'He's probably lying on his arse, down by the river. I will drag him back to the Tri-Spires for you soon enough.'

'Good. Meet us beneath the arena.'

She half-expected Kirika to say more on the matter, but instead, the scrier stood opposite her in silence. Kirika appeared to drift off suddenly, lost in thought, distracting her from the task at hand.

'Kirika.' she said, trying to focus the scrier's attention. 'Kirika!'

'Apologies, Rayna. I was…'

'There's more, isn't there?'

'It is Rarni. There is something off about the child.'

'What do you mean?'

'The way her visions have manifested is abnormal for those with our ability. Furthermore, the clarity of the images was impressive for one new to the art. Typically, such vivid images are only made possible through practice for tens of passes – she has only just begun her journey.'

'We can figure that out later. Our main priority should be to prevent the attack from happening, else deal with its aftermath. But, before we can proceed, we need to confirm the situation, immediately.'

'Yes, you are right. I can satisfy my curiosities later.'

'I do not mean to imply their lack of importance--'

'Of course not. The safety of the people needs to come first. Go find Lothnar. I will assemble the others, with the exception of Gaelin and Natalya; both are stationed amongst the farmsteads – I fear for their safety.'

'Nat can handle herself and Gaelin is no slouch in a fight, when the situation demands it.'

'Even so, events are in motion now that I do no fully understand, and that unnerves me.'

'You cannot follow that path, the one taken by Mirielle and your sister. Darlia hit rock bottom before realising the depths of its depravity, whilst Mirielle was completely undone by its destructive lure. With that said, this is not the time for second-guessing either. Make an informed decision, based on what you know, and see it through – no one can fault you for that.'

'I know. Believe me, I have learned that lesson well. Still, I cannot prevent its dark presence from lapping at my shores. The weight of the responsibility of managing the welfare of our people is overwhelming at times.'

'And that is why the revised council, the one you helped to put in place, exists, so that the burden can be shared – it is too much for an individual to shoulder alone.'

'Since when did you become so wise?' asked Kirika, expressing a playful grin.

'Since *someone* voted that I should command The Blades, robbing me of my carefree lifestyle.'

28

'Oh please, do not be so dramatic. That was a calling of your own making and you know it. Besides, you have both Nathanar and Natalya propping you up.'

'I am not so sure about that. Natalya has always been a misfit and I fear that her free-spirited ways have corrupted Nathanar.'

'Would it help to provide you with some much-needed perspective by going back to your mirror upstairs?'

'Oh, shut up!' she replied, followed by a grin of her own. 'Run along and send your Sky-Skitters, whilst I haul Lothnar back to the Tri-Spires for you.'

He missed the adventure of the borderlands, the excitement of not knowing what dangers would present themselves from one cycle to the next. By contrast, living in the vale was boring and routine, each cycle bleeding into the next, with very little to distinguish them. Despite the comforts of living in the vale – for him at least – existence within its confines felt dull and uninteresting. He missed the cycles when he and Ragnar would talk, drink and fight during his visits to the vale, between his numerous scouting sorties. Since the battle for Bleak Moor and the skirmish at Scrier's Post, the Narlakai ranks had been decimated. Furthermore, with no one to shepherd them, there was no longer a need for his scouts to manage and repel the soul stealers' random incursions. To the south, the Knights Thranis defended Freylar's southern lands, with little going on east or west of the vale. He sighed heavily. Essentially, the scouts had been benched, although Kirika had not worded his present situation as such, lamenting that his leadership and presence within the vale were paramount in helping to guide and embolden their kin in rebuilding

29

everything that their people had lost following the Narlakai invasions. Despite the safe, boring state of affairs, it was spring in the vale – his favourite season. The flora and fauna had returned, enriching the forest once more, enhancing its natural splendour. Though he missed the borderlands, there was nothing quite like sleeping on a bed of thick lush grass beneath the open sky, gazing up at the Night's Lights.

It was late morning. Unlike himself, his companion had barely moved from his spot since dawn broke. Krisis now lay comfortably sleeping across his lap, keeping him warm. Occasionally, the adolescent dire wolf's ears would twitch abruptly, honing in on distant sounds seemingly worthy of attention. Since he had no pressing concerns to attend to, he allowed his faithful companion to sleep whilst he lazily watched the world pass by. Though he had quarters within the Tri-Spires, he rarely used them, preferring instead to make his home outside – neither he nor Krisis were suited to enclosed spaces, especially those made of stone. On the few occasions that he slept within his quarters, it was typically on the floor, next to Krisis. Sometimes the dire wolf would take his bed, but he preferred sleeping on a hard surface, having grown accustomed to it over the passes. The verdant grass took the edge off the hard ground, but he had no complaints.

The sound of a faint crack suddenly caught his attention. Krisis leapt up on all fours, immediately turning to face the noise. He slowly rose to his feet, placing a firm hand upon the dire wolf's back.

'Easy boy. It is probably Rayna – at times, she is worse than Ragnar ever was.'

Krisis started to growl, clearly uneasy at the noise coming from the west. Focusing on the dense forest, he quickly picked out movement amongst the trees. Someone was moving awkwardly towards them. The figure's movements were horribly clumsy, like someone trying to walk for the first time. He perceived no immediate threat from whoever it was that approached them, nevertheless, Krisis continued to growl angrily. Sliding a throwing knife out from a sheath strapped to the underside of his left arm, he crouched down slowly, alongside his companion, quickly blending in with the surrounding growth to conceal his silhouette.

'Quiet boy, else you will give us away.' he said, using his telepathic ability to commune with the wary dire wolf.

The mysterious figure continued to advance, sluggishly, as though something impeded their progress. Krisis' growling abated slightly, like rumbling thunder slowly receding. Their gaze remained fixed on the figure, analysing its every move, looking for the smallest of details that would give their quarry away. The figure lurched forward on its right leg, before regaining its composure with the other. He had observed the same movement many times in battle, in each case the result of leg trauma.

'They're injured.' he communed, tucking his throwing knife back into its sheath. *'You take the rear.'*

Krisis immediately ceased his growling and slunk off into the undergrowth to circle their quarry. He crept forwards, advancing slowly, allowing his companion time to get into position. The distance between them closed, enabling him to discern the true nature of their target: a female Freylarkin, who carried a bow in her left hand. Stained cloth had been tied around the Freylarkin's right

31

leg, confirming his suspicion. He stood up, alarming the Freylarkin, who then tried to shuffle around upon hearing the sound of Krisis' vehement growling behind them.

'Drop your weapon!' he cried, in a deliberately intimidating tone.

The Freylarkin did as commanded, immediately releasing the grip on their bow, allowing it to drop to the forest floor with a dull thud.

Another crack sounded. This time, the noise came from behind him. With deft movement and alacrity, he slid a knife from its place of rest, turned and threw it towards their fresh target.

'Whoa!' cried the familiar sound of Rayna's voice.

The light bringer stepped out from behind a tree, before wresting his knife free from its thick bark.

'Next time, check your target, Lothnar!'

'You *are* still breathing.'

'Barely!' replied Rayna, who slowly jogged towards him.

'You got closer this time.' he said, sardonically.

'Hardly. You were distracted.' said Rayna, before handing him back his blade. 'Who is this?'

'A good question.'

He turned to face their quarry, before being quickly passed by Rayna, The Guardian's inquisitive nature getting the better of her once more.

'Rayna, wait!'

'Leyla, is that *you*?'

THREE
Appraisal

'This is Anastacia, the facility's practice manager. She effectively runs this place.'

'The Director is attempting to flatter me, as per usual, so that he does not lose his successor.'

'Did I mention that she is also incredibly sharp?'

'No, I do not believe that you did.' he replied, curious as to the relationship between the pair.

'Watch your step, young Callum. Anastacia does not miss a trick, nor does she take prisoners.'

The well-presented woman, in her early forties, had long, straight, dark brown hair. Her eyes, a similar colour to her hair, were sharp, assessing his every detail. Her tall, slender frame and professional attire granted her an imposing presence, suggesting that she was not to be trifled with.

'I manage the day-to-day operations here – nothing more. I facilitate The Director's vision for this facility, which you will fall in line with.'

'OK.' he replied, taken aback by the woman's direct approach.

'Well then, I shall leave you two to get to know one another.' said The Director with a subtle grin. 'I have a matter to attend to. Callum, I will catch up with you in a few days to see how you are settling in.'

After The Director left, there was a period of silence between Anastacia and himself. The stern practice manager appeared to be evaluating him, her steely gaze fixed on him as she made her critical assessment. Though her expression remained blank, giving nothing away, he sensed a feeling of disapproval towards him.

'I am not looking for trouble.'

'So say those who often find it.' replied Anastacia, bluntly.

'Have you already judged this book by its cover?'

'Yes.'

'Do you not believe that to be presumptuous?'

'No. The stereotype fits, more often than not.' replied the Practice Manager sternly. 'I do not have the time, nor the desire, to read each book. We lack the resources and motivation to apply such granularity to every case wandering these halls.'

'Empathy aside, at least we can have a candid relationship with one another.' he said, giving Anastacia a wide grin.

'Follow me.' replied the Practice Manager, ignoring his quip entirely.

Together, they walked towards the rear of the facility, along a series of drab-looking corridors – the place looked more like a medical facility than a typical children's home.

'Has this facility been repurposed?'

'Yes – you are perceptive.'

'Page one.' he said, looking for some kind of less-than-stale response, which he did not receive.

Their footsteps echoed along the gloomy corridors, giving the place a sinister feel, like some kind of depraved laboratory.

'This facility used to admit and treat those experiencing mental trauma. After the program was shut down, we began to operate out of this premise instead – it has the necessary space required.'

'What type of mental trauma did they treat?'

'Typically, the degenerative kind. Care was mostly palliative.'

'I see.' he said, staring blankly at the discoloured walls whilst Anastacia unlocked the door at the end of the corridor.

'You will receive your access pass shortly. It will permit you access to your dormitory and the communal areas of this facility. The remainder is restricted access only.'

'How many children have you admitted to this place?'

'One hundred and eighty six, including you. Currently, we have one hundred and seventeen residents, excluding staff.'

'Then you must have worked here for a while.'

'Three years, nine months.'

'What!' he said, astonished by the numbers. 'But that's an enormous turnover!'

'Of course. We serve teenagers. With each departing year group, we shed circa fifty residents. For a facility of this size, those statistics are to be expected.'

Previous children's homes he had lodged at had been significantly smaller and less sterile. He began to understand why Anastacia and The Director were so desensitised to their surroundings. This was his first time experiencing the endemic problem personally on such a large scale – the revelation was jarring. He knew that the issue of homeless children within the metropolis was at breaking point, but witnessing the scale of the crisis first-hand made the numbers even more real. The heart-breaking state of affairs saddened him.

'Does the government have any future initiatives aimed at tackling the issue?'

'To my knowledge, no. Growing disdain towards the Shadow class is restricting public spend. Providing free lodging for your kind does not win votes.'

Anastacia's words were brutal, though he could not fault their merit. As he pondered the cutting truth of the matter, the door connecting to the next corridor slowly slid open, its movement laboured and accompanied by the sound of grinding metal.

'Adequate maintenance is an ongoing issue. Limited funds are problematic.'

The corridor ended in a dead-end, with a door on each of its flanking walls.

'Your dormitory is on the right. Here is your access pass. Do not lose it.' said Anastacia, handing him a small security token. 'The dormitory has shared facilities for you to use. Contact me if there are any issues.'

After handing him the token, Anastacia tuned on her heels and began heading back down the gloomy corridor.

'Are you not going to introduce me to my dorm mates?'

'You are a big boy, Callum.' replied Anastacia sarcastically, who continued to walk away from him. 'I am certain that you can introduce yourself.'

The door began to creak. He leapt through its narrowing gap as it slowly slid shut, barely avoiding being squashed by the aging mechanism, whose obstruction sensor no longer appeared to function. Clutching the security token, he loitered for a while in the corridor, staring vacantly at the door to his new dormitory, wondering what fresh torment lay in wait. Until now, his life had largely

36

been spent bouncing between a succession of children's homes, each more arduous than the last. Now, his latest residency would be the last of its kind, ushering in an end to what had largely been a miserable chapter in his life. With the exception of Kaitlin, he had little to speak of for his time spent leeching off what remained of the planet's blasted landscape. Spending time in the company of the attractive young librarian had been the highlight of his teenage years. The remainder amounted to scavenging, avoiding fights – with only mediocre success – and, for the most part, general survival. In less than a year, the system would forever close its doors to him. He needed to keep his head down and use the remaining time to figure out his next move. Exhaling a deep breath, he walked silently towards the door, hoping that whatever drama lay beyond would not distract him from achieving his objective.

Something was shaking her, yet her eyes remained shut, her heavy slumber fighting in defiance, seeking to retain its control over her torpor.

'Wake up.'

Muffled words sounded in her ear, a murmur, muted by the comfortable embrace of the darkness that held sway over her body. She felt warm, contented, unwilling to answer the distant call in her relaxed state.

'Leyla, get up!'

Her eyes snapped open. Someone crouched over her, their arms gripping her shoulders in a vice-like hold, violently shaking her. She recognised the Freylarkin screaming at her, though she could not put a name to the face; her mind remained disengaged, still clinging to the hope of further rest.

37

'Get up!'

'What is--'

A blur of silver washed over her, taking with it the auburn-haired Freylarkin, dragging its victim towards the far-right corner of the barn. Screams pierced her ears, obliterating the remnants of her stupor. She rolled over, grabbing her bow with her left hand, snatching an arrow with her right. Rising to her feet, she hastily nocked the arrow onto her bowstring before quickly acquiring her target. The projectile slammed into the back of the assailant, causing it to release an ear-splitting yelp. The lupine creature toppled right, revealing the ghastly sight of Zealia, slumped against the corner of the barn, whose torn throat gushed crimson liquid onto the straw-covered floor.

'Zealia!' she cried, darting towards the young Freylarkin. 'Stay with me!'

It was too late. The Freylarkin's soul was already bound for the Everlife, no longer tethered to the world she knew. Realising the futility of her efforts, she grabbed her quiver before leaving the barn.

Panic had broken out amongst the people, fuelled by distant screams that tore through the night, sending a shiver down her spine. Civilians frantically ran about the farmstead, searching for family members amongst the labyrinth of wooden dwellings and outbuildings. They clashed against one another, paying no heed to their kin as they desperately sought out loved ones.

'They are here! The Louperdu are here!' cried a civilian close by.

She chased down the scared Freylarkin, grabbing them by their hood, pulling their face close to her own.

'You are causing panic!'

'We must leave.'

'We need to stay and fight!'

'It is too late for that – they have the drop on us.'

'The Blades will defeat them. That is why we are here!'

'There are too many of them. You cannot defeat them; they are like an autumnal mist, rolling in over the fields. We must run!'

'Useless.' she spat, releasing the coward from her grasp.

She began sprinting towards the distant yelps and cries emanating from the southern edge of the settlement. She felt vulnerable without her falchion and shield, longing for her weapons of choice. Instead, she would make do with the bow that she gripped tightly in her right hand. Although not ideal, given the reduced visibility caused by the night, the moon was waxing gibbous, bathing the farmstead in a silvery light. As she ran, she passed a number of skirmishes throughout the settlement. Lending aid where she could, she helped her fellow Blades to even the numbers by impaling their adversaries before pressing on, her will bent on reaching the front line.

At the edge of the settlement, silver mist sprawled out in all directions. Louperdu disappeared from sight, only to reform behind the farmstead's defenders amidst wisps of grey smoke. Coordinating the defence was Natalya, who stood defiantly at the centre of The Blades' formation. The Valkyrie's squad was cut off, victims of an ever-tightening noose orchestrated by the Louperdu, who quickly circled their prey, biding time whilst their ranks swelled. Though ephemeral when dissolving their form, the Louperdu still shared many traits with their dire wolf cousins; they were pack hunters, predominantly, and would garner numbers before wiping out their prey. Realising the situation, Natalya opened fire. The telekinetic guided her arrow, steering it towards its prey, ensuring that her agile target would not evade the projectile. The arrow curved mid-flight, arcing into its target's flank, causing the spirit wolf to yelp in pain prior to its inevitable release. Again, the Valkyrie fired, continuing to focus her wrath towards the west. The Blades reformed in unison, turning to face the fallen wolves. It was clear that Natalya sought to create a gap in the feral cordon whilst the others protected her. Most of the Louperdu held their ground, snarling and fidgeting. Whilst others reverted to their mist form, slowly circling their prey like angry spirits, waiting for the opportune moment to strike. Realising her mentor's gambit, she threw her bow onto the roof of an adjacent shack, before jumping up to grab the edge of its flat roof, using her arm strength and wraith wings to hoist herself up. Scrambling across the marginally sloped roof, she retrieved her weapon and began firing down towards the widening gap, catching one of the spirit wolves by surprise and narrowly missing another that quickly dissolved. As more of their numbers fell, the rest of the pack become increasingly agitated. Sensing that the wolves would not wait any longer, Natalya cried out, ordering The Blades to charge.

She dropped another of the spirit wolves, moments prior to Natalya's counter-charge, praying that they had done enough for The Blades to drive a wedge into the gap. The encircling smoke moved to fill the opening, attempting to plug the widening hole, but the Louperdu were slow to reform, allowing The Blades to run right though them. The remaining wolves bounded towards their prey, pouncing on those making up the flanks. Some of the wolves were sent reeling, as cold steel slashed deep across their muzzles, whilst others snapped at the heels of the withdrawing Blades, dragging several of them down before more of their lupine kin hauled the prone warriors into the throng of the pack. Chilling screams filled the night whilst the lupine predators mercilessly ripped the unfortunate Blades apart.

'Take flight!' cried Natalya, realising that she lacked the numbers to mount an effective defence.

She dropped to the ground, using her wraith wings to cushion her fall, then launched herself forwards, beating her wings furiously, allowing her to join the others.

'Head towards the treeline!' cried Natalia, 'We can lose them in there and regroup.'

In the distance, she could see the moonlit silhouettes of other Freylarkin fleeing desperately towards the trees. Some flew ahead – mothers mostly, cradling infants and shepherding the young – whilst others hopelessly ran.

'What are they doing?' she cried, bemused by the sight of those fleeing on foot.

'Providing a distraction.' cried Natalya, 'They have made their choice. Do not let their sacrifices be in vain; we must get to that treeline and defend the survivors.'

There was an unexpected recess in the surviving Blade's harrowing account; Leyla's voice broke, consumed by grief and emotion, causing tears to stream down the Freylarkin's grubby face.

'I have heard enough!' thundered Lothnar, pounding his fist on the large oval table, causing Leyla to flinch. 'My scouts and I will end the bastards.'

Krisis began to snarl, echoing his master's sentiments.

41

'You are coming with us.' said Lothnar, directing his attention towards the adolescent dire wolf, who straightened his back in response.

'What happened to the others?' asked Larissa.

'Is Natalya safe?' enquired Thandor.

The aloof Paladin was clearly worried, evidenced by the look of concern now etched on his normally deadpan face.

'I…do not know.' Leyla stammered.

'Leyla, what happened to The Blades?' asked Nathanar, calmly, trying to put Leyla at ease.

Lothnar stood up, before slamming his fist upon the table once more.

'They had the gall to come back! This time, I will ensure that I end them all!'

'Lothnar!' she said, shooting a hard glare at the Paladin. 'Can you not see that she is traumatised? Your outbursts are not helping. Sit down!'

'Rayna, surely you cannot be OK with this?'

'Of course not, but you can at least give her a moment to compose herself.' she said, trying to restrain her own emotions.

'Every moment we sit here ushers in further release.'

'Lothnar,' said Kirika gently, 'We *will* right this wrong. However, we must understand the facts before we go charging in – you know this.'

When not overcome with emotion, the nomadic Paladin was more than capable of rational thought and logical decision-making, though his passion often got the better of him in pressure situations. Lothnar favoured tracking and hunting his prey, not the other way round. By contrast, the former Captain, Ragnar, loved to meet his enemies head on in battle, seeing each challenge as an opportunity to demonstrate his mastery in combat. It was little wonder, therefore, that the two got on so famously well, each perfectly complimenting the other's skills.

'Please, Lothnar.' she said. 'I promise you that we will avenge this travesty. You *will* have your vengeance.'

The furious Paladin turned to her before releasing a heavy sigh.

'Very well, Rayna.' replied Lothnar, before seating himself once more. 'Your promise is good enough for me.'

'Good.' she replied, before turning to Kirika.

'There is something that you should all know.' said Kirika, rising from her chair. 'I assembled this council of war *prior* to learning of Leyla's return to the vale.'

'What have you seen?' asked Nathaniel, who until now had remained silent during Leyla's account.

'It is not what I have seen, but rather what has been seen by a young Freylarkin named Rarni.'

'What!' said Nathanar, clearly taken aback by Kirika's words. 'You are referring to Lyra's daughter, I assume? The young Freylarkin that your sister and I rescued, along with the Knights Thranis?'

'Correct.' replied Kirika, who began slowly pacing around the subterranean chamber. 'Both Rayna and I spoke with Rarni at Lyra's request. Her daughter has been experiencing terrible nightmares, and yet they are not nightmares at all – they are *visions*.'

'I know Rarni.' said Larissa. 'Her hair is not purple like yours; she was born during the wrong season. Besides, she is too mature to be developing signs now.'

'Agreed. Nevertheless, her ability is real – I have *seen* it.' replied Kirika.

'She *saw* the attack, did she not?' enquired Thandor suddenly, the Paladin's keen deductions as sharp as ever. 'That is why you allowed Leyla to attend this confidential meeting.'

'Correct. The two incidents are linked.'

'Then, you also saw this tragedy unfold, when you scried the young girl.' said Lothnar, who had since composed himself.

'Yes, albeit a different view of events, earlier this morning, after which, I immediately called this meeting.' replied Kirika. 'I asked Rayna to track you down whilst I assembled the others. Then you both encountered Leyla in the forest.'

'What did Rarni see?' asked Nathaniel once more.

'Although I cannot be certain, I think it was Gaelin – I recognised his slender, calloused hands from our numerous discussions around this very table. He was running from the Louperdu, along with a number of others, not all of whom survived. I believe that he was trying to lure the pack away from the settlement, once he realised their true numbers.'

'I saw Gaelin.' said Leyla suddenly, wiping the tears from her eyes.

She watched as Kirika moved slowly towards the troubled Blade before couching down alongside her. Leyla's physical wounds had been completely healed, courtesy of Nathaniel. However, the damage caused to The Blade mentally would take far longer to repair; in time, Leyla would likely recover from her recent trauma, although, there was no knowing how long the recovery process would take.

44

'I realise that this is difficult for you.' said Kirika, offering Leyla a sympathetic ear. 'However, if you are able, we should be grateful if you would kindly continue your account for us.'

They set down in front of the treeline, unwilling to risk flight within the forest, especially in poor light. The moon's touch barely penetrated the forest, making it difficult to distinguish friend from foe amidst the thick flora. They each took a moment to catch their breath whilst Natalia assessed the situation.

'We will fight them at the edge of the treeline.' commanded Natalya. 'That gives us the advantage; we will see their approach and, with any luck, the Louperdu will find it difficult to outflank us with the trees at our backs.'

The Blades quickly formed a cordon along the edge of the treeline, placing themselves directly in line with the surviving Freylarkai sprinting towards them. In the distance, two of the silhouettes suddenly disappeared from view, snuffed out by their lupine pursuers. Deftly nocking another of her arrows, Natalya drew back on her bowstring, prompting her to follow suit, before they each acquired a fresh target.

'Get ready to receive the charge. Allow the civilians to pass us. Slaughter the rest!' ordered the Valkyrie.

Natalya fired at the Louperdu, using her ability to strike down one of the pursuers from an incredible distance – an impossible shot for anyone else. She considered doing the same, but without their commander's skill and ability, she knew that she had no hope of success. Instead, she waited, watching in awe as the Valkyrie nocked another arrow onto her bowstring. The swooshing sound of two more arrows flying into the night filled their ears, followed by the dull thud of Louperdu bouncing lifelessly across the ground as their shots found their mark. Reaching for her quiver she hastily drew another arrow, before attempting to acquire a fresh target amidst the rapidly growing number of silhouettes fast approaching them. Adjusting her footing, she stepped left, narrowly avoiding one of the fleeing Freylarkin who bounded past her at breakneck speed. More of the fleeing Freylarkai broke through their lines, disappearing into the forest behind them. One of the fleeing civilians lost their footing upon the uneven camber of the forest's perimeter, causing them to bounce across the ground. Paying the unfortunate Freylarkin no heed, she released her arrow, sending another of the pursuers off course.

'Brace!' cried Natalya, moments before the Louperdu crashed into their lines, sending a good number of The Blades crashing to the ground.

Working in pairs, those who evaded the charge quickly got to work, slashing their falchions across the fur hides of the Louperdu viciously mauling their prone comrades. Using her ability, Natalya wrenched one of the wolves from its prey, launching the lupine into the air before impaling it, mid-flight, with another of her vicious arrows. Yet, despite their efforts, several of the spirit wolves broke through the cordon, quickly disappearing into the forest in pursuit of their initial prey.

'Protect the civilians!' cried Natalya, who shot her a brief glance through the bloody carnage.

Seeking to put her bow to better use, she darted into the forest, realising there was little she could do amidst the chaotic melee that had broken out along the treeline. She ran as fast as she could across the uneven ground, using her free hand to deflect the foliage slapping at her face. Fresh screams sounded from within the forest increasing her sense of urgency. If not for the haphazard placement of the trees, she would have broken into a sprint. Instead, the terrain forced her to adjust her heading continuously, narrowly avoiding several collisions, as she homed in on the harrowing cries.

Upon reaching a small clearing bathed in moonlight, she paused for breath, taking stock of the shapes dashing through the trees up ahead. The sound of a male voice, followed by several yelps, drew her deeper into the forest. When at last she discovered the source of the commotion, she saw a male Freylarkin lying on his back, pinned to the ground by one of the silvery wolves. The Freylarkin gripped his slender hands tightly around the lupine's throat, trying desperately to pull the creature's snapping muzzle towards the ground. The spirit wolf backed up fiercely, dragging its quarry with it, trying to wrench itself free. Nevertheless, the valiant civilian held on, using his long fingers to maintain the vice-like grip in a bid to control the head of his opponent. Seizing the opportunity to strike, she drew another arrow before quickly targeting her opponent. As her arrow took flight, the wolf melted away, leaving behind a plume of grey smoke.

'Where is it?' she cried, before nocking another of her arrows onto her bowstring whilst the dazed Freylarkin scrambled to his feet.

Turning slowly on her heel, she scanned the surrounding woodland looking for signs of movement amongst the shadows. Something moved to her left, but before she could adjust her footing, her opponent was

47

already upon her. She thrust her bow towards her assailant's head, using it as an improvised melee weapon, trying to stagger it. Regardless, the brazen lupine crashed into her, using its weight and momentum to knock her off balance. Reeling from the attack, she fell backwards before crashing hard on the ground. Something dug into her right leg, causing her to gasp in pain, following which the ferocious animal tried to snap at her face. She instinctively punched her weapon into the wolf's muzzle, thwarting its attack. The animal let out a yelp, followed by an awful whine as her newfound ally drove something sharp into its flank. The spirit wolf immediately backed off, limping away in pain. As their assailant withdrew, she identified the design of the fletch at the nock end of the arrow protruding from their opponent as one of hers.

'Thank you.' she said as the tall, slender Freylarkin quickly helped her onto her feet. 'That one should have hit the first time!'

'Do not beat yourself up about it. Without you, my soul would already be on its way to the Everlife.'

'Likewise.' she said, giving her ally a firm nod. 'Best we finish it.'

'Save your arrows; there will be more. It will not survive. Besides, we need to dress your wound quickly.'

'What is your name?' she asked, as they hobbled away from their crippled opponent.

'My name is Gaelin.'

FOUR
Acquaintance

The off-white door, with its light brown marks and black scuffs along the bottom, slid quietly shut behind him. He stood in a narrow corridor, painted in the same discoloured drab white as the entrance door, looking up and down the length of the passageway. There were gaps along the corridor at regular intervals, where doors should have been, each presumably leading to a separate sleeping area providing minimal privacy. He was familiar with the setup, designed to keep dorm mates honest at all times. The open access policy did not faze him, especially given that he had little of note worth stealing. Aside from the few books that he owned – which people rarely took interest in – he had nothing of value. As he stood in the corridor, wondering which of the sleeping bays had been allocated to him, a gaunt ginger-haired boy stepped into view.

'Hi, my name is Callum.' he said, taking the initiative.

'Are you the new kid? The Commandant told us to expect someone.'

'Commandant?'

'Yeah, that woman who runs everything. You met her, right?'

'You mean Anastacia?'

'Yeah, that's right.' explained the boy. 'We just call her The Commandant.'

'I see.'

The gaunt teenager stared at him awkwardly, unsure of what to do or say next. It was painfully obvious to him that the boy possessed little or no initiative of his own and was likely just a follower, subservient to whomever lorded it over the rest of the dormitory's residents. He had met the type on countless occasions before – submissive and obedient, all of them. The setup was no different to any other he had encountered and was essentially just a more civilised variant of the gangs roaming the streets. There was always a pack leader, one who, more often than not, maintained power using intimidation and coercion. He knew the arrangement well and was under no illusions that the setup would be any different at the facility.

'So, who's in charge around here?'

'Err…' the boy stammered, as though fearful of uttering his juvenile overseer's name.

'Come on, it's not as if you will take a beating for mentioning their name.'

The boy continued to stare mutely at him, as though suddenly paralysed by fear.

'I am in charge.' came a deep voice from the sleeping bay behind him.

He turned around slowly, determined not to exhibit any signs of nerves or intimidation. With all such encounters, it was crucial to start as one meant to carry on – he would not allow himself to be coerced by others. More often than not, self-proclaimed group leaders recognised him as being difficult to control. Those in charge would often let him be, provided he too refrained from kicking the hornets' nest, thereby maintaining an uneasy truce of sorts. However, when such truces inevitably broke down, he was more than capable of handling himself when it came to brawling in the dorms.

'And beatings are at my discretion. Incidentally, that is Jacob.'

'I expected you to be located at the end of the dorm; that is the normal arrangement.'

'I prefer the centre of the dorm; better to glean facts first-hand, as opposed to acquiring distorted information through the mouths of others.'

The tall, dark-skinned, muscular kid stood opposite him was not at all what he had expected. The gang leaders he had dealt with previously were uneducated runts, who, for the most part, had lived abusive lives. By contrast, the boy, if not a man, now towering over him appeared to be cut from a different cloth entirely.

'Makes sense.'

'Your name is Callum, correct?'

'Correct.'

'My name is Sebastian.'

'Good to meet you, Seb.'

'My name is Sebastian.' explained the boy once more, giving him a deadpan stare.

They stared at one another, each silently assessing the other. The lull in their conversation piqued the interest of the dormitory's remaining residents, who, one-by-one, poked their heads out from behind their sleeping bays to observe the encounter.

'Let me be clear, *Sebastian*.' he said, steeling himself for what would likely be an intense exchange of words. 'I am not seeking to challenge your authority, nor am I a team player. Therefore, I have no interest in running with your crew. My *only* agenda is to figure out my next move, after I have served my final year in this place. You want the middle – fine. I will take a bay at the end of the dorm and leave you and yours to it.'

51

An awkward silence ensued whilst the gang leader considered his response. Although Sebastian's unorthodox approach made him feel uneasy, nevertheless, it was refreshing dealing with someone who measured their words carefully. As they continued to eye one another up, more and more of the dormitory's residents poked their heads out to observe the encounter, which had evolved into a war of silence.

'Ivan,' said Sebastian in a deep voice, knowing that the boy in question would already be eavesdropping on their conversation. 'Kindly clear out your belongings and make yourself comfortable in one of the spare bays towards the end of the dormitory. I want Callum in the one next to me.'

'That is not necessary.' he said, immediately recognising the ploy for what it was.

'You are new here. It would be rude of me not to make you feel welcome among us.'

He watched as the boy named Ivan hastily threw his meagre belongings into the corridor as the others watched in silence.

'You see, Callum. Ivan is more than happy to offer you his bay. I trust that you will find it comfortable - once you have had a chance to settle in, that is.'

'I am sure that I will.' he replied flatly, secretly cursing the manner in which events were unfolding.

Because of his complacency, he had underestimated Sebastian. Now, his every word would be scrutinised, given his close proximity to the group's leader. He understood well now the reason for The Director's candid warning when first they had met. Yet despite the unexpected assistance, he was already caught in Sebastian's web.

Nevertheless, despite his apparent oversight, there was still time to escape.

'Gaelin, of the ruling council?'

'Yes, but we can discuss that later.'

Using Gaelin as a crutch, she hobbled deeper into the wood, putting the sound of the awful distant cries behind them. Abandoning the others grated against her soul, but she had her orders, and those on the front line had theirs. Once they had put sufficient distance between themselves and the fighting, Gaelin set her down on the ground before tending to her leg. She nocked another arrow onto her bowstring, fixing her sights on the surrounding woodland, whilst her companion used cloth from his own garments to wrap her wound.

'This will hurt.' said Gaelin, who then pulled the fabric tightly around her leg.

'It is what I signed up for.' she replied defiantly, unwilling to let the pain get the better of her.

'No one should have to witness such sights.' whispered Gaelin, wearily. 'We work the land and are peaceful folk, yet other people's wars seem to haunt us.'

'The Louperdu started this – *they* attacked us.'

'Yes, but what provoked such an attack?'

She had never considered the point of view before. As a Blade, she carried out her orders without question, trusting those in command to make the right decisions – the Order could not function without such discipline. That said, Gaelin's words struck a chord with her, giving her pause for thought.

'My orders were to protect the civilians.'

53

'Which you have done – the fact that I am still here is proof of that.' said Gaelin, who then stood up. 'Now, you must do something else.'

'You outrank Natalia; I will follow your orders.'

Gaelin laughed.

'I am not your superior. I am a farmer.'

'You sit on the ruling council.'

'I represent the working class, giving them a voice in matters that affect the domain – nothing more.'

'What would you have me do?'

'You must deliver word of the attack to the Tri-Spires.'

'But my leg is wounded – you will move faster than I can.'

'I realise that our people have become less reliant on them over the passes, slowly forgetting the old ways, however, have you forsaken your wraith wings entirely?'

She felt herself blush, embarrassed by her obvious oversight in the presence of one who was held in such high regard. Fortunately, the night veiled her embarrassment, masking her wounded pride.

'Apologies, I will consider my words more carefully in future.'

'Relax, there is no need for formality in my presence.' said Gaelin, earnestly. 'I will travel to the next settlement, east along the river, warning them of the attack. If I encounter any survivors, I will ask that they accompany me.'

'Very well.' she said, acknowledging Gaelin's plan.

'Speak with Kirika. Inform her that I request further support from The Blades. We require immediate aid to repel these attacks, of which I believe there will be more.'

54

'I am just a Blade Adept. Why is it that you believe that I can convince one such as Kirika to act?'

'You do not give yourself enough credit.' said Gaelin. 'You fought with heart, fending off that spirit wolf with a weapon unsuited for melee.'

She grabbed Gaelin's calloused hand, which he offered, aiding her back onto her feet. The former farmer was deceivingly strong for such a lean Freylarkin, pulling her upright with ease.

'Kirika is not the haughty politician some believe her to be – she grew up in the forest.'

'I guess that her lofty position has influenced my perception of her.'

'I can understand why that would be the case. Nevertheless, talk to her – she *will* hear you out.' said Gaelin, reassuringly. 'Besides, you can always ask that she uses her ability to corroborate your story.'

For someone who had predominantly worked the land, Gaelin's impromptu leadership reassured her. He was clearly no stranger to decision making, reasoning his point of view in a clear and down-to-earth manner. She felt comfortable following his lead and acknowledged his words with a firm nod.

'I will do as you ask.' she said, using her bow to steady herself. 'Please, do not take any risks; those wolves are still out there.'

'I trust that Natalya will thin their numbers, at least enough for me to reach the next settlement – she is ruthless with that bow of hers.'

'Indeed.' she said, releasing a gentle laugh. 'I have been fortunate enough to train with both Natalya and The Guardian.'

'Ah, that explains it then.'

'What do you mean?'

'When was the last time you saw either of them back down from a fight, eh? I suspect that Rayna has already given you one of her *talks*, given the way that you fought that spirit wolf.'

She thought back to her time in the barn, training alongside the pair during winter, and how both had encouraged her to persevere with the use of a bow. Without consciously acknowledging the fact, that cycle had wrought a profound change in her mind-set, serving as a reminder that the only person holding her back was in fact herself. Since that time, she had embraced change, along with the challenges that came with it, and in doing so had broadened her skills, considerably.

'Yes, indeed she did. I will not fail you; word will be delivered to the vale and you will have the support needed.'

She gave Gaelin a firm nod, bidding her new ally farewell, before moving towards the edge of the forest. Making her way towards the river, she unfurled her wraith wings. Concentrating on the use of her aetheric wings, she tried hard to focus her mind on beating them furiously, an art that she had all but forgotten. Her body became lighter as her feet slowly left the ground. Though she was drastically out of practice, only managing to hover a pace above the ground, nevertheless, it was sufficient to achieve her ends. She hovered towards the centre of the river, knowing that her enemies could not reach her there. Re-orientating her body westwards, towards the heart of the vale, she tightened her grip on her bow then sped off into the fading night.

There was a short pause after Leyla's account, whilst the others gave the surviving Blade a moment to consider any further information warranting dissemination. Unsurprisingly, Lothnar was the first to break the silence, once they realised that Leyla's report had been concluded.

'Let me deal with this. My scouts and I will track the pack's movements and cut them down at the source.'

'The scouts have been garrisoned all winter.' said Nathanar, turning to face Kirika. 'They are not built for guard duty and are becoming irritable. Giving them this assignment would allow them to scratch an itch.'

Kirika nodded in agreement.

'We need to discover the cause of these incursions.' she said to the group. 'Lothnar is the only one among us who can communicate with them, if only enough to discern the truth.'

'Agreed.' said Thandor. 'Rayna, you should accompany Lothnar and the scout regiment; your ability could prove invaluable.'

'Are the Louperdu vulnerable to light?' asked Larissa, curiously.

'Unknown. We know very little about them.' explained Lothnar. 'However, they do not attack during light – we know that much. Whilst it is possible that they could have an aversion to the light, they may simply be nocturnal creatures.'

'I will go.' she said. 'I trust Nathanar to manage The Blades in my absence.'

'Fine. Provided, that he remains in the vale this time!' said Kirika, before giving the Captain of The Blades a weak smile.

'I do not have a vacation planned.' said Nathanar, casually acknowledging Kirika's quip.

'Nathaniel,' she said, 'Are the Aspirants capable of assuming guard duties if we redeploy the scouts?'

'Yes.' replied The Teacher, leaning forward in his chair, revealing the many scars along the outer edges of his chiselled arms. 'Their training is sufficient to carry out such duties. The responsibility would be good for them.'

'That makes sense.' said Thandor. 'Then it is agreed, is it not? Lothnar and Rayna will take the scouts to learn the cause of these attacks, before putting an end to them.'

'Agreed.' said Lothnar, followed shortly afterwards by Larissa.

'What say you, Nathaniel?' she said, her gaze still fixed on her adopted father. 'Are you also in agreement?'

'I am not on the ruling council; I do not have any authority here.'

'Nor I. Nonetheless, your counsel is valued, and I for one am keen to garner your thoughts on the matter.'

'Speak freely, Nathaniel.' said Kirika, 'You, more than most, have earnt that right.'

Nathaniel sat back in his chair, making himself more comfortable, whilst he measured his response.

'I have had my fill of war.' said Nathaniel, earnestly. 'With that said, this council is duty bound to protect the *people*, not just those resident in the vale. Gaelin has requested assistance. His kin aided us in our time of need. It is only right, therefore, that we answer his call. However, in Gaelin's absence there is one here who should formally proxy his vote, before we commit our already depleted forces to another campaign. The decision to send the Freylarkai into further conflict should be unanimous.'

58

.   'Well said.' replied Lothnar, who nodded in affirmation before turning to Leyla. 'You witnessed the fighting first-hand. Furthermore, you fought alongside Gaelin. Nathaniel is right; you have the right to proxy Gaelin's formal vote in this matter. Either you chose to back down from this fight, turn the other cheek, and hope that these incidents do not escalate. Or, you choose to incite further bloodshed, theirs and ours – conflict is, more often than not, a gluttonous master, rarely content with the souls of a few. There is no abstaining.'

Leyla appeared caught off guard by the nomadic Paladin's frank summary. Nevertheless, Lothnar spoke the grim truth of the matter, presenting the options plainly. Leyla turn towards Kirika, no doubt hoping to seek guidance from one who could scry future events.

'She cannot help you. There are too many variables in battle, too many strands of fate to investigate, each capable of shifting their course in an instant.' she explained. 'Attempting to foresee the outcome of the maelstrom invites madness, courting the loss of one's sanity. Therefore, Kirika will vote last, so that she is not tempted to influence the council's judgement with potential folly.'

'You are asking me to vote on whether or not to place our people in further danger – I am not qualified to vote on such matters.'

'Are any of us?' asked Thandor inquisitively.

'Leyla,' said Kirika in a calm voice. 'Our kin are already in danger. You must decide now which path you believe is best suited to ending that danger.'

The Blade Adept bowed her head before fidgeting uncomfortably in her seat whilst making her decision. After another short pause, Leyla raised her head, fixing her gaze upon her intensely.

'Rayna, I agree with the others. Both you and Lothnar *should* take the scouts. However, I wish to join you.'

'Leyla, you are not a trained scout.' said Lothnar. 'You have not yet learned to use the battlefield to your advantage.'

'Nor have I.' she said, cutting the Paladin short.

'You are a light bringer; that gives you an advantage. Furthermore, you have those fancy blades of yours to deliver you from trouble.'

'Leyla is skilled in both melee and ranged combat and she has spent a good amount of time in the field.' she said, turning her head towards Lothnar. 'Besides, you know what it's like, that feeling you get when a score needs to be settled – will you deny her that?'

Lothnar narrowed his eyes and shook his head slowly.

'If she falls behind, we will not wait for her.'

'I am no one's burden.' said Layla defiantly.

Leyla's unfettered words reminded her of when she had first met Lothnar, in the very same room, shortly after her arrival in Freylar. She smiled, knowing that Lothnar would no doubt recall the moment when first they had locked horns across the oval table.

'Well said.' replied Lothnar, nodding his head, before taking a moment to consider his response. 'As you know, your father served under me in the borderlands. He was a staunch member of the scout regiment and a skilled fighter. What you may not know, is that I regarded him as a close friend – I miss him. He would be proud of you, his daughter. Therefore, I have made my decision. You may

60

accompany us, provided Kirika also agrees to the proposed campaign. However, Leyla is *your* responsibility, Rayna.'

She nodded in agreement, before turning to face Kirika at the head of the table. The scrier appeared to be lost in thought. Concern gripped her unexpectedly, as she briefly considered the possibility of Fate Weaver straying along the same path Darlia had once done. However, her fears were quickly allayed when Kirika gave her a brief smile.

'I agree.' said Kirika. 'We cannot abandon the outlying communities – the people need protecting. This situation needs ending before it can escalate further. Lothnar, I trust that you will finish what you started.'

'Hopefully you will both be comfortable here.' she said, watching as Rarni's eyes canvased their new quarters. 'I thought that it might be less jarring for you both at the base of the Tri-Spires. Although there are more people lodging in this area of the citadel, you can easily escape outside should you feel a little claustrophobic.'

'Thank you.' said Lyra, who appeared more at ease since their last meeting. 'I must admit, this feels very different to our home in the forest.'

'Indeed. The Tri-Spires can feel very...busy, at least in comparison to the forest dwellings. Though I spend most of my cycles here, I still find time to visit friends who make their homes in the forest.'

'As I understand it, you too were once a forest dweller.'

'Yes, that is correct. However, after my appointment to the ruling council, my duties warranted that I reside here instead.'

'I see.'

61

They both watched with interest as Rarni continued to cast her gaze over the chamber, scrutinising every little detail as she familiarised herself with the new lodgings.

'Do you like it?' she asked, curious as to the child's first impression of their quarters. 'If it is not to your liking, there are alternative quarters higher up in the Tri-Spires. However, you will need to use Waystones to access them.'

'This is perfect.' said Lyra. 'We will be comfortable here.'

'Mummy said that the queen made the Tri-Spires.' said Rarni unexpectedly.

'It is true.' she replied, eager to engage the child in further dialogue, regardless of the subject. 'Queen Mirielle made the Tri-Spires. She is the most powerful shaper that I have ever met.'

'Where did the Queen go?'

'She chose to leave the vale. Mirielle spent the winter at Scrier's Post.'

'Is she still there?' asked Rarni, whose interest had clearly been piqued.

'I do not believe that she continues to linger there.'

'She must be lonely by herself.'

'Mirielle has been alone for a long time.'

'Rarni, you have asked Kirika enough questions for now.' Lyra interjected. 'We need to unpack. Besides, I am fairly certain that Kirika has important work to do.'

'I will be back tomorrow, once you are both properly settled in. Then, Rarni, we can begin your training.'

'Rarni, what do you have to say to Kirika?'

'Thank you.' said the child, before resuming her thorough investigation of the chamber.

'You are most welcome.' she replied, followed with an earnest smile, before pulling Lyra to one side. 'If you are in agreement, I would like to begin Rarni's training in private tomorrow, free from any distractions.'

'Of course. You are one of the few people that my daughter has spoken to since the abduction. I am sure it will not be an issue.'

'Wonderful. I will return here tomorrow, mid-morning. I find that youthful minds are more astute during the mornings, before fatigue claims their fragile resolve.'

Lyra laughed.

'Perhaps you should give motherhood a try, Kirika.' said Lyra. 'It appears that you have a few tricks that will place you in good stead for such an adventure.'

'I am not sure that I am ready for such a heavy responsibility.' she said, taken aback by the comment.

'Kirika, you went head-to-head with Mirielle. Do not try to convince me that you are no match for a child.'

'Perhaps, one cycle, I will rise to the challenge. However, for the time being at least, chairing the ruling council is more than a handful.'

'I would have thought your role on the council to be good practice for motherhood.'

'Stop it.' she said, amused by Lyra's quip. 'I really must go. Just ask if you need anything.'

FIVE
Duty

'You do not have to do this.' he said, whilst assessing the size of the regiment skulking amidst the trees. 'There is still time to back out of this mission - no one would hold it against you.'

'Lothnar, I am not walking away from this.' said Leyla, vehemently.

'Very well. In which case, I will treat you no differently to the others. Fall in line with your comrades, you are part of the scout regiment now.'

He watched with interest as Leyla took her place amongst the veterans arrayed before him. Some paid her little or no attention, though there were others who gave her disdainful glares signalling their disapproval. Despite their obvious disrespect, he overlooked their slights given their veteran status – each had earned a degree of leniency given their lengthy service to The Blades' vanguard.

'Sir, may we begin the briefing?' asked Lazrik impatiently, clearly eager to return to active service. 'Furthermore, if I may, why are both The Guardian and this untrained Adept accompanying us?'

He had known the straight-talking scout for many passes. Lazrik had accomplished many feats under his command, and in doing so had earned his respect, in addition to the rank of squad leader. Nonetheless, the scouts were renowned for being cocksure, and at times even arrogant. Therefore, it was expected of him to rein them in on occasion.

'Because I said so. If anyone has a problem with my orders, they may voice their concerns now!'

The scouts stiffened their posture and saluted him, Lazrik included. Despite their idling in the vale, babysitting the inhabitants of the Tri-Spires, he was glad to see that the scouts had not succumbed to lethargy in light of their extended guard duties. It was high time that the scout regiment returned to active field duty. Although their mission meant that they would likely remain within the vale, a tour of the outlying communities would at least enable them to forego their shackles for a spell.

'Listen carefully, I will not repeat myself. The Louperdu have attacked one, perhaps more, of the outlying communities to the east. Report of these attacks was delivered to us first-hand by Leyla.' he boomed in a commanding tone, before pointing squarely at the Adept. 'Leyla fought at the farmstead and will guide us to its location. We will retake the position, which will become our forward operating base for the duration of the campaign. Our objective is to secure all of the eastern communities, rescue any survivors and locate the source of these incursions, then destroy it.'

'Yes, sir!' cried the scouts in unison.

'We have two with us who are untrained in our ways. I trust that you will *all* teach them. By the time we are done with the Louperdu, I expect both of these rookies to be trained to an acceptable standard – their failures will be *your* failures. Is that understood?'

'Yes, sir!'

'Lazrik, take point with your squad. Leyla is to remain at the rear of your vanguard. I am also assigning Krisis to your team – use him. Yandar, your squad has the left flank. Saralia's squad will protect our right. I have centre of the formation. Rayna, you are with me.'

The scouts expertly moved to their assigned positions as though each were part of an intricate piece of machinery, engineered to perform a singular function, flawlessly. They moved like wraiths, gliding smoothly into place despite the natural detritus littering the ground of the forest; fallen trees, large rocks and bushes were of no hindrance to the scouts, who flowed around them like water.

'*Go with Lazrik and put your keen senses to work.*'

The adolescent dire wolf bounded enthusiastically towards the front of the formation now rapidly taking shape. It felt good to have direction once more, a feeling clearly shared by his comrades, who moved with renewed purpose.

'I failed to appreciate the level of discipline amongst your scouts, Lothnar.' said Rayna, keenly watching as those in position prepared themselves, ready to move out.

'When off duty, we often come across as cocky, abrasive and even arrogant - managing public relations is not amongst our strengths. However, in the field, you will not find a more skilled group of predators.'

'Perhaps I should have better utilised them at Bleak Moor.'

'Open warfare is not our strong suit.' he said, turning to face the light bringer. 'We silently track our prey, then, when the time is right, strike hard from the shadows.'

'Which position did Alarielle assume, when she fought by you side?'

'I assigned Alarielle to the vanguard. When the Narlakai ambushed us, those up front were hit hardest by the attack. I am responsible for her release.'

'You could not have known that the Narlakai were being coerced at the time.'

'The signs were there, Rayna – fewer Narlakai aimlessly roaming the borderlands. However, we were not perceptive enough to acknowledge them. We underestimated our enemy that cycle. That will never happen again.'

'You are being overly hard on yourself.'

'There is no support out here. No room for error. One cannot be *soft* if they wish to endure in the scouts. A part of you must understand this, given your time in the Wild?'

'Yes, I suppose that it does.' Rayna replied, followed by a weak smile. 'Lothnar, try not to lose yourself in this – there is a life waiting for you beyond revenge, violence and bloodshed.'

Rayna's words caught him off guard. When Callum first arrived in Freylar – stealing Alarielle's body, as he had put it – their relationship had been nothing short of hostile. In truth, he had taken an instant dislike to the interloper for robbing the light bringer of her comatose body, denying him the opportunity to advance his affections towards Alarielle. Since then, he had grown to respect Rayna and the deeds that she had accomplished during her relatively short time in Freylar. Their relationship had become far less turbulent with each passing cycle, and, over time, he had developed a great deal of respect for the Valkyrie in light of her accomplishments. Hearing Rayna speak of concern for his wellbeing stirred emotions that he had once harboured – but never acted upon – for Alarielle. In terms of physical appearance at least, Rayna was Alarielle. Until now, he had always identified them as separate individuals. However, his relationship with Rayna was changing, and had been since their time working together to depose Mirielle. He could not tell if he was transposing his past feelings for

Alarielle onto Rayna, or whether he was growing fond of the light bringer for a second time. In any event, the situation had become complicated. Until now, he had believed the complex state of their relationship to be completely one-sided. However, Rayna's empathetic words now suggested otherwise. He was about to reply, but with a clear mind and his emotions in check, logic intervened, cautioning him not to dismiss her words or deflect them with humour. He forgot – more likely, he just never really considered – how difficult it must be for Rayna, formerly Callum, to come to terms with her lot. Were he in the same position, he had no clue as to how he would react in such circumstances. The idea of losing one's body then acquiring another, of the opposite sex, was lost on him. No doubt, one could only truly appreciate the complexities of such a scenario when directly exposed to it. In the end, his relationship with the light bringer would either flourish or wither depending on whether he chose to accept or reject Rayna for the person she now was, and not who Alarielle had once been.

'Thank you for your concern. I will heed your words.' he said sincerely, surprising even himself.

Rayna gave him a coy smile, which instinctively prompted one of his own. It had been a while since he had smiled in earnest. To his recollection, the last time was when Captain Ragnar still commanded The Blades - memories of the burly oaf's attempts to sneak up on him still amused him.

The formation was ready, with the scouts eagerly awaiting his orders. It felt good to be at the helm of the regiment again, despite their reduced numbers. At such short notice, it had been difficult to round up sufficient

69

numbers for the campaign. However, time was limited, thus they could not afford to wait any longer. He would send word via Sky-Skitter to Thandor of their movements. The wily Paladin would marshal the remainder of the regiment, which would later reinforce their position. Though he socialised very little with his fellow council member, he trusted Thandor implicitly.

For too long the scouts had languished in the Tri-Spires, their skills underutilised. Nevertheless, they remained as sharp as ever; he could see the predatory look in his comrades' eyes, dispelling the concern that the scouts had become a dull blade in light of their forced sabbatical. With sufficient numbers now assembled and waiting in position, it was time to commence the campaign against their lupine adversaries. He surveyed all those before him one last time, ensuring that preparations were complete, before issuing the command that his restless brethren had been waiting for.

'Scouts, move out!'

Ivan's former sleeping bay, now his own, was sparsely furnished. Aside from a metal-framed bed, there was a sterile-looking bedside cabinet and a wardrobe covered in scuff marks. Neither piece of furniture had a lock, which, although not surprising, disappointed him given the disposition of his neighbours. His initial encounter had already taught him one important lesson: he would be dealing with a more troublesome group this time round and not the usual ilk. Dim-witted or emotionally traumatised meatheads were easily managed. However, educated, devious and nosey acquaintances were far more problematic.

He sat down on what was now his bed. The mattress was lumpy and uneven. Though not ideal, he had slept on far worse. Pressing his back to the wall, he wondered if Sebastian lay directly on the other side, listening to every sound from his sleeping bay. Or instead, whether the arrangement was simply a bluff, designed to keep him on his toes and prompt him to question his every move. In any event, Sebastian was two steps ahead of him, already renting space in his mind. How could he be so stupid, he thought.

'Have you settled in?' asked the familiar gaunt figure suddenly stepping into his room.

'Jacob. Don't you guys knock?'

'On what?' asked the youth, directing his gaze towards the space in the wall where a door ought to have been.

'The wall, maybe...'

Jacob gave him a gormless stare, confirming what he already knew to be true: the boy was not overly bright. He supposed that was probably true for most of Sebastian's crew. No doubt, the more educated lot had been driven away by their leader in favour of more malleable replacements.

'Is that a book?' asked the teenager, suddenly.

He pressed his right index finger against his mouth, turning his head slightly towards the wall.

'Eh?' replied Jacob, clearly too dim-witted to understand his body language.

'Sebastian will hear.' he whispered.

'Oh... He left already. Probably in the common room.'

'How do you know that he left?'

'I saw him leave from my bay.'

71

'Do you spy on everyone?'

'Is that a book?' asked the boy again persistently, ignoring his question.

He pushed the book back into his satchel, along with his other meagre possessions. Given the frequency with which he changed accommodation, it made little sense to cart numerous belongings around with him. Aside from the few keepsakes in his satchel, from various chapters of his life, his only other possessions were a long holdall full of worn clothes and the odd grooming appliance.

'Yes, it is indeed.'

'Where did you get it?'

'I did not steal it, if that is what you're thinking. It was a gift to me.'

'Who gave it to you?'

'Has Sebastian ordered you to gather information on me?'

'Eh?' replied Jacob once more.

The youth either lacked intelligence or was a well-trained actor – he could not tell. Perhaps he needed to make more of an effort, he wondered. However, the facility was just another bump in the road that he needed to ride out before his release from the system. At which point, they would likely never meet again; Jacob was visibly younger than he was and would therefore cling to the facility's bosom for perhaps another year, before it disowned the clueless waif.

'Why are you here?' he asked, cutting to the heart of the matter.

'Was just seein' if you have anything to trade.'

'I don't.'

72

He felt bad rebuffing Jacob so abrasively, but history had taught him well not to get too close to his dorm mates. In his experience, everyone was out for themselves, including those not clever enough to realise it.

'What about the book?'

'I am not trading the book with you. Why are you so fixated on it?'

'I have never seen one.'

Jacob loitered before him uneasily, unsure of what to do next. He could see now that Sebastian had not been the one to instigate the awkward encounter.

'Look, why don't you give me a minute, then maybe afterwards you could give me a tour of this facility?'

'Sure, OK. I could show you the common room.'

'Sounds good.'

He waited for Jacob to leave his sleeping bay, but the moment never came, despite the prolonged silence between them. In that instant, he wondered what it must be like to be so oblivious to the nuances of social interaction. He felt sad for the boy, who clearly lacked proper education during his upbringing. The world, or what was left of it, was cruel and unfair. Only those with affluence prospered, receiving the education and protection needed to generate further wealth. This endless cycle repeated itself, spitting out the remains of those crushed in its wake, specifically, the Shadow class. His kin deserved better, but with no way to fight the system, the Shadow class would continue to war over its scraps.

'This is the part where you leave.' he said flatly, loathing the need for such plain speak.

Jacob started to move, paused, and then eventually left the sleeping bay. He sighed, knowing that in all likelihood the boy was loitering behind the wall. Pulling the book from his satchel again, he wandered over to the wardrobe. The cabinet was the clear choice, but he needed somewhere Sebastian would not search, ruling out the inside of the wardrobe. He considered stashing the book behind the piece of furniture, but it was an obvious ploy for someone of Sebastian's intelligence. As he stood there, assessing the wardrobe's usefulness, he remembered a trick he had used before, at previous lodgings. Flicking open the book, he read the message handwritten on the inside of the cover page before setting his plan in motion.

'Callum, your education is important – it will keep you safe. Make sure that you come back to the library soon. Keep reading. Kaitlin x'

Snapping the book closed, he placed it gently on the floor in front of the wardrobe. Wrapping his arms around the cumbersome piece of furniture, he slowly tipped the metal container to the right. It was lighter than expected, no doubt fabricated from wafer-thin metal sheeting. Its poor construction forced him to manhandle the wardrobe gently, easing the sound of flexing metal. Using his left foot, he gently nudged the literary treasure under the piece of furniture into the void beneath the base of the wardrobe, before quietly setting it back down. To complete the look, he haphazardly scattered his remaining effects around the room, before throwing his holdall into the wardrobe with a deliberate thump. Happy that he had sufficiently covered his tracks, the stepped into the corridor. Sure enough, Jacob was there, back pressed against the wall.

'Right then. Shall we crack on with this tour of yours?'

'Are you OK?'

When Rarni first laid eyes on the Waystone chamber, the child's darkening blue eyes seemed to visibly double in size, her interest piqued to new heights. However, since passing through one of the Waystones, Rarni now appeared a shade whiter, as though ill or about to retch.

'The experience can be quite jarring at first. However, you will get used to it.'

Rarni looked up at her, before quickly covering her mouth with both hands.

'You need to breathe. Take the breath into the pit of your stomach, right here.' she said, gently poking the child's stomach. 'Then release it, slowly.'

'Rarni did as instructed, inhaling deeply, before slowly exhaling.'

'Good, keep doing that for me. This breathing exercise is one that you should practice regularly; it will help you to focus.'

She waited whilst Rarni practiced the exercise as they stood opposite the imposing wooden doors leading to Mirielle's former chamber beyond. She rarely ventured to the apex of the Tri-Spires, instead preferring to live closer to the base of the citadel, as though doing so somehow connected her better to the people. She pitied Freylar's former queen, whose downward spiral into ruin had largely been self-inflicted. Although other contributing factors – herself included – had led to the sundering of Mirielle's reign, it was the queen's insatiable need for knowledge and control that had instigated the sad affair.

'I feel better.'

'I am glad to hear it.' she said, before ushering the child towards the ominous doors opposite them. 'Come, let us get started – you have much to learn.'

She pushed hard against the doors to Mirielle's former chamber, forcing them to give way. The doors creaked on their hinges, opening slowly to reveal the gloom beyond. A thick, heavy drape covered the circular room's large arched window and the air beyond the threshold smelt stale.

'It looks scary.' said Rarni, moving close to her side.

'There is nothing to be afraid of.' she said, trying to reassure the child. 'Very few people have been up here since the queen left. It has remained largely unused.'

'Why do you not use it?' asked Rarni, as she gingerly led the child inside the chamber.

'It does not suit me, it would feel too pretentious.'

Rarni clung to her side as she wandered across the room and tore down the drape, before pushing open the window. The fresh spring breeze rushed through the opening to meet them, quickly dispelling the stagnant air. She forgot how impressive the view was from the citadel's utmost vantage point. It was easy to fathom Mirielle's disconnect with the people when gazing down upon the domain from such height. Everything beneath them felt so small and insignificant, yet each moving dot on the ground below represented a lifetime of adversity and triumph. If only their queen had taken the time necessary to engage with the people, perhaps then, Mirielle's fate would have led the shaper along a different path.

'We are so high up.' said Rarni, the child now standing on tiptoe to better her view.

'Indeed. I know of no higher vantage in all of Freylar. Still, that is not why I have brought you here.'

'Why did we come up here?'

'Because, young Rarni, you are still a child. I am yet to meet someone of your age who is not easily distracted. We will not be interrupted up here.'

She strode towards the centre of the chamber, which now felt naked without Mirielle's sparse furnishings, before turning to face the once glorious stone tree that continued to stand in the room – another reminder of their former queen's power. She remembered the times she had been lost in awe of it, dumbstruck by its magnificence. Now, however, the elaborate stone construct looked sad and unloved, stripped of its beautiful crystal leaves in the wake of Krashnar's deplorable attack.

'What is it?' asked Rarni, the child's gaze following her own.

'One of Mirielle's many creations. Our former queen shaped this stone tree, along with the Tri-Spires in which we now stand – she is the most powerful shaper known to our people.'

'It looks sad.'

'Yes, it does. However, it was not always so. Once, its branches were covered with delicate crystal leaves that refracted light from the window around this room – it was beautiful.'

'What happened to it?' asked Rarni.

'It withered away, along with Mirielle's reign, its leaves smashed and long since discarded.'

She kept her explanation deliberately vague, deciding it best to withhold the gory details of the tree's demise given Rarni's age. However, her efforts to shield the child from such horrors would likely be futile if Rarni's newfound ability proved to be as advanced as she suspected. In any

77

event, the child's attention was now inadvertently fixed on the barren tree.

'Please do not concern yourself about the queen's former accomplishments and sit yourself down. I have something else for you to focus on instead.'

She took a step forward and gently grasped the child's hands. Slowly, she sat down on the stone floor, encouraging Rarni to do the same. Once seated, she pulled an intricate silver barrette from her hair, placing it upon the palm of the child's right hand.

'See if you can focus on this.'

Rarni starred at her blankly, as though her words held no meaning.

'Try your best to focus on it. Allow your curiosity to penetrate its exterior. Glimpse the winding path fate has bestowed upon it, both what has been and what will be. Allow its fate to fill your mind's eye, allowing you to witness the endless road upon which this object travels.'

Rarni did as instructed, trying hard to focus on the barrette. However, she could see the child's attention waning, betrayed by her pupils darting back and forth between the silver barrette and Mirielle's stone tree. She knew that training a child of Rarni's age would be difficult. Perhaps the room she had chosen was not sparse enough in its decor, yet her scrying had shown what appeared to be an emotional response to the exercise. Perhaps, in hindsight, her visions had misled her, she mused.

'Focus on the object in your hand.'

'But the tree--'

'You must cast aside such distractions. Focus on the task you have been set.'

'I am sorry. I cannot. The tree, it is calling me.'

78

Rarni suddenly stood up, allowing the barrette to fall to the floor with a sharp tap, before turning to face Mirielle's stone construct once more. She watched with interest, recognising immediately the signs of one about to engage their second sight. All other worldly concerns melted away, ceasing to exist within the child's mind's eye as Rarni stared intently at the tree, as if somehow bewitched by its presence. She stood up and quickly circled the child, looking to better observe her student. Rarni's pupils were dilated. The child's eyes looked like obsidian orbs that threatened to draw in the light surrounding them.

'Rarni, you may cease the exercise now.'

The possessed-looking child paid her no heed. Rarni seemed to be in some kind of disturbing trance, evident by the twisted look on the child's face that became ever more ghastly with each passing moment. She realised then that her student had lost control of her ability. Rarni was being assaulted by each and every scene the tree had borne witness to during its existence. From the cycle of its shaping, its awful desecration, to the present cycle and beyond.

'Rarni, that is too much – you must stop now!'

Once again, the rapt child ignored her instruction. What came next stabbed at her core, wounding her soul like the thrust of a sword might pierce one's heart. Rarni's mouth opened slowly, releasing frightening broken screams that mirrored the awful sight of the child's ghastly visage.

SIX
Discovery

'Rayna, you should learn to walk on the inside of your feet, to minimise heel and toe imprints.' whispered Lothnar, who seemingly moved like a wraith with preternatural speed. 'Also, you need to alter your gait and step inside my tacks – it will mask our true numbers.'

'I can't even see your bloody tracks!' she said, daring to raise her voice as she struggled to maintain her breathing whilst keeping pace.

Lothnar laughed softly – the Paladin clearly found her clumsy movements amusing. She recalled her late-night parkour runs to Kaitlin's library through the metropolis. However, skills from her former life did not always lend themselves to her new body. Poor vision in dim lighting aside, her lower leg strength was not what it had once been. Besides, the terrain was poorly suited to free running antics, especially when carrying her *fancy blades*, as Lothnar had eloquently put it.

'None of us are invisible out here; we all leave our mark on this world – you just need to know where to look.'

'Perhaps you could show me?'

'When we rest up, I shall.'

It was noon when the scouts reached their destination. Despite their numbers, the entire regiment had made swift progress, maintaining its formation for the duration of their journey. When word finally passed down from the front ranks that they had located the site of Leyla's attack, she hoped that Lothnar would grant the scouts a moment's respite. The muscles in her calves were tense from the strain of remaining low whilst traversing the woodland and

81

her back ached. She wanted nothing more than to stand upright and straighten her back. However, her hopes were quickly dashed when Lothnar ordered the regiment to go to ground whilst the vanguard pushed on ahead. The remaining scouts silently disappeared into the surrounding woodland and dug in, whilst they eagerly awaited the unit's return.

'Are you expecting trouble?'

'No.' whispered Lothnar. 'The Louperdu have likely moved on from this position. Nonetheless, it would be foolhardy not to confirm the situation before committing the scouts to retaking the settlement.'

'Did you send Leyla in with the vanguard?'

'Of course. She is one of us now – I will treat her no differently to the others.' Lothnar answered. 'Since we have some time before they complete their reconnaissance of the farmstead, I will make good on my earlier promise to instruct you.'

She listened intently to Lothnar's words as he explained in detail the signs one might look for when tracking another of their kin. Soil scatter, overturned dark rocks, disturbed grass, sideheading – it was clear that the Paladin knew his craft. Although delivered in hushed tones, so as not to draw attention to their position, nonetheless, the passion with which Lothnar gave his sermon told her a great deal about the Paladin. She began to realise why Lothnar had been so restless in the vale. For Lothnar, the surrounding woodland was home, not the shaped granite of the Tri-Spies, whose artificial construction defied nature. There were many, Kirika included, who described the Paladin as a nomad, one who preferred the company of nature to that of his kin. Previously, she had paid little attention to their words. However, she understood them now, witnessing first-hand how the Paladin truly came alive when in his natural environment.

'How did you learn all of this?' she asked, overwhelmed by the amount of information Lothnar rapidly imparted.

'I had a troubled upbringing, made harder by the sudden manifestation of my telepathic ability. As such, I spent a great deal of my childhood outdoors – I learnt through doing.'

There was an awkward pause between them following the Paladin's unexpected personal insight, as though Lothnar suddenly felt that he had disclosed too much. For someone who spent most of his time in the company of animals, she understood the Paladin's reservations, more so given her own experiences. During her time spent bouncing between children's homes, she had been equally reserved and distant towards others – Kaitlin being the exception.

'I haven't had the same experiences as you. Nonetheless, my own childhood was a mess, therefore, I believe that I understand where you are coming from.'

'I have many regrets, Rayna. Things that I did, moreover, the things that I never did... I treated Nathaniel poorly.'

'That is in the past. If I have learned one thing from my rebirth in Freylar, it is this: the past is exactly that. Accept it and move on. Do not allow your regret to consume you. Learn from your mistakes. Try to become a better version of yourself. Most of us whish that we could have done things differently. Some of us live in fear of making the wrong decision – Mirielle for example – but that is not a healthy way to exist.'

83

'Wise counsel, especially from someone so young. Your former life has made you wise beyond your passes.'

'My former life was a wreck. I simply have no desire to repeat it, or to see others do the same.'

'Do you ever wonder what would have been had you remained in your world?'

'All the time. However, I believe that it was the right decision for me to come to Freylar, despite the ongoing challenges I face. I needed a fresh start.'

'From what I have heard, the hardships that you endured in your previous life were not of your own making.'

'Perhaps. However, indecision, inaction…these things can be just as bad as making the wrong decision, or worse – some consider poor leadership better than none at all. I was guilty of this myself. There were those who looked to me to lead them, yet I chose not to. I distanced myself from noble causes. I chose not to fight the system. Because of my poor decisions, I lost friends.'

Lothnar looked away, but she could tell from his vacant stare that the Paladin considered her words and the parallels that he drew from them.

'I did not intend to steal Alarielle from you – for that I am truly sorry. However, I know now that I have earned the right to this body. Now I must learn to accept it.'

The Paladin turned to face her once more, fixing her with his gaze.

'That body is yours and yours alone – I respect that now. Alarielle was gone well before you came here, Rayna. Furthermore, if I am being truly honest with myself, the relationship between her and I would have never flourished because of my *own* inaction.'

'Then find a way to change. Say what you *really* think. This cycle, I watched you command an entire regiment with both confidence and ease. Everyone here respects your command, whether you make the wrong or right decisions. I want to see more of *that* Lothnar – not the vengeful Lothnar, pissed off because the domain's most powerful telepath bested him one time.'

Lothnar smiled.

'You are right. It is time that I, too, became a better version of myself.'

'I have got you. Calm down, you are safe.'

She pulled Rarni close to her chest, wrapping her arms around the child tightly. Her earnest embrace had an immediate effect, though it took some time before Rarni's screams abated fully. Stood in the centre of Mirielle's chamber, she rocked the terrified child gently, attempting to ease Rarni's pain. Although she had foreseen such a response, the images she witnessed did not convey the child's terrible screams, nor had she expected Rarni to react so quickly, the speed of it jangled her nerves. She had seen many scriers become overwhelmed by the visions they manifested, through the use of their second sight, over the passes. Yet, never before had she witnessed such a rapid, violent onslaught of imagery. Typically, scriers were subject to a steady stream of imagery, and those with experience were able to speed up or slow down the process. Therefore, it was unusual for those new to scrying to experience such a deluge of imagery so quickly, even amongst those who struggled to control their ability initially.

'It is over now.'

'They felt real.' blubbered the child, now sobbing in her arms.

'I will not lie to you – they *are* real. However, they are not happening right now and the visions you witnessed belong to the tree. They are not your own.'

Rarni said nothing, and instead continued to sob. Still, crying was preferable to silence – at least the child was not in shock, as with her previous experiences.

'I think that we should go for a walk outside to get some fresh air. I know how overwhelming it can be prior to becoming accustomed to the Tri-Spires.'

Rarni wiped her tearful eyes then held her hand. Together, they left the chamber and made for the Waystone before exiting the citadel.

The gentle warmth of the mid-morning sun felt good on her face. Of all the seasons, spring was her favourite. Seeing the flora and fauna return to the vale filled her with joy, even more so given the recent invasions and wars that had ravaged Freylar. The sound of Sky-Skitters nesting in the trees as well as the vivid bloom of plant life gave her hope, assuring her that the domain was already healing its wounds and that the Freylarkai would do the same, in time. There was a noticeable change in Rarni's mood the moment they left the Tri-Spires. She suspected that a brief stroll outside would do a child of the forest the world of good – and she was right. She immediately sensed that the child was happier outside, given the weak smile on Rarni's face and the relaxed grip of her hand. Already, Rarni's head was on a swivel, tuning this way and that, attempting to analyse everything at once. Together, they walked down the slope leading towards the river that cut through the vale. Upon reaching the old wooden bridge, they veered left, heading

86

westwards along the riverbank. They watched the sun glisten upon the calm water, disturbed only by the occasional flutter of Fan-Fish beneath its surface. Once she was satisfied that Rarni had calmed sufficiently following the ordeal, she sat the child down by the riverbank.

'Did you realise that you were scrying again, back in the queen's chamber, when you saw the stone tree?'

'No – I was not dreaming. It was scary.'

'Am I correct in thinking that you saw lots of images, or rather visions?'

'Yes. They were horrible.'

'Do you mean to say that *all* of them were horrible?'

'Yes. Every one.'

They sat in silence by the river, watching the Fan-Fish disturb the surface of the water whilst she pondered Rarni's words. The way in which the child's ability manifested troubled her; the trigger mechanism for Rarni's scrying and the exclusively dark nature of the visions concerned her. Typically, scriers experienced visions in sequence, be it forwards or in reverse, ergo filtering the images generated by one's second sight was not possible, at least not in her experience. Furthermore, Rarni, despite being asked to focus on her barrette, was drawn to the source of the dark visions as though they called out to the child, triggering Rarni's spontaneous scrying. These observations were not traits one expected from a scrier, be they an experienced user or a student beginning their training. Instead, Rarni wielded a vicious variation of the ability, one that had been forced upon her, without consent. Given everything that they had learned from both Rayna and Nathanar's reports, in addition to her sister's own accounts, it made sense that Krashnar's soul had been tainted by his prolonged exposure

87

to the Soulmancer, which had ultimately claimed dominance over the released shaper's body. From what she understood, both Krashnar and Xenia, of the Knights Thranis, had spent time with the Soulmancer. Both were able to push back against the possession of their bodies, in particular Xenia, whose strength of mind and staunch defiance had served the knight well. Rarni, on the other hand, was a child, therefore lacking the mental fortitude to fight back against her oppressor's will. Knowing that such a depraved being existed disgusted her; the notion of being at ease with dominating a child's will in order to achieve one's own agenda was abhorrent to her. No child deserved to endure such darkness. It was little wonder that the forced encounter had left its mark on Rarni.

'Tell me, did your mother mention anything to you about the outlying communities?'

'No.' answered Rarni, meekly.

'Did you overhear talk of them from others perhaps?'

'I heard some of the children in the forest talking about The Blades.'

'What did they say?' she asked, curiously.

'One of them talked about their brother.'

'Does this brother serve in the Order?'

'Yes. He is a Blade Adept. The child was sad because their brother had not returned home.'

The pieces suddenly fell into place. Rayna had tasked the Blade Adepts with protecting the outlying communities, shortly after Mirielle's departure. The primary focus of the mission was to provide reassurance for the communities, in addition to furthering their own skills in ranged combat, whilst serving in the field. In any event, that weak link was the connection to the settlement attack involving Leyla. For reasons she did not yet understand, it appeared that Rarni was capable of scrying events indirectly. However, as powerful as the child's ability was, it appeared to trace dark events exclusively. Rarni's ability was drawn to the darkness, feeding on it as though it offered her sustenance.

'Rarni, it is my belief that your time with that evil Soulmancer has affected you.'

'I am confused.'

'Understandably.' she said, empathising with the child. 'When the Soulmancer imposed his will on Xenia, her mind was both mature and strong enough to allow her to fight back. However, in your case, due to your young age, his will was absolute, meaning that you had no way of fighting its evil. Because of the Soulmancer's complete dominance over your soul, I believe that it has altered you in some way. Your ability to scry such awful events exclusively, and without a direct connection to their source, worries me.'

'How do I stop it?'

'That is what you and I are going to work on. With my help, I am confident that, in time, you will learn to control your ability, despite its violent nature.'

'I just want to be normal again.'

She could see the immense sadness in the child's eyes. Though not a parent herself, she understood fully now why Lyra had sought her out, albeit through pure desperation. How awful it must be to watch one's own child endure such a terrible legacy. Instinctively, she leant forwards and held the child in a tight embrace. Rarni burst into tears; the dam holding back the child's sorrow finally gave way. She rocked the child gently, trying to sooth the worst of the hurt, whilst Rarni sobbed uncontrollably in her arms. The vengeful part of her wanted to gather The Blades and storm the Ardent Gate, pass through the wretched Waystone that facilitated the fiend's escape and hunt it down. Yet she knew in her heart that such a scenario was both fanciful and fraught with danger. As powerful as she was, if her own sister had been unable to fully track the Soulmancer's movements, there was little hope that she would fare any better. The Soulmancer's ability to possess the body of another, on a whim, would confound her second sight as it had done with Darlia.

'Try not to worry yourself.' she said, trying to reassure the distraught child. 'I *promise* you that I will keep trying until we find a way to fix this – I am not going anywhere.'

'Leyla, I want you to remain at least twenty paces behind me at all times, is that understood?'

She nodded firmly, acknowledging her orders.

'Provide covering fire, should we need it.' commanded Lazrik. 'The rest of us will break down into pairs and advance silently, maintaining the line. When you breach the settlement, I want a search of every dwelling. If you encounter the Louperdu, issue the signal to withdraw to this position, where we will engage them on our terms.'

Krisis snarled, as though instinctively understanding Lazrik's orders. The remaining squad members nodded in unison, also acknowledging their orders. Their battle-hardened faces told countless stories. It was clear that the scout regiment's vanguard had fought innumerable skirmishes and battles over the passes. They had witnessed horrors that continued to haunt them to the present cycle – that much was painfully obvious by the grim expressions they bore. Each member of the vanguard was battle tested and not to be taken lightly. If the Louperdu were still

90

skulking in the shadows of the farmstead, she had no doubt that the scouts would root them out before releasing each one in turn.

'Good. Form up!'

The group immediately broke down into pairs as ordered, forming a long line that spanned the width of the field in which they stood. Krisis, too, joined the line, sliding into position along with the others. As instructed, she fell back twenty paces behind Lazrik, watching in awe as the line of scouts crouched outside of the settlement rapidly formed. Nocking an arrow onto her bowstring, she crouched low, doing her best to mask her presence. Had their incursion taken place later in the pass, the regiment would have benefited from the cover of the surrounding crops. Instead, the virgin shoots left them exposed. Nevertheless, hugging the landscape made it harder for the enemy to assess their numbers. Furthermore, their stretched deployment ensured that the pack would find it difficult to flank their position. Once the squad was in place, Lazrik gave the signal to advance.

The squad, accompanied by Lothnar's loyal dire wolf, stealthily approached the settlement. She could hear her heart thumping in her chest as she scanned the horizon, looking for signs of enemy movement. The ploughed field made her approach awkward. Yet, the line of scouts advancing before her showed no signs of hindrance, seemingly gliding across the field as though it were a flat surface. The unit advanced swiftly, quickly making contact with the settlement. As instructed, the squad penetrated the perimeter, maintaining its formation. Lazrik remained at the edge of the field, crouched low, whilst the others, Krisis included, permeated the settlement, like fallen rainwater

91

absorbed into fresh soil. She felt a sudden unease, the instant the scouts faded from sight. Eeriness clawed at her mind and the field in which she crouched no longer felt safe. Given the squad's veteran status, she knew that her fears were unfounded. Even so, the Louperdu's ambush had clearly had a profound effect on her. The muscles in her arms and legs tensed, and her breathing became heavy, causing her chest to rise and fall. Up ahead, Lazrik remained perfectly still. She wondered if the vanguard's commander, too, was affected by their current situation, indeed, whether the Freylarkin knew fear at all. Either way, Lazrik gave nothing away whilst he silently observed the scouts' infiltration.

After what felt like an eternity of waiting, a number of the scouts re-emerged from the settlement, quickly withdrawing to Lazrik's position. Shortly afterwards, the commander signalled for her to move up. Abandoning her position, she swiftly advanced towards Lazrik, remaining low whilst she joined the commander at his side.

'Early reports suggest that the Louperdu have moved on. However, I do not trust them and Krisis' nose seems to agree with me. Their ability makes them extremely difficult to track.'

'What are your orders?' she asked, instinctively tightening the grip on her bow.

'We will regroup at the centre of the settlement, which will become our forward operating base, as per Lothnar's orders. There will only be a handful of lupines left in the settlement, if indeed any remain at all; we would have seen at least some signs already of far greater numbers. Our open presence in the heart of the settlement will draw out any stragglers.'

'You are going to use the scouts as bait.'

'Indeed. However, you and a number of others will shadow us. Get to the rooftops and cover our position. Your job is to counter a potential ambush.'

'Understood.'

'I am assigning five scouts to you. They will be under your command.'

'Commander, please forgive me if I am speaking out of turn, however, I am new to the vanguard. I have not earned the right to a command of my own.'

'Leyla, out of us all, you have spent the most time here. You know this place better than the rest of us. You alone are most qualified to position the vanguard's forces for a counter offensive in this scenario. We will buy time on the ground should an attack occur. It is *your* job to snipe the enemy.'

'Please forgive me for questioning your orders.'

'You are forgiven. Do not do it again – you have not *earned* the right.' replied Lazrik, before flashing her a brief smile.

'Understood.' she replied, stiffening her back. 'Will they follow my command?'

'We are scouts – we do as commanded.'

Lazrik immediately began issuing orders to those closest. Having delivered their reports and now in receipt of fresh orders, the scouts promptly moved back into the settlement to relay Lazrik's plan. As they disappeared into the gaps between the outbuildings, she started to feel nervous. Until now, she had never known the burden of leadership. Despite her own reservations, Lazrik seemingly had no qualms appointing her for the daunting task of coordinating part of the vanguard's counter-offensive – the thought made her head spin a little. She found it difficult to accept that the scouts would trust her so easily, before promptly reminding herself that she was a trained Blade Adept. Indeed, and as Lazrik had keenly pointed out, she knew the farmstead well, having spent the entire winter at the settlement, including the best locations from which to snipe the enemy.

Before she could finish reassuring herself that Lazrik had not made an error in judgement by tasking her with the responsibility of command, five scouts swiftly emerged from the settlement. They moved towards her position, where they promptly lined up, crouched down alongside her. Each had their hoods pulled tightly around their faces and all carried a pair of dirks attached to their belts. Now that she was familiar with the scout regiment's standard armaments, she had no doubt that each also carried an arsenal of throwing knives strapped to their limbs. However, she was surprised to see that one also carried a bow, along with a quiver of arrows slung across his back.

'You are skilled with a bow?' she asked with interest.

'I am.'

'Klein excels at ranged combat. He is your second in command. Heed his counsel.'

'I will.' she replied, earnestly.

'The six of you will infiltrate the farmstead and take up positions overlooking the centre of the settlement. We will use the vanguard to lure out any lupines that may remain. In that event, we will hold the enemy. It is your job to release them. Is that understood?'

'Yes sir!'

'Good.' said Lazrik sternly. 'Leyla is in command. Now go!'

94

SEVEN
Guile

His gaunt guide was clearly eager to show him around the facility. Together, they wandered in and out of every accessible room and corridor of which Jacob possessed knowledge. At each stop, Jacob would tirelessly expound upon the use of each location. Even bland generic-looking corridors warranted some kind of description, including an explanation as to which parts of the labyrinthine construction they connected. He found the excursion dull and uninteresting, and caught himself wondering, on several occasions, if Jacob was the obsessive type, endlessly caught up in the minutiae.

'And this is where the cleaners store their cleaning materials.'

'Terrific. Although, do they actually use them?' he asked, trying to inject a little humour into their tiresome jaunt.

Jacob stared at him blankly, the joke clearly lost on the dim-witted teenager. He wondered at first whether he had offended the boy. However, Jacob's vacant expression quickly confirmed otherwise, that his guide was simply confused instead.

'We have been at this for what seems like hours now. Is there someplace more exciting that we can go to?'

'We still need to visit the kitchen facilities, plus there is the common room.'

'Perfect, let's go there.'

'The kitchen is down--'

'No, I meant to the common room.'

'Do you not want to visit the kitchen?' asked Jacob blankly.

'No, I do not.'

Though he enjoyed preparing his own meals, the thought of Jacob providing an inventory of the kitchen's equipment and utensils terrified him. At least in the common room they would find other residents to interact with; he prayed that they would be more switched on than his present company.

'OK.' replied Jacob, before escorting him in the opposite direction.

Eventually, they reached the facility's common room, though he had no idea how to locate the destination from their dormitory; Jacob's round-a-bout guided tour of the facility had left him feeling completely disorientated. Nevertheless, he was grateful to finally lay eyes on other residents. The common room itself was similar to others he had frequented at previous children's homes. However, in terms of size, it was significantly larger in order to accommodate the facility's large number of residents – it was essentially a hall. The space itself was bland and boxy. The walls were discoloured and sterile, much like every other room in the facility, and the paint had started flaking away from the tired-looking surfaces in large patches. There was an odd smell about the room too, probably caused by mould or water encroachment, likely the cause of the spoilt paintwork. However, despite its grim look and feel, there were plenty of residents present, most of whom were engaged in conversation or various gaming activities. As with any children's home, there were the usual introverts present who loitered in the corners of the room, observing silently from afar.

He scanned the room thoroughly looking for signs of gang congregation, typically present in communal settings amongst his kin. Sure enough, there were a number of large and stocky individuals, around whom others seem to congregate, denoting a clear segregation between the residents. Among these self-proclaimed kings of youth was Sebastian. The tall, muscular, dark-skinned youth sat at the head of a table, flanked by boys of a similar age. He appeared to be chairing some kind of council, no doubt discussing ways to maintain his influence within the juvenile society.

'Who holds the most sway around here?' he asked absentmindedly, whilst continuing to scan the room. 'I assume that it is Sebastian.'

'Yes. About forty percent are loyal to him.' answered Jacob.

'I guess in that case, I should thank my lucky stars that I am under his *benevolent* protection.' he said with a wry grin.

Once again, Jacob regarded him blankly, clearly confused by his sarcastic remark.

'What about the others?' he asked, glossing over his guide's painful ignorance.

'What do you mean?'

'What's the breakdown of power amongst the opposition?'

'Kyle's group make up about twenty five percent, same for Dylan's lot.'

'And the rest?'

'We don't have many girls here. But those that are here all fall under Kristen – she's a psycho.'

'I see.'

97

There was no need for further elaboration. He had encountered similar individuals before, including the likes of Kristen. When the male brutes took charge, their female counterparts invariably used their feminine wiles to manipulate the landscape, whilst others took on the role of the sociopath. Sebastian, however, was different. Despite his enviable physique, the gang leader did not conform to the usual gang leader stereotypes. Instead, Sebastian employed cunning over brawn to achieve his ends. Regardless, he continued to survey the common room, this time overlaying the statistics from Jacob in order to understand its social demographic in detail.

'Why have Dylan and Kyle not removed Sebastian from power?'

'They hate each other, more than they hate Sebastian. Also, Sebastian has Kristen in his pocket – so the rumour goes.'

'Nice. This room is about as messed up as the outside world.'

'What do you mean?'

'Forget it.' he replied, lacking the desire to explain his remark. 'Perhaps I should go acquaint myself with Dylan, or Kyle.'

Jacob's face suddenly drained of colour, accentuating the colour of his ginger hair. His guide stared at him mutely, as though having just witnessed some kind of ghastly apparition.

'Are you feeling OK?' he asked, genuinely concerned for the boy's welfare.

'Why would you say something like that?'

'Like what?'

'We're in the same dorm as Sebastian. Do you have any idea what he would do?'

'No, I don't – that's the problem.'

'I don't understand.'

'Sebastian doesn't use his muscle to control what goes on around here. I learned that lesson pretty quickly. If he did, things would be much simpler; we could have slugged it out already and gone our separate ways.' he explained, now turning to face Jacob. 'Sebastian knows that I am not another serf, willing to serve his every whim through fear. But in order to manage Sebastian's guile, I need to employ a level of cunning myself.'

'I still do not understand.' replied Jacob. 'How does speaking to Sebastian's rivals protect you?'

For reasons he could not fathom, he liked Jacob. Although the witless youth irritated him, he had no desire to see any harm come to the teenager. Perhaps it was pity, or maybe some misguided sense of righteousness on his part, thinking that he could protect them both. Either way, he had no issues with Jacob. That said, he knew that Jacob could not be trusted; cowardice ensured the boy's obedience. Ergo, Jacob was likely already in Sebastian's pocket. However, knowing this gave him an edge. Jacob's subservience provided him with a link to Sebastian, without the need to establish one of his own. He could use that link to manipulate Sebastian, by feeding the leader of the pack false information.

'You said that they do not get along. However, if I position myself as an intermediary – loyal to neither side – I can facilitate both gangs working in unison towards the common goal of ousting Sebastian. The balance of power will shift and both you and I will be protected at the heart of the new regime.'

'Sebastian would not allow it.'

'He is unable to prevent it.' he said, giving Jacob a hard stare. 'We all have daily access to this room. Of course, if Sebastian were to relent and leave me be, I would reconsider my position. I only want a quiet stay at this place so that I can prepare for what comes afterwards.'

Although a little colour had since returned to the boy's face, even so, Jacob looked incredibly uncomfortable. His guide lacked the mental capacity and foresight to realise that he was being manipulated. He knew that Sebastian would not fall foul of the same trick. However, it did not matter. The threat was real, and besides, surely the gang leader had far greater concerns than coercing one more lackey to his side. With a little luck, the matter between them would be settled, without a single punch being thrown and with no loss of face.

'OK, shall we visit the kitchen now?' he said, giving Jacob a sarcastic wink.

He watched with interest as a returning member of the vanguard withdrew silently through the treeline towards their position. The scout possessed a great deal of skill, quietly melting into the shadows cast by the canopy as the sun started its descent towards the horizon. Yet, no amount of stealth would enable the proficient scout to evade his eyes – his countless passes spent training beyond the vale ensured as such.

'Report.' he whispered, as the scout crouched alongside him.

'The settlement appears to be empty. However, Lazrik suspects otherwise.'

'He has a nose for these things. What about Krisis' own?'

'The dire wolf is restless – he suspects something.'

'Very well. If the Louperdu want a fight, here and now, we will give it to them.' he said, vehemently. 'What is the vanguard's current status?'

'Lazrik believes that only a handful of the spirit wolves remain. He intends to use the vanguard to lure them out.'

'He is a wily one.'

'Indeed.'

'And the counter-offensive?'

'Six members of the vanguard, commanded by Leyla, with Klein as her second. The squad is taking up positions overlooking the centre of the settlement.'

Interesting, he mused. He had not expected Lazrik to accept the Blade Adept so readily. Yet the decision to do so was sound. Leyla was both a skilled and staunch member of the Order. Furthermore, she knew the terrain well and was suited to the task, given the circumstances.

'Good. We will advance our position accordingly, providing a fall-back corridor in the unlikely event that one is required. However, we will not engage unless necessary. I do not want to commit the entire regiment unless absolutely required – we will only add to the congestion. If the mission goes against us, withdraw to our position and draw the spirit wolves out into the open.'

'Understood.'

'If the Louperdu *had* tracked our approach, we would have known about it already. Therefore, if any of the spirit wolves are indeed lurking within the settlement, we must

101

assume that their primary focus is to alert the pack. To that end, I will have Saralia's squad advance the right flank to cut off any runners to the east.'

The scout nodded in confirmation, then withdrew into the shadows and began making their way back towards the treeline to relay his orders. If the Louperdu wanted to play games, he was more than happy to oblige. He made a quick series of hand gestures, after which another member of the scouts quickly moved to his position.

'The vanguard are expecting contact with the enemy. Should this happen, they will draw them out into a counter-offensive. We will advance the line to provide support, if needed. However, I want Saralia's squad to push ahead of the line and cut off the east – take down any runners.'

'Sir!' replied the scout fervently, before taking their leave to relay his command.

After issuing his orders, he moved silently towards Rayna's position; the light bringer was slumped behind a fallen tree, firmly dug in.

'Are we moving out?' she whispered, as he neared her position.

'Yes. However, I want you to join Saralia's squad for a while. Some of our lupine friends may attempt to alert their brethren, in which case we will need to take them down, quickly – your ability may prove useful.'

'Have the vanguard made contact?'

'No, not at this time. However, it seems probable that they will. They are working to lure out any stragglers hidden within the settlement, who will likely seek to ambush us. I have therefore tasked Saralia with pushing up the right flank, ahead of Yandar and I, to cut off any escape to the east. Should that happen, the pack will be alerted to our position and we will lose our advantage in this hunt.'

'Understood.' replied Rayna with a firm nod. 'I will join Saralia's squad and bolster their offence.'

'Good. Be sure to use your ability sparingly; there is every chance that it will attract unwanted attention. However, if a runner does make it past her squad, we *must* take it down.'

'Agreed. I will do what I can.'

'I know that you will.'

Rayna flashed him a brief smile, before promptly abandoning her position. He watched with a sense of pride as the light bringer moved through the forest more deftly this time, unlike her previous clumsy attempts to navigate the woodland terrain. The Guardian was a fast learner. Unlike Leyla, who was eager to prove her worth, Rayna's determination to succeed at anything she set her mind to was terrifying. Although she could be a rough jewel, The Guardian's unmatched resolve allowed Rayna to push through the challenges she faced, no matter how bleak things got. However, her frightening determination was also the light bringer's undoing. Rayna needed her allies, for those occasions when she bit off more than she could chew. Thinking back, his own confidence had taken a massive knock during the Narlakai invasion, with Lileah repeatedly asserting her mental dominance over him. His defeat, by the now released telepath, was a sobering reminder that he was not the insurmountable opponent that his cocksure arrogance had fooled him into believing he was. Although a humbling experience, the lesson learned served him well. He prayed that Rayna would not require the same lesson. In any event, his musings aside, if the

Louperdu were indeed hiding within the settlement, they needed only to be patient in order to root out their prey.

After relaying the regiment's movements to Yandar, he re-took his position at the centre of the support squads, ready to issue the signal to advance the line. In all likelihood, the Louperdu would wait until nightfall to make their move; the creatures favoured the cover of darkness, which helped to mask their numbers. Furthermore, there were those who believed that the source of the spirit wolves' savagery and strength came from the silvery embrace of the Night's Lights; ergo, the sun was not their friend. Either way, the board was set, with all the pieces in place. With the light beginning to fade, he could sense rising tensions amongst the scouts. Although battle-hardened all, due to their extensive training and experience in the field, nevertheless, it was normal for all Freylarkin to experience some level of anxiety on the eve of battle. Still, he knew in his soul that every member of the scout regiment would quash any thoughts of self-doubt, focusing their all on the task ahead of them.

'Come and get it!' he whispered vehemently, before spitting on the ground, signalling his distaste for the enemy.

It was getting late; time for her to return to the Tri-Spires, and more importantly, to her lover's bed. Though she had been appreciative of the forest dwelling provided to her by the ruling council, after spending so long slumming it in the borderlands, nonetheless, she was long overdue a little luxury. As such, she was more than happy to take up residence with Nathanar in the Tri-Spires when he presented the offer to her in light of their developing relationship. Since their time together beyond the Ardent Gate, their unexpected relationship had blossomed. Lileah still occupied a special place in her heart, and in all likelihood would do so forever. Nevertheless, she was happy with Nathanar, happier than she had been in a long time, and had therefore promised herself that she would not bring her past into their relationship.

She crossed the old wooden bridge spanning the river that ran the length of the vale, nodding and smiling pleasantly to those whom she passed along the way. Despite her chequered past, the people had largely accepted her return to the vale. Though she would always have some detractors, they appeared to be few in number. Furthermore, she had vowed not to allow them to derail her efforts to put her past behind her, along with Mirielle's troubled reign. She powered up the grassy slope leading towards the Tri-Spires, determined to make it back to Nathanar's chamber in good time. The Captain of The Blades often prepared her lavish evening meals, and she had no intention of keeping him waiting. It had been both interesting and character-building living together. Although they got on well, enjoying one another's company, they were also two very different people – complete opposites in fact. Nathanar was tidy and possessed a good temperament, where as she was more emotional and habitually left his chamber in a mess, for which she frequently felt embarrassed – tidying her personal effects did not come naturally to her. She often wondered why the Paladin tolerated her sloth, and when asked one time, he had simply replied "I enjoy setting things right". Did that mean that she needed setting right? Maybe he felt that she needed fixing in some way. Then again, perhaps she was simply over-thinking the situation – she could not tell.

105

'Just stop it already!' she said aloud, scolding herself.

She knew that if she kept kicking the nest over such trivial things, that she would only bring about that which she least desired. She needed to let things go, find a way to detach herself emotionally from situations that grated on her. However, realising that a problem existed and remedying it were two separate things. She had the former down pat, having indulged in a great deal of introspection since Lileah's release. The latter was proving to be a fresh challenge, however, for which she currently had no solution.

Upon nearing the base of the Tri-Spires, she saw a young Freylarkin crouched on the ground outside the citadel. The child looked hauntingly familiar as she closed the gap to what appeared to be a young female. Though she could not be certain, since their face was turned away from her, she felt sure that she knew the child somehow.

'Rarni, is that you?'

The child was playing with some stones, flicking them towards one another, attempting to strike her targets. Hearing her name called, Rarni nimbly stood up and turned to face her.

'Hello Darlia.'

'Oh, it *is* you.' she said, surprised to see the child. 'What are you doing here?'

'My mummy and I are staying at the Tri-Spires.'

'Really, since when?'

'We arrived here two cycles ago.'

'I see.' she replied, intrigued. 'May I ask what brings you here?'

'I have been having scary dreams. Kirika is helping me to control them. She says that I am scrying.'

'Scrying? Are you certain that my sister told you that?'

'Yes.'

'Curious.' she said, fascinated by her sister's diagnosis. 'How strange. You certainly do not possess the usual characteristics of a scrier, although...'

She leant forwards, slowly raising her good hand towards Rarni's face. The child flinched at first, but a reassuring smile from her quickly put Rarni at ease, allowing her to run her fingers gently through the child's hair.

'Hmm, your hair is much darker than I remember. Was it not blonde before?'

'My mummy says that it is changing colour.'

'Most strange.'

'The Guardian says that my eyes are changing too.'

'Rayna, you mean? Is she involved in this too somehow?'

'Yes.' answered Rarni, shaking her head up and down energetically, providing exaggerated confirmation. 'They came to visit my mummy in the forest, and then we came here. Kirika is--'

Rarni's pupils suddenly dilated and her face twisted ever so slightly. The child's expression reminded her of Krashnar's sinister visage, during her time spent in the borderlands with the exiled shaper. She recalled the occasions when she witnessed the deviant flesh worker in his workshop, working fervently on his latest works, with a similar ghastly look on his face. The lines in Rarni's face deepened and a slight crease appeared across her forehead.

'Rarni, are you scrying?'

There was no response from the child. Rarni continued to stare at her, with a vacant look that made her shudder.

'Rarni, I think that you should stop.'

Again, there was no response. The child continued to fix her with an increasingly sinister glare that sent chills down her back.

'If you do not cease what you are doing, nothing good will come of it child.'

Again, Rarni ignored her. If the child possessed no self-control, the awful events that she had witnessed would assault Rarni's impressionable young mind. No stone would remain unturned, allowing unfettered access to her dark history, thus harming the child's fledgling mind.

'Stop it now!' she said, quickly grasping the child's shoulders and shaking her violently. 'You do not want this.'

Rarni's pupils returned to normal and the furrows marring her face immediately vanished, restoring her unblemished skin.

'You were scrying – you could not stop it.' she said, releasing her hold on the child.

Rarni withdrew from her, before turning this way and that, as though confused and unsure what to do.

'Whatever you saw, those images cannot hurt you.'

She tried to approach the child, but Rarni quickly stepped back, pushing her arms out as if to keep her at bay. The child was clearly in distress and had no means of coping with what she had witnessed. She recalled the time when she had laid on her back for cycles, on the dank floor of the meld beast's pen, when her bleak past had finally caught up with her, almost drowning her in a sea of melancholy. Having barely managed to escape from the depths of such overwhelming despair, she was now able to recognise the familiar sadness in the eyes of the terrified

108

child trembling before her. Rarni's lips parted slowly as she tried to speak, but the words never came. It was one thing to experience such events first-hand, slowly, enduring each one in turn. Though it would be quite another to relive them all through the eyes of another in a condensed space of time. Without engaging her own second sight, she had no way of knowing what the child had witnessed. She needed to know, though she dared not revisit her past in fear of what it might do to her.

'Please, tell me what you saw, so that I can help you.'

Once again, she tried to approach the traumatised child, but her attempts to reassure Rarni only served to push the child further away.

'Please, you must tell me.'

Tears streamed down Rarni's face. She did not know what to do. Aside from Lyra and her sister, there was no one uniquely qualified to help. In any event, she could not afford for her past to be dredged up, especially by others. If retold using the second-hand images of a child, the lack of context would skew the retelling of actual events, making the account far worse. She had worked tirelessly to atone for her past mistakes and continued to do so. She could ill afford to start over, knowing that she lacked the mental fortitude to endure the nightmare for a second time. Again, she considered the use of her second sight, but the thought of reliving her past caused her muscles to tense and her body to shake. Panicking, she snatched at Rarni's arm, seeking to escort the child away from the base of the citadel and its prying eyes. Rarni swiftly evaded her grasp, before shouting at her in a terrified scream.

'Go away!'

109

'Please, Rarni, you must talk to me, tell me what you saw. If you do not, it will consume you.'

'Leave me alone.'

'If not me, please go and speak to my sister, immediately. She will be able to help you.'

'Make it go away!' screamed the child, now clawing at her eyes.

'Rarni, stop it! You are going to hurt yourself.'

'I do not care!'

'Go and see Kirika – she will help you.'

Rarni turned and fled inside the Tri-Spires, her hands still clutching at her face. She staggered backwards, reeling from the emotional weight of the impromptu encounter, her body still shaking. She had not expected the threat of revisiting her past to have such a profound effect on her.

'It is happening again.' she muttered to herself. 'What must I do to escape it?'

EIGHT
Bait

They encountered no resistance when re-infiltrating the settlement. It felt strange revisiting the farmstead under such conditions. The once lively place of work now stood quietly abandoned, giving the farmstead an eerie feel. She felt sad seeing the place ravaged by the Louperdu's attack. Farming implements, knocked over outdoor furnishings and other detritus littered the well-trodden paths running between the dwellings. A foul odour was also present that lingered in the air. The stench was a familiar one, that of fresh bodies slowly decomposing under the sun. Though when combined with the otherwise fragrant scent of spring, a dreadful type of rotting perfume was inadvertently concocted. The abhorrent smell drew their attention to a number of fallen Freylarkai, whom the vanguard would shortly dispose of once her squad was in position. Fortunately, the body count appeared to be low, suggesting there were survivors or that the Louperdu had taken down their prey outside of the settlement.

Threading a path between the run-down outbuildings and poorly constructed dwellings, she led her team towards the heart of the settlement, where the bulk of the vanguard intended to congregate. From there, she moved the squad north towards several barns, still home to their Karlak residents.

'Clever.' whispered Klein, who was crouched low beside her. 'The mountain range to the south is colder, providing a lighter backdrop against which to spot our targets.'

'Yes.' she replied, giving the veteran scout a wry grin. 'Furthermore, the Karlak should help to mask our scent.'

'Lazrik was right to assign you a command for this mission.'

'Your support is appreciated.'

'I would have supported you regardless. However, I know now that I can focus my efforts on releasing the enemy, as opposed to the team's survival.'

'If my judgement becomes impaired, I expect you to inform me – I will not jeopardise the team.'

'That goes without saying.'

She nodded in response, appreciating the scout's inoffensive plain speaking.

'Tell me, Klein. Why is it that you carry a bow?'

'Over-specialising breeds weakness. A number of us train in the use of different weapons, so that the regiment is able to adapt to changing circumstances. Throwing knives provide both ranged and melee attack options. However, they excel at neither.'

'I had no idea that the scout regiment possessed such flexibility.'

'We play our cards close to our chest.'

'Indeed.'

They pushed forwards, weaving an efficient path towards their objective. She directed their attention towards the roofs of the old barns.

'We will break down into two teams, to maximise lines of fire. From up here we will be able to observe the fighting. Klein and I will maintain ranged support. The remainder of you will hit and run where the fighting is fiercest, using your wraith wings to stick to the rooftops. You will also keep the Louperdu off our backs in the event

112

that they discover our position during the conflict and modify their tactics.'

'Understood.' the group whispered in unison.

'Remember, when the Louperdu attack, they do so as a pack. Do not allow their rapid movement to blindside you.'

'We have our orders.' said Klein, affirming her command. 'You two, with me.'

'Move out.' she said to the others.

Using her wraith wings for assistance, she hoisted herself up onto the roof of the adjacent barn, before scrambling across the rooftop into position. She readied her bow and promptly began scanning the horizon, allowing her eyes to adjust to the dwindling light. It was getting late in the evening and would not be long before the spirit wolves made their move. She felt sure that the creatures would strike early, allowing them adequate time under the cover of darkness to consolidate their hold over the settlement in the event of a victory. However, she convinced herself that such an outcome would not happen. The Louperdu would pay dearly for the release of Zealia and the others. Even now, the awful memory of the Blade Adept's gushing throat made her shudder, more so knowing that her own fate might mirror that of her fallen comrades.

'Are you OK?' whispered one of the scouts closest to her, who had clearly noticed her brief trembling.

'I have seen what these *bastards* can do – it is not pretty. However, do not concern yourself with my wellbeing; I am simply ridding myself of any lingering nerves. I have a score to settle, and settle it I shall.' she said, fervently.

'I have seen many creatures whilst serving in the scout regiment. Many fought fiercely with tooth and claw. Yet none boast the same savagery told by those who have survived the Louperdu.'

'One cannot hunt the Louperdu; their ability makes it extremely difficult to track them. They alone dictate when and where a battle takes place – we can only react to their movements, pre-empting them at best. When they do decide to attack, they strike with preternatural agility and a terrifying ferocity. Do not underestimate them, and under no circumstances show them any mercy.'

'In that case, I will treat them with the respect that they deserve.'

'See that you do, else you will not survive an encounter with them. Moreover, you will not be able to provide adequate warning to the next Freylarkin to engage them in battle.'

She felt more at ease following their brief exchange of words, as though acknowledging their opponent's capacity for violence somehow had a calming effect upon her. Her mind wandered back to her time with Rayna and Natalya, when The Guardian duly reminded her of the importance of never giving up. Even though they were now apart, with Natalya's fate in particular unknown, Rayna's strange sermon and the lesson it imparted remained with her, ingrained on her psyche. It was as if the light bringer had emboldened her with part of her light, causing the light of her own soul to shine brighter. It was a warm feeling, like a parent encouraging their child to achieve the impossible, and one that would likely remain with her until fate inevitably claimed her soul. In any event, she had overcome her nerves, now all but vanquished. Comfortable with the likelihood of facing the Louperdu once more, she relaxed as she focused her attention on the battlefield below, easing herself into what promised to be a long night.

It was late by the time he returned to his sleeping bay in the dormitory. Jacob's obsessively in-depth guided tour had lasted for what seemed like forever. Just when he thought that they were done for the day, the gaunt ginger-haired teenager had insisted that they walk the grounds outside the facility – clearly one tour had not been enough.

He sat on the edge of his bed, removed his shoes, then fell back onto its hard mattress and stared up at the unfamiliar ceiling. Mould had begun to spread along the edges where the walls met the ceiling. Furthermore, tiny cracks were also visible, signs that the paint was starting to peel. He rolled onto his side and stared vacantly at the bedside cabinet. As he lay there, perfectly still, thoughts tumbling through his mind, something about the scene felt out of place. He sat up abruptly, his gaze still fixed on the small piece of sterile-looking furniture. The cabinet was out of position; it had been moved, he felt sure of it. The cabinet was now far too close to the bed, as though someone had inadvertently pushed it back too far. Quietly, he slid off the bed and began inspecting the item of furniture more closely. The effects that he had scattered across it appeared to have been jostled, with each now facing in a different direction. His attention quickly turned to the wardrobe containing his holdall stuffed with clothes. Moving swiftly across the room, he quietly opened the wardrobe's door. Lying at the base of the piece of furniture was his holdall, exactly where he had left it. Temporarily removing the bag, he manhandled the metal container once more, again tipping it towards the right. Placing his left foot underneath the cabinet, he used his toes to locate the book that he had hidden beneath the bland metallic piece of furniture. The ends of his toes quickly connected with the treasure he had secreted away in the void beneath the cabinet, allowing him to breathe a sigh of relief. Satisfied that the book remained within his custody, he replaced the cabinet slowly, careful not to make any unwanted noise.

Quietly, he lay back down on his bed, wondering if his mind played tricks on him. Maybe he had imagined the whole thing. Perhaps the cabinet had always been where it now stood, and that the placement of his effects had not been as regimented as he had previously thought. Then again, his instincts had always served him well in the past. Furthermore, his memory of events was usually extremely reliable. Perhaps someone had been in his sleeping bay, snooping around, searching for anything of value in order to make a quick sale, he supposed. On the other hand, it was possible that his vivid imagination was running rampant again – he could not tell. It had been an eventful day given the various introductions, tours and general familiarisation with his new surroundings. As a result, his mind was racing, and, in all likelihood, over-thinking things. Still, he could not shake the feeling that something was not right. Unable to put a finger on it, he rolled onto his right side and closed his eyes, attempting to clear his mind of the thoughts bouncing around inside his skull. It did not take long for his drained body to assert its dominance over his overactive imagination, forcing his mind to yield as the welcoming embrace of sleep claimed its newest prize. Slowly, his thoughts faded into oblivion. Finally relenting, he left his sub-conscious in charge, leaving it to deal with whatever it was that troubled him.

116

The frantic knocking startled her. She had been about to settle down for the night when the loud banging came from her door. She walked across her chamber before cautiously opening the door. Stood in the gloomy stone corridor outside was Rarni. The colour of the skin surrounding Rarni's dark blue eyes had a reddish hue, suggesting that she had been crying. Furthermore, Rarni was trembling, having clearly been frightened by some ordeal. She knelt down and took Rarni's hands, trying to comfort the child.

'Come in.' she said, inviting the young Freylarkin into her personal space.

Slowly, she led Rarni into her chamber and sat the frightened child down gently on her bed. Before she could utter a word, Rarni burst into tears once more.

'I did not know what to do.' blubbered Rarni.

'You were doing so well.' she said, trying to reassure her newest student. 'Tell me, what has happened?'

'Darlia told me to see you.'

'You mean my sister?' she asked, unable to conceal her surprise.

The turn of events that had led the child to her door caught her off guard. She considered scrying Rarni's past, but the lack of sound would not provide her with the context that she required to fully understand her student's alarmed state. Besides, using her ability for personal gain alone was both unethical and commonly frowned upon. Instead, she decided to seek the child's own account first-hand.

'Where did you both meet?'

'Outside.'

'When was this?'

117

'Not long ago.'

'Had you both arranged to meet one another, or was this a chance encounter?'

'I was playing outside.'

'That is when my sister approached you, I gather?'

'Yes.'

'I see.' she replied, somewhat frustrated by the child's one-word answers. 'Rarni, I am afraid that I am going to need a bit more information from you in order to help you.'

There was a brief pause between them, during which she wondered if she had tried to push her student too fast. However, her concern was quickly dispelled when Rarni unexpectedly blurted out the reason for her distress.

'I did not mean to do it!'

'Do what?'

'I used my ability on your sister – it just happened!'

'Oh no.' she said, suddenly fearing the worst. 'What did you see?'

'Horrible things.' said Rarni, 'The images scared me.'

She understood now; her student had understandably been traumatised by the inadvertent encounter with her sister and the awful things she had seen. She chided herself for not anticipating or foreseeing such an encounter. Given her relationship to Darlia, the chance of Rarni and her sister meeting was high. How foolish she had been, overlooking the prospect of such an encounter.

'I am not surprised. One of your age should not bear witness to that which my sister has suffered over the passes. This is *my* fault. I should have warned you to stay away from her. How could I have been so stupid?'

'It is not your fault.' said Rarni, wiping her eyes once more. 'Darlia was my friend.'

'Is my sister not still deserving of your friendship?'

'She is a murderer!'

'I do not disagree. Darlia was, albeit only in part, responsible for the Narlakin war. However, she also put a stop to it; she killed her former lover to end that atrocity.'

'She has released Freylarkai.'

'Yes, her actions led to...'

'No, you do not understand, because you have not *seen* it.'

'What do you mean?'

Rarni grabbed her right hand before lifting it and pressing its back against her forehead.

'See for yourself.'

Accepting her student's invitation, she cleared her mind and engaged her second sight, looking back to Rarni's encounter with Darlia. As before, the images were different. They belonged to her sister and were not those of Rarni herself. Moving sequentially through the images flooding her mind, she quickly learned the truth of the horror responsible for her student's distress.

Moving silently through verdant woodland, she came across a small dwelling nestled amongst the flora. After a moment's pause, she approached the dwelling, grasping its door handle with a bronze mechanical claw, causing the lock to splinter into tiny pieces. She entered the gloomy abode noting three Freylarkin, each lying asleep on separate beds, all sparsely clothed. A startled young female, clothed in a grubby linen dress, appeared from another room connected to the main chamber. The alarmed Freylarkin pressed a finger to her lips then directed her gaze towards one of the males. The Freylarkin rolled over in his cot. A

119

ceramic jug fell from its owner's grasp, breaking upon the floor. The young female quickly fled the room. She closed the door behind the fleeing Freylarkin, before dragging a small table across the main entrance, barricading the broken door firmly shut. The male who had dropped the shattered jug now stood by the side of his cot. The bleary-eyed male rubbed encrusted rheum from his eyes then appeared to cry out. She strode towards the male, who raised his arms in defence. She grabbed one of his arms using her claw, where her left hand should have been. Forcing the Freylarkin backwards, his bare feet trod upon the broken pieces of ceramic littering the floor. Again, the Freylarkin appeared to cry out, his feet cruelly cut to ribbons by the shards of ceramic slicing into both of his feet. She watched in horror as she violently pushed the male back onto his cot, before swinging her claw backwards, foreseeing an attack to her rear from another. She caught one of the male's companions flush, sending them reeling back. Her fresh opponent's face had caved in under the force of the impact, the nose and left cheekbone crushed by the violent backhanded strike. The injured male staggered backwards, clutching his ruined face, seemingly howling in pain. The third male immediately juddered towards her with a jug raised in his right hand. He hurled the ceramic container towards her head, causing it to smash across the back of her claw, which she used to shield her face. Liquid and shattered pieces of ceramic sprayed across the room, covering the floor with further detritus. Her newest assailant advanced towards her, only to receive her right foot to his groin. The Freylarkin doubled over in pain after which she brought her bronze claw up under his chin. The male's head snapped backwards and his body crumpled to

120

the floor in a heap, his lower jaw no longer attached to his head. The awful sight caused her to retch, yet she allowed the images to continue to assault her mind – she needed to know the truth of her sister's actions.

The second male, whose face was ruined, stumbled towards her brandishing a ceramic shard. She caught a glimpse of the other remaining male in her peripheral vision, who appeared to leap up, possibly in an attempt to restrain her in some way. She appeared to lurch forwards suddenly, before noting the unfortunate male fall back down onto his cot. She struggled to make sense of the visual onslaught, the absence of feeling and sound adding to her confusion. She then grabbed her second opponent's hand as it struck her, crushing his fingers around the sharp object in his grasp before dropping him to his knees. She swung her left arm once more towards the male's head, annihilating the little that remained. The force of the brutal impact sent his bloodied corpse rolling across the floor, leaving a trail of scarlet in its wake. Again, she retched, unable to stomach the bloody massacre orchestrated by her sister, which she was now reliving first-hand.

The surviving male cowered on his cot, shaking, his legs drawn close to his chest in a foetal position. Blood trickled from his ruined feet, cut to ribbons by the sharp ceramic littering the floor. His right arm was clearly broken, evidenced by the horrid angle in which it lay.

There was a long pause, during which the male appeared to be talking to her. The unheard words spoken to her sister clearly amounted to naught. She raised her bronze mechanical claw one last time, now steeped in gore, before raining it down upon the petrified Freylarkin's face.

121

She screamed in horror, immediately disengaging her second sight.

She stood up. Her legs felt weak and unstable, causing her to sway as she moved towards the window. Frantically, she opened the wooden shutters, allowing fresh air to enter the room. Inhaling deeply, she allowed the fragrant spring air to fill her lungs, slowly easing her nausea.

'Kirika, are you OK?' asked Rarni, sheepishly.

She wiped her mouth with the back of her hand, before turning to face the child.

'No. I am anything but.'

Her entire body shivered as she struggled to process the images that she had just seen. She knew that her sister was not averse to violence. However, the recent visions revealed an ugly side to Darlia, one that utterly terrified her.

'Can I help?'

'I think that you have done enough.'

She instantly regretted her choice of words the moment they parted ways with her lips. Rarni looked crestfallen, understandably so, in light of her unkind emotional response. Pulling the shutters closed once more, she returned to her student's side before giving Rarni a warm embrace, resting her head gently on the child's shoulders.

'I am sorry for my poor choice of words. That was unfair on you. I allowed my emotions to get the better of me.'

'I did not mean to upset you, Kirika.'

'It is not your fault.'

'Why did your sister release those Freylarkin?' asked Rarni sombrely.

'I believe that Darlia's actions are the result of past transgressions unfairly visited upon her by our former queen, Mirielle. My sister's past makes for a sad tale, one that I will share with you another cycle.'

'It was horrible.'

'Yes, it was. However, know that my sister's actions are never without reason. I must discover the motivation for her crime and learn why she deemed it just to carry out such heinous butchery. Once I have done so, punishment will be meted out accordingly.'

'But she is your sister.'

'Yes. Nevertheless, I am duty bound to ensure that she atones for her actions, which cannot go unanswered.'

'Am I in trouble?'

'Of course not.' she replied, squeezing Rarni tightly in her embrace. 'You must not blame yourself. Furthermore, please do not allow this incident to derail your progress. I realise that your ability is terrifying. However, in time, you *will* become its mistress, and not the other way round.'

'But I cannot stop it!'

'Once you learn to quieten your mind, you will. It may seem like an impossible task right now, but you will learn to control your ability with both time and training.'

'I wish that it would just go away. I just want to be normal again.'

'If Rayna was here, she would probably tell you that being normal is boring, or something like that.'

Rarni laughed softly.

'Not many Freylarkai have been to the Ardent Gate. Even fewer would have the mental and physical fortitude to endure the horrors that you have witnessed. For one of such young age, you have achieved a great deal. Could you

123

really go back to a boring existence, given everything that you have seen and done?' she asked as she withdrew from Rarni, before placing her hands reassuringly on the child's shoulders.

Rarni gave her a weak smile. Though not the response she had sought, nonetheless, it was a step in the right direction. The child had been through a lot. Therefore, it irked her that she had not foreseen Rarni's encounter with her sister, thus failing to insulate the child from further trauma. Now, her lack of foresight cursed her with knowledge that she would sooner forget - such was her penance.

'Rarni, I must ask a favour of you. Whilst I would rather not add further burden to your young shoulders, if I do not ask this of you, I fear for my sister's safety.'

'What do you need me to do?' asked Rarni, looking her directly in the eye.

'I need you to say nothing of what you saw, not for the time being at least.'

'Of course.' said Rarni, nodding in acceptance.

'Know that this does not mean that I condone my sister's actions. However, I must understand what drove her to such an end. Though the ability to scry is powerful indeed, it is not without its flaws. The images we see lack input from our other senses, often, therefore, depriving them of context. I seek that context now, so that I may fully understand why this horrible crime took place, before raising the issue with the ruling council.'

'I will say nothing.' Rarni said, earnestly.

'Thank you. I appreciate your patience in this delicate matter. For a child, you are wise beyond your passes young Rarni.'

124

Rarni smiled weakly; the child appeared embarrassed by her praise.

'I will need a couple of cycles to conduct my investigation, after which, I will apprise the ruling council of my findings.'

'What happens if you do not find what you need to...'

'Absolve; is that the word you are looking for?'

'I think so.' said Rarni, gingerly.

'Crimes, especially those of a barbaric nature, cannot go unpunished.'

'But Darlia is your sister!'

'Yes...she is.'

NINE
Blindside

It was late by the time the Louperdu finally made their move.

'Damn them!' she whispered under her breath.

She had expected the spirit wolves to attack sooner. Instead, their opponents had waited patiently, maximising their cover behind the veil of night, despite the Night's Lights doing their best to aid the scout regiment.

'Leyla!' said the scout closest to her.

'Yes, I see them. Signal Klein, I will alert the others.'

She nocked an arrow onto her bowstring, before loosing it towards the gathered scouts below. The shot landed close to one of the ambling scouts, immediately raising the alarm. Like water running into cracks, the scouts on the ground quickly dispersed, maximising the use of cover. Even Krisis slunk into the shadows, ready to counter the attack.

There was an eerie silence once the regiment had gone to ground. The mild spring air was perfectly still. Even the soft ambient hubbub of nocturnal wildlife was strangely absent, as though collectively holding its breath, waiting for the impending attack. Everything felt wrong, somehow, although she could not put her finger on it. She scanned the horizon again, desperately trying to locate their foe, which had disappeared from sight. There was nothing. The shadows were still and not a single sound dared intrude upon their silent night. That which she was clearly missing clawed at the periphery of her mind, taunting her with its hidden truth. Her subconscious tried to make sense of the situation, but the thoughts were too vague, the answers she

127

sought eluding her. She felt the weight of Lazrik's trust pulling her down, like a heavy chain. The last thing she wanted to do was to fail her new comrades, especially during her first command assignment. Damage to her reputation aside, the potential for casualties amongst them would increase significantly if the enemy managed to catch them by surprise. Furthermore, she did not want to let down her mentors, Rayna and Natalya, both of whom had invested time in her development. There had to be more to it. Why would their attackers offer them a glimpse of their location, only to then go dark? It made no sense, unless--

'Break cover!' she cried, standing up abruptly. 'They're moving between the buildings.'

'Defensive formation, now!' she heard Lazrik bark suddenly from below.

The scouts immediately withdrew from their positions and fell back towards the open space at the centre of the settlement. What was once a place of gossip and trade had now become a bulwark against an incoming wave of teeth and claws, its fortification hastily constructed from the minds and bodies of the vanguard. As the scouts formed up, she caught a glimpse of predatory movement from the corner of her left eye. The adrenaline pumping through her body compelled her to act. She turned and fired, giving little thought to her actions, now ingrained courtesy of the countless cycles spent training, constantly drilling the same techniques imparted by her instructors. The projectile hit its mark, causing her target to howl in pain from the arrow now embedded in its flank.

The spirit wolf's sonorous death throes served as a signal for its kin to attack. A silver-grey mist crept along the ground, slowly emanating from the surrounding structures, followed by wisps of grey smoke that began to manifest within the centre of the scout's defensive circle on the ground. Lazrik's team was clearly oblivious to the silent danger, their attention now focused on the inbound attackers noisily crashing through poorly shuttered windows and doors to dwellings left ajar. Realising the immediate threat to the formation, she screamed as loud as she could, praying that Klein would hear her cries.

'Klein, aim right!'

She loosed another arrow, this time towards the silvery lupine shapes in the centre of the vanguard's defensive circle. She caught her target on its rear hide, causing it to yelp before faltering in its movement. Another arrow sailed in from her right, impaling its target through the head. The masterfully placed shot released its victim immediately, causing the spirit wolf to topple onto its side, motionless, before dissolving into a plume of silver-grey smoke. Once dissipated, only a pool of silvery blood remained, slowly staining the ground where it fell, marking the beast's grave. Klein's unerring accuracy caused her heart to beat furiously in her chest, be it due to adrenaline or excitement – she could not tell. Hearing the commotion, one of the scouts quickly finished off her target, sinking a knife deep into the wounded creature's skull, spraying more of the spirit wolves' preternatural blood across the ground. Elsewhere, other members of the vanguard received the Louperdu charge, which savagely blitzed their defensive cordon. In an instant, a number of the scouts were on their backs, the vicious creatures pouncing on top of their prey, furiously snapping at their opponents' exposed faces with savage maws bearing razor-sharp teeth. If the regiment knew fear, it did not show it. Despite the terrifying screams echoing through the night from those unable to react in time, the scouts fought on, functioning at peak efficiency, working in unison to rebuff their attackers. At the heart of the maelstrom was Lazrik, who continued to bark orders, doing his best to manage the unexpected waves of Louperdu blitzing their cordon. She let loose another arrow, this time puncturing the flank of a spirit wolf that had broken through into the centre of the formation. Klein speared another, offering their opponents no mercy. His arrows whistled past her from the shadows, each one a harbinger of release. Together, they focused on keeping the vanguard's inner circle clear of foes, allowing Lazrik and the others to concentrate their attentions on the relentless waves crashing down on them.

Despite the vanguard's resolve, the Louperdu were far from lacking in their own. The spirit wolves pounced from one victim to another in a feral rage, seemingly attempting to incapacitate their targets as quickly as possible. With vicious teeth and claws, the Louperdu raked at their opponents, causing debilitating wounds. It became clear to her that the spirit wolves lacked the staying power for a prolonged assault. As such, their opponents had chosen to strike hard and fast, no doubt seeking to break the vanguard's morale.

'They are attempting to break us.' she cried, whilst loosening another arrow towards the carnage below.

'Let them *try*!' cried a voice from the gloom, causing a smile to spread across her face.

'Leyla, incoming!'

She recognised the second voice – it was a member of her team. She turned her attention to the roof of the old barn, where plumes of silver-grey smoke had suddenly appeared, rapidly condensing into recognisable shapes. Her protector sprinted across the rooftop towards their manifesting opponents at break-neck speed, desperately seeking to intercept the impending attack despite their numerical disadvantage.

'On the left!' she cried, drawing the attention of the third member of her team, praying that together they would be able to fend off the apparent flanking manoeuvre. She chided herself for allowing such an incident to occur. Distracted by the chaos on the ground, they had failed to protect their flanks adequately, allowing themselves to be almost blindsided by their opponents.

Waking early, and being unable to return to sleep, he gave up on his uncomfortable, lumpy bed in favour of a short walk around the facility's grounds. The fresh air felt good, although there was nothing pure about the pollution filling his lungs. Only Apex class citizens led long lives, relying on expensive drugs and treatments to take them beyond the life expectancy of the remaining classes inhabiting the metropolis. Farms of industrial air scrubbers worked tirelessly to purify the local atmosphere, but their effects were limited. The irony of it all, knowing that humanity had advanced technology both prolonging its existence yet also shortening it with devastating wars, along with the sad destruction of its environment, fascinated him. Only humans could be so arrogant, he mused. Then again, perhaps it was simply a case of stupidity on their part – he could not tell. Humanity, in the grand scheme of things, was still in its infancy. Perhaps, therefore, humanity was like a child, bumbling from one mistake to another, slowly learning during its painful, turbulent upbringing.

131

After growing tired of wandering around aimlessly, he found a metal bench upon which he chose to lie. Like his bed, it was uncomfortable – members of the Shadow class were not permitted the simple comforts enjoyed by those above their station. Lying on his back, his eyes closed, listening to the distant sounds of industry labouring tirelessly, he heard someone approach.

'Sebastian wants to see you.'

He immediately recognised the voice – it was Jacob. Unperturbed by the teenager's words, he continued to lie on the metal bench, resting, his back and head flat against its unforgiving surface whilst he stared up at the grey sky.

'Did you know that we, as in humanity, are responsible for this hellhole?'

'Sebastian wants--'

'It was *us* who scorched the planet, along with its once beautiful sky.'

'You need to--'

'Sebastian can wait – I don't answer to him.' he snapped, tired of the gang leader's proclamations.

He could see Jacob out of the corner of his eye now. The boy fidgeted uncomfortably, clearly unsure how to react to his blunt response.

'You can't let guys like that dictate your actions. You were born with free will. Although, I'll admit, that freedom seems to be in short supply these days.'

'But it's Sebastian.'

'What's the worst he can do, eh? A good beating? Surely you know how to take one of those by now?'

'You don't understand.'

'What do you mean?' he asked, curiously.

'He's more calculating than that.'

'Sebastian is clever, I'll give him that. Although, what power does he actually wield? After all, he's trapped in this institution along with the rest of us. What significant resources could he possibly have access to that we don't?'

Jacob said nothing. The obedient gang member lowered his head and stared mutely at the ground. Clearly, something he had said had triggered a profound emotional response, a previous incident perhaps that Jacob could not shake. He sat up, swinging his legs round to face the troubled teenager.

'What is it?' he asked, surprised by Jacob's sudden state of introspection.

Jacob said nothing, choosing instead to continue staring at the blotchy concrete pavement in silence.

'Did something happen?'

'I don't want to talk about it.' mumbled the teenager.

'Look, I'm sorry.' he said, feeling somewhat guilty for Jacob's changed mood. 'Obviously you know Sebastian better than I do – I should heed your counsel.'

Jacob raised his head slightly.

'You don't know Sebastian, not like the rest of us do at any rate. You need to be more careful, Callum.'

'Why? What is he capable of, besides hammering his fists into someone's face, or intimidating someone else to do his dirty work for him?'

'Like you say, he intimidates people. Then, if that does not work, he manipulates them instead, using information against them, often resorting to blackmail in order to achieve his ends.'

'I got that impression after our first meeting. However, he has nothing on me. I came here with nothing, ergo he has no leverage over me.'

133

'You're wrong, Callum; Sebastian always finds something to tug on – that's just the way he is.'

'How can you be so sure?'

'I don't want to talk about it.'

'Fine, I won't press you further on the matter.' he replied nonchalantly. 'Keep your secrets.'

'It's not like that.'

'Then what is it like?' he asked, agitatedly. 'Clearly you have something to say, yet you won't spit it out!'

'Because I can't!' cried Jacob suddenly.

Jacob's uncharacteristic, abrupt outcry caused him to take note. Whatever it was that troubled Jacob, clearly warranted attention. He had pushed the teenager as far as he could; he would not glean any further information. At this point, Jacob had become a pawn in Sebastian's escalating war with him. He had only been at the facility for a few days, yet he was already mired in gang-related politics. There had to be a way of breaking the cycle, he thought.

'I'm not looking for trouble, Jacob. I just want to do my time here and then move on.'

'He won't allow it.'

'As far as I'm concerned, Sebastian can go piss in the wind.'

'He has something to say and you need to hear it. Just go and see him, Callum.'

'Very well, I will pay him a visit – when I'm good and ready.'

Jacob lowered his head once more, before mumbling something to himself that he could not quite discern. The teenager looked forlorn, as though something bad had just happened.

134

'They're serving breakfast in the kitchen. You should get something to eat.' said Jacob, who turned and began slowly walking away.

The plumes of silver-grey smoke solidified into recognisable shapes that bounded towards them with frightening speed. She loosed an arrow towards the beast headed down their left flank, striking the spirit wolf cleanly in the forehead. At such close range, the force of the arrow's impact snapped the creature's head to its right, causing it to veer off line. The spirit wolf teetered on the edge of the barn roof, before toppling over the edge. She caught the flash of a throwing knife from the corner of her right eye as her protector sought to fell another of their attackers. The projectile struck its target, but failed to impede the assailant. The injured creature dipped its muzzle, continuing its charge. It crashed low into its opponent, taking out the scout's legs before sending them tumbling across the roof of the old barn. Momentum sent the dazed scout rolling over the edge of the barn roof, crashing onto the ground below with a sickening thud.

Unable to save her companion, she withdrew from her assailants whilst hurriedly attempting to nock another arrow onto her bowstring, the task made harder by her jangled nerves and the adrenaline now flooding her body. The two remaining wolves quickly spread out across the roof of the barn, adopting flanking positions, their piercing eyes fixed intently on her. Dipping their muzzles in unison, they sprinted towards her, with the sole intention of ripping her asunder. Realising the futility of holding her ground, she sprinted towards the right edge of the barn roof, still trying to ready another of her arrows. Launching herself off the roof with her left leg, she twisted her body whilst pulling back her bowstring, before immediately unfurling her wraith wings. Sailing backwards though the air, the silver light of the Night's Lights disappeared from view, obscured by the silhouette of a spirit wolf high above her. As the lights went out, she instinctively released her grip on her bowstring, loosing its savage payload towards her target. With no time to properly aim, and utterly reliant on her point-blank shot to find its mark, all she could do was offer a silent prayer, hoping that fate had not seen fit to release her this cycle.

The arrow impaled the Louperdu diving down towards her. It struck her target just below its left collarbone, the arrow embedding itself deep into her target, causing the spirit wolf to let out an ear-splitting yelp. Beating her wings furiously, she willed herself towards the sky, trying desperately to slow her descent. Razor-sharp claws from the wolf's outstretched paws raked her legs, causing her to cry out. Yet, the stinging pain was short lived, extinguished by the thump of her body against the ground. The violent impact winded her badly and her body felt numb. A loud ringing in her ears replaced the ambient sound of battle, and she felt heat rising in her arms and legs. Two large shapes approached her, yet she was unable to focus on either of her assailants. Her weapon was gone and she struggled to move. Her body was in shock – she realised that much at least – following its sudden impact with the ground. Completely disorientated, she tried to push herself away from her attackers, but the stinging pain in her legs resurfaced again, causing her to cry out once more.

'Leyla!' cried a distant voice, struggling to make itself heard over the ringing in her ears.

Breath filled her lungs again and her vision snapped sharply into focus. The Louperdu she had previously wounded limped towards her, snarling and baring its razor-sharp teeth. Its companion had turned its attention away from her, now focusing on a new threat instead. Glancing left, she saw the remaining member of her team, crouched low, in a knife forward stance, armed with a throwing knife in both hands. The pair stalked one other, ready to strike, yet she could ill afford giving the outcome of their battle any further attention, in light of more pressing concerns. She groped around with her arms, desperately trying to recover her weapon whilst her injured assailant continued its awkward advance. Unable to locate her bow, she could sense panic taking hold of her, causing her muscles to tense. She turned her head frantically in all directions, praying that something she could use as a makeshift weapon would present itself, all the while continuing to push her body away from her attacker. With nothing useful within arm's reach with which to defend herself, her heart began to sink and a wave of dread washed over her. In that sobering moment of inevitability, her thoughts turned to Rayna and Natalya, and how she had let them both down. Moreover, how she had failed Lazrik, who had trusted her to fulfil her duties and defend the vanguard.

The Louperdu now menacingly bearing down on her eclipsed her vision entirely. She could smell its stench as it closed in, its jaw lowered ready to tear off her face. Her entire body shook uncontrollably, fear gripping her with its cold embrace. The eyes of her attacker widened as it savoured her dread, as though sampling a delightful appetiser before consuming the main banquet. The noisy chattering of her teeth echoed in her skull, drowning out the

137

abhorrent sound of battle. Her breathing became shallow and erratic and she could feel the muscles tightening in her chest. Whether the Freylarkai's waning belief in the Everlife was still justified, or now irrevocably flawed in the wake of The Guardian's arrival, either way, it seemed fitting that fate now presented her with a similar end to that of her father; both were fated to meet the end of their physical existence whilst serving under Lothnar. Her only regret was not having done more to protect her comrades. Nevertheless, her resolve had not been lacking. Closing her eyes slowly, whilst trying to get a handle on her breathing, she attempted to quieten her mind, steeling herself in readiness for the next chapter of her existence.

She could sense Saralia's unease, nevertheless, the squad leader's scouts had a job to do – they would carry out Lothnar's orders, regardless. Still, it did not make listening to the distant screams emanating from the settlement any easier to stomach. Everyone present, herself included, wanted nothing more than to lend aid to their comrades. However, that was not the mission. Instead, theirs was to prevent the Louperdu from giving up the scout regiment's location. That meant sitting tight and maintaining a watchful eye over the eastern edge of the settlement. Ironic, considering her poor night vision. Nonetheless, as Lothnar had correctly pointed out, her ability would be crucial in thwarting any attempts to flee by runners seeking to alert the pack.

Saralia's squad had formed a thin cordon stretching almost the full length of the eastern edge of the settlement. The squad's unorthodox formation required its members to space out considerably, each some twenty paces apart.

Despite the thin coverage, the formation was the only sensible way of maintaining adequate surveillance across the entire eastern edge, whilst still facilitating meaningful communications between its members. Though she did not like the arrangement, nevertheless, it was necessary to achieve their goal. Although able to adopt a mist-like state, she had it on good authority from Saralia that the Louperdu could only hold their transient state for a limited period. Furthermore, the spirit wolves moved slowly when devoid of their physical bodies. Ergo, if any of the lupines tried to breach the cordon, they would know about it. Still, hiding in the field outside the settlement whilst listening to the cries of their comrades irked her. The Freylarkai had granted her the title of Guardian, tasked with overall responsibility of The Blades, and yet she felt useless given the current situation. Even so, she knew the stakes. Her days spent running around in the Wild, operating alone, were over. She had to function as part of a team in order for the scouts to succeed, which meant sitting on the bench, for the time being at least.

'Contact!' cried a distant voice suddenly.

She turned her head north, towards the direction of the warning. She could barely see a thing in the distance, such was the inadequacy of her vision in low light.

'Runner!' cried another voice, this time to south.

'Saralia,' she cried out to the squad's leader, just north of her position. 'I cannot see them!'

'Rayna, head south!' cried Saralia. 'Secure the south!'

She leapt up from her crouched position and immediately bolted southeast, looking to intercept the enemy. Unfurling her wraith wings, she leapt forward, beating her geometric, translucent wings furiously, giving

139

her the burst of speed needed to head off the fleeing spirit wolf.

'Where is it?' she cried.

With her vision impaired, she was utterly reliant on the sound of the scouts' voices in order to track their fleeing adversary. Although Lothnar had cautioned her against using her ability unnecessarily, without knowing her position, the scouts would find it difficult steering her towards the enemy.

Cupping her right hand behind her, she conjured a small sphere of white light into being, concealed within the palm of her hand. Speeding through the night, she allowed tiny flecks of light to peel away from its surface. The fleeting petals of light trailed behind her, forming a broken thread of faint light in her wake. Realising her intent, the scouts immediately began calling out to her through the night, guiding her trajectory. Adjusting her heading based on their instructions, she quickly located the spirit wolf, which was still in its transient form. The silver mist snaked a path across the field, hugging the uneven ground in a failed bid to obscure itself from sight – a sound tactic, if not for the keen eyes of her comrades. Upon locating the fleeing enemy, her prey quickly reverted to its physical form, as though sensing her proximity and the threat that she posed. Before her feet could touch the ground, the Louperdu bolted east on all fours. The creature bounded across the field desperately seeking to lose her in the night. She pursued her quarry fervently, beating her wings furiously once more, knowing that if she lost sight of the spirit wolf now, that her companions would be unable to lend aid in time. The spirit wolf accelerated, now travelling at break neck speed. It was fast and agile, able to change direction on a whim, causing her to almost lose sight of it.

'Damn you!' she cursed. 'Apologies Lothnar.'

With both arms outstretched, she released a concentrated beam of light from the palms of her hands, targeting the Louperdu. The searing light lit up the field, temporarily giving away the scouts' position, before striking the evasive creature, causing it to yelp in pain. The light quickly dissipated, after which she inadvertently overshot the injured spirit wolf. The beast cratered muzzle first into the ground before rolling across the field, its limp body bouncing from one furrow to the next, quickly swallowed up by the gloom. Coming to an emergency halt, she dropped to the ground and commenced backtracking on foot across the uneven terrain seeking to confirm the creature's release. Thandor's hunch about the Louperdu being averse to light, albeit at first glance, seemed to be true. Even so, she picked her way through the gloom cautiously, unsure if the creature still lived. Groping around in the dark, she soon discovered the body of the fallen Louperdu. Its head appeared to be snapped backwards, possibly due to its initial high-speed impact with the ground. It was impossible, therefore, to confirm Thandor's theory, given that she could have simply blinded the creature, thus causing it to lose its balance.

'Rayna!' cried a voice from in front of her.

A member of Saralia's squad suddenly stood before her, appearing abruptly, as though disgorged from the shadows.

'I have released it.'

'That was a decoy!'

'What?'

141

'The silver mist…there were two of them!' blurted the scout, whilst trying to regain their breath.

'Shit!' she said, cursing aloud. 'Which direction did it go?'

'East, towards the forest.'

'I'm going after it.'

'You will never find it – not with your sight – let alone catch it.' replied the scout. 'The others are falling back to regroup. We have failed in our mission.'

'No – I refuse to accept that outcome.'

'The spirit wolf's lead is too great.'

'Regardless, I'm going.'

'Rayna, I admire your resolve – we have won battles because of it. However, determination alone is not enough to close the gap in time. We misjudged the situation.'

'You are probably right. Nevertheless, I'm still going.' she said, before giving the scout a playful wink.

Their brief exchange of words had ended. With that, she turned about, beat her wings furiously, then disappeared into the night.

TEN
Predicament

After grabbing breakfast from the kitchen, he made his way to the common room so that he could sit and eat. The facility's communal hub was extremely busy; most of the tables were already at capacity, with a bum planted firmly on nearly every seat.

He stood awkwardly in the doorway, surveying the room, looking for a suitable place to sit down. A couple of empty seats caught his eye, though each was ensconced in rival gang territory. After briefly considering both options, he decided against riling Sebastian prior to their meeting by brokering any deals with Kyle or Dylan – he needed more information before making his move, and his residency at the facility was still young. Kristen, on the other hand, posed the least amount of threat to the others. Whilst it was rumoured that Sebastian tugged on the girl's strings, it was likely that neither Kyle nor Dylan saw the crazy female as a significant theat. Therefore, a seat at Kristen's table would cause less friction amongst the three juvenile kings. Even so, he had no desire to pass any time in the psychotic girl's company. Having encountered Kristen's type at other institutions, he knew well the ramifications of pissing off such unstable characters. Still, it was obvious now that Sebastian had taken an interest in him, therefore it would only be a matter of time before his female sycophant attempted to sink her claws into him. It made sense, therefore, to take the offensive and head off any manipulations by catching Kristen off guard.

'Wonderful.' he muttered to himself. 'It's too early for this shit.'

143

Slowly, he made his way across the room towards Kristen's lot. He could sense those around him watching his every movement, curious as to what he might do, their staring eyes boring into his skull. Unperturbed by the judgemental gaze of his onlookers, he continued his steady path towards Kristen's table. The girls congregated around Kristen quickly focused their attentions on him, fixing him with menacing stares. He looked towards Kristen who met his gaze with a crazy, wide smile.

'Like what you see, Callum?'

He knew better than to answer Kristen's loaded question, choosing instead to give her a weak smile as he continued walking towards her table in silence. Antagonising a crazy girl was the last thing he needed to do, meaning that diplomacy and tact were his best weapons. If the stereotype indeed fit, there was also a good chance that Kristen was a narcissist. If needed, he would feign quiet interest in the girl's boastful achievements whilst eating, before promptly taking his leave. However, before he could take a seat, Sebastian rose quickly from his chair.

'Callum, we have a seat reserved here, especially for you.' boomed the gang leader from across the room, his deep voice silencing the ambient chatter.

He paused, watching the leering smile on Kristen's face. Showboating, Kristen puckered her lips then blew him a kiss, reinforcing his supposition that the girl possessed low self-esteem.

'Looks like Sebastian wants to play with you. Shame.'

'I don't *play* games.' he said, immediately regretting indulging the girl in conversation.

'Don't be such a bore, Callum.'

Unsure how to respond, instead he gave Kristen a wink.

144

The girl responded with a puzzled look, suggesting that his efforts to confound her - and thus evade her attempts to pin him down - had indeed worked.

'It would be unwise to disrespect my hospitality, Callum.'

'I could not care less where I sit.' he said, turning to face Sebastian. 'So long as I am not disturbed whilst eating.'

Sebastian signalled for one of his lackeys to pull a seat away from his table. The chair scraped across the floor noisily, after which Sebastian motioned for him to take the vacant chair opposite.

Everyone in the room now stared at him, curious to see how he would react. Sebastian said nothing; the gang leader sat at the opposite side of the table, arms folded, waiting for him to take his seat. With little gained by rebuffing Sebastian's offer, he approached the table slowly, displaying no signs of urgency, before quietly sitting down. The room's occupants continued to stare at him intensely, Sebastian included, whilst he methodically ate his cereal. After finishing his breakfast, he dropped his spoon noisily into his bowl. The sound echoed around the large, sparsely furnished room, causing some of the residents to flinch. Reaching for his glass of water, he consumed the drink slowly, gulping noisily as the liquid flowed down his oesophagus. Once finished, he placed the glass firmly on the table, folded his arms and stared intently at his host.

'Jacob informs me that you wish to discuss a matter with me.'

'He is correct.'

'Let's hear it.' he said, pushing the bowel and glass away from him.

He did not fear Sebastian, unlike most of the residents in the room. Brushing aside the obstacles between them was a symbolic act, informing those present that he required no additional means of protecting himself from the gang leader. It was a small gesture, yet one that conveyed a clear message. Sebastian narrowed his eyes then gave him a hard glare, during which there was a lull in their conversation following their brief exchange of words.

'Give us the room.' said Sebastian suddenly.

The gang leader's deep voice reverberated around the hall, giving it the gravitas necessary to enforce a mass exodus of residents. Even Dylan and Kyle eventually relented, amongst the last to take their leave.

'Do you not wish them to hear me speak?'

'I do not want them to hear what I have to say.'

'Why is that?' he asked, curiously.

'I maintain control through fear – you know this. People fear what they do not understand.'

'So, you believe that you can manipulate me. That I will walk out of here as your obedient lackey, and that others will then fear my sudden unexplained change in disposition.'

'Correct.'

'You have nothing on me.'

'Incorrect.'

He gave Sebastian a cold stare. Jacob had warned him that the gang leader would attempt to manipulate him, given that intimidation would fail in his case. He considered his actions during the last few days, specifically, any breadcrumbs that he may have inadvertently left in his wake. He had been so careful, taking extreme care not to let anything slip that could ultimately be used against him.

146

What was it then that Sebastian supposedly held over him, he wondered.

'You're bluffing.' he said, tersely. 'I know that you went through my possessions – there was nothing of note to be found.'

'Not true.' replied Sebastian, pausing briefly before continuing. 'I quote: "*Callum, your education is important – it will keep you safe. Make sure that you come back to the library soon--*"'

'Fuck you!' he said, immediately standing up. 'Touch her and I will end you.'

'We live in a dangerous world, Callum. Now sit down!'

Overcome with rage, he violently flipped over the table between them, causing an almighty racket to echo around the room. So explosive was his response, that he barely had time to consider his reckless action. One of the table legs came close to hitting Sebastian, yet the gang leader never once flinched, displaying no sign of fear. Instead, Sebastian continued to sit calmly before him.

'Callum, I have a condition called EDD, Empathy Deficit Disorder – so the doctors tell me. It is probably the result of a shitty childhood, something that I am sure you are familiar with.'

'What's your point? Because right now there is no longer anything between you and my fists!' he said fervently, taking several steps towards the gang leader.

'Assault me and you will undoubtedly mess me up – I can see the hatred that boils inside of you. However, I will ruin you in the process. After which, I *will* find her! Furthermore, I have ordered a number of the others to lend assistance, if I press *this*.'

147

Sebastian pulled a small device from his right pocket before displaying it in the palm of his left hand. He was about to kick Sebastian's outstretched arm, denying the gang leader his advantage, when Sebastian clearly realised his intention, and quickly withdrew his ace to a safe distance.

'Despite your commendable determination, that alone is not enough to win against superior numbers. Furthermore, I know this institution well. I have every exit covered. Now sit down!'

'Report!'

'Sir, the vanguard has engaged the Louperdu. There were far more than we anticipated. However, we have broken the enemy. Multiple runners were spotted, fleeing east, as you predicted. Regrettably, one of the spirit wolves managed to sneak past Saralia's cordon – The Guardian is in pursuit.'

He released a deep sigh. There was always the possibility that one squad alone would not be able to cover enough ground effectively to form an impenetrable cordon; Saralia's squad had clearly been stretched too thin. Still, it had been impossible to counter every possibility, given the rapid manoeuvrability and elusive nature of their foe, especially with the limited resources at their disposal. Besides, he was through questioning his own decisions. The enemy had broken ranks. It was only a matter of time before the scouts secured the farmstead.

'Inform Yandar that he has command of the support squad. Once the fighting is over, I want all three squads to move into the farmstead and dig in. Heal the wounded and rest the scouts.'

'Understood.' replied the scout. 'Sir, what of yourself?'

'Unless Rayna is able to bring down the fleeing spirit wolf quickly, she will lose it. I will assist The Guardian; there is every chance she will require my skills to track it.'

'Can we catch it in time?'

'The enemy is fatigued – I am not. With that said, if I do not return before dawn, I want preparations underway to counter any future Louperdu offensive. Either way, the enemy will not attack us again this night. I leave Lazrik in command.'

'Sir.'

He gave the scout a firm nod, after which he unfurled his wraith wings before immediately heading northeast.

The Louperdu had a sizeable head start, plus the spirit wolves possessed good stamina. Even so, they could not run forever. Fatigue would eventually set in. Furthermore, whilst in their transient state, the Louperdu moved slowly. Although small, there was still a chance that he could catch up to the enemy, especially with Rayna harrying it – The Guardian's resolve was her defining characteristic. Blessed with his night vision and unparalleled tracking skills, he was convinced that he could locate the pair. As he sped across the fields leading away from the settlement, his keen eyes soon detected crop displacement, indicating signs of a chase. Having picked up the trail, he dropped to the ground and proceeded to move quietly on foot so that he could better study the terrain. Although his wraith wings provided a significant speed advantage, he was keen to follow the spirit wolf's tracks as opposed to Rayna's own, and that required significant concentration, which he could not apply at speed.

It was late and the temperature had dropped noticeably. The early morning dew had begun to settle on the crops, the welcome moisture reinvigorating the virgin shoots. Light from the Night's Lights reflected off the tiny droplets, giving the vegetation the illusion of a majestic halo. Yet, in places, the condensation appeared to be strangely absent, as though something had gently swept it away with its passage. A more apparent trail veered away from the phenomenon, evidenced by a clear abundance of damaged plant life. Regardless, he chose to ignore the obvious signs of disturbance, choosing instead to pursue the strange trail southeast, convinced that his prey now moved in its transient state. His gut told him that the enemy's change in tactic had confused The Guardian, causing Rayna to lose sight of it. If his supposition proved correct, there was every chance that he would soon hear the light bringer moving noisily on foot.

He swiftly followed the trail out of the field and into the adjacent woodland. The surrounding moisture rapidly vanished, no doubt held at bay by the thick canopy above, along with the increased temperature amongst the trees. The change in terrain prompted him to look for fresh signs of disturbance as he continued moving eastwards into the heart of the forest. The nature of the old woodland forced him to travel at a slower pace. Careful not to disturb the detritus littering the floor of the forest, he slowly picked his way through the trees, his eyes dancing across the relief searching for signs of his quarry. He soon detected fresh signs of movement, suggesting that the Louperdu had now resumed its physical form. Knowing that the spirit wolves possessed phenomenal hearing, he slowed his pace further, sensing that he was nearing his prey. Moving deeper into

150

the forest, his mind tried to play tricks on him by conjuring up strange images amidst the woodland. Experience taught him to filter such distractions, allowing him to discern truth from the dancing shadows.

As he continued to track his prey through the ancient woodland, he eventually caught a glimpse of its outline weaving an irregular path between the trees. Slowing his pace even more now, he focused on foot placement and regulating his breathing. Silently stalking the enemy, he noted obvious signs of fatigue, no doubt responsible for the creature's inefficient direction of travel. Occasionally, the spirit wolf would pause, its ears twitching during its brief periods of rest, before resuming its ponderous journey. Deftly closing the gap between them to within fifteen paces, the opportunity to take down his quarry at last presented itself. He slid a throwing knife from its sheath, careful to obscure the small weapon lest what little moonlight penetrated the canopy should catch the surface of the compact blade. Slowly taking aim, careful not to make any sudden movements, he drew back the weapon, ready to release his unsuspecting opponent.

A sudden cracking noise sounded faintly in the distance, to the northwest of their position. The spirit wolf's ears twitched rapidly, homing in on the source of the disturbance. He instinctively threw his knife, striking the spirit wolf, his subconscious realising in an instant that his quarry would surely bolt in response to the sound. The blade's impromptu flight lacked the stopping-power he would have liked. Nevertheless, the hasty shot pierced its target's flank. The spirit wolf released a sudden yelp, before quickly staggering forwards into the gloom, trying desperately to conceal its presence amongst the shadows. In

151

its wounded state, he prayed that the creature would be unable to shift back into its transient state. Unwilling to gamble, however, he immediately broke cover, bounding across the woodland towards his prey. The time for stealth and cunning was over, now he would take a leaf from Ragnar's playbook; Nathanar's predecessor frequently introduced his opponents to the smile of his double-handed axe prior to any faux introductory pleasantries.

A rush of air swept past her face and the sound of vicious snarling filled her ears, followed by an odd sense of pressure stabbing at her legs. She opened her eyes. A swirling maelstrom of black and silver fur blanketed her vision. The vicious snarls increased in pitch, followed by several ear-splitting yelps that made her flinch. Dust and dirt from the violent struggle forced her to recoil; she tried with all her might to drag herself away from the fighting, hindered by the close proximity of the attackers trampling over her feet. The scout she had witnessed engaging the other spirit wolf limped urgently towards her, his left leg gushing with crimson. She reached for his outstretched arm, grabbing it tightly, before her body was dragged unceremoniously away from the fierce fighting.

'Leyla, I have you!'

Her prone body bumped along the uneven ground, her left arm feeling as though it was being torn from its socket, the heat in her shoulder joint immense. The adrenaline flooding her body began to abate and her disorientation quickly subsided as she began to make sense of the situation.

Krisis savagely fought the injured Louperdu that had driven her from the top of the barn. The adolescent dire wolf's impressive physique made a mockery of his opponent's own. Even so, with its back to the wall and with everything to lose, the spirit wolf doggedly fought on with a ferocious intensity akin to the stuff of nightmares. It pounced repeatedly on Krisis, with zero regard for its own preservation as it relentlessly attacked. Its sharp claws raked across Krisis' fur, scoring the dire wolf's flesh, leaving glittering crimson lines in their wake as it desperately sought to grapple its superior adversary. The smaller, nimbler, animal repeatedly circled Krisis, diving in and out with its teeth and claws, trying to wear down its opponent. Realising his tactical disadvantage, Krisis backed off, breaking the cycle of attacks, before engaging in a renewed charge. The two wolves smashed violently into one another, though Krisis' muscular bulk held a clear advantage. Both fell to the ground in an awkward heap, the full weight of Krisis' mass crushing his opponent. Once more, the spirit wolf released an awful yelp, though it would be the creature's last, as the powerful dire wolf wrapped his jaws around his opponent's throat before ripping out its jugular. Blood sprayed from the Louperdu's savage wound, covering both the ground and Krisis, causing the dire wolf's fur to become matted. Krisis backed away from his ruined adversary, his piercing yellow eyes fixed on his fatally wounded opponent. Never before had she seen the dire wolf look so terrifying, soaked in the gore of its fallen opponent.

'Krisis!' she cried out, raising her right arm. 'Here boy!'

The dire wolf plodded towards her, lowering its muzzle so that she could stroke his head. He sat down beside her,

153

opened his mouth and began to pant whilst she affectionately rubbed his neck.

'Goooood boy' she said, before gingerly reaching up to wrap her arms tightly around the dire wolf's neck.

'We owe you one buddy.' said the injured scout behind her, now collapsed on the floor nursing his own wounds.

The fabric clinging to the scout's left leg was soaked in blood. Twisting her torso, she awkwardly aided the scout by applying pressure to his wounds using her hands. She pressed firmly against his leg, stemming the flow of blood.

'Thank you.'

Had Krisis not shown up, they would have both been released. In his injured state, after dispatching their other attacker, there was no way that the injured scout would have succeeded in fending off her opponent.

'Hang in there. Once the fighting is over, Lazrik will call for the aid of a renewalist.'

The scout's breathing was laboured and his eyelids appeared heavy. The pair of them were a mess. Even Krisis looked the worse for wear; the dire wolf slowly licked the matted fur on his chest, trying to rid himself of the blood of his fallen opponent.

'There is some linen in one of my right pockets.'

'Do the scouts always carry medical supplies?'

'We are scouts. Aside from each other, we are on our own out here.'

She twisted her body slowly. Sharp, stabbing pains in her legs made her wince, causing her eyes to water. After awkwardly fumbling around in the scout's numerous concealed pockets, she located the linen and began wrapping it tightly around her comrade's injured leg. Whilst tending to his wounds, the sound of battle began to abate. She ripped the end of the linen into two thin strips before tying off the end tightly above the scout's knee.

'It is far from my best work, but it will do the job.'

'Thank you.' said the scout, who then lay on his back.

'Keep your eyes open.'

Given the loss of blood, she was conscious that her comrade needed to remain awake.

'I want you to keep talking; sing me a song or something.'

'There is one I know; a few of us used to sing it together in the borderlands.'

'Perfect' she said, giving the scout a warm smile.

To her surprise, the scout had a dreamy, melodic voice, the sound of which somehow soothed the pain in her legs, putting her at ease. Krisis, too, seemed content. The dire wolf continued to chew his blood-matted fur, doing his best to cleanse himself of the gore. The scout finished his song, and was about to sing it once more when Klein suddenly came bounding over towards them.

'Is everyone OK?'

'Release has not come for us yet.' she said, giving the injured scout a wide smile. 'We have Krisis to thank for that.'

'I am sorry. Abandoning my post would have denied the regiment much needed covering fire. I had little choice but to send Krisis in my stead.'

'I appreciate the dilemma you were faced with. You made the right decision. Thank you!' she said, raising her right arm towards the archer.

Klein stooped down and grasped her forearm tightly before giving it a firm shake. The veteran bowman gave her a warm smile.

'I will send for a renewalist – our team needs its leader back on her feet.'

She rose early that morning after a restless night. The visions she had witnessed through Rarni still tormented her. Her heart refused to believe that her sister would be capable of such abhorrent acts, yet the logical thought processes running through her mind told her differently. Darlia's morals were very much grey, noticeably more so after losing her hand. Whereas she was expected to - and ultimately tried her best to - adhere to a path seen as acceptable and good by the people, her sister walked a different path. Although not inherently evil, Darlia had committed what many would consider to be acts of an evil nature. However, despite this, the majority had pardoned her sister due to extenuating circumstances and the opposing acts of benevolence Darlia had also performed. The rigid dichotomy between acts of good and evil held no sway over her sister. Darlia chose to thread a risky path between both extremes, pulled constantly from one polar opposite to the other, refusing to submit to the exclusive whim of either. Even so, these latest visions depicted acts of violence that went too far. What possible justification could her sister offer that would validate such heinous butchery, she wondered. Moreover, if Darlia failed to provide adequate reasoning for her actions, could she find it within herself to sentence her own sister to release?

It felt good to get outside, as though a heavy weight had been lifted from her shoulders, despite the burden of knowledge that she still bore. She inhaled deeply, allowing the fragrant air to fill her lungs as the morning sun spilled across her exposed arms and face, its gentle caress warming

156

her pale skin. Pausing for a moment, embracing all that spring had to offer, she then woke from her pleasant reverie and set off down the grassy slope towards the old wooden bridge spanning the river that cut through the heart of the vale. As was typically the case, the aging timber bridge was a hubbub of gossip, with Freylarkai from across the vale gathering to share information.

'Morning, Kirika.'

'Good morning.' she said, as she weaved a path between the throng of Freylarkai gathered on and around the bridge.

'Kirika, has there been any update on the grain situation from the farmsteads?'

'Kayla is investigating the matter for me. I am awaiting her report.'

'Our son has enlisted with The Blades – we are so proud of him. He has his first class with The Teacher this cycle.'

'Nathaniel will instruct him well; of that I am certain. I am sure that your son will be a tremendous asset to the domain.'

'Kirika--'

'Please accept my apologies. There is something that I must attend to.'

'Good cycle to you Kirika!'

She dipped her head and quickened her pace, trying hard to avoid further engagement with the gathered crowd. Given her lofty status, she found it almost impossible to wander the vale unnoticed. It was then that she began to wonder if her intended course of action was wise, given her station. Though she had never actively sought such an elevated position, the path she had pursued in trying to hold

157

the domain together had ultimately given rise to her role within Freylarkin society. Yet, part of her would happily give it all up, so that she could disappear into the forest and carve out a far simpler existence alongside those who dwelled there, Rayna included. Constantly managing the domain's affairs became tiresome on occasion, despite reaping satisfaction from her work. Though she worked as part of a team, her role within the ruling council was such that the other members looked to her to navigate their way through the endless hardships that threatened the domain. Despite the ongoing taboo associated with scrying - hence her reluctance to indulge in the use of her ability in public - she knew that the other members, at least for the most part, secretly approved of the use of her ability in private to help guide the council's actions.

'Kirika, have--'

'I cannot right now I am afraid. Please speak with Kayla.'

She felt bad throwing her aide to the wolves. Still, Kayla had proved herself repeatedly, now rarely panicking when under pressure. Despite the young Freylarkin's heavy exposure to the ongoing politics that still dogged the vale, Kayla remained enthusiastic and eager to please – she could not ask for a more willing and capable assistant to help her manage the domain's affairs.

She pushed on, weaving a convoluted path through the press of Freylarkai eager to engage with her. She felt awful dismissing their concerns, but she knew that the people would forgive her this one time given her habitual devotion to the domain and its residents.

Leaving the bridge and its continued hubbub behind her, she pressed on, deep into the forest, the distant chatter eventually giving way to the choir of Sky-Skitters perched in the canopy above. The pleasant song enhanced the woodland's natural splendour, which, along with the shafts of golden light that speared down through small gaps in its thick canopy, gave the ancient forest an enchanting feel. Though she now resided within the Tri-Spires, she had not entirely forgotten her childhood stomping grounds. There were scenes from the images that Rarni had shown her that felt familiar. However, her absence from the forest meant that she would have a decent amount of walking ahead of her, no doubt spent chasing down numerous dead ends. Nevertheless, she was confident in her ability and that eventually, before the cycle was out, she would detect the presence of her sister's recent past within the woodland.

ELEVEN
Revulsion

'What! You want me to help you commit a robbery? Against an Apex class citizen, no less. Are you out of your fucking mind?'

'It is time that we took something back from those privileged arseholes in power.'

'Clearly, the immoral way in which the Shadow class is treated is something that we can actually agree upon. However, what you are proposing is straight up theft.'

'What of it?'

'It won't change a thing!'

'Will it not? It will take riches from those with, delivering them into the hands of those without.'

'You mean *your* hands.'

'To be shared amongst those who support my cause – a means of motivation, if you will.'

'Sebastian, this will not alter the public's perception of our kin – it will likely worsen it! We need to play by their rules.'

'Their rules are broken, the odds heavily stacked in *their* favour. Callum, do you really want to play a losing game for the remainder of your life, whilst you eke out a hollow existence surviving on the scraps that they toss us?'

'We need to win by their broken rules, else a victory will mean nothing, breeding only further contempt towards those in our position.'

'That is where you and I disagree. Direct action is necessary!' said Sebastian sternly, leaning forwards across the table. 'Given the Shadow class's pitiful status, we cannot afford to appear soft.'

161

'Look, I am sympathetic to your - sorry *our* - cause. I was born into this shitty life – I have known nothing else. That does not mean that I have become complacent and accepting of our lot. However, if you give them further cause to hate us, it will spell disaster for our kind. You know as well as I that the government would jump at the opportunity to sweep our last pieces from the board. Do not give them the ammunition they need to do so.'

'Callum, I can see that you are intelligent; you are not like the others here. Which is why I want you by my side on this, ideally willingly. There is little chance that we can improve our lot by playing their game – you know this.'

'Little chance, yes. Nonetheless, there is a chance.'

'You would have us gamble everything on a sliver of hope, as opposed to taking the fight directly to them?'

'We have a greater chance of altering people's perception of us, rather than assembling a militant order using stolen funds with which to oppose them.'

'I disagree, Callum.'

There was a long pause between them. Sebastian was resolute on the matter. He knew nothing of the teenager's past, therefore he lacked the knowledge required to affect the gang leader's thinking. Nevertheless, he remained unperturbed, deciding instead to use what little he did know.

'You cannot apply the model that you have employed here, within the confines of this facility, to the outside world, simply by scaling up your operation.'

'See, I knew you were intelligent!' replied Sebastian, who slowly eased back into his chair. 'Nevertheless, fear is a powerful motivator – you would do well not to underestimate its potential uses.'

162

'If we employ such tools to achieve our ends, we become no better than those oppressing us.'

'Righteous thinking like that has no place in our current society, Callum. Humanity's thinking has regressed, defaulting to its tribalistic ways. There is no greater good mentality or a common goal to unite us. Now, there is only survival of the fittest.'

'Or most cunning.'

Sebastian laughed.

'You still think that you can play a crap hand and win.'

'Yes.'

'Then prove it. Maybe then, I will reconsider my thinking. However, for the time being, you *will* follow my direction – is that clear?'

Loath to become an accomplice to Sebastian's agenda, he narrowed his eyes, giving his adversary a hard stare. If he could not sway the gang leader, how could he expect to alter the public's mind-set, thus changing their perception of the Shadow class, he wondered. Sebastian was cunning, which meant that he was also dangerous and liable to act on any threats. Without leverage, he could not risk Kaitlin's safety.

'I would rather you and I were friends, Callum. There is a severe lack of ingenuity and forward thinking around here. Most cannot see past the physical walls of this cage, let alone the future and their place in it.'

'They feel hopeless. Like a leaf carried downstream by a strong current – they do not fight to alter their destiny.'

'Yes.' replied Sebastian, before giving him an unnerving smile.

The gang leader tucked the small device back into his right pocket, a clear sign that their discussion had evolved into something more than manipulation versus hatred.

'You have made good use of your friend's library. Know that I have no desire to bring harm to one who would provide education to a member of our class. Indeed, she could be an asset.'

'I do not want her involved in this.'

'Then I will respect your wishes. However, you will work for me. I cannot afford to surround myself exclusively with simple-minded drones. Whilst they have their uses, they do not bring anything fresh to the table.'

Sebastian paused for a moment, considering his next words carefully.

'In order to oppose the system that suppresses us, we need to counter the natural disadvantage that our social status bestows upon us. Brute force and fear are natural counters. However, they do seed resentment, which causes other issues. Therefore, I am open to a fresh approach, something that incorporates cunning and guile. But, before I can get behind more unorthodox means of coercion, you need to prove to me that you are capable of such feats.'

'What do you propose?'

'This *robbery*, as you put it--'

'What else would you call it?'

'Distribution of resources.'

He laughed, unable to contain his amusement, though the gang leader chose to ignore his obvious lack of respect.

'Devise a means of achieving my goal that does not require painting the floor red. Do that and, provided it is successful, we will discuss your views further.'

164

Despite fatigue and the wound he had inflicted, the injured spirit wolf moved at an impressive speed through the verdant woodland. Desperate to escape the reach of his blades, the beast weaved a complex path through the undergrowth, trying its best to lose him amongst the thickets. The wolf's superior agility and low stance enabled the creature to fade into the background. Even with the assistance of the light of dawn seeping through the gaps in the canopy, the velocity with which the wolf travelled made it difficult for him to maintain a visual lock on his target.

As he bounded through the woodland in pursuit of his prey, he sensed another closing in on their position. Whoever it was that followed them could not match their agility, instead being forced to bludgeon a path through the forest in order to maintain pace, evidenced by the sound of snapping branches and the frequent rustling of leaves. He caught a glimpse of movement in his periphery, confirming the presence of another moving as the Sky-Skitter flies, with no regard to their own welfare as they trampled through the woodland.

'*Rayna!*' he communicated telepathically, instantly recognising the light bringer from the ochre colour of her skin. '*Left flank!*'

Such brazen pursuit served The Guardian well, plus she was light on her feet, but charging headlong through the dense terrain would not go unpunished for long. Yet, the light bringer's dogged determination frequently meant that Rayna disregarded her own safety if it meant achieving her ends. He admired her resolve, although such impetuous behaviour was foolhardy given the nature of the terrain and without others to support her.

The injured wolf steered right, away from the incessant noise caused by The Guardian. He slid one of his throwing knives from its sheath in readiness for the inevitable shot that would soon present itself. As predicted, the spirit wolf crossed his path, looking to evade its fresh pursuer. He released the projectile in his right hand, guiding its path towards the Louperdu. The blade embedded itself deep into the spirit wolf's right flank, causing it to yelp in pain. Buried deep into its target, the knife severely hindered the creature's movement, allowing him to close the gap between them rapidly. Pulling one of his custom dirks from his leather belt, he pounced upon the injured spirit wolf. He sunk the blade deep into the neck of his prey, before promptly wrestling it free, silver blood gushing across the forest floor signalling the Louperdu's demise.

Within moments of the creature's release, Rayna skidded to a halt less than five paces from his kill. The Guardian doubled over, clearly out of breath, trying hard to regulate her breathing.

'Stand tall and breathe deeply, into your belly; remember what Nathaniel taught you.'

Rayna did as instructed, placing her hands on her hips as she stood upright, allowing her lungs to fill with air.

'Recovery breathing is key to outlasting your opponent in a fight – never forget that.'

Rayna flashed him a quick smile whilst continuing to inhale deeply, as she sought to regulate her breathing.

He wiped his dirk on the creature's silver fur before its body dissolved into a plume of smoke that slowly dissipated through the undergrowth. Standing perfectly still, he looked towards the thick canopy above, listening to the ambient sounds of the forest accompanied by Rayna's deep rhythmic

166

breathing. As he gazed up at the canopy, he felt an odd sensation. Despite having taken down their prey, something felt wrong, or rather, out of place. Using his telepathic ability, he cast his mind adrift, searching for the presence of anything unusual or amiss.

'What are you doing?' asked Rayna, inquisitive as ever.

'Shh! Let me concentrate.'

Allowing his mind to wander, meandering through the woodland, he searched for whatever it was that troubled his subconscious. In addition to his keen senses, it was normal for his ability to detect the presence of others passively, though his mind had become somewhat desensitized to the proximity of other Freylarkai. However, now he sensed something different. The forest was shielding something that his mind had not felt the presence of before. Whatever it was, the unusual presence stirred up a mixture of emotions, namely sorrow and dread, leaving him with a feeling of unease.

'We are not alone.'

'What is it?'

'I am not--'

Before he could complete his sentence, a spine-chilling howl sounded from deep within the forest. The trees rustled ominously and scores of Sky-Skitters abandoned their perches, the sound of their wings beating fervently filling their ears. Turning their attention towards the disturbing sound, they both stared into the gloom, trying to ascertain what it was that lurked within the depths of the forest.

'We should investigate.'

'The mission comes first, Rayna.'

'Surely it knows that we are here. We could lose this opportunity to assess a potential threat if we do not act now.'

The Guardian made a valid point. Besides, Lazrik, Yandar and Saralia each knew how to command the regiment in his absence.

'Very well. However, you cannot go barrelling though the forest like before.' he said, pointing to several scratches marring the light bringer's skin. 'We need to approach with caution.'

'Agreed.' said Rayna, followed by a curt nod. 'I will follow your lead.'

Slowly, cautiously, he threaded a path through the forest towards the harrowing sound, using his ability to hone their route. Whatever it was that lurked within the woodland lay just beyond the reach of his senses, luring him deeper into the forest, eluding his grasp.

'Are we clo--' whispered Rayna, clearly eager to discover the source of the howl before it cut their conversation short once more.

The foreboding sound thundered across the forest once more. It felt heavier this time as it reverberated through his body, carrying with it a sense of sorrow, like the sound of an animal in distress. Yet his ability told him a different story, one of hatred and resentment. In any event, he could feel a growing sense of dread as they neared their target. He wondered whether Rayna felt the same, or instead if her dull senses shielded her from the unease that he felt.

It was mid-morning when eventually she detected the past-presence of her sister. Using her ability, she discerned the route Darlia had taken through the forest. Following the

168

breadcrumbs laid out in her visions, she diligently travelled the same path as her sister, careful not to deviate from her scrying. It was a painstaking process overlaying the scenes in her mind with the surrounding woodland, doing her utmost to interpret the images correctly, despite most trees looking alike. Nevertheless, her attention to detail, along with her local knowledge, served her well, allowing her to - albeit slowly - retrace her sister's footsteps.

Eventually, she came to a small dwelling in the heart of the woodland, identical to the one she had seen in Rarni's vision, the sight of which made her anxious. She took a moment to observe the abandoned-looking home from a distance, using the time to attempt to quell the feeling of unease in her stomach. The ancient gnarled tree's door was ajar due to its smashed lock, and a sense of dread emanated from the narrow, dark gap between the door and its weather-beaten bark. Steeling her nerves, she slowly advanced towards the artificially swollen tree, silently cursing the shapers responsible for its sinister appearance – why they had chosen to shape such an ominous tree to begin with was beyond her.

There was nothing left of the door's lock, now well beyond the repair of even the most skilled shaper. Sliding her fingers around the edge of the door, she pulled it open gently before peering into the gloom, her eyes slowly adjusting to the dark interior. The main room was sparse and tidy, consisting of three empty beds and a small wooden table. There were no soft furnishings – the cots were bare – nor did she see any traces of ceramic or blood on the floor. The room was clean – too clean. It felt sterile. There was nothing inviting about the room, indeed its sparse condition gave it an eerie feel. Her eyes drifted towards the entrance

169

to the adjacent room, from where she had seen the young female emerge during the visions. Reluctantly, she entered the main room, despite her growing dread, before engaging her second sight. She allowed the past to flood her mind's eye, directly this time, knowing that she needed to confirm her sister's crime first-hand before pursuing the matter further. Once again, the abhorrent scenes played out before her as she scried Darlia's macabre actions. Witnessing the images again, now in greater clarity, made her shudder.

Feeling nauseous, she ceased her scrying and promptly vacated the dwelling, returning to the fresh air outside. There was no lingering doubt in her mind. Darlia had indeed released all three of the victims, but for what reason? She engaged her second sight again, this time moving forward from the previous events that had transpired. She watched in horror as she witnessed her sister unceremoniously drag one of the ruined corpses from the dwelling into the woodland. Darlia dragged the body from where it had fallen, using her bonze, mechanical claw to grab the victim by its right foot. A feeling of revulsion started to well up inside her; the ugly sight of the victim's head, or at least what remained of it, bouncing along the ground, whilst her sister tugged on the prone body, made her retch. After wiping her mouth clean with the back of her hand, her eyes began to water, followed shortly by tears that streamed down her cheeks.

'Why?' she cried aloud, suddenly losing all composure. 'After everything…it was finally over. Why would you do this?'

She dropped to the floor, quietly sobbing to herself, unable to understand why her sister had committed such a heinous act. It was some time before she managed to compose herself, eventually finding the emotional strength to wipe the tears from her face and continue her investigation.

Using her ability once more, she followed her sister deep into the woodland to an area of particularly thick undergrowth. She watched with her mind's eye as Darlia painstakingly dug a large hole in the ground using her mechanical claw, grafted onto the stump of her sister's left arm by the accursed shaper, Krashnar. She felt sure that the cursed prosthetic held sway over her sister, the twisted will of its maker somehow influencing Darlia's actions, causing her to stray down paths best not trodden. As with any scrying, it was difficult to get a sense of time. Although, given the amount of dirt that attached itself to her sister's clothing, Darlia had surely spent a considerable amount of time excavating so much earth. It was then that the true horror of her sister's crimes hit home. Though she had already anticipated that her sister would bury the bodies, she had not expected the process to be so macabre.

The hole was clearly not large enough to accommodate all three bodies, not if they were laid out decently. Furthermore, her sister was obviously in a race against time, with each passing moment increasing the chances of her discovery. Ergo, Darlia proceeded to arrange the body that she had dragged through the woodland, bending its limbs into positions that best fit her hastily dug grave. Although the images lacked sound, nonetheless, she vividly imagined the noises made by the bones snapping under the vice-like grip of her sister's claw. With each imaginary crack, her body shook with fear. She could feel the blood drain from her face whilst the air around her seemed to drop in temperature. Though she had witnessed many horrors in

171

her time, be it directly or otherwise, none had affected her quite like the images now cascading through her mind.

After completing the dreadful deed, Darlia made her way back to the scene of the crime to retrieve the remaining corpses. Unable to stomach the rest of the awful burial process, she disengaged her second sight. Standing at the edge of the abhorrent site, her pale skin more ashen than usual, she silently regarded the loose foliage and lumpy earth below that had been used to mask the communal grave. Tears began rolling down her cheeks once more as the gravity of her sister's actions crystallised in her mind. Her thoughts shifted, now focusing on the aftermath, in particular, how the situation would be successfully managed – if indeed that was even possible.

'Come in.'

The sound of Lazrik's voice made her feel anxious. After her wounds were healed, by one of the regiment's renewalists, she found herself repeatedly questioning her actions, wondering if events could have played out more favourably. Both of the regiment's renewalists had worked overtime, doing their best to patch up those who had taken wounds in the fighting. They had only lost one of their members, regardless of the large number of injuries suffered. Therefore, despite the fatality it had caused, statistically speaking at least, the mission had been a resounding success. Even so, losing one comrade was a blow to the regiment's morale – to some it had meant the loss of a life-long friend.

She stepped inside the barn. Lazrik was bent over a large wooden table, studying various objects neatly arranged before him that had no place being together. It

172

seemed that Lazrik was using them to portray the layout of the settlement, so that he could better plan its defence. Beside him stood Yandar and Saralia. Both looked towards her as she entered the room.

'I am glad to see that you are still with us Leyla; we cannot let the males have all the fun.' said Saralia, before giving her a subtle grin.

'If not for the renewalists, it is likely that I would have lost the use of my legs.'

'True.' said Lazrik, raising his head. 'However, without your team's covering fire, the Louperdu would have broken our defensive circle.'

The squad leader stood upright, folding his arms across his chest. Though none of them came across as intimidating or unapproachable, even so, she felt anxious whilst they carefully studied her.

'Leyla, you can relax.' said Yandar. 'This is not the arena, nor are we The Teacher.'

'That is a relief; I am not certain that I could go another round with Nathaniel right now.'

The squad leaders laughed heartily, putting her at ease.

'Klein spoke highly of your actions in the field. I value his opinion. You served the regiment well, which is why I have asked you to join us.' explained Lazrik. 'You know this settlement well – Klein confirmed as much – therefore it would be remiss of us not to consult you during our preparations.'

'You believe that the Louperdu will return?'

'They fought hard to take back the settlement after allowing us to enter it unchallenged. Furthermore, the ferocious nature of the ambush suggests that we are dealing with a level of cunning that should not be underestimated.' said Yandar.

'They lured us in, with a view to our release, using stealth and guile in an attempt to root us out. It is therefore logical to assume that they intend to finish the job. That being the case, the Louperdu might consider the use of alternate tactics. Superior numbers seems like the obvious choice given that we are now fortified.' Lazrik explained.

'You are assuming that the pack has been alerted to our position.'

'We have to make that assumption.' said Saralia. 'Though this battle was a victory, we failed to entirely seal off the area. Lothnar and Rayna are chasing down a runner that managed to evade our cordon.'

'You doubt their success?'

'Not at all – they *will* release it.' replied Lazrik. 'Both are equally stubborn and determined, hence their inevitable fight in the arena. However, we cannot be certain that more spirit wolves did not elude our grasp.'

'I see.' she said despondently, unable to mask her feelings.

'Try not to feel so glum.' said Saralia. 'If you wanted a quiet life, you would not have followed in your father's footsteps.'

'Did you know him?'

'Not personally. However, others here did, Lothnar included, all of whom speak highly of him. Therefore, I *can* tell you that you are a credit to his name.'

'Which, again, brings me to why you are here.' Lazrik interjected. 'I would appreciate it, Leyla, if you offered us your counsel regarding this place, along with your knowledge of the enemy, so that we can better prepare ourselves in the event of a further assault.'

'Of course, I will tell you everything I know.'

She walked towards the remaining table edge and took her position.

'Good.' replied Lazrik. 'Together, I want us to have a working plan that we can implement prior to sundown. I do not expect the Louperdu to offer us any respite, therefore we must make haste in our preparations.'

'Before we get started,' said Saralia, 'I want you to know that we found Zealia.

'Can I see her?'

'Of course. However, your friend was badly mauled by her attacker – you should prepare yourself. Even so, we thought that you would like to be the one to bury her.'

TWELVE
Fear

'It is here – straight ahead.'

The forest was silent now, save for the sound of their anxious breathing. He had never seen Rayna so on edge, though he too felt the same following the ominous howls that had drawn them deeper into the ancient woodland.

'I will lead.'

'No.' he whispered, giving The Guardian a hard stare. 'Stay behind me.'

'You don't need to mollycoddle me, Lothnar.' replied Rayna, fervently.

'I have no idea what that--.' he replied, cutting himself short.

Rayna was not a scout, nor did she answer to him within the chain of command. He realised then his error in judgement, that his abrupt words might be misconstrued as either condescending or dismissive, especially given The Guardian's headstrong disposition.

'I mean no disrespect.' he said, looking to diffuse any tension. 'Your ability is likely to be of greater use than my own, if the situation develops into conflict. Therefore, you should remain behind me until your skills are required.'

Rayna paused for a moment, considering the merit of his words before nodding in agreement. The light bringer's willingness to consider alternate perspectives, regardless of differing viewpoints, was a trait that he greatly admired. He wondered if the rare quality was ingrained, or whether she had developed it due to her otherworldly experiences. Thandor was the same; the aloof Paladin considered every angle before casting his lot.

Pressing forwards, he slowly parted the last of the undergrowth obscuring their view, revealing a large clearing nestled within the dark woodland. At its centre stood a colossal tree, its massive canopy blocking out the fledgling light of dawn that held no hope of penetrating its verdant shield. Leaning against the ancient wooden pillar was a massive creature covered in unkempt, matted fur, standing some four to five paces in height. The towering creature possessed features similar to that of the Louperdu. However, it had large fists and crimson, hate-filled eyes. It appeared to be squatting on its muscular hind legs, making it difficult to gauge its exact height. The creature's body was a mess of silver and black fur, as if the skins of multiple animals had been stitched together to create its patchwork hide. That hide undulated and rippled, as though parasitic worms writhed beneath its skin, trying to escape their organic prison.

'My god, what is that?'

There were no words, at least none that he could fathom, that would adequately sate the light bringer's need for answers. Never before had he witnessed something so monstrous in all the passes that he had spent in the borderlands. Even the deplorable nightmare that had consumed Krashnar in the arena somehow failed to surpass the level of depravity exuded by the sinister thing before them, now hunched over the ancient tree, using it as some kind of oversized crutch.

'Ragnar!'

'What?'

'The thing that released Ragnar, you remember it, do you not?' he asked, turning to face the light bringer whose ochre skin had paled significantly.

178

'This looks different.'

'Yes, but the hallmarks are still there – look at it closely.'

He watched as the concerned light bringer studied the wretched behemoth squirming at the centre of the clearing, the low light clearly hindering her sight. Armed with the knowledge reaped by his superior perception, Rayna's face darkened as the truth of his words sunk in.

'You could be right.'

'Rayna, that is not natural. *He* is responsible for this monstrosity.'

'Krashnar is gone – I immolated him!'

'Indeed, but this…*thing*, it is old.'

'Will this nightmare ever end?' asked Rayna, turning to face him.

'We need to leave, now, and report our--'

His words died on his lips as the monstrous creature released an ear-splitting howl, forcing them both to cover their ears due to their close proximity. The deafening cry sent a shiver down his spine, a response only heightened by what was happening physically to the creature. Silver-grey mist seeped through the monster's hide, like puss oozing from a festering wound, accompanied by a pungent odour that made him feel ill. The foul-smelling vapour forced its way through the beast's skin, before slowly assuming a number of physical forms. The amorphous beings gradually took shape, still clinging in part to their host, slowly adopting the form of that which they had pursued from the settlement. Once fully realised, the newly manifested Louperdu fell to the ground, now free of their host. Dazed, the newly birthed lupines lay still where they had fallen, presumably recovering from the trauma of their genesis.

179

The creature responsible for their birth released an awful whine, after which its muscles appeared to relax, its skin no longer undulating, thus providing it some respite from the pain. Some time passed whilst the disorientated fledglings slowly righted themselves, after which the spirit wolves ponderously made their way deeper into the woodland, where they soon vanished from sight. The monster responsible for their manifestation recomposed itself. Pushing itself away from the tree, which it seemed to have used as a birthing aid during their creation, it dropped to the ground on all fours before stretching its muscular limbs. The creature seemed more threatening now, no longer weakened by its vulnerable birthing state. Raising its muzzle high, it sniffed at the air.

'This is not good.' he whispered under his breath.

The monstrous, patchwork creature turned in their direction, its menacing, red eyes fixed intently on their position. Holding his gaze with its own, they stared silently at one another, the creature now acknowledging his and Rayna's unwanted presence in what was presumably a private sanctuary for the birthing of its children.

'We must leave. Now!'

He slowly released his grasp on the undergrowth, which he had been holding back. The creature staring them down detected his subtle body movement, causing it to open its maw and release another of its ear-splitting howls. The deafening sound reverberated through him once more, causing his body to tremble involuntarily. A sense of foreboding washed over him, the wave of dread threatening to drown him. Refusing to succumb to paralysis borne from fear, he parted the undergrowth once more, this time fixing the terrifying creature with a formidable glare of his own.

'You were foolish to come here. Know now that I see the fear within you, which makes you mine!'

'Callum, why are we here?'

'Shh, be quiet.'

Crouched behind a line of grime-stained waist-high containers, he gingerly peered round the edge of their cover, trying to gauge the situation. It was not technically illegal to steal from refuse sites – at least, that was how he interpreted the law. However, it was illegal to trespass on private land. Furthermore, the Shadow Class had been looting such facilities for years. Therefore, it was only a matter of time before the authorities decided to address the problem with more heavy-handed tactics. For now, all they needed to concern themselves with was lunch breaks, shift changes and metal fencing.

'Is this really necessary?'

'Look, Sebastian ordered you to assist me. Besides, you owe me for snooping around my affairs.'

'Callum, I--'

'I don't wanna hear it.' he snapped, tuning to give Jacob a hard glare. 'You allowed Sebastian to use fear to control you, and because of that, I, too, now have something to lose.'

'Then you know how it is; like me, you are also being coerced.'

'Do not compare us – I am nothing like you.'

He peered around the edge of their hiding place once more, watching with interest as several of the machine operators powered down their systems before breaking for lunch.

181

'This is our chance. Get the mat ready.' he said, reaching for the length of rope in his satchel.

'I can't do this.'

'Shut up. I am the one taking all the risk; all you need to do is keep an eye out and help me carry the stuff back.'

'But if you get caught, they will come after me as your accomplice.'

'You should have thought about the consequences of your actions before taking on the role of Sebastian's lap dog.'

'I had no choice.'

'There is always a choice – you could have lied to him, told him that you found nothing.'

Jacob went quiet. It was then that he regretted allowing himself to be drawn on the matter; now was not the right time. He needed Jacob to focus. Instead, the gaunt orphan was no doubt questioning his own actions in light of his terse words.

'We can discuss this later. Right now, we have a job to do. Follow me.'

They moved in a line towards the tall metal fencing constructed from thick vertical bars, the top of which were studded with vicious metal spikes. Most would have deemed scaling such defences impossible. However, he had learned from his kin how best to deal with similar obstacles. He threw one end of the long rope over the top of the fence, allowing it to drop down the other side. Reaching through a gap between the vertical bars, he grabbed the free end of the rope and proceeded to tie a noose knot, which he then pulled tight so that the rope hung down from the top of the fence.

'You should have knotted it first.'

He responded to Jacob's flawed insight with an audible sigh.

'That would have prevented me from tightening the knot. Tell me, how *did* you know where to look for my book?'

Jacob averted his gaze, choosing to stare at the ground instead.

'Never mind; I know it was Sebastian. Although I am loath to admit it, he and I are similar in some respects. In any event, we have a job to do. Hand me the mat.'

His reluctant accomplice passed him a small, grubby, hessian mat, to which they had fastened a piece of cord at both ends, allowing him to hook it around his neck during his ascent. Before commencing his climb, he quickly changed his shoes; forgoing his thick tread for a pair with a more flexible rubberised sole would offer him greater purchase when scaling the metal fence. As a precautionary measure, he had coated the bottom of the plimsolls with a rubber-based adhesive to provide further traction. Doing so, however, meant losing time whilst changing his footwear either side of the barrier. Satisfied with his preparations, he pulled on the rope one last time, ensuring that it was indeed secure, before beginning his climb.

Ascending the fence was much harder than he had anticipated. Still, the thick rope and appropriate footwear allowed him to reach the top, albeit incredibly slowly. Harder still was dealing with the spikes. The thick mat they had brought allowed him to cushion their points. However, hauling himself over the summit was an inelegant process; he fell awkwardly down the other side, landing on his feet before crashing onto his backside. The mat promptly followed him down, catching the side of his face as it landed on the ground beside him.

'Callum! Are you OK?'

'I'm fine.' he replied in a disgruntled tone, rubbing the carpet burn on the side of his cheek. 'Pass me the other shoes.'

Jacob handed him his original shoes, allowing him to change his footwear yet again. It was a hassle continuously swapping shoes, but he needed to ensure that the adhesive on the plimsolls remained free of grit and dust in order to maintain their effectiveness. Although a ladder would have been far more appropriate for scaling the fence, carting one through the metropolis would have been highly suspicious.

'OK, take cover and wait for my signal. I will need at least fifteen minutes.'

'That's cutting it fine.'

'We've gone over this already. The workers break for forty-five minutes. That gives me more than enough time to find what we need.'

'If Anastacia realises our absence, we are fucked.'

'Relax.' he said, trying to placate Jacob's obvious panic. 'Sebastian has us covered. I may dislike him, but the guy has talent. He is more than capable of covering for us.'

The tension in Jacob's face eased a little, but it was clear that the boy still had jitters.

'Go and take cover. Remember to signal me if anything starts to go sideways.'

Jacob scampered off back towards the containers. He held onto the plimsolls, choosing to hide them himself. It was unlikely that Jacob would abandon him; the boy's fear of Sebastian was far greater than that of actually being

184

caught, or worse, facing Anastacia. Even so, he had no reason to trust Jacob, particularly given the boy's previous actions. Therefore, he decided that it would be best not to rely on Jacob in the event of saving his own neck.

Wasting little time, he sprinted across the site towards the large refuse containers located at the opposite end. As he made his way quickly across the yard, he made sure to maximise the use of any available cover, trying his best to conceal his presence. Although the facility's amenities were located on the other side of the site, there was always the possibility of an early shift change or a rogue worker deciding to stretch their legs – the last thing he wanted was to be spotted scurrying around the grounds.

'Lothnar, what is it?'

Taken aback by the creature's words, he was barely conscious of Rayna's own.

'Loth, talk to me – you look like you've seen a ghost.'

How could such a base creature formulate such articulate words, he mused. Only moments prior, whilst giving birth to several of its kin, the abhorrent thing was barely able to stand. Now, however, it was like a completely different beast, one that threatened to end their existence.

'It spoke to me.'

'What!' replied Rayna, clearly shocked. 'How is that even possible? I heard nothing.'

'Its muzzle cannot formulate words directly. However, I can hear its thoughts clear in my mind.'

'What did it say?'

'Something about using fear to control us – it makes no sense to me.'

185

The light bringer's ochre skin paled even more – he had never seen The Guardian look so bleached of colour. Though the creature's words meant nothing to him, something about them clearly had the light bringer rattled.

'I need to speak with it.'

'Why?'

'I just do – I cannot explain to you why just now. Please, just trust me on this.' implored Rayna.

The Guardian's request made even less sense to him than the creature's menacing words. Nevertheless, he trusted Rayna implicitly.

'I could try using my telepathic ability to communicate with you both, simultaneously. Provided that you do not oppose me, I should be able to use my ability to relay your own thoughts to the creature and vice-versa.'

'I see. So, you would act as a bridge.'

'Something like that. However, you need to open your mind to me in order for this to succeed and that means letting down your guard. As I understand it, you have made great strides to let go of your past. Yet a dark shadow still looms over your mind – I can sense it – which your subconscious is trying to shield you from. That mental barrier will make it difficult for me to connect with your thoughts, despite having mastered my ability.'

'You seem to communicate with Krisis with ease, as though conversing audibly with another.'

'Krisis is a dire wolf. An animal's mind is far less complex than our own. They think of things in such simple terms, largely concerning themselves with basic needs such as food and shelter. By contrast, your own mind is a cacophony of complex thoughts and emotions, some of which have been suppressed so that you can function. The

186

memories of your dark past have been compartmentalised and locked away, caged by your mind that only allows them freedom as and when it is advantageous to do so. If you do not unlock at least some of those cages for me, I will continuously bounce off of them as I try to navigate the maze that is your battle-hardened psyche.'

'I thought that I had dealt with my past.'

'You have come a long way. However, if you want this mental dialogue to take place, you need to take another step forward on your journey. Otherwise, I will try to relay the creature's thoughts to your verbally as best I can. However, this experience will not be the same; you will lose some of its meaning from my own interpretation of its words. Either lower your mental guard or settle for second best – the choice is yours, Rayna.'

He studied the subtle changes to the light bringer's face as she considered his words carefully. It was plain for someone of his ability to see that Rayna was confounded by his analysis, clearly unaware of the state of her own mind. The Guardian was still keeping secrets from herself, shielding her mind from the trauma of her past, thus instinctively protecting herself without even realising it. Rayna's inception into their world had been both sudden and violent. The changes to both herself and the world around her had been a lot to digest. It was unsurprising then that the shock of it all had caused her mind to block out any painful memories, therefore reducing the strain on her psyche. There were limits to what the mind could endure; sometimes the mind needed to protect itself in order for its host to function. As time wore on, he could sense that Rayna's mind was slowly giving back that which it had locked away, albeit only when she was ready to bear the

187

secreted information once more. A lot had happened since the light bringer's arrival in Freylar. Even now, he was conscious of the fact that they were, once again, being dragged towards danger. He suspected that Rayna needed time to reflect on everything that had happened to her, so that she could properly come to terms with her new body, in addition to the world in which she now lived.

'You do not have to do this.' he said, trying to be empathetic towards Rayna's unprecedented situation. 'Your mind may not be ready to revisit certain aspects of your past.'

'I cannot continue to flee from my past, albeit subconsciously.' said Rayna thoughtfully. 'I find it frustrating not knowing when I am actively running away from it – I would rather just deal with it head on.'

'Your soul would, yes – it is in your nature. However, your mind will not actively seek out more than it can bear. That said, sometimes it *will* take on additional load when forced to by external stimuli. Although, this is risky; if you are not ready, mentally, the results can be detrimental.'

'I understand, but I need to do this, Lothnar. I have managed to let go of the hatred that manifested from the darkness that once festered within my soul. Even so, that achievement is meaningless if I cannot reconcile my past and clear my mind.'

'Very well. In that case, I will initiate the mental bridge. But know this: by letting me into your mind, I will share whatever it is that you experience during the connection.' he explained, satisfied that Rayna had properly considered the potential ramifications. 'Prepare yourself!'

188

'You both look like shit. Furthermore, Callum, you smell like it.' said Sebastian, his arms folded across his broad chest. 'What happened to the pair of you?'

The sight of Jacob shrinking under interrogation irked him – the addled boy needed to find a backbone before his disposition became ingrained. Perhaps the inevitable beatings from Sebastian's lackeys would eventually wake the boy up, he thought. In any event, their journey back from the refuse site had not gone without incident. Rifling through the piles of discarded clothes had taken longer than he had anticipated. Furthermore, their time spent packing the used garments into their sacks had taken too long. None of which was helped by Jacob's incessant panicking whilst he had struggled to haul himself back over the metal fence, fatigue getting the better of him. Regrettably, they had run out of time to properly cover their tracks; he chided himself for leaving the noose knot behind, still tied to the fence. Regardless, it was unlikely that the poorly paid workers would give it much thought. Besides, that tool alone had not been enough to achieve their ends; he managed to sell himself the lie that their bungled withdrawal would not hinder future attempts made by their class.

'We ran into a bit of trouble.' said Jacob, meekly.

'Oh?' queried Sebastian, giving them both a hard look. 'What of your reassurances, Callum?'

'It was nothing – Jacob needs to learn when to shut up.'

'Is that so?'

'You do not need to concern yourself with such trivial events. I promised you that we would retrieve the tools that we require – we did exactly that.'

'A pile of tatty clothes – what do you propose that we do with these?'

189

'These belong to Apex class citizens.' he explained.

He said nothing further. Instead, he allowed adequate time for the words to crystallise in Sebastian's mind as the possibilities they incited occupied the gang leader's thoughts. The prolonged silence between them made Jacob anxious, causing the boy to babble needlessly, further embarrassing himself.

'Callum, they're a mess. Some have stains on--'

'Shut up!' boomed Sebastian in his characteristically deep voice. 'Do not disrupt my thoughts with your inane prattle.'

Jacob took a step back, almost physically cowering, as if the gang leader had offered him the back of his hand. Whilst he felt some sympathy towards the boy, regardless, Jacob's own stupid actions invariably prompted such treatment. If the boy could just learn to hold his tongue, life would go more smoothly for the gaunt orphan.

'So...' said Sebastian, fixing him with a hard stare. 'You want us to pass as upper-class citizens, using these clothes?'

'Yes.'

'We have means of infiltrating the heart of the metropolis without these. Whilst security measures are becoming increasingly more challenging with each year that passes, they are not beyond our ability to circumvent at this time – I suspect that you already know this.'

'I do.'

'Therefore, you have an angle – enlighten me, Callum.'

'You want to steal from the one percent and use the funds to empower those with nothing, with a view to creating some kind of rebel militia. However, as I said previously, that approach is too blunt – it will further sully

190

the way other classes perceive the Shadow class.' he explained, laying the foundation for his proposal. 'Based on my dealings with you thus far, Sebastian, the threat of blunt action appeals to you. Although, I do not believe that approach is your sole strategy. You are obviously educated, somehow. Therefore, either you have an ace up your sleeve or are motivating *me* to develop one for you. Given the general lack of respect that you possess for those you have chosen to surround yourself with, I suspect that you view other humans as little more than tools to be manipulated.'

'An interesting deduction.'

'As you say, these clothes – albeit with some minor remedial work – will allow us to pose as citizens above our current station. They will elevate our status enough to achieve the desired result.'

'Which is?'

'Sullying the perception of classes other than our own.'

There was another long pause between them whilst Sebastian considered his proposal. He could sense Jacob fidgeting awkwardly from the corner of his eye. Fortunately, the runt stayed his tongue, likely because of Sebastian's earlier dressing down.

'Very well – that approach works for me.' said Sebastian. 'Prove to me that your stratagem of misdirection has real merit and I will consider adjusting my long-term strategy accordingly.'

'If you would like proof first-hand, consider joining us.'

Sebastian smiled ominously – it was an unsettling sight.

'I will remain here.' replied the gang leader. 'Do not make me regret backing your play, Callum – there are still plenty of *books* worth my while checking out.'

191

Sebastian turned and began walking away from them, issuing one last order before taking his leave.

'Clean yourselves up. As it stands, the pair of you will be lucky to pass as sewage treatment workers.'

THIRTEEN

Motivation

'You do not have to do this now.' said Klein,
sympathetically. 'Perhaps you should get some rest first?'

'Now that I know she is here, I *must* perform my duty.
Besides, she was my friend – I cannot leave her this way.'

She stared at the hessian sack laid across Zealia's body.
Knowing that the deceased Blade's ruined body lay beneath
filled her with dread. She had so many fond memories of
her time spent with Zealia – the last thing she wanted to do
was contaminate those memories. However, she had a duty
to perform. She needed to be the one to dig her fallen
comrade's grave. Under no circumstances would she
disrespect the Blade by delegating the task to another,
regardless of how difficult and upsetting burying her friend
would undoubtedly prove to be.

'I apologise on behalf of the scout regiment that we
cannot permit a pyre at this time.'

'You do not need to apologise, Klein. I understand,
and I know that Zealia would too.'

'If we were certain that all of the spirit wolves were
released, giving away our position would not be--'

'It is fine – I completely understand.'

'We can be an overzealous lot sometimes.'

'The regiment operates independently when in the
field, it is imperative, therefore, that it protects itself at all
times.'

They both stood in silence, paying their respects to the
fallen Blade. She sensed a heavy weight burdening the
veteran scout. No doubt, Klein had said his goodbyes to

many fallen comrades over the passes given his length of service to The Blades, in particular the scout regiment.

'I take it that you have seen many comrades journey to the Everlife?'

'Too many.'

'I realise that this is not your responsibility, however, will you help me move her body to its final resting place?'

'Of course – I will also help you bury her.'

'You do not need to do that.'

'Digging her grave by yourself will take far longer and you need time to properly recover. The team needs its leader fully rested, ready for whatever challenges we face next.'

'Thank you.'

'It is the least that I can do.' replied the scout. 'Now then, have you prepared yourself?'

'Yes – I need to see her, one last time.'

'Very well.'

The scout crouched down and pulled back the hessian sack. Zealia's ruined body was horribly mutilated. Deep gouges and lacerations raked across Zealia's torso and face showed the graphic horror of the Louperdu's savagery. Zealia's left cheek was split in two, with her lower lip torn free from what remained of her mouth. Her throat had been slashed, resulting in a stream of dried blood that ran from the deep wound on Zealia's neck down to her abdomen. Furthermore, she noticed exposed bone along Zealia's right arm, likely a result of the sprit wolf dragging her former comrade across the barn floor. Seeing Zealia's ruined body was even ghastlier than she had imagined. How could one ever prepare for such a sight, she wondered, as her head began to spin, causing her to feel unsteady.

194

'I think it is best that we get some fresh air.'

'Agreed.' she said, fighting back the bile rising in her throat.

The air outside felt like a blessing compared to the awful odour within the barn. Inhaling deeply, she allowed the clean air to fill her lungs. Quickly regaining her composure, the world stopped spinning and the burning sensation in her throat receded.

'Your first time?'

'Not at all, far from it in fact. Although, I have never seen wounds like that before. Also, she was my friend – that makes it personal.'

'I understand.' said Klein. 'Although perhaps of little solace to you, your friend would not have suffered. The body goes into immediate shock when sustaining wounds of that calibre – I have seen it before – followed by a swift release. The brutal savagery of the Louperdu rarely leaves any survivors; it is one of the reasons why we know so little about them.'

Tilting her head backwards, she looked past the rising sun towards the clear blue sky above, wondering if Zealia had passed into the Everlife, or whether something else awaited the Freylarkai upon their release. The Guardian's arrival had altered the belief of many, calling into question the next chapter of their existence. Prior to Rayna's arrival, there was no doubt in her mind that she and her fallen comrades would meet each other again in the Everlife, but now she was not so sure.

'Klein, do you believe in the Everlife?'

'No.'

Taken aback by the scout's blunt answer, she turned towards Klein, seeking further clarification.

'The Guardian's presence, specifically talk of how she arrived in Freylar, strengthens my belief.'

'What do you suppose happens to us when we are released?'

'Who can know for certain? However, it is my belief that our souls return to their place of origin, ready to repeat the cycle of rebirth and release once more.' explained Klein.

'I see.' she said, struggling to know what to believe.

'Regardless of what happens to us next, do not allow the future to distract you from the present – your friend needs burying.'

'Yes, you are right.'

Between them, they carried Zealia's body to the edge of the settlement, where they dug a deep hole for the fallen Blade. She marked the grave using a pile of stones that she diligently gathered from the bank of a nearby stream. The water felt good, washing away the mud clinging to her hands along with the irksome dirt that had collected beneath her fingernails. Whilst paying their respects, those scouts within earshot temporarily abandoned their assignments in order to accompany them, forming a crescent around Zealia's grave. Together, they stood silently, allowing memories of the fallen to occupy their thoughts, ensuring that those who had found release in battle would live on in the hearts and souls of the living.

'Farewell, Zealia.'

He could feel the light bringer subconsciously fighting him. Even so, with each mental push, Rayna's mind relented a little more, permitting him further access to the darker recesses of her mind. By contrast, the beast in the clearing up ahead welcomed his intrusion, allowing him full

196

access to its thoughts without any resistance. It was a strange, eerie sensation; he imagined it being similar to when the vanguard infiltrated the settlement. Was he straying into a trap or did the creature genuinely wish to make contact, he wondered. Given that it was the first one to initiate contact, he chose to believe the latter, hoping that the monstrous creature would permit them to converse further telepathically, since it was unable to do so physically. He continued to push deeper into the dark crevices of The Guardian's mind, unlocking fragments of repressed memories that, when assembled into some kind of logical order, began to tell a tale of coercion and deceit. Rayna groaned and squirmed under the mental strain, nevertheless, he pressed on, knowing that the dogged light bringer would not accept failure.

More of the memory fragments revealed themselves the further he descended into Rayna's mind until, ultimately, he understood what it was that she was protecting herself from. Rayna groaned once more, responding to the dip in his concentration, which he quickly fought to correct. The beast, too, reacted, snarling in a deep disgruntled tone, like the sound of thunder rumbling across a distant horizon.

'Damn it!' he said under his breath, scolding himself for his lapse in concentration.

Redoubling his efforts, he concentrated harder still, pushing himself to the limit in order to repair the mental bridge between them. When finally he was satisfied, he allowed himself to relax a little, conscious of the sweat slowly rolling down the side of his face.

'*Rayna, can you sense my thoughts?*' he said, pushing his way through the light bringer's maelstrom of thoughts.

'*Yes, I can hear you.*'

197

He refrained from correcting Rayna's inappropriate choice of words, instead satisfied that the mental bridge to her mind was holding. Focusing his attention on the creature, he attempted to make contact, praying that his fears of a trap were unfounded.

'What are you?'

'Something that should never have been.'

He was taken aback by the beast's immediate response; there was no hesitation in its reply, just clear, seemingly honest, dialogue. Although, before he could converse with the creature further, Rayna intervened, steering their conversation along a different path.

'Do you have a name?'

'My birth name is no longer relevant; my bastard children refer to me as The Moon King.'

'You were not born this way?'

'I was not. Although, my memories prior to this chapter of my existence are unclear – I am ancient.'

'Did something bring you here?'

There was a brief pause in their exchange. Given the creature's age, he surmised that The Moon King needed time to collect its thoughts. By contrast, Rayna's own were sharp and concise. Given the knowledge recently gleaned from her mind, it was clear to him that the light bringer was investigating an angle that he did not yet fully understand. Based on the pointed nature of her interrogation, it was obvious that Rayna had already made a connection between herself and the strange creature and was now pursuing another lead.

'Yes.'

'Was there a choice?'

'Yes.'

198

'*Do you regret that choice?*'

'*Yes.*'

'*How so?*' he asked, wading in on Rayna's terse exchange with the creature.

'*Would you not loathe your own existence if you were reborn into this patchwork, bestial form of mine? Would you not seek an end to your suffering if forced to bear unwanted offspring by the mere light of the moon? Tell me, would you seek such a miserable existence?*'

'*No, I would not.*'

'*I grow tired of your questions.*'

'*Do you serve another?*' enquired Rayna, taking the lead in their exchange once more.

'*A curious question – who are you?*'

'*Just another agent of The Deceiver, turning the wheel of fate.*'

'*I serve no one!*'

'*Yet you are forced to give birth to the Louperdu, who in turn release the souls of others, feeding your master.*'

'*Enough! I told the other one before that you were foolish to come here. Despite my wretched existence, this is my domain and you are not welcome here.*'

'*If you cease to attack us, we will have no quarry with you.*' he intervened, steering their dialogue back on track.

'*My children do as they please. However, you will obey my will: leave this place and this land.*'

'*This land is not yours.*'

'*Everything you see here is mine.*'

'*We will not abandon our homes.*'

'*Then you will be slaughtered defending them. Consider this your choice – you are fortunate that I am offering you one. You have until nightfall to decide.*'

'*We do not fear you!*' Rayna interjected once more.

'*Of course you do – you just do not realise it, yet.*'

'*I will destroy you, again!*'

'*Release from this miserable existence is welcome. However, your promise is hollow, one that you cannot hope to achieve. Therefore, I will settle for ripping apart those who you care about the most, should you oppose my will. Let me be clear on that point. I will find them – you let me into your mind! I will have my way, Callum!*'

'*Go to hell, Sebastian!*'

The Moon King shielded his mind, abruptly severing his link to the creature. The sudden disconnect was jarring, disorientating both himself and The Guardian. Despite his head still spinning, he grabbed Rayna's arm tightly.

'We are leaving, now!'

'I am not done with him.'

'Nevertheless, he is done with you.'

He tugged on the light bringer's arm signalling his intent. Realising the truth of his words, Rayna relented and together they quickly withdrew into the undergrowth. As they fell back, The Moon King released another of its terrifying howls that reverberated through the woodland once more. It was an obvious ploy, one intended to instil fear in light of the beast's ultimatum.

'I *will* release that bastard!'

'This is neither the time nor the place. We can discuss the animosity between you two later. Right now, we need to focus on placing some distance between us and it.'

'Don't tell me the *mighty* Lothnar fears such a miserable creature?'

There was a time when such comments would have riled him. However, his mind was clear – it was not the time for childish retorts. Others were depending on him, Rayna included – he had a regiment to lead.

'Not at all.' he said, nonchalantly, maintaining his composure by taking a leaf out of Thandor's book. 'What I fear is the effect this creature is having on *you*.'

Sebastian's plan was simple enough: infiltrate the heart of the metropolis and coerce a wealthy entrepreneur into transferring funds to an account that one of his associates had set up. Their target was a woman, single, who lived alone in one of the tall buildings near the centre of the metropolis. Somehow, the gang leader had managed to secure the access codes necessary to gain entry to the woman's hab unit. Furthermore – he had no clue as to how – the gang leader appeared to have knowledge of the woman's schedule, knowing when she would return to her home; Sebastian was very specific regarding the date and approximate time. The whole thing unnerved him. Without complex social engineering or hacking expertise, it would have been almost impossible to acquire such information. How then, did someone like Sebastian, operating out of a children's home no less, gain access to such detailed information, he mused. He kept analysing the operation in detail, unable to leave it alone, wondering whether the planned heist was some kind of test or elaborate setup, or perhaps simply a delusional aspiration that would see them all caught. The whole thing stank. Nonetheless, Sebastian's threat was very real, therefore, he had little choice but to play along. Given his preaching comments to Jacob regarding freedom of choice, he felt hypocritical in his willingness to comply. However, Kaitlin's welfare was at stake – he could not allow the innocent librarian to be

201

dragged down by his social status and the garbage it entailed.

Casting his eyes around the common room, he continued scrutinising its occupants, searching for the best candidates available for the mission. He saw Kristen laughing disingenuously along with her menials, no doubt doing so to remain in their good social graces. The girl's arms were perpetually in motion, everything a grand gesture, as though anything less would diminish her existence in the eyes of others. It was a sad spectacle to behold. Kristen seemed to be of the belief that such gaudy movements were necessary to maintain the attention of her audience, when in reality the precarious leader had become a slave to them, ever the constant spectacle. Regardless, the girl was insufferable, both too loud and unstable for anything requiring a modicum of stealth or tact, ergo he cast his eye elsewhere.

He turned his attention to Dylan next. The rival gang leader stood in a corner with several muscular boys loitering by his side. Cut from the habitual gang leader cloth, he would have had no difficulty dealing with someone of Dylan's stereotypical disposition. However, Sebastian was an entirely different beast, refusing to conform to the normal tropes of society. Kyle was no better than Dylan; if not for the pack leaders' mutual disdain for one another, they would have likely formed an uneasy alliance to rival Sebastian's power base. However, that scenario had not played out; he could not help but wonder if Sebastian was responsible for their hatred of one another.

'That is not going to work.' said Sebastian, startling him.

So immersed in his thoughts, he had failed to notice the gang leader's silent approach, despite Sebastian's imposing physique – he chided himself for lowering his guard.

'Those two will never see eye to eye.'

'No doubt, you made sure of that.'

'You are so untrusting, Callum.' replied Sebastian, with a deadpan stare that gave nothing away.

'Why are you here?'

'To let you know the members of your crew.'

'It was agreed that I would choose those who would accompany me.'

'I am altering our agreement.'

'It is *my* neck on the line!' he said vehemently, struggling to hide his annoyance.

'Calm down.' Sebastian said patronisingly. 'The team members I have selected for you are sound.'

'Which members?'

'Ryan, Ezra and Jacob.'

'Jacob is liable to panic and run under the pressure – why would I want him?'

'You took him to the refuse site.'

'As I recall, you ordered him to accompany me. In any event, I saw first-hand how he operates in the field – he hesitates too much. Besides, he is your lackey – your eyes and ears.'

'Which is why you are taking him.'

'Do you want this mission to fail?'

'Ryan and Ezra are reliable. They will do whatever it takes to accomplish our objective.'

'This ridiculous heist is all *your* doing.'

'Not so – *you* are a part of it now too.'

'Once this is over, I am out. Furthermore, you will leave Kaitlin alone.'

The gang leader leant in closer towards him. He could see Sebastian studying the common room's occupants, analysing the behaviour and mannerisms of its residents. In all likelihood, the gang leader was devising a means of bringing those not already under his sway to heel, indoctrinating through fear an army of obedient children in readiness for life outside the facility.

'Look at them, Callum. They are sheep, waiting for a shepherd to lead them.'

'Is your intention for this to be some kind of deep and meaningful moment, or a religious sermon perhaps?'

'Neither. I only share information that I *want* people to know and I only believe what I have *seen* with my own eyes.'

'So, what are you implying? That you're their saviour or something?'

'They are nothing more than tools to me, Callum. I already told you about my EDD – I could not give a fuck about them or their feelings. But they are useful to me and, whether they realise it or not, I am helping them to better their lot in life.'

'Am I just another of those tools, which you seek to manipulate?'

'Like me, you are capable of great things. However, you seem to be *waiting* for something, like the collapse of society or some shit like that. You lack motivation, which is why I am providing it for you.'

'I do not need motivating.'

'If you continue to wait, life will pass you by and you will achieve nothing – neither you nor I will get another chance, Callum.'

'I apologise for my awful behaviour. I did not mean what I said earlier; you are one of the bravest Freylarkai I know.' said Rayna, sincerely. 'It's just that…'

'You are letting him get under your skin – that is what he wants.'

'I know. Even so, I am unable to prevent it.'

'Rayna, I let Darlia and Lileah do the same to me. It almost led me to ruin. You are better than this. Others look to you to lead the way; you are a source of inspiration to many, myself included.' he said, with a level of conviction surprising even himself. 'Do not allow Sebastian to derail you.'

'You saw all of that?' asked Rayna, genuinely shocked by his frank disclosure.

'When you let me in, I saw the memories that you have been hiding from yourself.'

'I do not want to be that person again.'

'Most are destined to repeat history. However, provided you learn from your past, as opposed to continuing to bury it, it is within your power to avoid this trap. *"Do not allow your regret to consume you. Learn from your mistakes. Try to become a better version of yourself."* – that is what *you* told me.'

Rayna grasped his right hand and smiled affectionately. Though he welcomed it, the act caught him off guard. She had a way of doing things that was both bold and direct, whilst still being acceptable. Rayna possessed charm and a likeability that somehow permeated almost everything that she contacted, himself included. He realised now that, historically at least, his own actions had often made it difficult for others to engage with him. Perhaps, if he softened his approach a little, it would improve his own relationships, he mused.

'Thanks, Lothnar – I needed that. I fell off the wagon for a moment back there.'

'You are most welcome.'

Together, they sat in the woodland for a while, not saying a word. There was no awkwardness to their mutual silence, just a pleasant moment shared by both before their inevitable conversation.

'Given what I witnessed, I do not believe that any attempts to reason with The Moon King will be met with success. Yet despite his disposition, if we *could* alter his perspective, would you find it within yourself to forgive him?'

'If you had asked this of me back in the clearing, my answer would have been different. But yes, I believe that I could – though that still does not mean that I *like* him.'

'Good, because I need you clear-headed when we fight him.'

'Then you had no intention of me making amends?'

'No.' he replied sternly. 'Sebastian's behaviour is likely far too ingrained for our words to have any effect, no matter how sincere their meaning, especially in the short time available to us. In addition, he has been touched by Krashnar; The Moon King is another victim, another one of the vile shaper's abominations. Lileah, the beast that released Ragnar and even Darlia, all have struggled with the mark left upon them, regardless of the size of its stain. Once touched by evil, that evil must be exorcised entirely if

206

one is to be truly free from its taint. However, your former associate inhabits a body comprised entirely of that evil; the only way to free Sebastian now is to release his soul from the wretched trap that has ensnared it.'

'So, after successfully altering my perception, *now* you want us to release it?'

'For the *right* reasons, yes; not to sate your anger. If we do not, its children will continue to release our people. Furthermore, The Moon King is essentially a mobile army, based on what we have seen and assuming that the moon does indeed facilitate the birth of his kin. If he decides to move away from the birthing tree, we could have no clue as to where the next wave of attacks will come from – we might end up needlessly chasing Sebastian across Freylar, all the while casualties continue to mount in his wake.'

'Then we should consider attacking him now; the element of surprise will work to our advantage.'

'There is merit to that strategy. However, we do not know how many of the Louperdu there are in the forest right now. I can sense The Moon King's children watching us, but not their exact numbers. In addition, he has issued his ultimatum and we have no reason to believe that Sebastian will renege on his threat. Therefore, if we fall back to the farmstead, we will have the advantage of a fortification.'

'But the Louperdu can easily breach our defences.'

'That is true. However, they cannot all come at us at once if we contain the fighting to within the settlement. There is also no evidence to suggest that The Moon King can move through solid obstacles, unlike its children. Furthermore, we will have the advantage of higher ground, if we maximise use of the rooftops.'

'That strategy risks the lives of the scouts, not just our own. Although, it does have a greater chance of success given that our knowledge of the enemy's numbers is limited.'

'Also true. With that said, I believe in the scout regiment and its ability to complete the mission assigned to it. When, finally, The Moon King comes for us – which he will – your battle with Sebastian will likely devolve into the common brawl you initially thought it would be. Are you ready for that outcome, Rayna?'

Judging by her vacant expression, Rayna's thoughts had strayed – her mind was elsewhere now. No doubt, the light bringer was rehashing her past once more, trying to make sense of the chain of winding events that had led to their current situation. He suspected that The Guardian felt responsible for those already released by the Louperdu, that her actions in her former life had paved the way for the present.

'You must not blame yourself for this.' he said, trying to reassure the light bringer. 'Rayna! Are you listening to me?'

'Sorry.' she replied, snapping out of her reverie.

'You are not to blame for Sebastian's actions. Besides, we all need to share this responsibility – you cannot keep it all for yourself.'

Rayna smiled.

'I know. And yes, I am ready. This ends tonight!'

FOURTEEN
Insight

It was late morning when she eventually returned to the Tri-Spires. The sun was now high in the sky, indicating that she was late for her lesson with Rarni. Nevertheless, she decided to clean herself up first, given her prolonged trek through the forest. Although Rarni had already witnessed the grim events conducted by her sister, there was no need for her to give any further credence to the terrible visions by turning up to class with her hair unkempt and the hem of her dress covered in soil. She changed her outfit for one made from a lighter fabric and brushed her hair, which had become tangled and knotted.

Once she was satisfied with her appearance, she left her chamber to seek out her student. After speaking with Lyra, she learned that Rarni was playing down by the river with one of the other children. She decided to go and watch Lyra's daughter play with her new friend, intrigued that such a development had even occurred. Sure enough, she found Rarni beside the riverbank, just east of the old bridge, though there were no other children present. Confused, she chose to hang back and observe the situation. Rarni's behaviour seemed odd, as though the child was conversing with another, yet there was no one else present. Eventually, the young girl spotted her, calling out her name.

'Kirika!' cried the child, who began skipping along the riverbank towards her. 'I thought that you had forgotten my lesson.'

'Not at all. I was conducting the investigation that we discussed.' she replied, working her way slowly down the long sloping riverbank towards the excited child. 'Tell me, who were you talking to?'

'I was playing with my friend.'

'Does this friend have a name?'

'Her name is Mohraine.'

'I see.' she replied, trying hard not to sound patronising. 'Is Mohraine still with us?'

'No, silly.' replied Rarni, followed by a gentle laugh that surprised her. 'She just left.'

There had been no one else with the child, of that she was certain. She suddenly became concerned, worried that Rarni's mind had devised a means of coping with the horrible, unwanted visions that the child had been experiencing.

'Do you think that Mohraine will come back?' she enquired, curious about Rarni's new friend.

'I know that she will.' said Rarni, confidently. 'Mohraine is shy of adults though, so you might not get to meet her.'

'I understand. Nevertheless, perhaps one day she and I will be able to talk.'

'Maybe.' said Rarni softly, before turning her attention to the river.

The sound of running water and the occasional plop of Fan-Fish jumping in the water filled their ears as they stood quietly beside the riverbank, watching Freylar's more idyllic nature go about its business. She remained silent, wondering if Rarni might say anything further about her new friend, yet the child remained tight-lipped on the subject. Though she had implied full disclosure to Rarni regarding the outcome of her investigation, the situation had now changed. She wondered if burdening the child with

210

further distasteful information was wise. Perhaps, in light of new events, it was best to withhold the details of her investigation, she thought.

'Are you going to speak with your sister?' asked Rarni, suddenly, taking her aback.

'Regrettably, it seems that I must now do so.'

Rarni went silent once more. She wondered if perhaps the child was hoping for a different response, one that might discredit the awful visions that she had witnessed. However, the troubled young girl would find no solace in her words. Instead, the path they now both travelled was destined to follow an even darker route that would likely result in conflict between Darlia and herself.

'I intend to speak with her later this cycle.'

'What do you think will happen?' asked Rarni, meekly.

'We will argue, fiercely – I can predict that much.'

'Can you use your ability to find out?'

'That would be unfair on my sister – I cannot ambush her like that. The last thing I want to do is rile her. If I take that approach, I will not learn the truth of the matter. Instead, I will repeat past mistakes by embellishing her guilt before she has had a chance to form any kind of defence.'

'Can she be defended?'

'I do not know if such heinous actions can ever be justified. I suppose that all I can do at this stage is to hear my sister out. Once I have discovered the truth of it, a terrible decision will likely…'

She was unable to finish her sentence; the words stuck in her throat and her eyes began to water. Rarni saw her distress and immediately wrapped her short arms around her, trying her best to provide comfort.

'I am sorry for burdening you with this. You are just a child. You should be leading a nor--'

'Both you and Mohraine are my friends.' said Rarni, cutting her short and squeezing her tightly.

Tears rolled down her cheeks upon hearing Mohraine's name once more. It upset her, knowing that the child's mind had resorted to such coping mechanisms in order to function. She thought back to her experiences with Rayna and how the light binger's own mind had erected defences, locking away memories that were too awful to process. Although, in Rarni's case, it appeared that her mind sought to distract the child instead by giving her something more positive to focus on – a friend. What upset her most was that her own friendship had clearly not been enough, placing her in an awkward position going forward. Either she fought Mohraine for Rarni's sole attention or she allowed the child to indulge her fantasy, in the hope that she would eventually grow out of it. Regrettably, she knew very little about the mind. Perhaps Lothnar would be able to provide counsel regarding the matter upon his return.

'Thank you.' she said, receiving Rarni's heartfelt embrace. 'Know that I value your friendship very much.'

Rarni craned her neck back. The child's dark blue eyes now bordered on black and her once blonde hair, now a shade of dark brown, was continuing to alter in colour. The rapid ongoing physical changes to Rarni's body disturbed her.

'*We* do too.' Rarni replied, still clinging to her tightly.

'These clothes are uncomfortable.' said Jacob, who looked thoroughly out of place.

They had washed and pressed Jacob's reclaimed clothes and had managed to remove most of the stains. At a glance, they were more than passable, proving adequate for their needs. The remainder of the boy's transformation also appeared to be sufficient. They had neatly combed Jacob's typically scraggy hair. Furthermore, they managed to cover most of the ginger with a dark-coloured dye. Jacob had also grown a weak moustache, which they had also dyed, further elevating the gaunt runt's normal appearance.

'Stop complaining.' he said, trying to concentrate on the unlikely ensemble, looking for anything that might give them away.

Both Ryan and Ezra also looked the part. Their impressive builds meant that their clothes fit them more snugly, unlike Jacob's, whose attire was extremely loose fitting and a little odd looking in places. Nonetheless, all three would pass for his needs.

'It's going to be difficult to move around in these.' said Ryan, clearly more interested in the practicality of their attire than the aesthetics.

'Yes, they are restrictive. However, we will not be running.'

'What about after we've completed the job?' asked Ezra.

Sebastian is handling that; he is organising go bags for each of us, which we will rendezvous with at an agreed location *after* we have completed our mission.

'Where is this location?' asked Jacob.

'You do not need to know that.' he said matter-of-factly. 'I need each of you focused entirely on your assignments. If any one of you fucks up, this mission could go sideways very quickly. Do you all understand?'

213

Both Ryan and Ezra nodded in unison. In another life, the pair could have been trained elite soldiers, ready to give their lives in service for someone else's grand desires. Instead, they were little more than brainwashed thugs, just waiting to be released from their master's chain so that they could pound their fists into something ripe.

'Remember, we are not looking for a fight – that is not the purpose of this operation.' he said, sternly. 'We go in, casually. Find the woman, coerce her into transferring the funds, tie her up and then leave. Once we get to the go bags, we will change clothes and leave the heart of the metropolis.'

He turned towards Jacob, looking for confirmation of his orders. Upon meeting his gaze, the anxious boy nodded quickly, signalling his understanding of the details of their assignment. Though he had not sought it, he could sense rising fear in the teenager. It was as strange feeling, watching someone squirm before him whom he had not lamped with his fists. It was then that he realised the true extent of Sebastian's manipulations; the commanding position bestowed upon him by the gang's leader had given him a taste of power. No doubt, Sebastian had sought to offer him the feeling as a means of leashing him, thereby bringing him into the fold, willingly, of his own volition.

'*Bastard!*'

Admittedly, it would make life easier, though he did not hunger for power. Even the slightest bit tasted bitter and was not something that he wished to sample further. For all his cunning, Sebastian had failed to underestimate his resolve. Regardless of his position, he would resist the lure.

214

'So, you just need us to rough her up a little?' asked Ezra.

'No, absolutely not.' he said, tersely. 'Just intimidate her – that's all we need. This has to look like an act committed by a class other than our own. If we wander around the metropolis beating up its citizens, eyes will turn towards the Shadow class – that is the exact opposite of what we want to achieve.'

'Is that why we are performing a transfer of funds?' asked Ryan.

'Precisely. They do not believe that we have the means to make such transfers – we do. Furthermore, fencing goods will draw unwanted attention, plus there is the logistics involved.' he explained. 'This is the best play for us.'

Ryan and Ezra nodded in unison once more. He was beginning to understand why Sebastian had handpicked the pair for his crew. Still, Jacob was another matter entirely. He remained convinced that the boy was a liability. As such, he sought to limit Jacob's direct involvement, relegating him to menial duties instead.

'What do you need me to do?' Jacob enquired.

'You will cover our rear by keeping a look out.'

'Is there nothing else that you need me to do, Callum?'

'No. You have done enough already.'

The teenager shrank back, realising exactly what it was that he was referring to; if it were not for Jacob's snooping around, he would not be dangling from one of Sebastian's strings.

'Now, do you all understand what is expected of you?'

All three nodded this time, signalling their understanding of the plan.

215

'The operation will commence this evening. Once Anastacia finishes for the day, we will make our move.'

'Why not leave earlier?' asked Jacob. 'It will give us more time.'

'It would. However, if we wait for Anastacia to knock off, she will be one less variable for us to worry about.' he explained. 'Besides, we will have plenty of time as it is.'

In truth, the less time they spent in the field, the better; the last thing he needed was Jacob's nerves getting the better of the teenager, which more time would surely facilitate. Once the mission was over, he could get back to planning his future outside of the facility, at least that was the lie that he told himself.

'Any other questions?'

Everyone stared at him mutely.

'Good. I suggest that you all go and get some rest – it's going to be a long night.'

It was noon when they finally returned to the settlement. Krisis was the first to spot their return; the muscular dire wolf came bounding across the field towards them as they made their approach.

'*I have missed you, boy!*' he communicated telepathically whilst affectionately rubbing the dire wolf's thick black fur, under his neck.

Krisis pointed his nose towards the sky and opened his muzzle revealing his large pink tongue, as he continued to stroke the dire wolf enthusiastically. Rayna, too, crouched down and began stroking Krisis' head – the dire wolf craved the affection.

After sating his companion's needs, they continued their approach towards the farmstead, acknowledging the

216

scouts assigned to guard duties as they entered the settlement. Lazrik had clearly done well to command the regiment in his absence. He watched with paternal joy as the scouts busied themselves with fortifying the settlement. No doubt, Lazrik had pre-empted imminent further conflict and had therefore ordered the scouts to prepare for such.

'Welcome back, Sir!' cried Yandar, who quickly noticed their presence in the settlement.

'Yandar.' he replied enthusiastically, pleased to see the squad leader again. 'Assemble the others, The Guardian and I have urgent news to disseminate.'

'Sir!'

They gathered at the edge of the settlement, far enough away to prevent any inadvertent eavesdropping.

'Sir, I have brought Leyla in on this; both her skill and counsel have proved valuable in this campaign.'

'Very well. I am pleased that her experience has served the regiment well.' he replied, before giving the newly inducted scout a curt nod. 'You honour your father's memory.'

Leyla nodded in return. He could sense the pride that his acknowledgement instilled in her, reminding him of the importance of publicly valuing the efforts of those serving under him.

'I am pleased to see that work has already begun on fortifying the settlement against further attacks, and there *will* be further conflict – mark my words.'

'Have you learned when the next attack will take place?' asked Lazrik, getting straight to the heart of the matter.

'Tonight!'

He allowed a moment for the notion of another imminent attack to sink in, watching as the eyes of all those present widened in anticipation of his next words.

'Rayna and I released the Louperdu that managed to evade our cordon. Unfortunately, we have since discovered a greater threat.'

'I am to blame.' said Saralia, 'I led the squa--'

'There is no blame to assign, Saralia.' he said, cutting the squad leader short. 'If the Louperdu were not so savage and cunning, we would not be here. I may abhor the enemy, but I still respect their ability in battle.'

'Thank you, sir. However, we *will* redouble our efforts, nonetheless.'

'I have no doubt. Regardless, I will now hand over to Rayna, who will explain what we have discovered.'

Everyone, himself included, focused their attention on The Guardian, eager to learn of the latest threat to the regiment. The light bringer's ochre skin had darkened and she bore a grim expression, uncharacteristic of her normal cheerful appearance.

'An evil dwells in the forest, east of here. A huge beastlike creature, known as the The Moon King, is responsible for both giving birth to and commanding the Louperdu.' said Rayna, ominously. 'Our foe plans to attack us tonight, unless we abandon this place.'

'Which we will not!' he interjected.

'What do we know about this Moon King?' asked Lazrik.

'We know that he is both brutal and cunning. Furthermore, he will not think twice about sacrificing his kin to achieve victory, making him extremely dangerous.'

'You said "he". Rayna, do you *know* the Moon King?' asked Leyla.

'To an extent; the creature is connected to my past. However, I cannot say exactly how for certain at this time.' The Guardian explained. 'What is important is that we know that it gives birth to the Louperdu; more than several per cycle, the exact number of which may be determined by the lunar cycle. Therefore, we do not know what numbers we will be facing.'

'Then it could be hundreds.' said Yandar.

'Indeed.' he replied, in a foreboding tone. 'Yet, we cannot afford to give ground to the enemy. Furthermore, we must release The Moon King to prevent his numbers from swelling.'

'You said that this thing is huge – how big exactly?' asked Saralia.

'Some four to five paces in height.' Rayna explained. 'Also, the cursed shaper, Krashnar, *may* have had a hand in its conception.'

'Then it is a demon!' said Yandar, vehemently.

'Perhaps.' he said, acknowledging the hate in Yandar's eyes.

The veteran scout had lost a number of close friends to the abomination that they had fought in the arena, back when the infamous shaper had lost control of his form. Some of the possessed Freylarkai that had hurled themselves into the arena had been friends of the scout, prior to their untimely release. It was understandable then, that Yandar would harbour such disdain towards one of the shaper's abominations.

'The creature's size does not concern me.' said Rayna, flatly. 'However, its level of intellect does.'

219

'We saw, during the previous encounter, that the Louperdu are capable of strategy; they wanted us in the settlement so that they could ambush us.' said Lazrik.

'Indeed. In addition, The Moon King cannot be reasoned with. Therefore, we must not allow it to continue to exist.' he said, ardently. 'If we fail to stop The Moon King here and now, the potential for civilian casualties is extremely high – wherever it goes, its children will surely follow. Therefore, we must use this opportunity to strike it down, now!'

'Based on what has been said, the enemy is likely to attack us where we least expect it.' said Saralia.

'The Moon King knows that we will draw such a conclusion.' explained Rayna.

'Our enemy has the advantage of speed, agility, they know us as well as we know them, they could well have superior numbers and they can dissolve their form and then reappear – what then, is our strategy against such formidable opponents?' asked Saralia.

'They are a gang; take out the leader and they *will* break.' replied The Guardian.

Yandar balled his right hand into a fist, which he then pounded noisily into the palm of his left hand. His expression hardened, causing the weather-beaten lines etched into the scout's face to deepen. It was clear to all present that the scout wanted nothing more than to be the one to release The Moon King in order to avenge those he had lost. Such hatred made the scout exceedingly dangerous, but also impetuous too – he could not afford reckless action against their foe.

'Then that is our strategy. We work as a *team*.' he said, fixing Yandar with a hard stare, 'Our primary objective is to take out The Moon King, swiftly, then the others will fall into disarray. If the Louperdu do break and flee, we will track them down and eliminate them – time will be our ally in this endeavour.'

'What if they hold their lines?' asked Saralia.

He turned his attention from Yandar, fixing his gaze on Saralia instead. Though not his intent, he flashed the squad leader a wicked grin, inadvertently setting the scout's teeth on edge.

'Then we will be in for *another* long night.'

After their meeting, Lazrik gestured for her to join him, taking her to one side.

'You were very quiet during the meeting. Are you OK?'

'Thank you.' she said, acknowledging the squad leader's concern for her wellbeing. 'I am fine. I think that burying Zealia has just made things more real for me.'

'Losing comrades is rough, nor does it become easier with time – not really.'

'I just hope that both Natalya and Gaelin made it out in one piece.'

'Natalia is tough. She is probably in the forest right now, laying waste to the Louperdu. Maybe she will release them all before we get a crack at it.' replied Lazrik, followed by a gentle chuckle. 'And, from what I know of Gaelin, his cautious nature will serve him well.'

'Thanks.' she said. 'Please do not think me fragile, but I think that I needed to hear someone say that.'

'None of us are above worrying or from letting fear affect us in *some* way, regardless of one's bravado. Indeed, fear is healthy – it keeps us alive.'

221

'Is that why Lothnar took issue with Yandar?'

'Ah, so you noticed that too?'

'I was always acting that way myself.'

'What changed, Leyla?'

'Spending time with Rayna and Natalya, listening to The Guardian's stories – they helped me to focus and manage my frustrations.'

'Why were you frustrated?'

'Because I want to do better. I see all of you protecting the people, each performing such great feats, and I want to be like that.'

'Is this to do with your father?'

'I joined The Blades because of him. Although, I had not expected that serving with the scouts would bring my memories of him to the fore once more.'

'I appreciate your motivations, Leyla. Know that you already protect the people and you more than honour your father's legacy with your own actions. Even so, you must not become a slave to the past. Do not blindly do what you *believe* is expected of you, or allow the past to control your destiny. You need to live for yourself.' said Lazrik, giving her a warm smile.

She had not expected such words of encouragement from the cocksure commander, who until now had been difficult to approach. Although, upon reflection, she supposed that it was the squad leader's job to get the best results from those following his command. In order to achieve such, it made sense that Lazrik might choose to alter his disposition to suit his target audience, when needed.

'Thank you.' she said. 'Although, may I ask why you are...'

'Being friendly?' replied Lazrik, who then laughed at this own words.

'Yes, exactly that.' she said, smiling in return.

'Some of us need discipline. Some of us need shouting at. And some of us need competition in order to extract the best from us. You are motivated enough, Leyla. Furthermore, I do not believe that you are the type that needs me blasting away in your ear, unlike some.' explained the squad leader. 'I think what you lack is affirmation. Someone to tell you that you are on the right path – a guide if you will.'

'Are you that guide?'

'We all are. The Guardian, Natalya, Lothnar, me… Each of us is here to guide you and each another.'

'You all seem pretty sure of yourselves – surely you do not require such guidance?'

'We all get lost now and then, Leyla. Even the commander. That is why Lothnar has me, Yandar, Saralia and Krisis to support him. Having people around you to support you and to show you the way when times are dark is a sign of strength.'

'Recognising one's weaknesses and finding solutions for them.'

'Exactly.'

She thought back to the Louperdu ambush and how the veteran scout, Klein, had supported her.

'You are capable of even greater feats of heroism, if that is truly what you seek, Leyla. However, you will need to surround yourself with the right people.'

'Like Klein?'

'He respects you, Leyla. I believe that both you and he will support one another and that in doing so you will *both* continue to grow and ultimately reach your potential.'

There was a lull in their conversation whilst she considered Lazrik's counsel. In doing so, her mind began to wander, her subconscious working furiously to solve the issue of how best to fortify the settlement given the nature of their enemy.

'What is it?' asked the squad leader, his keen perception recognising that her mind had suddenly latched onto something important.

'I believe that I know what we must do.'

'What do you mean?'

'I think I know how we can defeat The Moon King's children.'

FIFTEEN
Ambush

'The door is unlocked.'

Pushing the door aside gently, she took a single step into the chamber, peering around its thick wooden door. Her unexpected coyness took her back to the cycles when she had first begun her studies with Aleska. She recalled the intense feeling of intimidation that she frequently experienced during her lengthy education with the politically astute scrier, whose cool demeanour took her some time to become accustomed to.

'I apologise – I am disturbing you.'

The Captain of the Blades sat alone at a desk, where he appeared to be writing furiously. Nathanar looked up, before setting aside the lengthy documents.

'Stop hiding behind the door and come in, Kirika.'

'I can see that you are busy.'

'Not at all. Come in. You will be doing me a favour by saving me from this penance of mine.'

She slipped inside the chamber and gingerly approached the Paladin.

'Is there something wrong, Kirika?'

'Perhaps, although, I am not certain.' she replied, cryptically, unwilling to divulge all the facts. 'I was hoping that I might speak with my sister. However, I can see that she is not here.'

'Darlia left early this morning.'

'Do you know where she went?'

'Yes. She said that she was headed into the forest to meet with another of the families affected by the Narlakai.'

'I was under the impression that she had finished apprising those who had lost loved ones during the past conflict with the Narlakai – is her work still ongoing?'

'It has taken her some time to track down those affected.' explained the Paladin, 'Also, there are some families, single parents in particular, whom she visits on more than just the one occasion.'

'I had no idea.'

'Your relationship with Darlia is better now, is it not?'

'Yes. Although, I can tell that she still keeps secrets from me.'

'I am sure that will abate in time. Returning to the vale and taking up residence here in the Tri-Spires has been a massive change for her. It is going to take some time before she fully adjusts to her new life and begins to let her guard down.'

'I know. I just wish that she would confide in me more – I am her sister after all.'

'She finds it difficult to trust others, especially, I gather, since the loss of her hand. However, I cannot tell if the reason for such is due to her actual physical loss, or instead, Krashnar's prosthetic replacement.'

'Then you have noticed it too?'

'Yes, but I cannot explain it. I get a sense that she is conflicted.'

'This may seem like a strange question, but, have you ever seen her staring at her claw?'

'That is indeed an odd question.'

Nathanar leant back in his chair, giving the question some thought before responding.

'Perhaps I have, without realising it. I *have* seen her lost in thought, with her head bowed low. I guess that it is possible that she was staring at it. Was she scrying it, do you think?'

'She used that replacement hand of hers to release her former lover, Lileah, thus ending our war with the Narlakai. That kind of brutal memory does not just fade away quietly, especially when one is cursed with the ability to relive it.' she said, sombrely. 'A sword can be sheathed and its wielder can relinquish ownership of the weapon at any time. The weapon Darlia used to release Lileah is fused to the bone in her left arm – it is part of her.'

'I had never really considered that point.' replied Nathanar. 'Your sister has been working hard to put the past behind her. However, in light of your words, I see now that her past will always be her present and that she literally carries her sins with her.'

'From the moment she wakes until the sun sets, her prosthetic claw is a constant reminder of her actions, ones that she would no doubt rather forget. Ergo, it is a curse.'

Her downcast words killed their conversation. Nathanar exhaled deeply then rose from his chair. The Captain approached the window, allowing the sun to spill over his face, as if washing away the stain of their gloomy discussion.

'It is a new cycle, Kirika. Winter is long gone. The sun shines upon us and the war is over – surely, there is a way to move past all of this?'

'There may yet be a way. However, first I need to find my sister and talk with her.'

'She has made such good progress, Kirika.' Nathanar said sincerely. 'Whilst I understand your words, is it wise to dredge all of this up?'

'Burying it does not make the problem go away. Besides, those with the ability to scry are only capable of digging shallow graves.'

Nathanar sighed heavily.

'Very well. You should find Darlia with the Rochenko family, on the west side of the forest.'

'Thank you, Nathanar.' she said, sincerely. 'And for everything that you have done for my sister. You have been instrumental in helping her to turn her life around.'

'I appreciate your kind words, Kirika. Although, judging by the look on your face, I fear that you may be about to undo all the good progress that she and I have worked hard to achieve.'

'I share your concern. Nevertheless, if left untreated, the festering wounds that my sister hides will have their way with her, regardless.'

'Have you actually *seen* it – with your ability that is?'

'Possible outcomes, yes. Darlia's future is murky, even for one of my ability. However, there is another: a child who sees into the dark recesses of this world – one who you already know. It is this one's portents that terrify me.'

'Klein, we have a new mission!' she cried, signalling for the scout to join her.

The veteran scout jogged towards her, Krisis loping along in front. The loyal dire wolf bounded over to her, his wounds since treated by the regiment's renewalists. Krisis sat on his hind legs before her, mouth open, with his tongue hanging out. The dire wolf glanced over his shoulder, no doubt wondering if Klein was going to join them.

'Slow down boy!' said Klein, 'You know that I cannot run that quickly.'

'Krisis giving you a work out, is he?'

Klein came to a halt before them. The scout stood upright before quickly regaining his breath – a testament to the scout's peak conditioning.

'Both Krisis and I have been eagerly awaiting your return. How did the meeting go?'

'Based on new information, we have a revised strategy.'

She proceeded to explain the nature of the threat now facing the regiment. After recounting all of the relevant details, she expected Klein to show at least some signs of alarm, but instead, the veteran scout maintained his cool demeanour.

'You do not seem overly concerned.'

'The threat we face has clearly escalated and is indeed dire; we are no longer dealing with a simple skirmish. However, you mentioned that we have a strategy to counter the impending attack. That being the case, I am certain that this strategy is a product of sound tactical decision-making. The regiment does not act recklessly, Leyla – I take solace in that fact.'

'I see.' she said, in awe of the scout's unwavering faith in the scout regiment. 'There is no doubt in your mind that we will succeed?'

'None at all.' said Klein, resolutely.

She watched as the scout raised his weapon whilst pulling on its bowstring, before guiding it back, testing its tension. Satisfied that his weapon was in good working order, he hooked the bow over his shoulder.

'What is the plan?'

'We intend to take out The Moon King. If we do that, the pack will beak.'

'That seems sensible. Although, that will not be *our* job, I assume – more covering fire?'

'Indeed.' she said, giving Klein a firm nod. 'However, since we command the battlefield and have time on our hands, I would like to make some changes to the terrain.'

'That makes sense – we should alter the battlefield to accommodate both our objective and fighting style.'

'Yes!'

Krisis barked loudly, letting them know of his mutual approval. She smiled, before stroking the top of the dire wolf's head, causing Krisis' eyes to widen and his ears to flatten.

'What do you have in mind?' asked Klein.

'To the best of our knowledge, The Moon King is unable to assume a mist-like state, unlike its children. Therefore, we need to create a channel through the settlement in order to guide its path.'

'If the beast is indeed cunning, it will not willingly follow such a path.'

'True, therefore it must be subtle. We will find as much detritus as we can and litter the streets with it, ensuring that the route we wish The Moon King to take is slightly less congested – we must engineer it so that the enemy believes that they are responsible for their chosen path.'

'I see.' said Klein. 'This approach will also hinder the Louperdu from charging those on the ground.'

'Correct.'

'Clever – I like it.'

The veteran scout suddenly flashed her a wicked smile, completely out of character. Klein's unexpected action wrought a smile of her own that prompted further loud barking from Krisis.

'There is one problem.'

'Go on.' she said, curiously.

'Based on what you told me, there is no guarantee that The Moon King will even enter the settlement. He may choose to stand back and watch the massacre of his children instead, hoping that our numbers will be eroded in the process.'

'You are right – that is a problem.'

'How do you propose that we manage that possibility?'

'There is a way, but that is not *our* job.' she said. 'We have been tasked with preparing the battlefield. Lazrik has given us responsibility for ensuring that the terrain is to our advantage. To that end, he has given us authority to both co-ordinate and oversee the battlefield preparations, using the other teams as we see fit in order to ensure that the work is completed on time – it is vitally important that we get this done.'

'Understood.'

'The regiment will lure The Moon King into the heart of the settlement, where we were ambushed. From there, we can attack the beast on all fronts, using the high ground to our advantage once more.'

'So, we are now laying an ambush of our own – an obvious ploy.'

'Yes, therefore it must not appear that way.'

'Our bait, whatever it is, must be compelling in order to sell this trap, regardless of how well we manage to conceal its existence.'

'Indeed. However, we will leave that concern to the others. Right now, we need to ensure that the terrain is to our liking.'

Klein nodded firmly in agreement. She turned to Krisis and slapped her thigh, immediately attracting the dire wolf's attention.

'Come on, boy! We have a battlefield to prepare.'

Not wishing to distract the family and their business with her sister, she chose to wait outside for Darlia, some distance away from the family's tree, ensuring that she remained out of their line of sight. When at last Darlia emerged from the Rochenko's dwelling, the sun was beginning its slow descent towards the horizon.

'Darlia!' she cried, immediately garnering her sister's attention.

'Kirika, what are you doing here?'

'My apologies – it was not my intention to ambush you. Although, I needed to speak with you regarding an important, sensitive matter.'

'Is it so urgent that you needed to come and see me all the way out here?'

'Yes, I am afraid that it is.'

'Very well.' replied Darlia with a puzzled expression.

'I thought that maybe we could walk to the Eternal Falls together, where we will have privacy.'

'Kirika, there is hardly anyone here.'

'Yes. However, what I have to say will likely cause things to become heated between you and I.'

Darlia's features suddenly hardened. The stern look on her sister's face increased her anxiety. She sensed that

Darlia was deciding whether to use her ability to confirm her expectation.

'Please, do not do that.' she implored. 'Can I not enjoy a walk with my sister?'

'Very well.' replied Darlia. 'Since the war is over, I am hopeful that whatever it is that you have to say cannot be that bad.'

Forcing herself to smile, she moved to the right of her sister, locking her arm around Darlia's own, before leading them north through the forest. Their walk together was pleasant, bringing back fond memories of their time spent together prior to Darlia's exile. Sadly, her growing anxiety, no doubt sensed by her sister, marred the occasion. She tried hard to clear her mind, trying her best not to think about the ensuing conflict, yet her efforts were largely unsuccessful.

'You are worried – I can tell.'

'I am trying hard not to be.' she said, quietly. 'It is just that...I do not want to lose you again, Darlia.'

'That will *not* happen.' Darlia said vehemently. 'What has happened to warrant such talk?'

'I will explain everything, shortly.'

The atmosphere between them became awkward as they continued their walk. She tried to think of something meaningful to say in order to ease the tension between them. However, Darlia was the first to break their silence.

'Do you remember when we served Caleth?'

'How could I forget – that Freylarkin left his mark on us both.'

'Yes,' said Darlia, sombrely. 'Even so, I remember us sneaking out into the forest on more than one occasion, looking to escape our cage, if only for a while.'

'Yes.' she said, laughing suddenly, catching herself by surprise. 'You always were a mischievous influence.'

'And afterwards, when Nathaniel and Heldran freed us from The Blade Lord's charge – that was a good time.'

'Life was less complicated back then.'

'It certainly was.'

They heard the sound of crashing water long before they arrived at the picturesque waterfall. The breath-taking landmark existed long before their time and would continue to do so, easily outlasting them both. One could spend cycles scrying the majestic falls, learning of its long history and the secrets it undoubtedly held. Upon reaching the falls, they first chose to pay their respects to Lileah, both spending a moment's silence by the Freylarkin's unmarked grave. After which, she directed her sister towards a number of large rocks along the eastern edge of the pool, where they could sit and make themselves comfortable.

'It has been a while since I visited her grave.'

'We should come here more often – it is nice.'

'I think Lileah would appreciate that.' said Darlia, directing her gaze towards her former lover's unmarked grave once more. 'Besides revisiting my past, why are we here, Kirika?'

'Actually, that *is* the reason why we are here.'

'I thought that I had been pardoned for my actions leading up to the war?'

'Leading up to, yes.' she said, meekly. 'But what concerns me is what you did afterwards.'

'Speak plainly, sister.' said Darlia, fixing her with a hard stare. 'You brought me all the way out here for a reason, so whatever it is that you have to say to me, just say it.'

She took a moment to compose herself, using the breathing techniques that she had learned from both Aleska and Nathaniel to calm her beating heart.

'Out with it, Kirika!' Darlia snapped, clearly not wanting to drag out their wait any longer. 'This is to do with Rarni – specifically, what the child saw – is it not?'

'Yes.'

Darlia stood up, abruptly. A dark shadow formed across her sister's face, reminding her of the depths that her sister was prepared to sink to.

'Please, sit down – this does not have to be this way.'

Her sister began to pace back and forth, as though the act of doing so would somehow help to diffuse the situation, which it did not.

'Darlia, please sit down.' she implored. 'We need to talk about this calmly and rationally. I am scared that if we allow our emotions to get the better of us, that a rift could form between us – one that can never be healed.'

The settlement was a hive of activity since Leyla and Klein had put the regiment to work reconfiguring the terrain. Meanwhile, the remaining scouts tended to other duties assigned to them by the regiment's squad leaders. Though not expected of him, he lent his strength where needed, assisting the scouts with their assignments. Although tasked with the burden of command, he was not above pitching in when needed, nor was he the type to sit around on his backside. Like Ragnar, he needed to be on the front line, so that he could remain in touch with the regiment and understand its needs. He could not sit by idly, commanding from the rear ranks whilst those in his charge did all the heavy lifting, even sacrificing their lives following his orders. Besides, forming good relationships with the scouts was important. Watching him work and fight on the front line, understanding that he believed ardently in their work ethic and strategy with the conviction to execute it, emboldened those choosing to follow him. The Guardian, too, adopted a similar approach, which in turn had propelled her standing amongst the people, although he freely acknowledged that his rough social interactions needed more work, unlike Rayna, whose mere presence seemed to embolden all those around her. The light bringer's playful demeanour made her instantly likable, unlike himself, who often let pride and heated emotions get the better of him. Still, it was a new cycle. The past was just that, with the future yet to be written – in his eyes at least. Recognising one's own character flaws was the first step towards self-improvement.

Feeling like a third wheel, with the regiment set to purpose, he decided to go and find Rayna. He found The Guardian sat on the ground, leaning against one of the settlement's smaller dwellings. The light bringer stared at the sky, watching the reddish hues on the horizon slowly infect the ocean of blue above them.

'Even if you saw it – as Mirielle did – would it make a difference?'

'Actually, it would probably just piss me off even more.'

He laughed.

'Then it is best that you cannot see it.'

'True. Even so, knowing that it is there irks me. Somehow, I have let it get under my skin.'

'Like Sebastian?'

'I guess so – I am not doing very well, am I?'

'It is not too late to correct all of that.' he said, taking a seat on the ground beside the light bringer. 'I have a request – feel free to reject it.'

'Oh? What is it?' asked Rayna, curiously.

'Since we have some time before the impending conflict, I wondered if you would mind telling me your story – about you and Sebastian that is?'

'But you have already seen my memories of my time at the facility.'

'True. However, they are a combination of images and emotions. They still lack context, which your dialogue can provide.'

'I see. Although, my words would only present one side of the story.'

'You have always been truthful, renowned for calling things as they are.'

Rayna laughed. The light bringer shifted her gaze from the sky, now focusing her attention on him instead.

'Don't you have better things to do, like commanding those in your charge?' said Rayna, who followed up her words with a beaming smile, somehow making them acceptable.

'Knock it off. Besides, the regiment does not need me right now – the scouts know what is required of them. In any event, learning more about our quarry is a tactically wise move, do you not think, Guardian?'

'You *know* that title still grates on me.'

'I know.'

Rayna playfully jabbed him in the ribs, prompting a smile of his own. Their good-natured mood was a far cry from the atmosphere between them when they had first met, seemingly a life-time ago now. So much had happened since Rayna's arrival.

'Very well. I shall narrate for you.'

'I would like to hear it all: your thoughts, how you believed that you felt at the time, moreover, how you perceived others around you felt.'

'Looking to get inside of Sebastian's head?'

'Something like that – I want to fully understand the rift between you two.'

'Trouble?' he enquired, turning his head towards the kitchen entrance.

Ezra stood watch, diligently peering through the gap between the grimy double doors. The boy chose not to answer immediately, instead confirming the situation before making his report.

'Nah. It's the ginger kid – slipped on the floor.'

'He's a liability.' he said.

'Sebastian said tha--' said Ryan, before he rudely cut the boy short.

'I know what Sebastian said!' he interjected, tersely, 'But it does not alter the facts.'

Ezra opened the doors, permitting Jacob to enter the Kitchen.

'You can't run for shit.' said Ezra, critically.

'It's not my fault – the floor was slippery.'

'Moron, what did you expect?' he said, tersely. 'We are hiding in here specifically to avoid the *cleaners*.'

'I did not realise that they had actually cleaned.' replied Jacob. 'Is it safe in here?'

'The floors are the *only* thing that they clean – you've seen them walking the corridors with that machine of theirs.

In any event, they are not contracted to clean the kitchen area – hence this is our rally point.'

'Why is that?' asked Jacob.

'Something to do with insurance.' Ryan explained.

'Does that *really* matter?' he said, unable to contain his annoyance.

The three boys suddenly went quiet. Like scolded children, they stood before him in silence, awaiting his instructions.

'Jacob, you had a simple job to do. Has Anastacia left the facility yet?'

'Yes.'

'Are you certain?'

'Yes. I saw her leave through the main entrance.'

'OK, good. We have a long walk ahead of us. I do not want us looking like a dishevelled, sweaty mess once we arrive in the heart of the metropolis – we need to blend in.'

All three nodded in agreement.

'Good. We will leave via one of the windows here. Ryan, be sure to leave it ajar so that we can sneak back in.'

One by one, they clambered through one of the kitchen's unlocked windows before sneaking their way across the grounds towards the perimeter. The poorly maintained fence marking the edge of the estate posed no challenge to them, although, the few obstacles they faced were harder than expected to navigate due to their attire. They were all keenly aware of the lengths they had gone to in obtaining and preparing their disguises, thus the need to protect them; they could ill afford ripped trousers, scuffed shoes, unkempt hair and the like, for fear of onlookers seeing through their carefully orchestrated guise. Things became easier once they approached the heart of the

239

metropolis. The wide-open roads and pristine walkways meant that they could maintain a distance from the public without the need to concern themselves too much with their appearance. However, their awkwardly fitting attire meant that they – Jacob in particular – were forever tucking in excess fabric or adjusting their belts to maintain their appearance.

'Tighten your belt another notch.' he said, half-expecting Jacob's trousers to fall down during their brisk walk.

Although the sight amused him, they could ill afford any setbacks to their plan. It had been his choice to leave later that evening, thus the need to quicken their pace. Managing baggy clothing during a brisk walk seemed, to him at least, more favourable than idle thumbs in the field, especially where Jacob was concerned. Ryan and Ezra were far less of a concern; it was clear that both boys had the benefit of experience – no doubt they had been put through their paces previously by Sebastian during other assignments. However, Jacob was incredibly twitchy due to his lack of experience operating in the field.

'What do we do if we are caught?' asked Jacob, nervously.

'You have already been briefed on all the contingencies for our assignment.' said Ryan, in an annoyed tone.

'Be quiet and just concentrate on walking.' said Ezra.

It was clear that all of them were now starting to feel the pressure. If their plan were exposed, no doubt they would all be expelled from the facility, or worse.

'I do not want to do this.' Jacob blabbered.

Several members of the public walking in the opposite direction gave them odd looks. He smiled politely at them in return, doing his best to paper over the cracks.

'Shut up!' he whispered tersely, 'Else you will get us all caught.'

Even when Jacob did manage to remain silent, the dazzling lights and extravagant displays in shop windows did not help; the boy's head was constantly on a swivel, looking this way and that, like some kind of tourist. All he could do now was pray that they did not attract further attention from the public, or worse, a Peacekeeper, before reaching their target.

SIXTEEN

Pressure

'What did she see?'

'It is what *I* saw that is the issue here.'

'Just get to the point, Kirika.'

She felt physically ill. Her stomach churned and she felt light-headed. The colour of her skin was even paler than usual and she felt cold all of a sudden. No matter how she dressed the truth, her sister would not take kindly to her words, of that she was certain. She exhaled deeply one last time, before hitting Darlia with the blunt end of the stick.

'You heinously butchered three Freylarkin and then dumped their mangled bodies in a shallow grave.'

'They deserved it.'

'Darlia!'

'I carried out justice.'

'You released them! That is not justice, it is murder!' she said, the words sticking in her throat.

'You cannot understand, Kirika.' said Darlia.

'Why can I not understand?' she asked sincerely. 'Darlia, you need to talk to me – now is not the time for secrets.'

'I was the eldest, so things were different for me, back then.'

'What do you mean?'

'Caleth only beat you.'

'What does this have to do with the former Blade Lord?'

Darlia paused for a moment. She could tell that her sister was finding it difficult to talk about events concerning the issue. She grasped Darlia's good hand with her own, squeezing her sister's hand tightly.

'Take your time.'

'After I was exiled by Mirielle, I had *nothing*, at least until I found Lileah.'

'I know that. My heart breaks every time I think about it. I was not there for you. I should have done more.'

'You brought an end to her reign.'

'But it did not happen soon enough to save you. What happened?'

'Just scry my past, as Rarni did. Hopefully that will give you all the answers that you seek.'

'You know that it will not.' she said, patiently. 'Your actions could undo all the good we have done since the war. Everything could come crashing down on us if this is dealt with poorly. You need to tell me everything, Darlia, so that I can try to manage the situation.'

'Do not make me talk about it, not again, Kirika.'

'I need words, not just images. The bits and pieces you have previously told me about Lileah are not enough. I need to understand your motive for such a crime. I need proper context if I am to understand your actions.'

'I do not want to talk about this.'

'You *have* to. If word of this gets out, the people will demand your release!'

'I probably deserve it.' her sister replied sombrely.

'Maybe. Although, I do not want to believe that. Give me *something* to work with.'

'Just leave me to the whim of the mob, Kirika.'

'Stop being so selfish!' she said, no longer able to contain her anger.

'You have *no* idea!'

244

'Because you will not tell me!'

'I said that I do not wish to talk about it.'

'Your actions will likely damn us all, Darlia.'

'This is my burden to bear.'

'No, it is not! If they drag you through the mud, I will quickly follow, which in turn will affect the ruling council.'

'It will not come to that.'

'You do not know that – not for certain. Besides, think about Nathanar.'

'He has nothing to do with this!'

'Of course he does – he *loves* you, Darlia!'

'You have no idea what it was like, or what *she* felt!' cried Darlia, who suddenly stood up, pointing her good hand towards Lileah's grave.

She rose from her uncomfortably hard seat and grasped her sister's outstretched arm. Slowly, she pulled Darlia's arm downwards, bringing it close to her chest as she held her sister's watery gaze.

'I realise this is difficult for you. However, your silence affects more than just you.' she said, before pausing for a moment to consider her next words carefully. 'You have resigned yourself to accepting whatever blame others choose to lay at your feet. You may have given up, but I will not give up on you! I failed you once and I will not let that happen again. In order for me to mount some kind of defence in your name, I *must* know what motivated you to commit such an act. Please, Darlia, I am begging you. If you will not do this for yourself, please do it for your little sister and Nathanar – he does not deserve the wrath of the people.'

Her sister began to sob. She pulled Darlia's head down to her shoulder, stroking her sister's long, straight, purple hair affectionately. Together, they stood by the Eternal Falls, listening to the calming sound of water crashing into the pool at the base of the falls. Whilst comforting her sister, her mind began to wander. She thought back to their time with Caleth, and how the paranoid Blade Lord had treated them poorly. It was then that her sister's words suddenly held fresh meaning to her. Darlia had been the eldest of them, thus her body would have come into bloom well before her own. A dark cloud formed in her mind, casting a sinister shadow over her developing thoughts.

'Did Caleth take advantage of you?' she asked, the words escaping her lips before she could fathom their ramifications.

Darlia said nothing, but she could feel her sister violently trembling.

'Darlia, *did* he abuse you?'

Her sister burst into tears, prompting ire that she had never experienced before, even when Marcus had severed her sister's hand.

'He forced himself on you, did he not?' she asked, pushing her sister back so that she could look Darlia in the eye, thus confirming her suspicion.

'Yes.' replied Darlia, in a broken voice.

'And the Freylarkai that you butchered. Did they do the same to Lileah?'

'Yes.'

'Why did you not tell me all this?' she implored.

'I am ashamed.'

'You cannot think like that – the shame is theirs alone!'

'It is difficult…it did not happen to you…I…'

'Oh Darlia, you should have told me all this.'

'You are my little sister – it is my job to protect *you*.'

246

'I can protect myself!' she said, ardently. 'Darlia, murder is not the answer; you cannot release others, despite their sin – they must be held to account for their atrocities.'

'I did not want this to land on you. I secretly dispensed the justice they deserved.'

'You slaughtered them! You butchered them all, smashed their faces, broke their limbs and then dumped their bloodied corpses in a shallow grave – do you not see how awful that is?'

'I could not stop it.'

'Because you are tainted by his evil!'

'Whose?'

'Krashnar's!'

'The Guardian destroyed him.'

'But not his legacy.'

'What do you mean?' asked Darlia, wiping the tears from her watery eyes.

'That wretched claw of yours!' she said vehemently, unable to hide her growing anger. 'Look at it!

Darlia focused on her ornate, bronze, mechanical claw. Whatever people's feelings towards the notorious shaper, the artisanship of the prosthetic hand was outstanding – there was no denying Krashnar's talent for the perverse. During the many passes that her sister had played host to the replacement hand, not once had it failed her. The construct was a mechanical marvel, one that was well beyond the technological understanding of anyone she knew, including its current owner.

'I know that he was evil – but I am not!'

'Darlia, I too believe that you are not inherently evil. Yet, you have committed numerous acts of brutality since becoming its custodian: your part in the war, the way you ended Lileah and now this bloody massacre.' she said, her voice breaking once more. 'These are not the actions of the sister that I grew up with.'

'So much has happened since then, Kirika.' Darlia said meekly. 'My emotions get the better of me – I am unable to prevent it.'

'The stain of Krashnar's repugnant soul is infused into your claw – it is literally the hand that guides you.'

'Then what am I supposed to do, Kirika?' cried Darlia. 'This *is* me – it is a part of me.'

'I believe that there *is* a way to divorce you from Krashnar's evil, but I am not strong enough to exorcise his malevolence.'

'Then who is?' Darlia implored.

'There is one, pure of heart and with the strength to do what is required. However, this final act would need to be sold to the people in order to absolve you of these murders, which you call justice.'

'It *was* justice, for her!'

'Darlia, justice comes in many forms, but as individuals, what right do we have to decide if another lives or not?' she said, briefly pausing to consider her next words. 'Ours is not a black and white society, where a simple set of rules can govern our way of life. Take yourself, for example, and the brutal way you were treated. Mirielle ordered Marcus to sever your hand and then she separated *us*. You were not the only one who suffered that cycle. Marcus crossed a line that he had not intended to, tarnishing his otherwise unsullied reputation, and I lost my big sister! It was not justice that was served that cycle. Instead, one individual's insecurity was sated, albeit temporarily, setting in motion a long series of events that would affect all those living in the vale. Now, you have done the same. We do not know what the release of the three males you butchered will lead to.'

'I can scry that outcome.'

'No! That is what triggered all this mess in the first place! Your quest to *know* every possible outcome enflamed Mirielle's need for absolute control, leading to your inevitable exile.'

'Then what do you propose?'

'We need to get ahead of this and erect a dam, to prevent the ripples from spreading, as opposed to forever chasing them down stream.'

'What does that mean?' asked Darlia.

'It means that it is time that both you and I took responsibility for your actions.'

The sun slowly kissed the horizon, causing the light to fade – it was getting late. Her stomach rumbled loudly, though she could not tell if it was due to hunger or nerves.

'When did you last eat?' asked Klein.

'I am not sure – things have been pretty hectic.'

'Stay here.'

The veteran scout jogged off, presumably to find them something to eat, leaving her alone with Krisis. She crouched down and began rubbing the dire wolf's neck once more, watching in amusement as his eyes narrowed from the joy of having more affection heaped upon him. Krisis was nothing short of a vicious beast when engaged in battle, yet entirely the opposite when the opportunity for attention presented itself. As she massaged the dire wolf's fur, she felt hidden scars underneath Krisis' thick pelt from previous confrontations. Although still relatively young, the adolescent dire wolf had endured his fair share of conflict, both prior to and after aligning himself with Lothnar. Since the incident at Scrier's Post, the pair had become almost inseparable, both loyal to the other regardless of any adversity they faced during their travels together. Indeed, the scouts saw the dire wolf as one of their own, treating him no differently to any other member of the regiment. Now completely under her spell, Krisis' eyes had all but disappeared, his tongue now hanging from the left corner of his open maw.

'I got us something to eat.' cried Klein, quickly jogging back to their position.

'Thanks. I feel quite hungry now.' she said, patting Krisis on the head before standing up.

'You need to keep your strength up – you are going to need it.'

'Thanks, *mother*.' she said, jokingly.

Klein laughed whilst handing her some thick bread.

'How do you think this evening will play out?' she asked, before taking a large bite of her meal.

'The terrain looks good. Provided the bait is sufficient, I believe that we have a chance.'

'What if it is not?' she asked, her gaze drifting towards the gloomy treeline along the eastern horizon.

'I would not be too concerned; we can always send Krisis in to deal with The Moon King.'

Krisis barked on cue. She found it strange how the dire wolf behaved as though he understood their conversations, even though Lothnar was the only one capable of communing with him, albeit telepathically.

'Yes.' she said, laughing aloud. 'I believe that he would be up for the task – provided that I lavish enough affection upon him fist.'

'He is easily motivated.'

Klein tossed some of his bread towards the dire wolf, who quickly snapped up the meal before it could hit the ground.

'And with reflexes like that, The Moon King's defeat is assured.'

'I sincerely hope so.' she said. 'I do not wish to bury another comrade this cycle.'

The sun continued to dip in the sky as they quietly enjoyed their meal together. The shadows between the outbuildings began to stretch and elongate, doing their utmost to merge with one another, forming a sea of darkness that slowly swallowed the earth. As the ground beneath them gave way to the creeping black ocean, so too did the optimism in her heart at the sight of the ominous looking shadows. Unable to hide her concern, Klein caught her eye. She could sense the veteran scout reading the deepening lines on her face, as though reading a book.

'Our strategy is sound. Have faith in the regiment and its ability.'

'You are right. I must dispel such gloomy thoughts from my mind and focus on the task at hand.'

'Leyla, I cannot promise you that we will not lose comrades in this fight. Casualties are the inevitable result of any conflict. However, the scouts *will* prevail.'

'I am concerned that my leadership may falter and that as a result I may jeopardise the team.'

'Why would you say this?'

251

'I messed up during our last encounter with the Louperdu. I allowed myself to be injured, thus resources needed to be diverted towards my aid.'

'That is rubbish!' said Klein, ardently, taking her by surprise. 'Most of us took a beating, one way or another. Despite this, we all fought with heart and we all had one another's backs – that is what it means to be a scout.'

Klein's sudden unexpected change in demeanour, along with his raised voice, attracted the attention of those nearby, unbeknownst to the fervent veteran.

'We look after our own in the field, regardless of personal relationships or tolerance for one another. It is the unwritten founding principle of our creed: protect the Freylarkin standing alongside you in battle and they will do the same for you. By protecting our flank, you saved the lives of many scouts, who in turn offered their own to protect you. No matter how hard you train or how well you develop your skills – even if you master them – you cannot win a fight of this magnitude alone. We are a regiment. We fight together as one, with a singular purpose. That pack of animals looking to slaughter us have no respect for one another – fear and instinct alone govern their actions. We are better than that. We fight out of loyalty, with courage and an unshakable resolve!'

The lingering doubt clouding her mind was cast aside immediately upon hearing Klein's impromptu sermon. Unable to supress her emotions, she gave the veteran scout a beaming smile whilst clapping her hands enthusiastically, prompting their onlookers to do the same. Several cheers sounded in the background. Krisis, too, joined in, the dire wolf barking loudly. Taking a step forwards, she slapped

252

Klein's left shoulder with her free hand, acknowledging his words of encouragement.

Although inducted by the scouts, she was still a Blade – as were they all – and had therefore sworn to protect the domain. Regardless of the challenge they faced, or the growing dread festering inside her, she would face the enemy head on in battle, knowing that she would not be alone.

'Nice speech.' she said, her smile widening even further as the cheers continued to sound in the background. 'You certainly know how to start a fire.'

Klein's sudden bashfulness suggested that the scout had not intended to speak so enthusiastically, nor had he expected such an emboldened response from their impromptu audience. Although not a leader – not yet at least – a brilliant ember burned within the veteran's soul, one that, if nurtured, had the potential to set ablaze a path inspiring those choosing to follow in its wake. She fully understood now why Lazrik had paired them together, the purpose of the exercise to further Klein's development as well as her own. She remembered the commander's words about supporting one another, moreover, how Klein had supported her. With these thoughts in mind, she clapped even harder, before stepping forward to grab Klein's left wrist. She raised the scout's arm, thrusting his hand towards the darkening sky. The simple act of unity prompted further cheers from their onlookers, who had now grown in numbers. Swept up in the moment and inspired by her comrade's words, she suddenly cried out, her moment of spontaneity surprising even herself.

'Victory *will* be ours. Take it!'

It was getting late in the evening by the time they reached their destination. Despite several odd looks from members of the public, in addition to adjusting their route to avoid unnecessary contact with an unexpected Peacekeeper patrol, they eventually located the hab unit where their target resided. They entered the tall building, using the access codes provided by Sebastian, confidently strolling through its main entrance to ensure that the building's surveillance systems logged their entry. If their plan was to succeed, they needed to make certain that blame for their actions was assigned to one of the other social classes – which meant being seen.

'Callum, that was too easy.' whispered Jacob.

'Be quiet.' said Ryan.

He could see that both Ryan's and Ezra's moods had changed. Both bore stern expressions and were completely focused on the task at hand. Now was not the time to indulge Jacob's nervous, idle chatter and neither were prepared to tolerate it, given their proximity to their objective.

'Remember to act confidently. You will give us away if you show any sign of nerves.'

After stepping foot into the building's foyer, it was Ezra who initiated their faux conversation, deliberately raising his voice to attract attention.

'Did you see the state of that filthy Shadow class runt loitering near the perimeter?'

'You mean the rat?' replied Ryan, before laughing loudly.

'I could smell his stench from across the road.' he said, playing along with the others.

254

'It is the government's fault; they need to migrate the lot of them, give them a plot of contaminated land to farm, beyond the Midden Belt.'

'It is a shame that ground vehicle did not mount the pavement and remove the vermin from our sight.' said Ryan, vehemently, leaning into the role of an Apex class member.

'More jobs are needed – a task for the middle classes perhaps?' he said, continuing their disparaging conversation as they leisurely strolled towards the main elevator.

They passed a bored-looking security officer as they approached the elevator. He noticed the guard quickly raise his head as they passed by, specifically focusing his attention on Jacob, whom they had tried to shield in the middle of their pack.

'What do *you* think?' he said, turning to face Jacob, realising that the boy's silence had piqued the guard's suspicions.

Caught off guard, Jacob paused awkwardly for a moment, before realising the need to act.

'That does not sound very ethical.' said Jacob, meekly.

'Ethics!' said Ryan sternly. 'We are discussing the metropolis' pest control issues – ethics are irrelevant.'

'It is true.' said Ezra, disdainfully, promptly calling the elevator using its holographic access panel. 'Their kind do not warrant any rights.'

'They are a blight on the metropolis.' he said, chiming in once more.

The guard turned his attention back to the device in his hands, clearly uninterested in their staid conversation, no doubt having heard such thoughts aired in public repeatedly before, by others of the same social class.

255

'Agreed. You need to adjust your way of thinking.' said Ryan sternly.

The doors to the elevator slid open, after which they all promptly entered the metal box and ascended to their desired floor. They continued their faux conversation whilst huddled together in the elevator, conscious that security devices would be monitoring their every action. After exiting the elevator, they quickly found their target's hab unit, entered the access code – provided by Sebastian – via its holographic display before entering the lavish living quarters, shutting the door behind them. Jacob immediately released a sigh of relief, signalling his continued unease.

'Pull it together.' he said, concerned by the fact that they still needed to exit the building cleanly.

'You fucking idiot!' said Ezra, 'You nearly gave us away back there.'

'I panicked.' said Jacob.

The boy slumped to the floor and bowed his head low. It was clear to him that Sebastian's lackey now understood the very real danger they faced.

'I get that.' he said, deliberately softening his voice, deciding not to flagellate the boy any further. 'However, you have to be more careful – if you are caught, we *will* leave you behind.'

Leaving Jacob to consider the reality of their situation, he pulled four sets of latex gloves from his pockets, issuing three pairs to the group.

'Put these on immediately; we cannot afford to inadvertently leave any trace of *us* having actually been here.'

After putting on the gloves, both Ryan and Ezra began canvasing the hab unit, quickly acquiring a feel for their new surroundings. They were careful not to disturb or touch anything unnecessarily, mindful that doing so could potentially spook their target upon return.

'Callum,' said Ryan flatly, 'These storage compartments will work for us.'

'Good.'

'I will take the door.' Ryan continued. 'You, Ezra and Jacob should remain out of sight.'

Ryan's words made sense. Out of the pair, Ryan possessed the more muscular build and was seemingly more focused and composed than his associate. Furthermore, something about Ezra's mannerisms concerned him. Though he could not put a finger on it, the boy's erratic disposition made him more unpredictable.

'Agreed.' he said. 'Depending on the accuracy of the information Sebastian provided us, we may have a long wait ahead of us. If you need the bathroom facilities, go now. Then I want these lights off and us hidden. No one is to utter a word unless I say so. Is that understood?'

Both Ryan and Ezra nodded firmly in agreement. Jacob too stood up and nodded, acknowledging his instructions.

'Good.' he said. 'Take your positions and make yourselves comfortable – we could have a long wait.'

After drinking some water and taking a piss, they each got into position, doing their best to make themselves comfortable. He reluctantly chose to share one of the storage compartments with Jacob. Of those in the group, he was less likely to set the boy's already frayed nerves on edge. Besides, Ezra's impressive build did not lend itself to sharing one of the compartments and he was reluctant to leave Jacob alone in the dark. Ryan took up position

257

adjacent to the door, doing his best to press his body close to the wall. Although he could have concealed his slimmer frame better, Ryan possessed the strength to subdue their target with minimal fuss. After extinguishing the lights and closing the doors to the storage compartments, they silently hid in wait. It was difficult to decide what was worse; Jacob's incessant worrying or the boy's nervous, shallow breathing, now the soundtrack to his distasteful evening.

SEVENTEEN
Prey

'Enemy sighted!'

He detected the sound of those closest to him adjusting their stance in light of the ominous, distant cry. It had been a long wait, following The Guardian's in-depth account. After taking their positions, the entire regiment had lain in wait, keeping a watchful eye on the horizon for early signs of their foe. Although expected, given the tardy nature of their previous encounter, it would have been remiss of him to make assumptions. After listening to Rayna's story, it was clear that The Moon King favoured tactics based primarily on fear and manipulation. Even so, The Moon King was not above changing the rules when it suited his agenda. With The Moon King's will now bent on securing his expanded territory, Sebastian would not allow anything to get in his way; as such, there would be no rules of engagement during their bloody confrontation. Sebastian's disorder meant that loss of life, on both sides of the inevitable conflict, would mean nothing to The Moon King. Therefore, they needed to adjust their way of thinking to allow for, what they would typically perceive as, reckless commands – The Moon King would not think twice about sacrificing his children if doing so increased his chances of success.

'Eight hundred paces, northeast, advancing quickly!'

'Southeast!' cried another voice. 'Same distance and closing fast!'

At those distances, it would not be long before the Louperdu set upon them. Given their conspicuous charge, it was possible that the enemy would attempt to infiltrate their formation during the initial maelstrom.

'Secondary spotters, look to the west for signs of encroaching mist.' he cried.

'That's too obvious for someone like him.' said Rayna, crouched low beside him.

'I know.' he replied sternly. 'But if he has got behind us, I fully expect a delayed incursion from the north and south. It is imperative that we position ourselves correctly.'

'Mist!' cried another voice. 'Encroaching from the west, five hundred paces.'

'Rayna, take Leyla and Klein. Use their team to hold the rear.'

'You believe that Sebastian will approach from that direction?'

'It is a hunch. He will be the last to commit and I do not believe that he will lead the main group when it links up to the east. From what you have told me, Sebastian prefers operating from the shadows. Furthermore, I am certain that he will seek to cut off any means of escape.'

'I see.' replied The Guardian. 'He expects us to split the regiment by engaging his open charge on two fronts, diluting our numbers further to deal with the rear incursion.'

'At which point, I expect him to infiltrate us from the north and south.'

'If he intends to hit us on all fronts, will that not push us towards a defensive circle?'

'We know that, but The Moon Kind does not. I believe that he expects us to commit to the charge.'

'Good luck.' said Rayna, who then quickly turned and left.

260

'*Krisis, my friend. Go with Rayna, Klein and Leyla –
keep them all safe for me! You and I will meet again, after
this is done.*'

As he watched the muscular dire wolf bound across the
sloped roofs of the outbuildings, he opened his mind,
seeking to link with those of his squad leaders. Only those
with the ability to master their telepathy possessed the
means to connect with more than one mind concurrently.
The technique required total concentration and unerring
precision; fortunately, Lazrik, Yandar and Saralia had not
moved from their locations, making the task of locating
their minds simple enough. However, the strain of
communication with them simultaneously was another
matter entirely.

'*Saralia, take your team and engage the pack to the
northeast. Yandar, head southeast. Both of you draw the
enemy in – whittle their numbers down as you fall back to
the rally point. Lazrik, divide your team and be ready to
push north and south if needed, else you will support the
others. Take the few telekinetics that we have, in case they
try to flank us in their mist state. The Guardian, Leyla and
Klein will cover our rear. I fully expect The Moon King's
forces to surround the settlement. I wish you all good
fortune – now go!*'

He could hear the distant cries of his squad leaders,
immediately relaying his orders. After which, the regiment
promptly redeployed throughout the settlement, each squad
diligently following its assigned duties. The scouts leapt
between the rooftops like shadowy assassins, using their
wraith wings to glide elegantly from one building to the
next. It filled him with pride, seeing the regiment's
individual components function as one, each team working

261

harmoniously with the others towards a common objective. Although Blades, all, the scouts in particular excelled at working together to take down their prey. Their fluid movements and exceptional agility made them ideal for complex skirmishes, reconnaissance and vanguard assignments, with hit and run tactics forming the backbone of their military strategies. Furthermore, his own ability lent itself well to their covert operations, in addition to Krisis' unerring agility and speed, thus each member was an integral part of the regiment.

It would not be long before the familiar sound of battle rung out across the settlement. Soon, the still air would carry the awful screams and howls of pain that would inevitably ensue, the awful song of battle no doubt providing him with a wealth of information, prompting him where to redirect their forces. Confrontation was not something he actively sought out – his true calling being exploration and adventure. Nevertheless, he was one of the domain's appointed wardens and as such would do everything within his power to protect his kin, even if his duty meant sacrificing his own life to do so.

His muscles tensed at the faint sound of heels clacking against the marble floor of the corridor outside. Shortly afterwards, they heard a swooshing sound as the hab unit's door slid open, followed by the unmistakable noise of heavily muffled squeals.

'Go, now!' he whispered, sliding the door to the storage compartment wide open.

Light from the corridor poured into the room. Ezra was already running to assist Ryan, who had his muscular right arm curled around the neck of a well-dressed woman, covering her mouth tightly with a large hand. Ezra scooped up the woman's feet, gripping them tightly, before the pair carried their prize towards the dining area. With their target secured, he quickly closed the door.

'Lighting, low!' he said, prompting the automated controls to engage the hab unit's low-level lighting, marking the perimeter of the room.

The woman fought desperately against her captors, moaning incessantly, trying to attract the attention of anyone within earshot. He felt sick, watching her futile struggle as Ryan and Ezra gagged, then bound, the woman to one of the dining table's chairs. He turned his attention to Jacob. The gaunt boy looked the other way, refusing to watch the horrible show of force. He could see Jacob trembling, his hands fidgeting as though wanting to cover his ears. Desperate to ease the awful mood, he quickly approached the woman, kneeling down beside her, careful not to reveal his entire face.

'We are not here to hurt you, but we *need* you to be quiet.' he said.

The woman continued to struggle. She writhed violently, causing the thin straps binding her wrists to the chair to chafe.

'Please, calm down. If you do not, you will hurt yourself.' he said, softly, tying to instil a sense of calm.

The woman continued to struggle, desperate to free herself from her bonds. No doubt, the skin around her wrists and ankles was already tuning red, though it was impossible to confirm his suspicions given the dim lighting.

'Give us a moment, please.' he said, looking to Ryan and Ezra to create some space, before tuning to Jacob. 'Go, listen out by the door.'

263

The group slowly dispersed, leaving him alone with the frightened woman.

'I meant what I said: we are not here to hurt you. However, I cannot loosen your gag unless you are quiet – can you do that for me?'

The terrified woman was shaking uncontrollably. He was unsure whether his words even registered with their captive, or instead if she was operating on base instinct alone, interpreting the sound of his voice as a sign of further harm and aggression.

'I will not let them hurt you.' he said, gently.

He thought about placing his left hand on the scared woman's lap to reassure her, although, there was every chance that physical contact, in her current state, would have the opposite effect.

'I just want to have a quiet conversation with you.' he explained. 'If you are able to calm down, I will release your gag for you – do you understand?'

It took a moment for the woman to process his words, although she did eventually nod, prompting him to reach for her gag.

'I am going to pull down your gag. Please, promise me that you will remain quiet – I am sure that neither of us wants the others over here.'

The terrified woman almost shook herself apart as he slowly pulled down her gag. She inhaled deeply before gulping loudly, trying to clear her throat, whilst he slowly stood up.

'I cannot give you my name. However, please believe me when I tell you that I do not intend to cause you any harm.'

264

'Why…are…you doing…this?' asked the scared woman.

'I can tell you what we want from you, but not why.'

'What…is it that you want…from me?' blabbered the terrified woman.

'Put plainly: access to your funds.'

'What?'

'Once we have emptied your accounts, we will leave. After that, you will be free to contact the authorities – you are insured against such acts, I presume, given your social status?'

'Take it and leave – you *disgust* me!'

The frightened woman's words gouged a deep wound within him. He could not determine the means with which to justify their deplorable actions. Their captive spoke the truth: what they were doing was wrong. He realised that now. The gulf between social classes was not reason enough to bring fear or harm to others. He chided himself for allowing Sebastian to sully his ideals. He was not naive enough to believe that those of a higher social class possessed an enlightened disposition. However, his core values did permit him to consider the existence of those, regardless of class, capable of pragmatic, logical reasoning, uncontaminated by base tribalistic thought processes.

'I disgust myself.' he whispered, unable to contain his disappointment. 'I will require your personal details, along with a scan of your biometrics to initiate the transfer.'

'Just do it and go.'

Their captive's compliance ensured that the transfer went smoothly, albeit the process took longer than he had anticipated. On several occasions, he was forced to wave both Ryan and Ezra away, ensuring that they kept their

265

distance. He could see the scared woman's eyes flicking towards them, terrified that the ones directly responsible for restraining her would return.

'They will not come near you. I give you my word.'

After the transaction was complete, he knelt down beside the woman, doing his best not to reveal too much of his face.

'I am going to replace your gag, then inform the others that we are done here, after which we will shortly take our leave and you will never see us again.'

'Who will release me?'

'I will ensure that the door is left open and that you are visible to those walking past your hab. You will be released by one of the other residents in the morning, by which time we will be long gone.'

As he moved to replace the woman's gag, she started to shake once more, whilst giving him a watery stare.

'You have…violated my home. How…am I supposed to feel safe after this?'

He paused for a moment, struggling for the right words to say, but there were none, at least, none that would make things right. Instead, he offered her the truth, unwilling to insult the woman further.

'You're not. We have taken that privilege away from you – we must now live with that shame.'

After receiving her orders, she quickly left the veteran Paladin to command the remainder of the regiment's forces, seeking instead to link up with Leyla and Klein. She followed Krisis, who bounded effortlessly across the settlement's rooftops. Despite her head start, the powerful adolescent dire wolf had already overtaken her and was

266

reliably following his nose – no bad thing, given her poor vision in low light. Although the moon did its best to bathe the landscape with its silvery light, nevertheless, she still found it difficult to make out anything beyond fifteen paces. Unlike the others, she was the only light bringer in the regiment. Although she possessed the rare ability to both manifest and manipulate light, empowering her with an array of offensive tricks that she had since learned, her inability to see as well as the others often hindered her. Unaware of her disadvantage, Krisis powered on until they reached the pair, forcing her to user her wraith wings to keep up.

'Leyla, Klein!' she cried. 'Your team is to defend the west.'

'Understood.'

She watched as the once short-tempered Blade took immediate control of the situation. After a brief exchange with Klein, Leyla calmly issued a series of commands to the team, prompting the scouts to adopt a pre-established formation. The scouts quickly assumed their positions and immediately moved west following Leyla's order to engage.

'Advance!' cried her former student, with an iron will that caused her to smile.

Krisis barked loudly, as if affirming Leyla's command, following which the team quickly moved west, maintaining its formation. They moved in two columns, with Leyla and Klein at the middle of their respective groups. Each team's strategy relied on keeping their two archers firing, whilst slowly falling back. The remaining scouts would engage at short range using their throwing knives, the leading member of both columns withdrawing to the back of their line after placing their shot. The ephemeral formation would allow

267

the teams to continue firing at short range whilst they withdrew into the settlement, all the while holding the high ground. They would force the Louperdu to flow around the well-placed detritus on the ground, the plan being to slow the Louperdu down and negate the enemy's ability to charge. The other squads had instructions to follow suit, albeit in greater numbers, no doubt forcing them to fight on the ground in addition to the rooftops. Lothnar had kept Leyla and Klein's squad intentionally small, not wanting to add to their mounting pressure. Besides, she was assigned to accompany them, along with Krisis, ensuring that the fledgling leaders had additional support. Furthermore, the bulk of the Louperdu charge would come from the east, managed by veteran squad leaders Yandar and Saralia.

Since neither Leyla, nor Klein, had expected her support, her role and position in the squad, along with Krisis' own, had not been discussed. She chose to take up position between the two columns in order to support the team's archers and protect the forward scouts if needed. Krisis stood alongside her, placing himself at the centre of the formation. The dire wolf's astonishing speed and agility meant that Krisis could support the squad where needed once the fighting began.

'Contact!' cried one of the lead scouts as the Louperdu moved into range. 'Mist, fifty paces out.'

'Hold ground!' cried Klein, causing the squad to halt suddenly.

Leyla and Klein each nocked an arrow onto their bowstrings and took aim. The situation reminded her of Scrier's Post. Back then, she had only been able to imbue weapons with her ability one at a time. However, since then her power had grown substantially, furthered by Alarielle's experience, which had been passed down to her directly. Having learned to greater control her ability, she could now – as she had at Bleak Moor – imbue the squad's weapons en masse with minimal effort on her part.

'Lower your heads and close your eyes.'

Few had served under her at Bleak Moor, though most had since heard the stories, thus the squad immediately obeyed her order, ready to receive her gift of light.

After rapidly manifesting two balls of light within her clenched fists, she released the pent-up energy, causing it to explode outwards in an expansive wave that engulfed them. Using her will, she pulled the light back, guiding it towards the scout's weapons, where it came to rest, causing their armaments to glow vibrantly with the imbued light energy. During her previous conflicts, the stored light energy had diminished quickly. However, now that her power had grown, she felt confident that the enchantment would last considerably longer.

'Open your eyes!'

She watched the scouts' faces bathe in the golden light of their imbued weaponry. Whether or not the light would benefit them in combat remained unknown. Nonetheless, the enchantment clearly had a positive mental effect on the squad; even with her poor sight, she could see backs stiffening and smiles creeping across the faces of the scouts. Even if the light served only to embolden the squad, that in itself was enough to warrant spending the energy required to pull off the feat.

'Ready yourselves!' Leyla cried once more.

The front-runner from each column moved to the edge of their respective rooftops, with those further back defending the flanks in the event that the enemy managed to push past them towards the heart of the settlement. Rotating out the foremost scouts would allow the teams to withdraw steadily, providing a constant rate of fire whilst steadily falling back. The strategy, in theory, would allow them to whittle down the enemy's numbers before coming together in a defensive circle at the heart of the sprawling farmstead. With the ground littered with carts, crates and other detritus, they sought to slow down the Louperdu's advance and deny the spirit wolves the opportunity to both charge and pin down their ranks. If they could maintain a fluid formation whilst eroding the enemy's numbers, there was a chance that they could deal with superior numbers and avoid being overwhelmed.

'Thirty paces!'

'They're right on top of us.' she said, turning towards Leyla first, followed by Klein. 'It is time. Both of you, give the order.'

Both of the squad's fledging leaders stood upright and took aim. They briefly turned their heads towards one another and nodded, acknowledging their unified commitment to battle, before shouting loudly together.

'Fire!'

Two trails of light arced through the night sky, descending towards the encroaching haze. The imbued arrows struck the pool of mist advancing towards them, the light penetrating the vapour, spreading outwards like a golden pestilence, eroding everything it touched. The foremost scouts immediately followed suit, indiscriminately throwing their imbued projectiles into the fog before withdrawing, hoping to suppress the enemy's advance. Again, the light devoured the surrounding mist, like hot water poured onto snow, melting everything with its touch.

'They're reforming!' cried one of the scouts, who now headed up Klein's column.

'Continue holding the edge of the roofs until they are within striking distance.'

Her lack of sight meant that she found it difficult to comprehend the maelstrom of battle unfolding before them. It was only when the light struck the enemy that she truly gained a feel for the enemy's numbers. Realising their vulnerability to the light, the Louperdu quickly abandoned their incorporeal forms, reverting to their physical lupine states instead. Although now exposed to physical attacks, in their natural form the Louperdu benefited from impressive speed and agility. Sensing that things were about to get bloody, Krisis eased into an attacking stance and began to snarl viciously.

Taking in a slow, deep breath, she drew her twin Dawnstone falchions, gifted to her by Nathaniel and Heldran. Translucent, ephemeral smoke trailed from Shadow Caster as she gently wielded the blade into a defensive guard. She could sense the ravenous appetite of the starved Narlakin trapped within the Dawnstone blade, eager to devour the souls of her opponents. By contrast, The Ardent Blade in her left hand was completely inert, patiently awaiting the inevitable swipe of her thumb across the Waystone masterfully embedded into the top of its grip, just beneath the weapon's cross-guard. The Dawnstone twins had served her well in previous battles and would undoubtedly do so again, provided that she did not give in to their bloodlust. Heldran, in particular, had warned her of the weapons' penchant for acts of evil, as intended by their architect, the twisted shaper Krashnar. Both former owners had agreed, given the blades' ability to compel their

271

wielders, that she would be their custodian going forwards. Having finally vanquished the darkness that had once plagued her own soul, she was now a suitable candidate for managing the sinful weapons without succumbing to their dark desires. As with all the abhorrent shaper's creations, Krashnar had poured his deep-seated malice and twisted desires into the blades' creation, tainting them with his evil. Yet despite their questionable genesis, if wielded by one immune to their gradual corruption, the vicious weapons possessed the means to annihilate their enemies.

Exhaling slowly, she looked to Krisis. The adolescent dire wolf continued to snarl at the enemy, now knocking on their doorstep.

'Get ready boy – blood is about to be spilled.'

'You are back late.' Nathanar said sleepily, as she tried to sneak her way into their bed. 'Did you speak with your sister?'

'Kirika was here?'

'Yes.' replied Nathanar, rolling over to face her. 'She spoke with me briefly this morning – said she was looking for you. I got the impression that it was about something important.'

'She caught up with me in the forest.'

There was a lull in their conversation whilst she tried to make herself comfortable. Her prosthetic hand made it incredibly difficult for her to relax, forcing her to lay awkwardly on her right side, or else on her back, which she loathed. Aside from during her time of deep depression, whilst laying on the hard ground of the Meldbeast's filthy pen, she could no longer recall a time when she had ceased to fidget prior to eventually falling asleep due to sheer

272

exhaustion. To make matters worse, Nathanar – like herself – was a light sleeper. Still troubled by their past, neither of them managed to achieve the deep slumber that their bodies craved, their over-active minds denying them the privilege. Still, they were both trying hard to move on – Nathanar more successfully than herself – despite their troubled past desperately clinging to them.

'She spoke with you then?'

'We did indeed speak.' she said, still trying to get comfortable.

'I realise that I am only half awake right now. However, I get the feeling that you are being evasive – do you not wish to talk about the matter?'

She rolled onto her back and flicked her long purple hair away from her face. As she stared upwards into the gloom, the sprawling dark shadows across the ceiling began to shift, slowly forming images from her past, no doubt conjured by her mind working subconsciously to make sense of her life. At first, she imagined the Meldbeast again, this time sulking in its stinking pen, followed by Rarni, when she and Nathanar had first found the traumatised child back in the canyon. Unwilling to release her from their grasp, the shadows continued to shift, seeking to manifest further facets of her past. The dark imagery morphed once more, this time forming the outline of Lileah. The eerie portrayal reminded her of when she had stumbled across the waif whilst wandering the borderlands. Lileah had looked gaunt, even back then, and even more so after her horrific injury, followed by the twisted ministrations wrought upon her ruined body by Krashnar.

'Darlia...'

The dark images morphed again, this time showing her Krashnar's awful visage. She recalled the insidious shaper's disgusting dry and dirty cracked lips, along with his flicking tongue, the thought of which made her feel uneasy. The image of her tormentor quickly morphed into something else entirely. At first, she mistook the ephemeral image for that of an arachnid creature, akin to the Septlari. However, there were only five digits, as opposed to seven. The manifestation slowly descended towards her, reaching down from up high, as though seeking to crush her in its menacing grasp. Her breathing became shallow and her body started to tremble, yet despite being aware of the changes and the fear that she felt, she was unable to dispel the apparition, which continued its advance towards her.

'Darlia!'

She suddenly flinched. The images had gone. Her skin felt clammy and she was breathing rapidly. Nathanar's hand rested upon her right shoulder in a bid to calm her whilst she tried to compose herself.

'What is going on, Darlia?'

She said nothing at first, instead focusing on her breathing, trying to get a handle on her frayed nerves.

'Talk to me.'

'I am fine, really.'

'Do not lie to me.'

'This is my problem. You have your own fair share to deal with, given that you are the Captain of The Blades.'

'We share the same bed; your problems *are* my problems.'

'I am dealing with it – I really am.'

'You do not need to keep secrets from me – or your sister for that matter. We are both here to support you. However, we cannot help you if you keep us in the dark.'

'I do not mean to shut you both out, it is just that…'

'Just that what?'

'…I, am not…'

'What is it, Darlia? What prevents you from asking for help?'

'I am not *weak* like that!'

'We are *all* weak. None of us is perfect; we all have character flaws and fall down on occasion. But there is no shame in accepting someone's hand to help each of us get back on our feet.'

'Nathanar, I have been alone for so long, dealing with my own problems. Even when I was with Lileah, it was my job to protect and care for her – not the other way round.'

'I accept that – you can protect yourself. However, I am now making it my job to *care* for you.'

'I do not need looking after.'

'Yes, you do – you still do not know how to tidy up.'

She sat up, grabbed one of her pillows and proceeded to bash Nathanar's face with it lightly, all the while the Paladin smiled at her annoyingly, whilst taking his punishment.

'You jerk!'

'You first called me that when I came over to your tree that time – the place was a dump.'

'I had only just woken up!'

'Shameful.'

She bashed him once more, before realising the futility of her actions, then laid back down.

'I know what you are doing.' she said.

'What am I doing?'

'Putting me at ease, caring for me.'

Nathanar moved closer, before placing his hand gently on her stomach.

'Look, it is late. I appreciate that now is not the time. However, you cannot keep this, whatever it is, locked up inside of you indefinitely – it will eat you up.'

'I know.' she said reluctantly.

'Tell me everything in the morning. After that, we will find a solution to your problem, together.'

'Very well.' she said, before closing her eyes.

Unbeknownst to her lover, Kirika had already scried the answer to her problem, yet they lacked the strength to execute the solution themselves. Come the break of dawn, she would present the course of action to Nathanar, praying that the Paladin possessed the conviction necessary to execute their wish. Despite all that Nathanar had seen and done, she knew – without the aid of her second sight – that her request would be a true test of the Paladin's mettle. If the Captain of The Blades truly did care for her, he would see to it that her sister's brutal proposal was done.

EIGHTEEN
Withdrawal

After completing the transfer and reassuring the woman of their imminent departure, he replaced her gag, then signalled for Jacob to give him a hand. Together, they gently manoeuvred the woman's chair so that she sat directly opposite the door to her hab. Upon their departure, he had promised the woman that they would leave the door open, so that other residents could come to her aid after they had taken their leave.

'Are we set?' asked Ezra.

'Yes. I have completed the transfer.'

'Then let's go find those go bags.' said Ezra.

'What is their location?' asked Ryan, curiously.

'I will update you all once we get out of here.' he said, deciding it best to play his cards close to his chest.

He chose to ignore the subtle sneer on Ezra's face – there would be ample time for bickering once they were back at the facility.

'Let's go.'

Doing his utmost not to engage with their victim, he bowed his head as they crossed the main living area. He told himself that his lack of acknowledgement was for the safety of their mission, but in truth, he was ashamed, doing all he could to hide his guilt. He was about to reach for the door's controls when a high-pitched yelp sounded from behind. He spun around to see Ezra slowly pulling his fist from the woman's stomach, with her now doubled over in pain and clearly struggling to breathe, tears streaming down her face.

'You fuc--' he started to cry, before Ryan covered his mouth and pressed him hard against the wall of the hab.

'Do not make a scene. *He* ordered us to rough her up a little.'

Ezra pulled his right arm, before striking the woman hard across the face with the back of his hand. Again, the woman let out a muffled yelp. He writhed, trying to break free from Ryan's powerful grasp. Jacob stood motionless, as if frozen, paralysed with fear. The boy's eyes were wide with terror.

'It is done.' said Ryan, loosening his grip.

'You fucking shits!' he said, as Ryan removed his large hand from his mouth.

'Let's get out of here.' said Ezra, who turned and left the winded woman still tethered to her chair.

'We are leaving.' said Ryan, moving towards the door's controls.

'Fuck you – find your own way back.' he said, moving to assist the injured woman.

'She's young, rich and insured – she'll get over it.' said Ezra.

The callous statement fuelled his anger, causing his rage to boil over. He tuned and threw a reckless punch towards Ezra's face, falling just short of his target. Ezra quickly grabbed his hand, twisting it hard, forcing him to the ground in pain.

'I never liked you!' said Ezra, vehemently.

'Where are the go bags?' asked Ryan.

'As if I wou--'

Ezra immediately applied further pressure, forcing him onto his back to avoid his wrist being broken.

'We do not have time for this.' said Ryan.

278

Thinking fast, he rattled off a fake set of coordinates, hoping that the urgency of their situation would be enough to convince them of his words. The pain in his wrist was immense, causing his eyes to water. Ezra released the grip on his hand before heading towards the door.

'Come with us, or stay here – it's your choice.' said Ryan.

'Get lost – both of you.'

'She's not worth it.'

'I said, get lost!'

'Screw him.' said Ezra, 'Let the Peacekeepers deal with him.'

'Fine.' said Ryan, who then turned towards Jacob. 'You coming?'

The ginger-haired boy was clearly petrified. Unable to deal with the volatile situation, Jacob stood motionless – the gaunt teenager had not moved from his spot since the violence began. He felt sorry for the kid, who was clearly paralysed by fear; theirs was a world where such inaction meant that you were invariably caught, leaving the authorities to mete out punishment. Fight or flight, those were the responses that provided any hope of surviving. Yet Jacob had learned neither, choosing instead to go to ground, cowering in the hope that things would naturally abate, without any ill lasting effects.

'Stay here and the authorities will soon pick you up – is that what you want?' asked Ryan.

'Look at him – he's no good to us. I say that we cut him loose.' said Ezra, spitefully.

'Fine. We are leaving. If either of you have any sense, you will follow us.'

Ryan opened the door, after which the pair promptly left, making their way calmly back down the corridor. He quickly moved to the door, closing the exit behind the two thugs before returning to the injured woman.

'Help me untie her.' he said, hoping for some assistance, yet Jacob remained rooted to the spot. 'Fine, go and get her some water.'

He removed the woman's gag before scrambling to untie her restraints. She continued to gasp for air following the savage blow to her abdomen, all the while making terrible noises that sounded like broken cries of pain. The awful chorus made Jacob shudder, eventually causing him to abandon his position and make for the kitchen area.

'You are going to be OK.' he said, desperately trying to reassure the woman.

The sound of glass shattering sounded from the kitchen, followed shortly afterwards by that of running water. Jacob's nerves were obviously shot. Nevertheless, the boy had at last found a means of coping with the stress, moving him to action.

After a short while, Jacob returned, by which point he had fully untied the woman.

'Follow me.'

Regardless of his aching wrist, he hurriedly scooped up the injured woman and carried her towards, what he assumed would be, the hab's sleeping area. The door to her bedroom quietly slid open.

'Lights.' he said, illuminating the room with a soft glow.

Gently, he laid the woman down upon the room's large bed, careful not to make any sudden jerky movements.

'Pass me those.' he said, directing Jacob towards the pillows scattered across the bed.

He slowly elevated the woman's head, using the pillows to prop her upright before requesting the glass of water from Jacob. Bringing the glass towards the woman's lips, he slowly tipped it forward, allowing her to sip the cool liquid. She gulped noisily, before gently pushing the glass away with her left hand.

'Why…are…you doing…this.' she said, still trying to catch her breath.

'I am so sorry that this has happened to you.' he whispered, his words wracked with guilt. 'If there is--'

'Leave…me alone.'

'I need to ensure that you are--'

'Go away!'

The woman continued to wheeze, still struggling for air. Her eyes were red and tears streamed down her cheeks. He felt truly awful, like some kind of evil monster. As he turned his head away in shame, he noticed a picture of the woman on top of a bedside cabinet. There were two women in the picture, one of whom now lay beaten before them, struggling to compose herself. Yet, it was the other one who prompted his jaw to drop suddenly. He turned to Jacob, directing the boy's waning attention towards the image. Jacob turned and stared at the image. The boy's ruddy face immediately became ashen, drained of all colour. Jacob's reaction confirmed his own understanding of the situation – there was no mistaking it. Panic stated to gnaw at him, doing its best to cloud his judgement. Sensing that Jacob was about to break, they could not afford to linger any longer. Satisfied that the woman could now take care

281

of herself, they needed to start digging themselves out of the hole into which Sebastian had thrown them.

'We are leaving.'

There were more Louperdu to the west than they had anticipated. The mist had masked the pack's presence well, making it difficult to read their numbers. Having learned of their vulnerability to the light, the spirit wolves reverted to their physical states and were now aggressively assaulting their position in waves. The scouts' unerring accuracy with their weapons was a marvel to behold, with each projectile connecting flush with its target. The awful sound of the Louperdu yelping in pain filled her ears, but the squad's combined talent alone was not enough to enable them to hold their position. Despite maximising the use of the high ground to their advantage, the spirit wolves had significantly reduced the gap between them and were now leaping towards the western edge of the rooftops.

'Fall back!' she cried, initiating the squad's planned withdrawal.

Both teams immediately fell back, with the space occupied by the former front-runners no longer being filled as the scouts continued to withdraw to the rear of their respective columns. Although a well-conceived strategy, in practical terms at least, executing the teams' manoeuvres proved more difficult than expected due to the gaps between the outbuildings. Their wraith wings allowed the scouts to glide from one rooftop to the next, whilst their comrades maintained the teams' rate of fire. Even so, the task became increasingly difficult with the enemy slowly lapping around their position. They could no longer solely focus their attention to the west, as the spirit wolves started leaping up the sides of the outbuildings.

'Watch your flanks!' she heard Klein cry in the distance, before striking another of the creatures in the face, sending the lifeless corpse rolling over the edge of the rooftop.

She quickly glanced towards Rayna whilst nocking another arrow onto her bowstring. The Guardian had her hands full, but appeared to be phasing in and out of sight, allowing her to cut down her foes with relative ease. Accepting the situation for what it was, she focused her attention on acquiring her next target before releasing her next deadly arrow. The projectile embedded itself into the torso of a spirit wolf leaping between the outbuildings. The released animal cratered upon impact with the roof opposite, its limbs now lifeless and therefore unable to absorb the impact of the creature's landing. The scout at the front of her column withdrew, after taking their shot against the same foe. The inefficiency of attacking the same target was not lost on her. Yet, the urgency of the situation, in addition to the lack of communication in battle, had resulted in the outcome nonetheless, allowing the Louperdu to close the gap between them further. The awkward situation placed further pressure on the scout next in line, increasing the team's risk of faltering. Recognising the strain on their formation, she called out to Krisis, hoping that the adolescent dire wolf could buy them enough time to re-establish their rhythm.

'Krisis! We *need* you!'

Two more spirit wolves leapt up onto their roof; one approached from the west whilst the other hit them form the northern edge, catching the team off guard. Whilst nocking

283

another arrow onto her bowstring, she took several steps back, trying to put some distance between herself and their opponents. The lead scout took aim at the spirit wolf to the west. She glimpsed the flash of moonlight reflecting off the small blade as the projectile struck its target, yet the amorphous silvery shape in her periphery continued to press its attack. Cold logic dictated that she ignore the incident, leaving fate to decide the scout's outcome. However, her heart demanded otherwise. Ignoring the threat to herself, entrusting her team to protect her, she pointed her arrow west, taking aim at the injured Louperdu now crouched low, ready to pounce on its prey. Having witnessed the beasts in battle several times, she now had a good feel for their speed and movement. Taking aim two paces in front of the creature's muzzle, she released her arrow the instant the spirit wolf twitched. The injured Louperdu unwittingly leapt into the path of the projectile, the arrow impaling the side of its skull, bringing immediate release. The creature's body sailed lifelessly through the air, following its original trajectory. However, its sudden loss of agility allowed the scout to evade the incoming corpse with ease. She could see the immediate relief in the scout's eyes. Yet, their expression quickly became one of concern.

'Leyla, to your right!'

With no time to prepare another arrow, she had little choice but to defend herself with her bow, using it as a poor means of blocking her assailant's incoming attack. Before she could finish turning, the weight of her opponent crashed down upon her, violently knocking her down. The back of her shoulders thumped against the roof. However, this time, she was able to keep her head up, staring down the open maw of her attacker with only the grip of her bow between

284

them. She heard shouts and cries around her, none of which made any sense due to the acrid stench of the creature's open maw overwhelming her senses. Before she could fully comprehend what was happening, the unbearable weight was wrenched from her, followed by a spray of silvery blood that splattered across her face.

Something pulled her body backwards as she wiped the blood from her eyes, before blinking repeatedly to restore her sight. When her vision finally corrected itself, she saw one of the scouts wrestling with her opponent, tightly gripping a pair of knives sunk deep into the spirit wolf's neck. Krisis was also present. The dire wolf had engaged another of their attackers towards the western edge of the rooftop, buying the team time to recover its formation.

'Thanks for the assistance.' came a strained voice from behind her.

It dawned on her then that the scout she had saved was now the one dragging her down the column, away from the font line.

'I can stand.' she said, placing her free hand upon the roof to steady herself.

The scout ceased dragging her body, helping her to stand instead. Glancing down at her body, she saw no obvious physical damage, aside from the few aches and bruises that she felt.

'Thank yo--'

Before she could finish offering her thanks, an awful scream pierced their ears. Two more spirit wolves had leapt onto the roof and were savagely mauling one of the scouts at the head of the column. Despite aid from both Krisis and The Guardian, the enemy's superior numbers were beginning to take their toll. The thought of abandoning one

285

of their kin was anathema to her, but in close combat, the Louperdu clearly possessed the advantage. It was now apparent to her just how awful the burden of leadership could be, how it forced one to question their ideals when weighed against the survival of those under their command. They desperately needed space to re-establish their formation. The prospect of abandoning one of her kin sickened her, yet the needs of the many took priority, despite the wound to both her heart and pride, let alone the imminent loss of life.

'G...go!' screamed the ravaged scout.

The two Louperdu had their jaws clamped around the scout's limbs, now gushing crimson, and were viciously pulling their prey in opposing directions. The heinous sight drained the colour from her face, yet she knew deep down that they could ill afford to squander the opportunity gifted to them courtesy of the scout's valiant sacrifice.

'Withdraw, now!'

'Callum, what are we doing?' asked Jacob, in a panic-stricken voice.

'Do *not* say my name!' he said, infuriated by the boy's stupidity. 'We need to leave the building at once.'

As fortune had it, when they reached the foyer, the security officer on duty had abandoned his post. In all likelihood, the guard was busying himself with his rounds – that or taking a piss. Either way, he did not care. Given the shit that had gone down, they were due a reprieve. A sense of relief washed over him as they vacated the building unchallenged. Once outside, he waited until they were a good fifty meters from the building before picking up the pace.

'Where are we going?' asked Jacob once more.

'To the agreed rendezvous site, followed by a detour.'

'But the others will be there.'

'Doubtful – I gave them a false location.'

'Callum, we are screwed; when we get back, they will pound the shit out of us!'

'They may not come back.'

'What do you mean?'

'I think that Sebastian planned all of this.'

'Eh?'

'Think about it. He knew that I would not react well to that assault. Furthermore, he knew that you would panic and freeze.'

'You're saying that Sebastian deliberately sabotaged us?'

'Yes.'

'Callum, that makes no sense!'

'Sebastian wants me out of the way, quickly – that much is obvious. I do not buy his working together bullshit for one minute. Whereas you, on the other hand, have proven that you cannot be trusted, that simple coercion will steer your path – that is not a quality he needs once he leaves the facility.'

'OK, I get that. But why would he throw Ryan and Ezra to the wolves?'

'Ezra is a fucking sociopath and Ryan is a little too calm and intelligent for my liking. If they fail to make it back, Sebastian will have fewer problems going forwards.'

'What do you mean?' asked Jacob, whose face was awash with panic. 'Of course they will make it back!'

'Are you so sure? Do you really think they will stroll back to the facility wearing *those* clothes, given that surveillance will be tracking our movements once the authorities get wind of the assault?'

'Ezra's not going to give a shit about that!'

'True, but it was Ryan who wanted the coordinates. Also, you more than most should know that I am no stranger to the heart of the metropolis – you snuck a peek at my book after all.'

'That woman friend of yours!'

'Yes. As such, I know the Peacekeeper patrol routes in and around the library pretty well. Where then do you think I sent Ryan and Ezra?'

'Why would you endanger her?'

'You idiot. I directed them towards one of the surrounding patrol routes.'

'Oh.' replied Jacob meekly.

'This group was carefully designed to fail – Sebastian made sure of that.'

'Then the true rendezvous location is probably--'

'A dud – of course it is. Which is why we are headed elsewhere, once we have confirmed my suspicion.'

'But--'

'Enough.' he said abruptly, having grown weary of Jacob's incessant worrying, not helping his own mental state.

'If you want to get out of this mess, please, just do as I say and stop constantly questioning me.'

Jacob remained silent for the remainder of their journey, giving him time to think. It was probable that the rendezvous point was a trap, designed to implicate them further. Therefore, he decided to hang back and observe the location from across the street. The coordinates directed them to what looked like shared office premises, based on the signage affixed to the front of the building. The likelihood of Sebastian previously infiltrating the building or – as was the more likely the case – having directed one of his pawns to do so in his stead, was low; there was something not right about the choice of premises, though he could not place his finger on it. Either way, he had accomplished his objective: he had seen the location for himself, furthermore, the stop facilitated an indirect route to their next location, helping to cover their tracks. With no intention of using Sebastian's escape route, he proceeded to direct Jacob to their actual destination.

It was getting late, with very few people still wandering the streets, which would make them look suspicious if they inadvertently encountered a patrol. Despite the late hour, he felt sure that Kaitlin – recently promoted to the position of assistant curator – would still be up, poring over her books. When they finally arrived at the library, the heavens opened, releasing a deluge of heavy rain. He banged noisily on the door to the library, trying desperately to attract the librarian's attention. By the time the door gingerly opened, the rain had soaked them through.

'Kaitlin, it's me – Callum.'

'Callum, what are you doing here at this hour?'

'Mind if my friend and I come in to dry off?'

'Yes of course, come in, both of you.'

Jacob was shivering when finally they entered the building, not surprising given the lack of meat on the boy. Although, he could not tell if nerves were in fact responsible for Jacob's visible unease, likely caused by Kaitlin's long-sleeved dress shirt, fitted pencil skirt and black-framed glasses.

'Given your ridiculous attire and those poor excuses for moustaches, dare I even ask what the pair of you have been up to?'

'Perhaps we should move onto the next question.' he said, not wishing to involve the librarian any more than was necessary.

'Oh, Callum – I always knew that you would be a work in progress.' she replied, giving them both a wide smile. 'Who is your friend?'

'Jacob.' he said. 'We attend the same orphanage.'

'I see.' replied the librarian, studying them both with a curious expression. 'You could have at least picked some clothes that fit you better. Still, it is a slight improvement, I guess.'

'Cut it out.'

Kaitlin giggled, making the most of her opportunity to ridicule him. Jacob's face was pale, like that of someone suffering from anaemia – the youth looked like he was about to die.

'I may have embarrassed your friend.'

'No – I'm pretty sure that you terrify him.'

Kaitlin instinctively swept back her silky, raven-black, long, straight hair. The attractive twenty-something young woman had no business working in a library; in his mind, Kaitlin should have been a model or working some other role in the beauty industry.

'So, I guess that I better get you both undressed?'

Jacob started to shake even more, so much so that he thought the boy would soon pass out. He turned to Kaitlin, giving the librarian a pointed stare.

'You've had your fun. Perhaps you could pay us for your late evening's entertainment with a change of clothes?'

'I believe that we have some bits upstairs in storage: old uniforms, lost property – that kind of thing. Nothing particularly glamorous though, I am afraid.'

'That will do, we just need to change our appearance.'

'Callum, what have you done?'

'He did not do anything wrong – this is entirely my fault!' blurted Jacob, suddenly.

The librarian studied the nervous boy with interest, tying to discern more information.

'Kaitlin, despite what you may hear, I *will* put things right.'

'Callum, I do not doubt you. If you say that you will do something, I know that you will – you are the most determined, strong-willed, person I know. In any event, you are both drenched. Let me get you both a change of clothes and a hot drink.'

'Thank you – you are the best.'

'I know.' said Kaitlin, before giving them both a playful wink.

NINETEEN
Conflict

Both columns withdrew. Slowly, they were pushed towards the heart of the settlement due to their enemy's oppressive nature. No matter how many spirit wolves they released, more took their fallen kin's place. Although the terrain worked to their favour, hindering the enemy's movements, they had not anticipated such large numbers. As their limbs began to tire, the scout's rate of erosion increased, with each loss taking a heavy toll on the teams' morale. The Guardian continued to slaughter her foes using her strange, but equally deadly, falchions, providing a symbol of hope for those within sight. However, Rayna's tenacity alone would not be enough to hold the teams together. Frayed nerves, fatigue, and the mistakes that inevitably ensued would be their undoing. Most of the regiment's forces had been deployed to the east and were busy dealing with the main visible threat. However, now that the mist had cleared, with the Louperdu taking on their physical forms, it was clear that they lacked the numbers to maintain their formation. They needed another strategy, but amidst the turmoil, there was precious little time to think. Furthermore, the distance between them, coupled with the growing discord of battle, made communications increasingly difficult.

'Come together!' she cried. 'Single column! Rayna, take point!'

Recognising the urgent need to reform, the scouts quickly gave ground, adopting their new formation. Klein joined her at the middle of the fresh column.

293

'We are running low on arrows, knives and scouts!'
said Klein, as another horrible scream pierced the air, as if
to punctuate the veteran scout's words.

'Resupply is not possible.'

'Then we must shortly engage in close combat.'

She knew all too well that their rate of attrition would
increase, exponentially, the moment they ceased firing, yet
their options were limited.

'Agreed.'

She pulled another arrow from her dwindling supply,
nocked the projectile onto her bowstring and took aim. Her
arrow tore through the night, finding its mark with deadly
alacrity, reducing the enemy's numbers again. Yet despite
their training and combined skill, the silver tide continued to
rise as more of the Louperdu leapt onto the surrounding
rooftops, gradually encircling them.

'Defensive circle, now!' she cried, desperate to meet
the enemy's change in tactics with at least some kind of
resistance.

Once again, the scouts quickly reorganised, with Klein,
Krisis and herself at the heart of their deployment. The
Guardian, too, fell back, joining the western edge of the
formation. Rayna was drenched in sweat, her dark red hair
clinging to her face and neck.

'This…is it – last stand!' cried The Guardian. 'Do
whatever it takes!'

She could feel her heart pounding in her chest, as
though about to explode from the stress of battle. She had
three arrows left. Assuming that each found their mark, it
would not be enough to repel the invaders. In that moment,
as she watched the enemy continue to encircle them, her
thoughts turned to Zealia, her mind tormented again by

images of the Blade Adept's savage release – would she meet the same ghastly end?

Before her mind could reach the obvious logical answer to her morbid musings, a volley of arrows struck the Louperdu, causing several to fall from their rooftop perches. Each of the arrows was an impossible shot, striking their targets from unimaginable directions. One of the spirit wolves suddenly bent and contorted, its limbs snapping backwards, as though wrenched by invisible hands, wrapping around its body whilst it howled in pain. The violent scene, compounded by more invisible heinous acts, continued to unfold with the adjacent lupine's head rotating up and around, violently snapping the creature's neck. Another launched sideways, as though struck by an invisible boulder that smashed into its flank, causing the creature to release an ear-splitting yelp.

'Fire!' she cried. 'Break them!'

Emboldened by their change in fortune and her fresh call for battle, the scouts unloaded the last of their projectiles onto the enemy. Every shot found its target, whether through skill or manipulation from their unseen ally. Another volley of arrows rained down on the enemy, sending more of the creatures from the rooftops, crashing to the ground with sickening thumps. Unable to fathom the sudden cause of their demise, several of them dissolved into mist, prompting others to follow suit.

'These bastards are *mine*!' cried Rayna. 'Cover your eyes, all of you – now!'

She did as instructed, closing her eyes whilst raising her free arm to shield her face. Amber hues briefly lit the back of her eyelids. After opening them, following The Guardian's all clear, the enemy's numbers had dwindled

295

significantly. Unable to get a handle on their revised tactics and with their numbers diminishing fast, the Louperdu began to break and flee. The enemy's offensive circle fell apart, their formation falling into disarray as they fled in all directions. Despite having beaten the enemy back, more spirit wolves were launched though the air, their bodies horribly twisted and contorted before contacting with the ground. Some bent in half like folded cloth, whilst others had their heads twisted, causing their necks to snap like twigs. Whilst the macabre sight disturbed her, there was no denying its effectiveness.

Few of the spirit wolves now remained. Those still defiantly holding their ground snarled at them from the rooftops opposite.

'Recover as many of your weapons as possible.' ordered Klein. 'Take from our fallen comrades if you must.'

'Here, take these.' said a familiar voice behind her.

She spun around and was immediately taken aback by the presence of a female Freylarkin with shoulder length blonde hair. The Freylarkin's magnificent wraith wings were unfurled, glistening in the moonlight along with beads of sweat adorning the Valkyrie's brow.

'Natalya!' she cried.

'Did you miss me?'

'You survived!'

'Take my bow and these arrows – I can defend myself without them. Put them to good use.'

Hooking her bow over her shoulder, she gave her remaining arrows to Klein before accepting Natalya's gifts.

'It packs more punch than that toy you are accustomed to – should give you another ten paces.'

'Thank you. What about you? You look exhausted.'

'That exchange took a lot out of me. Nevertheless, I will recover.'

'Ah, so you decided to show up at last.' The Guardian jibed, giving Natalya a playful grin.

'You can go back to sleep now Rayna – like that time at Bleak Moor.'

Before Rayna could retort with further joyful banter, a thunderous howl rung out through the night, demanding their immediate attention. The harrowing noise caused a shiver to run down her spine. Though she had not heard a sound quite like it before, regardless, the source of its origin required no introduction. As promised, The Moon King had come for them.

They said their farewells to the Library's custodian and proceeded to make their way back to the facility, trying hard to avoid detection of any kind. It felt good to be out of their stuffy attire, which allowed them to move more swiftly. They barely spoke during the return journey; there was a lot for each of them to process. He could tell that events weighed heavily on Jacob in particular.

'Please, Callum, accept my sincerest apologies.' said Jacob softly, as they neared the facility. 'It was not my intention to endanger your friend.'

'What did you think would happen? Did you honestly think that Sebastian wouldn't use the information against me?'

Jacob paused for a moment, before responding meekly. 'I didn't think.'

'Obviously – but you *need* to.' he said, earnestly. 'This world loathes our kind. Do not give it more ammunition than it already has.'

'I am truly sorry.'

He paused for a moment, studying the downcast expression on Jacob's face. Jacob's apology was indeed sincere. Though reluctant to absolve the boy of his actions, it was clear that he had not intended any harm to come to Kaitlin. In addition to fear, Sebastian had preyed upon Jacob's naivety. He truly despised the gang leader, especially given that Sebastian had barely sullied his own hands in the matter.

'I accept your apology.'

'Will *she*?'

'Who, Kaitlin?'

'Yes.'

'She is to never know of this matter. I do not want the friendship that she and I have to be her undoing – I hope that is clear?'

'I understand.'

'Good. Now let's get moving – we only have a few hours left until dawn.'

'Wait…what about the photograph?' asked Jacob, appearing to panic once more. 'We will be found out for sure – we cannot go back to our dorm.'

'You remember what I said, right?'

'Yes, but, what if Ryan and Ezra *did* make it back? Plus, Sebastian will be there too.'

'I will deal with it.'

'How?' asked Jacob, who was now beginning to freak out as the reality of their situation fully sunk in. 'They're

298

going to catch up to us. Sebastian will make sure of it, once he realises that we made it back.'

'At last, you're finally starting to think ahead.'

'But what good does that do for us? Either way, we are screwed, Callum.'

'Not if we get ahead of the situation. You said yourself, Sebastian does not yet know that we are back – we can use that to our advantage.'

'How?'

'Leave that with me. All we need to do right now is find somewhere in the facility where we can remain out of sight and lay low until morning.'

'Then what? Sebastian will be on us before we can put our side of the story forward.'

'He will not get the chance – you and I are going on the offensive.'

'What does that mean?'

'It means that you and I need to take responsibility for our actions, instead of shrinking from them. Sebastian is able to smell the stink of fear all over you – he will use your cowardice to his advantage. It is time that you stopped avoiding confrontation and instead, dealt with it.'

'Like you say, I am a coward, Callum. I cannot *deal* with this.'

'You are only a coward *if* you allow your actions to define you as such. It is within your power to alter your destiny, instead of allowing others to forge a path for you.'

'But--'

'Do you want to keep endangering others indirectly through your actions, or lack thereof?'

'Of course not!'

'Then *deal* with it, Jacob – I will be your guide.'

It was huge – much bigger than she recalled from their earlier encounter in the clearing, where they had first met The Moon King, slumped against its birthing tree. Even with her poor night vision, she could see for herself that the beast's silhouette towered over the surrounding outbuildings at over twice their height – her lack of visual definition could not mask the terrifying fact.

'It is enormous!' said Klein, clearly astonished by the height of their opponent.

'How can we hope to defeat that!' said Leyla, clearly unnerved by The Moon King's indomitable presence.

'Don't think like that!' she said, 'That is exactly what it wants: to feed on your fear. Do not give it the satisfaction, or allow terror to govern your actions. It is just another opponent; we will deal with it as such.'

The Moon King howled again, before raking the claws of its right hand across an adjacent outbuilding, tearing through its roof. The roof sheared off, its dark silhouette sailing through the night, briefly obscuring the Night's Lights, before crashing noisily on the ground.

'Rayna – your orders?' asked Leyla nervously, rattled by The Moon King's monstrous display of strength.

She stared intensely at the beast, her furious glare boring into the creature's skull. She could sense her past hatred rapidly surfacing once more, the loathing and disdain towards her old rival wrenched from the depths of her soul by Sebastian's deliberate actions, designed to goad her.

'It wants me.' she said, in a grim voice unbecoming of her.

'You are the bait!' said Leyla, quickly assembling the few scraps of information that Lothnar had granted her. 'Rayna, what is your relationship with that monster?'

'That is a story for another cycle. In any event, it wants me to go to it.'

'You cannot.' said Klein. 'The terrain is to our advantage. We cannot break cover – it must come to us.'

'Klein is right, Rayna. Do not let it goad you.' said Natalya, still weary from the extended use of her ability.

'This creature has manipulated me before – that will not happen again.' she said, vehemently. 'I want you all to fall back and lend aid to the others.'

'Rayna, we will not abandon you!' said Leyla, ardently.

'It will not come for me if the numbers remain in our favour.'

The Moon King smashed its fists into another outbuilding, causing the structure to list before slowly crumbling to the ground. It howled again, in what was an obvious ploy to incite dread.

'Fall back, now! Make it appear as though we are panicking. It needs to believe that it has broken our morale, else it will not advance.'

'All scouts, run back to the others – put on a show.' ordered Klein, before giving her a subtle nod.

'I *am* coming back for you!' said Leyla.

'I will be disappointed if you do not. But for now, at least, you must play the role of the coward – play it well!'

The Blade Adept gave her a fierce stare before fleeing, along with the others. As instructed, the scouts abandoned their positions, falling back in small groups, thus providing the illusion of desertion amongst their ranks. Klein and Leyla were amongst the last to leave, followed by Krisis –

the dire wolf was duty bound to protect them, therefore where Leyla went, Krisis quickly followed.

'Natalya, you need to leave.'

'A Valkyrie does not flee – you know this, as will The Moon King. It will look suspicious if you remain here alone. Ergo, if you want our ploy to seem convincing, I should stay.'

'This is a fight that I cannot possibly win, am I right?' she said, giving the Valkyrie a sidelong glance, before turning her attention back to her real opponent.

'You and I, we fight together, Rayna.' said Natalya, before turning to bark a series of faux orders at those fleeing. 'Hold your ground – get back here, now!'

'We don't need them!' she cried, leaning into the role. 'Deserters are of no use to me.'

The Moon King howled once more before lowering his stance, easing into what appeared to be a position conducive for a charge.

'Perhaps you should have held onto that bow of yours.' she said, considering their limited options.

'Klein said that the objective is to lure the beast fully into the settlement. Once we have achieved that, we will use superior numbers to bring it down, using the terrain to our advantage.'

'You saw how easily it tore those buildings apart. What makes you think they will be of any use to us?'

'Would you rather its fists struck the wood, or your pretty face instead?'

'A fair point.'

The Moon King lurched forwards suddenly, before pushing itself forward using its powerful hind legs. Unable to pursue a direct route though the settlement, it weaved an awkward path towards them using its preternatural agility to maintain good pace. The manner in which the beast moved around the obstacles within its path was truly astonishing, the sight of which caused her blood to run cold.

'Shit, we have a *big* problem.' she said, readying her twin falchions. 'Go, now! I will blind it!'

The sound of splintering wood and falling debris filled the air as the patchwork juggernaut bounded towards them, paying no regard to the structural damage caused by its thunderous advance. Natalya quickly abandoned her position as instructed, rapidly moving southwest using her wraith wings in an attempt to get around their opponent. The Moon King paid the Valkyrie no heed, instead choosing to focus its attention exclusively on her.

'Come and get me, you *bastard*!'

With less than ten paces separating them, she released two intense beams of white light from the palms of her hands, allowing her falchions to hang loosely, gripped only by her index fingers and thumbs. The Moon King dipped its head as the twin beams seared the fur along the top of its head, leaving trails of burnt flesh running from its brow across the top of its dome. Irrespective of the pain, The Moon King continued its advance, raising both of its fists, intent on obliterating the outbuilding upon which she stood. With its torso exposed, she darted forwards using her wraith wings, striking the beast on its right flank. The creature moved with frightening speed, forcing her to use The Ardent Blade's unique ability far earlier than she had hoped. The tip of the blade had barely penetrated the flesh of her opponent, meaning that disengaging would be difficult. Nevertheless, she had no choice but to engage the weapon's Waystone to avoid being smashed by the beast's massive

303

bulk. She slid her thumb over the Waystone embedded into the grip of The Ardent Blade, just below its cross-guard. The Moon King blurred and stretched into a streak of fast-moving light. Her body felt light as the familiar sense of displacement pulled her through the fabric of reality, causing her vision to fade rapidly. After being mercilessly stripped away, her surroundings were immediately reinstated, albeit she was now facing the rear of her opponent. Her hasty attack meant that the angle of her exit was all wrong, made worse by her lack of measure, meaning that The Ardent Blade was now lodged in the beast's torso. The failed attack caused her to lose her grip on the blade. In her mind, she could already hear the low-sounding groan of Nathaniel's disapproval, scolding her for letting go of her weapon. Regardless, she had missed her opportunity and now needed to focus on her escape.

The Moon King's huge fists smashed into the outbuilding where she had stood only a moment before, instantly reducing it to ruin. The beast then swung its fists around towards her, rotating its upper torso, sending rubble, splintered wood and other detritus headed her way. She backed off immediately using her wraith wings, but failed to react quickly enough to evade the hail of shrapnel flying towards her. Something caught her right arm, numbing it instantly, though she managed to maintain her grip on Shadow Caster despite the jarring impact. Bits of rubble scraped across her face and dust filled her eyes, temporarily blinding her. She fell to the ground, impaired by the fallout from her opponent's brutal attack. Directing her free arm towards The Moon King, she channelled an enormous amount of light energy, releasing the searing blast point-blank into the beast's rear. The Moon King released a deafening howl, causing her ears to bleed due to the close proximity, as its back immediately caught fire. Through the maelstrom of dust and flames that had engulfed the ruins behind her opponent, she saw the beast's massive bulk hit the ground with an earth-shaking thump. The Moon King rolled around on the ground, doing its best to smother the flames attempting to consume it. She tried to stand, but her body was too weak, drained of strength by her devastating counter-attack – she needed time to recover. Before she could finish assessing her precarious situation, her body lurched backwards, pulled by invisible hands that sought to drag her away from the burning hell of her own creation.

'Callum,' said The Director, 'What on earth are you doing here at this hour?'

It was six o'clock. They had spent the remainder of the night hidden in the storage cupboard designated for the cleaners' cleaning materials, before making their way to The Director's office moments prior to his arrival. He could still smell the potent stench of bleach and other cleaning products, as though the chemicals had somehow taken up permanent residence in his nostrils. At best, both he and Jacob had managed to snatch an hour's sleep. His eyes were heavy and his body felt sluggish. Nevertheless, he needed to liaise with the facility's director of operations before Sebastian could spin events, presenting a skewed version of reality.

'And why is Jacob with you?'

'May we speak privately in your office?'

'Of course, come in.'

The Director unlocked the door to his office before inviting them both in.

'Take a seat, the pair of you.'

It felt good, slouching into one of the office's worn leather chairs, as though a great weight had been lifted from his shoulders. He had barely spoken to The Director since their initial meeting upon his arrival at the facility. Even so, he felt safe in The Director's presence, as if protected by the man's power and influence over the facility and its residents.

'You two look awful – what has happened?'

'We're in trouble.' he said, cutting to the chase.

'What have you done?' asked The Director, who lent back into his seat.

'Sebastian!'

'I cautioned you to stay away from him, did I not?'

'It is my fault.' blurted Jacob, interrupting their conversation. 'Callum was coerced by Sebastian because of what I did, it was--'

'Stop!'

The Director stood up and walked over to the office's small window where he peered into the gloom outside. He remained there for a while, staring at the blurry lights outside before turning to face them.

'Does this have anything to do with Anastacia's sister, dare I even ask?'

'Yes.' he said, unable to mask the shame in his voice.

'How did--' Jacob began to ask, before The Director waved his hand, demanding silence.

'I had a call with Anastacia less than an hour ago. She is taking a personal day to care for her sister, who was violently assaulted last night.'

'We did not hit her!' blurted Jacob.

'Yet you were clearly complicit! Hence you are both here – do you think that my office is some kind of confessional?'

'Callum tried to stop…' said Jacob in a cracked voice, before giving way to tears.

The gaunt teenager had finally reached his limit. Jacob was no longer able to cope with the mounting pressure. He watched as Jacob bent over and began to sob whilst murmuring incoherent words that made little sense.

'Callum.' said The Director sternly. 'Start from the beginning – I want a candid account of *everything* that has transpired.'

It was fast approaching seven o'clock by the time he finished his detailed account. He left out nothing, ensuring that he described events as accurately as possible. For the entire duration of his account, The Director had stood by the window, barely moving whilst he recited the awful events. Jacob had continued to sob and was now listing in his chair, as though about to fall onto the floor.

'Callum, this information puts me in an extremely awkward position. If I do not report this, I will also be complicit in this crime.'

'Yes, I realise the gravity of the position that we have put you in.'

'If you understood this to be the case, why did you bring this information to my attention?'

'Sebastian needs to be held accountable for his crime.'

'But in order to achieve that outcome, you, too, will be burned at the stake.'

'My options were limited. Besides, I must atone for my own part in this miserable affair.'

307

'So, you would sacrifice yourself to take down another?'

'Yes.'

'And what about him?' asked The Director, pointing his right index finger towards Jacob.

'He is no longer able to cope with the situation.'

'Indeed.'

The Director paced around the room, before finally retaking his seat.

'I am bound to follow due process. However, it is within my power to massage that process.'

'So, what does that look like?'

'In the eyes of the law, you are still minors. Given that you have no living parents, the system has placed me in charge of your care. Whilst I cannot turn a blind eye to these events, or change the inevitable outcome, I can slow the process down, at least for the two of you.'

'Will that not harm your career?'

'My career is over, Callum. I am due to retire and Anastacia will take over the running of this facility – do not pretend that you were blind to the fact, else it will undermine the validity of your forthright account.'

'My apologies.'

'In truth, you have given me an unexpected parting gift, one far greater than any recognition of service for my time spent here.'

'I do not follow.' he said, his curiosity piqued by The Director's candid words.

'Sebastian is a loathsome individual. He preys on others, forcing them to carry out his agendas. However, for all his faults, he is well educated and cunning. Until now, I have been unable to find a way of deposing him from this facility. Your written testimonies will give me the ammunition I need.'

'Then you will do this?'

'Yes. However, be under no illusion, you will all be held accountable for your actions.'

'As it should be.'

'I will process both you and Jacob last. Given that I am due to retire, there will be no ramifications for my tardiness in executing your expulsions from this facility – you *should* be able to see out the remainder of your time, or at least most of it, here, provided that you stay out of trouble.'

'Thank you. May I please ask that you process me before Jacob? He needs the time to prepare, far more than I.'

'Very well. Of course, you realise that Sebastian will potentially come after you?'

'Sebastian does not shoot from the hip, he will play the long game. He and I will likely cross paths in the future, beyond the walls of this facility. In the meantime, he will no doubt have more pressing concerns vying for his time.'

'And should you two meet again, how do you propose to deal with him without my protection?'

'I *know* him now – I have seen him for what he is. That gives me an edge, or at the very least, puts me on an even footing.'

'I wish you good luck in the future, Callum. Although, please refrain from using such suicidal tactics going forwards.'

'Despite their effectiveness?'

'You were fortunate on this occasion. There are few in this ruined world of ours who are able to retire.'

309

TWENTY
Destruction

'Are you crazy? That was near suicide!' said Natalya angrily.

The Valkyrie had pulled her to safety. Together, they watched The Moon King collapse several neighbouring outbuildings, blindly smashing into them, reducing them to ruins with its massive bulk as it rolled across the ground smothering the greedy flames licking at its body.

'Why does release not come for it?' asked Natalya, wiping the sweat from her brow. 'How is it possible for something so malformed to withstand such a devastating attack?'

After dousing the flames, The Moon King slowly rose to its feet, absent The Ardent Blade, which had since lost its purchase on its host. The seared flesh across the beast's body, caused by the ravenous flames bred from her intense light, shimmered under the light of the moon's caress. The silver light bathed the creature's body, its healing touch slowly reversing the damage wrought by her powerful conflagration.

'What is going on?' asked Natalya, clearly dumbfounded by what they were witnessing.

'It's regenerating – the light of the moon is restoring its flesh'

'How is that even possible?'

'I do not know. Regardless, we must finish it quickly, whilst it is still recovering.'

Natalya turned her attention to one of the battered dwellings, now little more than a ruin, barely standing in the wake of The Moon King's violent rampage. Using what

311

strength she had left, the Valkyrie used the power of her mind to wrestle one of the fallen roof timbers free of the mangled wreckage. The pitted length of wood hovered above the ground, turning slowly in the air until it orientated itself to align with The Moon King's position. Natalya grunted loudly, before sending the wooden shaft flying towards its target, violently spearing the beast's torso. The length of wood ruptured the creature's right shoulder, punching though its charred skin, spraying silver blood across the ground. The Moon King released another deafening howl, before grabbing the wooden shaft with its left hand. The dogged creature painfully wrenched the length of wood impaling its body free, before hurling the bloodied timber towards them. They immediately ducked, pressing their bodies against the ground. She could feel the displacement of air above them as the lump of wood sailed over their heads, smashing into another of the dwellings behind them. Something hit Natalya, causing the Valkyrie to cry out in pain.

'Natalya!'

'Rayna, go!' cried the Valkyrie, whose left leg had taken a nasty hit from shrapnel.

'I'm not leaving you.'

'You have to release it. Now go!'

She groaned, willing her body to move despite needing more time to recover. Her muscles resisted her; they felt tired and sluggish, like waking up from a bad night's sleep. Nevertheless, she had to move in order to put some distance between herself and Natalya. It was her that Sebastian wanted; in all likelihood, her old adversary would pay the injured Valkyrie no heed now that she stood opposite the monstrous creature in battle.

312

The Moon King glared at her with piercing red eyes, all the while basking in the restorative light of the moon that illuminated the destruction surrounding them.

'Like me, you were a fool to accept its offer.' she cried. 'You should have stayed in the Wild, you *bastard*!'

The Moon King continued to fix her with its sinister stare; she could not tell if Sebastian understood her words, or whether he was simply trying to intimidate her. Either way, it was clear that she was at a disadvantage, giving up strength, agility, height and raw power to her opponent. Furthermore, she was keenly aware that Sebastian possessed a shrewd mind, making the chances of beating her opponent even worse. Still, despite her worsening odds, something nagged at her, like a loose thread demanding to be pulled. She recalled the words telepathically communicated to her by her opponent during their initial encounter, when Lothnar had temporarily bridged their minds.

"I am ancient."

What exactly did those words mean, she wondered. Just how long had Sebastian been in Freylar. Furthermore, if the beast was indeed ancient, as he claimed, had his mind waned during that time? Certainly, the creature's senses had not dulled, and yet he had allowed himself to be lured into the heart of the settlement with no provocation on her part – the Sebastian she knew would have demonstrated greater restraint.

The Moon King hunched over before swinging the back of its left forearm towards a battered crate lying on the ground. Splintered wood hurtled towards her, akin to grapeshot fired from artillery. She dived right, seeking cover amongst the detritus littering the ground, but was unable to evade all of the beast's incoming projectiles. Her

313

left leg went numb, taking a heavy knock from a piece of flying debris, although it failed to penetrate her skin. She scrambled to her feet and began limping towards her opponent, desperate to close the gap between them. Clenching her left fist, she began manifesting a ball of light within the palm of her hand, ready to blind her opponent once more. The Moon King outstretched its muscular arms, before howling again whilst it forced its claws to elongate. Silver blood dripped from the tips of its fingers as its blackened claws extended outwards. The creature's monstrous claws grew in length, each one now akin to a poorly maintained short blade. Saliva dripped from the beast's open maw, splattering across the dusty ground with a wet patter that made her stomach churn. She willed herself forwards, trying her hardest not to give into fear, yet the terrifying sight made her shudder.

Satisfied with his gruesome new weapons, Sebastian crouched on his hind legs, ready to run her through. However, before the beast could charge her position, she heard the familiar snarl of Krisis. The dire wolf darted out from behind one of the ruins to the rear of her opponent. With lightning speed, Krisis leapt onto The Moon King's back, wrapping his jaws around the rear of the beast's thick muscular neck. The loyal dire wolf sunk his razor-sharp teeth deep into the charred flesh of their opponent, seeking to put an end to the conflict. The Moon King responded, bringing its left arm around the right side of its neck, impaling Krisis with its menacing claws, causing the dire wolf to release an awful yelp that made her stomach churn. Sebastian drew back his arm, wrenching Krisis from his neck, before hurling the dire wolf into one of the burning ruins.

'I'll kill you!' she screamed, overcome with rage.

Still limping towards her opponent, she released a beam of searing white light from the palm of her hand, directing it towards Sebastian. Consumed by her hatred, she paid little attention to the placement of her attack, content for it to connect with her opponent, wherever the shot landed. The beam struck The Moon King's right arm, slicing through muscle and tendons, almost severing the limb under the shoulder joint. Still clinging to its host, hanging on by fraying tendons and a sliver of charred meat, the damaged limb hung uselessly by the beast's right side. Yet despite the devastating wound, the damage was already starting to repair itself. Wisps of silver-grey smoke coiled around the strands of exposed tissue, slowly taking form in an attempt to reconnect the immobilised limb. Although dawn was approaching, it would be some time before The Moon King lost its advantage. Before the light of day could lend its aid, the outcome of their battle would already be decided.

'*Rayna, stay on him.*'

Lothnar was sprinting towards The Moon King, fast approaching from the east, treading the path of his fallen lupine companion. Acknowledging the Paladin's orders, she dug deep, drawing on what little strength she had left, desperate to burn her opponent one more time. She tried to manifest her inner light again, but the ball of light struggling to take form in the palm of her hand winked in and out of existence. Seeing her falter, Sebastian lumbered towards her, nursing his right arm, which was now urgently seeking to reattach itself properly. The savage wound hindered the beast's advance, making the charge impossible. Nevertheless, one-on-one, she was hopelessly outmatched and would likely fall to a single swipe of her

315

opponent's good arm. Even so, she would not concede; the act of giving up was simply not part of who she was. Doggedly, she continued to limp forwards, tightening her grip on Shadow Caster whilst slowly closing the gap to her opponent.

'Here!' he cried, looking to draw The Moon King's attention away from Rayna. 'Do not ignore me, you bastard!'

It grated on him, using a throwing knife taken from a fallen comrade under his charge. Nevertheless, the enemy's superior numbers demanded such distasteful behaviour, forcing the scouts to rob from those no longer in need of a weapon. Releasing the stolen projectile, he targeted the tendons reforming above the beast's right arm, using his expertise to spin the blade on its horizontal axis. The blade sailed towards its target, slicing through the remaining tendons still attached to the beast's arm. The weight of The Moon King's damaged limb was too much for the fledgling tendons to bear, causing them to elongate and snap. The massive arm fell to the ground with a sickening thud, causing The Moon King to roar in pain.

In spite of its loss, the monstrous beast stooped to grab the discarded limb using its remaining good arm. Sebastian turned around, swiping towards him in the process, using the severed arm as a makeshift club, enabling his opponent to attack in a wide arc. He dived over the incoming strike, narrowly avoiding being pulverised in the process. Despite his sharp reactions, the attack managed to clip his feet, sending him head first towards the ground. His face hit the dirt hard, the sudden impact disorientating him in the process. His vision faded – only for a brief moment – and his head felt numb. The only noise he could hear was the sound of his own laboured breathing – everything else was muffled – accompanied by the familiar metallic taste of blood on his lips.

Before he could right himself, The Moon King readied its sinister club once more, intent on swinging it back towards him, looking to finish the job. However, despite its murderous intent, the beast was robbed of the chance to release his soul when two arrows viciously slammed into the creature's skull. The Moon King staggered forwards, rocked by the sudden attack. One of the arrows protruded from behind the beast's left ear, whilst the other was buried deep into the back of its head. Regardless of the brutal damage inflicted upon it, The Moon King continued to stand. The enraged beast hurled its severed limb towards its fresh opponents, obliterating the dwelling upon which they stood. With his vision restored, he watched in horror as both Leyla and Klein disappeared from sight, engulfed by the structure collapsing beneath them.

'Come on!' he cried, deliberately goading the juggernaut once more. 'Turn and face me!'

The Moon King directed its bloodied muzzle towards him whilst simultaneously drawing back its left arm, ready to beat him to a pulp. In a single fluid motion, he pulled both custom dirks from his belt, releasing the deadly projectiles towards The Moon King's face with unerring accuracy. The twin blades found their mark, impaling the beast's eye sockets causing their crimson residents to explode. The Moon King roared in pain again, before brushing the dirks aside with its massive fist. The weapons fell to the ground, causing blood to trickle from The Moon King's ruined eye sockets.

317

'*Rayna, you have to finish it, now!*'

With no more physical weapons left at his disposal, he opened a conduit to The Moon King's mind, desperately hoping that in the creature's weakened state he could use his will alone to dominate that of his opponent. That, or serve as a useful distraction in order to buy The Guardian more time, so that Rayna could bring an end to their brutal encounter.

When eventually they returned to their dormitory, Sebastian was gone. Upon investigating the gang leader's sleeping bay, it quickly became apparent that Sebastian had cleared out. The space was a mess; the bed was unmade, the doors to the wardrobe hung open and the bedside cabinet lay on its side. There was a small empty void on the underside of the cabinet, previously concealed by a thin wooden panel now lying on the floor. Any personal effects had gone, along with the essential items one might need to get by beyond the walls of the facility.

'He's gone.' he said, casting his eye over the few effects that remained. 'So much for delaying my departure.'

'I made you a promise, Callum, one that I intend to keep.' replied The Director.

'How did he find out so quickly?' asked Jacob.

'It's possible that Sebastian foresaw this outcome if one of the others made it back and tipped him off.'

'But you said that was unlikely to happen, Callum.' said Jacob in a frightened voice.

'In truth, I do not know how this happened – Sebastian had informants throughout the facility. Either way, he has gone. Dylan and Kyle will be vying for dominant control over this place now. If Ryan or Ezra did manage to make it back, they are not here now, which means that you are safe - they will have more pressing concerns than dealing with either of us.'

'But now that they're outside, what am I supposed to do once I am forced to leave this place?'

'Jacob, you've got to relax. Assuming for one minute that they weren't picked up by the Peacekeepers, that scenario is far from now – you have plenty of time to plan your exit strategy.'

'I need to file a report.' said The Director. 'One that I intend to sit on after it has been submitted.'

'I am in your debt.' he said, acknowledging The Director's favourable decision.

'Think nothing of it – you have provided me with some solace prior to my retirement.'

He nodded gently and smiled, content that his protector could enjoy a moment's reprieve from Sebastian's constant scheming during the final days of his directorship.

'Please see to it that this mess is cleaned up. Also, Callum, I would like you to broker some kind of deal between Dylan and Kyle – I do not want this place descending into chaos now that there is a power vacuum.'

'I will sort something out.'

'No doubt.' replied The Director, who gave him a weak smile before leaving them to tidy up.

After putting Sebastian's sleeping bay in order, they decided to get some rest. It had been a long night, during which they had received little sleep. When pulling back his bed cover, he discovered a small note partially tucked beneath his pillow. He sat down and unfolded the note, which had been hastily written, though, its author clearly

319

possessed a degree of skill with a pen – an art rarely practiced by his kind.

'*You can find me in the Wild. We shall conclude our business there.*'

He remained seated for some time, carefully studying the note, thoughts tumbling though his mind as he reread its words. The Wild was an enormous artificial wilderness at the heart of the metropolis. Most considered the achievement to be a beacon of hope, a reminder of the wondrous accomplishments that humanity could attain, when not consumed with bringing about its own destruction. Still, he had come to view the Wild in a different light. To him, the artificial wilderness was nothing more than a living memorial, a reminder of what humanity had lost. Either way, he had no reason to go there – especially now.

He crumpled up the handwritten note, crushing it in the palm of his hand, before lazily discarding it on the floor. He fell back onto the bed, pulling the cover over the lower half of his body. A heavy weight lifted from him as he allowed himself to relax, finally releasing the tension in his muscles. The only thing that mattered to him was Kaitlin's safety, which he had now ensured. In time, Sebastian would fade from memory, becoming little more than another dreary footnote in his miserable life. Closing his eyes, he smiled, content that he would never cross paths with the manipulative sociopath again.

'Leyla, Klein!' she screamed.

Her heart immediately sank as the dwelling beneath them collapsed in on itself, swallowing her comrades as it fell into ruin. The Moon King roared furiously, warranting her full attention once more. As she continued to limp towards the beast, thin steams of blood tickled from its empty eye sockets, glistening in the moonlight as they slowly ran down its face. The Moon King's sinister red eyes were gone, replaced by a pair of small blades that protruded from the bleeding empty recesses of the beast's ruined face. Lothnar stood defiantly before Sebastian, absent of any physical weapons. The Paladin bore a grim expression, one of fierce concentration, as he no doubt sought to use the only remaining weapon in his arsenal – his mind. She grimaced in pain, forcing her damaged leg to propel her forwards towards her age-old adversary, determined to put an end to its miserable existence. In light of his status – a fellow agent of release – Sebastian's soul was one that she had no qualms feeding to her omnipresent overseer, The Deceiver. Yet, despite the death and destruction The Moon King had wrought, she could not shake the feeling of guilt gnawing at her, knowing that – in part at least – she had been responsible for Sebastian's path to ruin, along with the violence that had ensued.

The Moon King brushed aside the blades digging into its skull, knocking them to the ground. Robbed of its sight, the beast's muzzle twitched, using its keen sense of smell to locate its opponents. Raising its left arm high into the air once more, the monstrous creature readied itself, seeking to release the Paladin from his mortal coil.

'It's me that you want!' she cried. 'It's time for us to conclude our business.'

Sebastian paid her deliberate attempts to goad him no heed; the cruel ex-gang-leader knew that in order to destroy her, he need only to release those that truly mattered to her.

Krisis, Leyla, Klein – all had been snuffed out by the merciless killer's supreme might.

'Get away from him!' she screamed, doing her best to block out the burning pain in her leg. 'I'll kill you!'

The feeling of hatred she once harboured towards her past resurfaced once more, despite her many previous attempts to quell the anger deep within her. The waning light in her free hand flickered into existence once more, growing in intensity along with her feelings of revulsion towards her enemy. The muscles in The Moon King's arm became tense as it sought to pulverise its opponent. Yet it struggled to rain down its remaining fist, its surviving arm wavering in the air whilst invisible forces fought valiantly to hold its enormous fist in place. Sebastian released another deafening roar, no doubt attempting to use the blast of sound to disrupt those responsible for its restraint.

'*You must release it – neither Natalya nor I can hold it for much longer!*'

Releasing the pent-up light jittering in her left palm, she blew a hole clean though The Moon King's left leg, causing the beast to fall with a ground-shaking thump. The Paladin cried out in pain, clawing at his eyes, which she had inadvertently blinded with her ferocious light. Fuelled by rage and adrenaline, she willed her exhausted body forwards then fell onto her opponent, sinking Shadow Caster deep into the beast's right leg. The wisps of smoke that continuously wreathed the edge of the sinful blade reacted vigorously, sensing the presence of a meal fit for the ages. The Moon King's body went into immediate spasm, juddering violently as though something sought to possess its ruined body. What remained of the patchwork fur still lining the beast's hide rapidly fell out, spirited away by the breeze. Once revealed, the beast's exposed skin darkened in colour, before fading to a greyish-white, devoid of any pigment. Patches of The Moon King's skin rapidly desiccated, those sections still charred from the flames being the first to wither. Before long, The Moon King's enormous corpse became hollow, an empty, dried up husk since parted from its malevolent soul, now incarcerated within her gluttonous blade. After devouring its meal, Shadow Caster felt heavier, fat on the venerable soul it had greedily consumed. She released her grip on the blade, causing The Moon King's desiccated remains to deflate as the Dawnstone falchion dropped to the ground, crushing part of the husk-like structure as it fell.

Her rage quickly subsided, and it was then that she realised that the battle with her nemesis was finally over – but at what cost? And what of its children, she wondered. Lothnar was writhing on the ground in pain, clutching his eyes, and she spied Natalya, face down in the dirt, less than ten paces away. The settlement was burning and she could hear the familiar howls of the Louperdu in the distance. With their leader gone and dawn close to breaking, it would not be long before the remaining spirit wolves broke and fled, retreating to their dens to lick their deep wounds.

She dropped to her knees and leant back, resting on her heels, trying to ignore the pain in her injured leg as she looked up at the fading night sky. Droplets of rain fell from the sky, landing on her cheeks before rolling down the side of her face. Drained and exhausted from the battle, she sat quietly, unable to move, listening to the cries of those injured during the fighting. When trying to will her body to action, it rejected her commands, no longer able to carry out her wishes due to fatigue.

'*That soul belongs to me. The Guardian is not permitted to retain it.*'

'Go...to hell!'

'*The Guardian has failed in their task.*'

'I am...happy...to disappoint you.'

'Rayna!' cried a familiar voice from behind her.

She tried to turn, but her body felt stiff and unresponsive.

'Rayna, it is me, Gaelin.'

'Gae...lin... When di--'

'Those who survived the original attack have returned, along with others from neighbouring settlements. I found most of the survivors cowering in the forest, before I rounded them up. We heard the distant screams through the night and came at once. Where are the others?'

'Gone...buried in...the rubble.'

'No, I cannot accept that. Where are they?'

She turned her head slowly towards the ruined buildings where she had last seen her friends. She watched in awe as the farmstead leader quickly began rallying those surviving scouts, along with the others he had mentioned, who suddenly appeared around her. Working together, Gaelin's hastily assembled crews began sifting furiously through the burning wreckage, desperate to locate other survivors.

'There is a survivor, over here!'

'Gaelin, are you there?' he said, struggling to make sense of his surroundings.

He stood up, almost tripping over in the process. His sight had forsaken him, affecting his sense of balance. Blind, he fumbled around in the dark, following the sound of unfamiliar voices. Groping around, sightless, his arms outstretched, all he could do was follow the cries of those calling out.

'Gaelin!'

'I am here, Lothnar – take my arm.'

'Who have they found?'

'It is Leyla.'

'How is she?'

'Not good; she was crushed by debris – she needs a renewalist.'

'Get word to Lazrik, he will make that happen.'

'Your eyes.'

'Forget that. How is Rayna? Where is Krisis?'

'Rayna will be fine. Her leg is in bad shape and she is physically exhausted. We are still sear--'

'You have to find him!'

'We are doing everything that we can. Please, sit down.' pleaded Gaelin.

'Find him, Gaelin. Please, you must find--'

'We found another one.' a voice suddenly cried out.

'Come.' said Gaelin, pulling his arm.

The farmstead leader strode towards the distant voice, directing him to where the latest body had been discovered. The reliance on another frustrated him, yet he had little choice but to allow himself to be led around by his fellow ruling council member.

'Be mindful of your footing – there is debris everywhere.'

'It is Natalya!' the voice cried again.

'What is her status?' asked Gaelin.

'She is unconscious.'

'Find Lazrik. Get every available renewalist over here at once!' Gaelin commanded.

'Yes, Gaelin!' someone close to them replied.

'There is another!' cried someone else.

The sound of voices all around him was disorientating. Without his sight, he had no proper sense of direction. He felt helpless, unable to lend aid to those in urgent need. Without Gaelin to direct him, he was truly lost.

'Who is it?' asked the farmstead leader.

'He carries a bow.'

'Klein, it has to be Klein.' he said. 'Is he alive?'

'Barely. If we do not get him to a renewalist immediately, release will surely follow.'

'See to it, now!' he commanded, unsure whether or not he faced the person to whom he spoke. 'Gaelin, *where* is Krisis?'

'I do not know – we are searching.'

'Search faster!' he replied angrily, instantly regretting his words. 'I am sorry. I did not mean to offen--'

'Lothnar, *you* must be the one to help us find him.'

'How? My sight has abandoned me. I canno--'

Gaelin released the grip on his arm, before placing them squarely on his shoulders. He could sense the farmstead leader move closer, in all likelihood a ploy to reaffirm his words that followed.

'It is not your sight that we need right now my friend, it is your *mind*.'

The humble, plainspoken nature of the farmstead leader's voice helped to calm him. The words Gaelin spoke cast his thoughts back to the battle for Scrier's Post, in particular, his mental duel with Lileah. Unable to best the telepath's unprecedented ability, he recalled the moment

326

when he projected his mind in search of aid from another.
Gaelin was right, they needed him – they needed his ability.
Opening a conduit to his mind, he projected his psyche
outwards across the burning wreckage. His astral projection
jumped between the minds of his kin, offering each a
cursory scan as he formed the briefest of connections to
them, in search of Krisis. What seemed like an eternity of
searching passed. Frustration started to get the better of him
as he struggled to locate the dire wolf.

'Damn it, where are you.'

'Relax, breathe and keep looking.' said Gaelin. 'You
will find him.'

After probing the minds of those scattered around them,
he began to lose hope. Having turned over every stone,
what more was there to do? Chiding himself, he started
over, trying to convince himself that in his haste he had
overlooked something. Whilst jumping from the mind of a
young male, he inadvertently detected a weak presence
amongst the ruins to their left. Willing his projection
towards the faint sign, he discovered a mind far simpler
than that of one belonging to a Freylarkin. He detected no
response from the fading presence, which slowly
diminished with each passing moment.

'I have located him!'

'Where?'

'Follow me.'

The irony of the blind leading the blind was not lost on
him. Taking Gaelin's hand, he stumbled across the debris-
strewn battlefield, homing in on the dying mind ahead.
Inevitably, he tripped and fell, finally falling foul of the
detritus littering the ground, seeking to impede his efforts.

327

Gaelin helped him to his feet, placing a long slender arm around his waist to aid him.

'I see him!' said Gaelin suddenly. 'Up ahead.'

'Take me there!'

Together they stumbled through the ruins, the dying mind's proximity drawing ever closer.

'Here.' said Gaelin, guiding his hands towards the ground. 'Krisis is here.'

His hands contacted with the dire wolf. Krisis' body was cold and his fur felt damp. His companion barely drew breath, making virtually no sound at all.

'He is leaving us. Gaelin, we need a renewalist, now, else he will not make it.'

Bending over, he slipped his right arm around Krisis' limp neck, cradling his fallen comrade. Slowly lowering his body to the ground, he gently pressed his face against his dying friend's muzzle, trying hard to fight back the tears of anguish that he felt.

'*Do not leave me. Help is on its way. You cannot leave me – that is an order from your master!*'

TWENTY ONE
Fallout

'You cannot ask this of me!'

The Captain of The Blades paced furiously around the chamber, like a caged animal seeking to escape its confines.

'We did not mean to break this to you so suddenly. However, this situation cannot wait – we need to get in front of this.' she said, trying to quell the Paladin's uncharacteristically foul temper.

'No – there *has* to be another way!'

'Nathanar.' said Darlia quietly, trying to ease her lover's obvious fury. 'This is the right thing to do.'

'How can you say that? Besides, this does not solely affect *you*!'

'I realise that we are asking much of you. Still, you are the only one that I could bear to perform such a task.'

'That which you ask of me is both sick and barbaric! I will not do it!'

'It is the *only* way that we can bring an end to Krashnar's legacy.' she said.

'Nathanar, please do not hate me – I could not bear it. I know that our proposal is anathema to you. Still, it is time that I accepted my original punishment. My sister is right; I must atone for my crimes. The people *will* find out about this – it is only a matter of time – and I cannot be seen to be flouting our laws. Doing so will bring down the ruling council, which Freylar can ill afford.'

'This is the best outcome that we can hope for, Nathanar.' she said, taking her sister's good hand before pressing it gently against her face.

'I get that! I understand what you are both saying. However, I cannot bring myself to commit such an act – it goes against my very being.'

'The Guardian has become a symbol of passion and unity for our people. However, you, Nathanar, represent the ideals that we strive towards: you are pure, untainted and incorruptible in the eyes of our people. You alone can serve this miserable sentence without its lingering stain clinging to you.' she said, sincerely, as she gazed deeply into her sister's violet eyes. 'We humbly beg your assistance in this matter – you are the only person who can make sense of this wretched task for the rest of us.'

'Damn it, Kirika!' cried Nathanar, who promptly turned and kicked the granite wall next to him, seeking a means of venting his anger. 'When am I supposed to do this?'

'I need time to convince the ruling council of this course of action – I may encounter some resistance.'

'You mean from Lothnar?'

'Perhaps.' she said, releasing her sister's hand before turning to face the Paladin. 'I received word via Sky-Skitter earlier this morning. The scout regiment has successfully completed its campaign against the Louperdu. They have suffered heavy losses. However, the threat has been dealt with.'

'What! Why am I only learning of this now?'

'I wanted to meet with you privately first, to discuss everything that has passed. None of this information can be made public in its raw form. The domain needs stability. Lies, constant wars, a change of leadership – all of these things have destabilised Freylar. We must put all of that behind us and close the circle of violence that has dogged us for so many passes.'

Nathanar leant back against the wall and folded his arms. It was clear that The Captain of The Blades felt uneasy with their proposal. Even so, Nathanar was the pragmatic sort, who considered his actions carefully. Furthermore, he was politically insightful, with a good understanding of what made the domain tick. Yet despite his virtues, the Paladin was not so righteous in his ideals that he was beyond the realms of being led astray – both Rayna and Natalya had proven such on a number of occasions. Therefore, with enough coaxing, both she and Darlia were confident that Nathanar would support their endeavour. Besides, it was unlikely that Nathanar would burn his lover – if it were within his power, the Paladin would choose to save all of Freylar's wayward souls.

'I *hate* this.'

'We are asking a lot of you.' said Darlia, softly.

'And you are truly alright with this?' asked the Paladin, fixing Darlia with a commanding stare.

'I have made my peace with it. Krashnar's legacy needs to go away now, for the good of our people and so that I can move forward.' said Darlia, sincerely, who then moved towards her lover. 'I want us to have a future together, but, in my current state that is not possible. I need to rid myself of my past.'

'But the past defines us, at least in part – it is who we are.'

'Yes, but I am incessantly reminded of it, every cycle. It is that constant reminder that impairs my judgement. I know that I can never truly forget my past and all the questionable things that I have done. Even so, if I can separate myself from it, that burden can be left behind me, allowing me to move forwards towards a brighter future.'

331

'I presume that you have both scried this outcome?'

'Yes – a decision of this magnitude demanded it. We would never leave something this important to the whims of fate.'

'You two are worse than Rayna and Natalya.'

'I would not necessarily say that we are any worse – neither of them share a bed with you.'

Nathanar gave her a weak smile. They both knew the hurt that their proposal would cause him. Nevertheless, the Paladin was strong enough, mentally, to carry out their request.

'I will do as you ask. However, I need to sit with this for a while.'

'Thank you.' she said, fully accepting the Paladin's need to come to terms with the situation. 'Know that you have my eternal gratitude, Nathanar, along with my sister.'

Darlia wrapped her arms around Nathanar, who in turn reciprocated. The Paladin dipped his head, resting it gently on that of her sister's.

'I am not oblivious to your feminine wiles – they do not define my actions. I will do that which you both ask of me for the stability of the domain and for no other reason. Should either of you ever ask me to commit an act that goes against the interests our people, I will step down and leave this place.'

'Understood.' she said, accepting the Paladin's just response. 'Should it ever come to that, I ask only that you run me through with a sword, before turning your back on us.'

'How are you holding up?'

'I have had better cycles.' replied the weary Paladin.

'They have managed to restore your sight I see – no thanks to me.'

'You did what you had to. Besides, I was lucky – Klein was not.'

'I heard that his face was crushed beneath the wreckage.'

'Yes. They have repaired most of the damage, but his right eye is lost – there was nothing left for the renewalists to repair. Leyla is with him, helping him to recover from his ordeal.'

'What of Leyla herself?'

'Her legs were badly crushed. Fortunately, her bone structure has been repaired. Given enough rest, I am told that she will fully recover.'

She slowly approached the bed upon which the injured dire wolf lay. Lothnar sat on the floor, slumped against the wooden cot, gently stroking Krisis' matted fur. It filled her with hope to see the dire wolf's diaphragm contract and expand, a sign that the animal was "out of the woods". She sat down beside Lothnar, joining him in comforting his companion.

'I nearly lost...'

The words stuck in the Paladin's throat, preventing him from finishing his sentence. She had never seen the nomadic scout look so vulnerable; Lothnar's habitual steely expression had gone, replaced by one of deep concern. Those who knew the Paladin well were aware of how deep his relationship with Krisis ran – if it meant giving his right arm to save his loyal friend, he would gladly make the sacrifice. Instead, all he could do was pray that the work of the regiment's renewalists was enough to help Krisis pull through.

333

'He's tough – he won't be going anywhere. Besides, do you really think that he will want to miss out on more of Kirika's cuddles?'

'You make a good point.' said Lothnar, who laughed sombrely. 'Incidentally, how is Natalya doing?'

'Oh, she seems to be her normal mischievous self; getting wiped out during the battle has not changed her much. She is supposed to be resting. However, I saw her earlier, limping around the settlement teasing some of the scouts.'

'That is good news. Given the losses the regiment has sustained, a bit of normality is very much welcomed – I am sure that she is aware of this.'

'I think so; despite her carefree demeanour, there is always a reason for her antics.'

She ran her hand along Krisis' back, watching the dire wolf's slow, heavy breathing. It would be some time before he was fit for travel.

'I assume that you know that we have been called back to the vale?'

'Yes – I read the message scroll that was received earlier.'

'Will you be returning with us?'

'I do not wish to leave him. However, it is important that the people see the scouts return. As their commander, I should be the one to lead them home. In addition, I must personally address the family members of those released in battle.'

'Would you like me to assist you in this?'

'Thank you, but no. It is my duty as their former commander – I must shoulder the burden.'

'What about Krisis?'

334

'Gaelin has kindly offered to watch over Krisis for me. Since he has been tasked with overseeing the repairs to the settlement, Gaelin will be remaining here for some time with his people – they need his leadership during what will be a tough time. As such, he has asked me to proxy his vote at the ruling council meeting.'

'About that, do you know what the council intends to discuss?'

'Yes. It is a politically delicate matter requiring careful management. That said, I fully support the proposal put forward by Kirika – Gaelin, too, is in agreement.'

'Which is?'

'Rayna, your battle with Sebastian has not diminished your curiosity I see. Nevertheless, I am not permitted to discuss the matter with you. You will learn of it soon enough.'

There was a lull in their conversation. Hearing Sebastian's name mentioned again cast her mind back to the events that had transpired during her brief stay at the facility. After the delayed investigation into the matter, she had been forced to leave the facility, at which time she moved into the metropolis' abandoned business district, home to the Shadow Class. It was a rough transition, proving to be an incredibly difficult time in her life. Nevertheless, the hardships she faced only strengthened her resolve. Despite the handwritten note, it was not until she foresaw the Rout when she eventually stepped foot into the Wild – strangely enough, out of necessity as opposed to curiosity. In any event, Sebastian was not to be found by the time she relocated into the artificial wilderness. Still, knowing that, at the time at least, they shared the same space, ensured that her guard was continuously up during her first couple of years of residency. After which, she soon forgot about the sordid affair, her mind burying the incident so that she need not relive the assault on Anastacia's sister over again.

'Tell me.' said Lothnar. 'What happened to Ryan, Ezra and Jacob?'

'I couldn't say.' she said, surprised by the sudden question. 'I gather that Jacob remained at the facility until the age of eighteen; he and I never met after I left. As for the others, Ryan and Ezra never returned – I do not know what became to them.'

'Then it is over.'

In truth, it was not over. Blinded from the truth, the Paladin failed to realise that Sebastian's soul was, in fact, incarcerated within Shadow Caster. Her hatred towards the former gang leader had compelled her to take Sebastian's soul, as if some kind of morbid trophy. Instead of feeding The Moon King to The Deceiver, she had taken her opponent's soul for herself, offering it to the Narlakin trapped within her Dawnstone blade, whose ravenous appetite ensured that the soul stealer accepted its glorious prize. Had she shown her opponent mercy, denying her master the spoils of war, or had she claimed her position of dominance purely for selfish reasons? She could not tell.

'What am I, Lothnar?'

'I do not follow.' replied the Paladin, giving her a curious look.

'I have been given the title of The Guardian. Yet, I was brought to this world under false pretences, to carry out the bidding of an overseer who I cannot see. One that demands the release of others though my actions – I am its reluctant harbinger of release. Since my arrival in Freylar, I have been a catalyst for war and unrest, both of which seem drawn to me – I even managed to piss you off, when I robbed Alarielle of her body.'

'Nonsense!' said Lothnar, who suddenly grabbed her arm and stood up.

Before she could react to Lothnar's sudden outburst, the Paladin marched her over to the door, pushing her outside into the settlement. It was light outside; the warmth of the sun bathed the farmstead, encouraging the surrounding flora to flourish and the crops in the fields to grow. The sound of construction filled the pleasant air, accompanied by the chorus of Sky-Skitters perched in the trees. It felt good to be outside; her spirits were quickly lifted, now that she was away from the melancholy of watching others recovering from their wounds.

'Without you, this would not exist! Furthermore, the community living here, along with others like it, would not be able to work the land. Our people would go hungry, with the prospect of release knocking at their doors. Do not lose sight of all the good that you have achieved since coming to Freylar. This is your home now. You fight to protect it – having never once given up – and that is how you have *truly* earned your title, not by serving some faceless overseer.'

'Thanks – I needed to hear that.' she said, giving Lothnar a heartfelt smile.

'You must not shoulder this burden alone. Also, you cannot do everything by yourself; some challenges are just too great – I have learned this lesson the hard way. There will be times when you need friends to support you, which you have.'

She thought about the Paladin's words. Lothnar was right. She had friends and there would be times when she would need them to lean on.

'I'm sorry. I have these moments, occasionally, when I seem to relapse.'

'We all get knocked down from time to time – that will likely never change. Even so, if we keep getting back up and, most importantly, learn the lessons that life's challenges impart, those events will make us stronger, allowing us to continue forward in our journey.'

The way in which the Paladin spoke to her triggered an emotional response that she could not fathom. When she first met Lothnar, beneath the arena, the Paladin had rebuffed her vehemently, demonstrating nothing but loathing towards her. Since that time, they had gradually learned to coexist. Yet, the nature of their relationship eluded her. It did not feel like a friendship, and for a time she wondered if it was simply a case of developing mutual respect. But now, their relationship was evolving into something different, something that her body longed for, though her mind struggled to embrace the simple biological fact. Tired of trying to understand the changes she was going through, she acted on impulse, grabbing his hand as he had done when leading her outside.

'Care for a walk?' she asked, playfully tugging at Lothnar's hand. 'It is a nice da--. I mean, cycle.'

Lothnar regarded her with a bemused look – she had clearly caught the Paladin off-guard. Given a moment to compose himself, Lothnar's expression quickly mellowed, giving way to a warm smile that put her sudden nervousness at ease.

'I would like that.'

'I think it suits you.'

Klein turned to face her, rotating his head more than usual on account of his injury. The veteran scout had tied a long piece of folded fabric around his head, ensuring that it covered his right eye socket, now robbed of its former tenant. The long scars on either side of the empty hole had almost faded, a testament to the skill of the scout's renewalists. However, as talented as they were, they could only repair damage; regrettably, the renewalists tending to Klein's injury were unable to fabricate a new eye to replace the one lost when the dwelling beneath them collapsed so suddenly.

'What does?' asked the scout, giving her a bemused look.

She playfully tapped him on the right cheek, just below the fabric, mindful of the fact that the empty socket might be causing him some discomfort.

'Oh, I see what you mean.'

She laughed gently, due to the scout's choice of words.

'What a fool I am.' said Klein, quickly acknowledging his inadvertent quip.

'A fool does not shoot an enemy who stands close to three times their height, through the back of the head – you are certainly no one's fool!' she replied, ardently. 'If anything, you are a hero!'

Klein looked away towards the pyres burning opposite them. She could tell that she had embarrassed the scout due to the sudden rush of colour to his face.

'The flames of our fallen comrades burn fiercely, as did their hearts in battle.' said Klein, trying to hide his embarrassment.

339

'It saddens me that we were unable to give Zealia the same send off.' she said.

'It is regrettable. However, you can visit her grave the next time you choose to remember her – those burned on the pyres leave no such lasting mark upon the land.'

'Why do we burn those fallen in battle?'

'It was believed that the act would hasten the departure of our souls, towards the Everlife.'

'*Was* believed?' she queried, puzzled by Klein's choice of words.

'For many, The Guardian's arrival in Freylar has caused them to question their beliefs. In any event, the released warrant our respect in equal measure – their sacrifices allow our people to prosper.'

She silently contemplated Klein's answer as they stood beside one another, watching the bodies of the departed scouts crackle and burn atop the lit pyres. Although Gaelin and his farmstead crews were the ones responsible for hastily building the wooden constructs, it was Lothnar who set them each ablaze the moment the sun dipped below the horizon. As commander of the scout regiment, it was Lothnar's duty to conduct the ceremony – she recalled the brief words spoken by the Paladin moments prior to lighting the pyres.

"You each know these Freylarkin, along with their countless deeds – they were family to us. Know that their final selfless act was to ensure that we each carried on living. We honour them and their sacrifice."

Had Rayna not released The Moon King when she did, the regiment's casualties would have been significantly worse. Even so, the toll on the regiment's numbers was a costly one. Nevertheless, despite their reduced numbers,

340

those that remained were combat veterans, each having fought in numerous battles, including herself.

'What will you do, now that this is over?' asked Klein.

'I…would like to remain with the scout regiment.' she said, 'Provided that Lothnar will have me, of course.'

'I would like that too.' said Klein, catching her off-guard.

It had never been her intention to follow in her father's footsteps, or at least, not so closely. After spending time with the scout regiment, she understood the freedom one felt when serving under Lothnar's command. She wondered if it had been the same for her father, whether he had felt the same sense of liberation when serving in The Blade's vanguard. Furthermore, she was reassured, knowing that the regiment comprised of veterans, led by those who favoured strategy over brawn. Despite operating on the fringes without any immediate support, functioning independently of The Blades' main force, she still felt safe amongst her comrades, knowing that they each had one another's backs. It was a curious feeling, one that she was not ready to give up. Previously, as an outsider, like others, she had perceived the scouts to be aloof and unfriendly, possibly even abrasive. However, things were different now. The scouts were not the difficult child she had once perceived them to be; they were professionals with impossibly high standards, who craved adventure, unwavering in achieving their objectives and dogged to the end. In many ways, the scouts mirrored her own needs and desires. The thought of returning to her previous assignment, a custodian of the vale, no longer appealed to her – she could not go back to her gilded cage after experiencing the thrill and excitement of wandering the

341

land. As such, she was not ready to part ways with the regiment. Once they had properly rested and fully resupplied, she was eager to engage in their next adventure, wherever that took them. Indeed, not knowing where they would be stationed next was what excited her the most.

TWENTY TWO
Atonement

It had been some time since she had publicly addressed such a large crowd. The arena was at capacity; the tiered stone seating was barely visible, its presence masked by the throng of spectators crammed into the amphitheatre. In addition to those seated, there were three standing rows on the floor of the arena, with a fourth sat upon the ground in front. Typically, the arena floor was off limits to civilians. However, some of the space had been permitted for use, at the council's discretion, given the high-profile nature of the events about to take place. Although the act they were about to commit sickened her, she needed as many of the people as possible to hear her words first-hand, so that her reasoning would be delivered as intended and would not be diluted through hearsay.

Her fellow ruling council members stood alongside her, with the notable exception of Gaelin. The farmstead leader's absence was understandable in light of Lothnar's report, following the welcome return of the scout regiment after their successful campaign against the Louperdu. In addition to the ruling council members, Rayna was also present, along with Nathanar, Nathaniel, Natalya, Kayla and her sister. The last time they had come together, united by a single purpose, was during the climax of Mirielle's rule. Now, they were gathered for an entirely different matter, albeit one that was equally distasteful. Given the abhorrent act she was about to command, she had requested that Rarni remain in the Tri-Spires with her mother, Lyra. She realised, of course, that the young Freylarkin had already witnessed the act that was about to transpire. However,

343

scriers like herself could only see past or future events –
they could never be heard.

Raising her left hand slowly, she held it high above her
head, respectfully waiting for gathered crowd to settle.
Once all those present fell silent, she took her place at the
centre of the arena, trying hard to hide her nerves. Though
her confidence had grown much over the last pass, she still
found it difficult to address the public in large open spaces.
In particular, the personal nature of the matter ensured that
her levels of anxiety remained high.

'Thank you all for gathering here this cycle. I realise
that my addressing you all like this is sudden. However, the
ruling council is in agreement that this matter cannot wait
and that you should all be apprised of its outcome swiftly.'

She took a moment to clear her throat, conscious that
those towards the rear might struggle to hear her voice.

'To the matter then.' she said, raising her head so that
everyone could see the sincerity with which she would
reason her case. 'My sister, Darlia, played her part in
instigating the Narlakai invasion at Scrier's Post – most of
you gathered here this cycle will already know of this. You
will also likely be aware that she alerted our people to the
vale's subsequent invasion, allowing us to fight the Narlakai
at Bleak Moor, therefore mitigating civilian losses and thus
protecting our children. Also, she released her former lover
in order to end the war between the Narlakai and ourselves
– she has atoned for her past transgression.'

She paused again, allowing the audience a moment to
sit with her words.

'Even so, it is my grave duty to report to you all that
there is another crime, of which my sister is guilty – a crime

that I recently learned of which, due to the nature of its brutality, cannot go unpunished.'

The audience gasped, taken aback by her candid delivery.

'I am a member of this domain's ruling council, therefore I cannot turn a blind eye to the knowledge that I have gained, even though the information I am about to impart is damning for my sister. Know then, that what I am about to say to you all…fills me with dread. I can only hope that you all concur – as the ruling council has done – that the punishment served here, this cycle, is sufficient, given the extenuating circumstances that I am about to explain to you all. Darlia, will you please join me.'

She turned to face her sister, deliberately holding out her left arm so that she could receive her sister's good hand. Darlia looker paler than ever whilst slowly crossing the floor of the arena to join her, almost tripping in the process as nerves sought to get the better of her sister. Nevertheless, Darlia remained steadfast, the scrier refusing to turn from her fate. Grasping her sister's hand, she turned to face the crowd once more.

'Put plainly, Darlia released three of our kin – she did this brutally, murdering them in cold blood!'

A loud gasp, followed by shocked silence descended over the arena. Shortly afterwards, whispers and murmurings ensued as the Freylarkai turned to one another in bewilderment, seeking to validate her words amongst themselves. She gave her audience only a brief moment to digest the news, thereby preventing the crowd from drawing its own conclusions and – of greater concern to her – reacting too unfavourably, thus potentially lobbying its own collective form of punishment.

345

'My sister's actions cannot go unpunished – the crime is severe! However, her motive was just, albeit not justifiable. The individuals in question *abused* and *raped* my sister's former lover, Lileah, with the intention of harming another whom Darlia has since freed.' she said, vehemently, pausing for a brief moment once more. 'Our former queen, Mirielle, did nothing to balance the scales of justice. This inaction, in turn, caused Lileah to rise up against our people, fuelled by anger and the need for revenge, thus prompting the Narlakai invasion. My sister was also complicit in the initial invasion. For different, but equally valid, reasons, both Darlia and Lileah were consumed and motivated by hatred, which led to their actions. In the case of my sister, the reasons were two-fold: firstly, due to the severing of her left hand by Marcus, at Mirielle's behest, and secondly, because of *this*!'

She swiftly circled around the back of her sister, grabbing Darlia's mechanical claw and thrusting it high above their heads.

'This, *abomination*, is the work of the twisted shaper Krashnar, whose mutated being was released in this arena – immolated by The Guardian.'

She paused again, allowing the Freylarkai to get a good look at Darlia's grim prosthetic hand.

'This punishment, wrought by Mirielle's poor judgement, was too severe! It did not fit my sister's original crime: over-stepping the boundaries imposed on the use of her ability. By exiling Darlia, our former queen condemned my sister, forcing the need for this monstrosity so that she could survive in the borderlands. Over time, it has tainted my sister, who must fight, every cycle, to prevent the malice Krashnar poured into the construction of this cursed artefact from consuming her soul. Ergo, Darlia's own poor judgement was not of her own volition, but instead derived from the evil that still lingers in this construct! Therefore, it is *this* that must be reckoned with – Krashnar's legacy – and not my sister, who has already suffered enough!'

Once more, she allowed the audience just enough time for her words to sink in, yet denied them the opportunity to pursue their own thoughts on the matter – a trick she had leaned well from her former mentor, Aleska.

'Krashnar corrupted our kin, in this very arena, forcing many of us here to release friends and family members. His evil knew no bounds. Therefore, his legacy *must* be extinguished, so that it cannot corrupt our people any further. To this end, the ruling council has decided that Mirielle's original punishment – the severing of Darlia's left hand – will stand, albeit now for the *right* reasons!'

The crowd gasped again, following which many began to nod in agreement, affirming their approval of the proposed sentence.

'Once this punishment has been meted out, Darlia will be formally exonerated, no longer forced to live the life of a pariah due to the actions of others. Therefore, if any of you wishes to challenge the council's judgement on this matter, please do so now! Otherwise, we will now put an end to the misery that had dogged our people, Darlia in particular, for too long now. This cycle of violence must end, so that we can move forward and build a brighter future for ourselves.'

Silence descended over the arena once more, her fierce and well-constructed delivery ensuring that no challenge dared to present itself.

'Very well. Kayla.' she said, turning to face her aide who stood behind them, alongside the others. 'Please bring forward the box.'

The youthful, hazel-eyed aide nervously dragged a wooden box towards them, leaving scrape marks in its wake, carved into the grit and dust of the arena floor. The awful grating noise, caused by the underside of the box scraping against the gravel, made her stomach churn. She started to feel lightheaded and could sense her body swaying as she rocked on the balls of her feet, as though about to faint. Kirika moved to stand behind her, before wrapping her arms around her waist to steady her.

'You and I, we will face this together – I will not abandon you this time!'

'Thank you.' she whispered, acknowledging her sister's attempts to comfort her.

Kayla dragged the box around them, placing it between themselves and the stunned onlookers. Kirika slowly guided her towards the ground, helping her to kneel down before the ominous wooden crate, before moving her mechanical claw into place upon its topmost surface.

'Nathanar, Nathaniel, both of you, please take your positions.' her sister commanded with authority.

Her claw shook violently on top of the wooden box, as though possessed by an evil spirit desperately seeking to escape its bronze, mechanical prison. She tried to steel herself, but her mind kept recalling the awful events at Scrier's Post, when first she had lost her hand. Sensing her anxiety, Kirika maintained the grip around her waist with her right arm whilst they knelt together before the ominous box, using her left hand to steady her jangling claw.

'Kirika, I do not...know if I can do this.' she said, unable to control the sudden burst of tears that streamed down her face.

'It will be over shortly – Krashnar will no longer hold sway over you.' replied her sister, who also began to sob, no longer able to maintain the stoic composure with which she had delivered her compelling argument to all those present.

'I am...not strong enough to do this – I am too weak. Please, I cannot do this, not again!' she said, now trembling in fear.

She looked up, gazing vacantly into her lover's eyes, tears still streaming down her face. The Captain of the Blades loomed over them. Despite her watery vision, she could see the tortured anguish in Nathanar's face; the Paladin looked crushed, as though his world was falling apart. Yet, they had all agreed that he was the most suitable candidate for the awful task, given his untarnished standing with the people. In her mind, she tried to plead with him, but the words would not pass her lips. Instead, she just stared at him mutely, shaking, dreading the foreboding moment when he raised his sword.

'Step aside, Nathanar.' said Lothnar suddenly, who strode quickly towards them. 'Go comfort her – you should not be the one to do this.'

'I thought that I cou--'

'Give me your sword.'

Nathanar passed his impressive double-handed sword to Lothnar, before kneeling beside her, wrapping his left arm around both her and her sister.

'Loth, get it done!' said Nathanar, turning her face towards his own. 'Look at me!'

349

'I am scared.' she blubbered, unable to stop herself from shaking.

'We are both with you this time.'

'Darlia.' said Lothnar, in a sympathetic voice. 'I do this, not out of hatred or spite, but instead, as a gift to you, the most powerful gift of all – freedom.'

There was a sudden swooshing noise as Lothnar wielded her lover's blade cleanly though the air, promptly followed by the stark realisation that her left arm no longer weighed as much as it once had. She turned her head to look at her left arm, fighting her lover's attempts to prevent her doing so. The top of the box had caved in from the impact of Nathanar's sword, now wedged between its wooden batons. Beside the ruined box, lying upon the floor like an upturned Septlim, was her claw – no longer attached to her left arm. Lothnar had cleanly severed the prosthetic hand from her, expertly landing the cut just above its flesh-metal join so that nothing remained of the vile shaper's work. Blood spurted vigorously from her fresh stump, furiously tended to by The Teacher, who was already at work, masterfully healing her severed limb.

'Hold on child, be brave – just a little longer.' said Nathaniel, his words imparted as a father might to a daughter.

She sensed a build-up of heat around the end of her bloody stump. It was slow at first, before rapidly reaching a crescendo and manifesting as searing pain.

'It hurts – Nathaniel, it hurts!' she cried, the pain consuming her, quickly becoming unbearable.

She felt growing pressure around her waist, both her lover and her sister squeezing her tightly, refusing to let go.

350

'It hurts!' she screamed, no longer able to cope with the awful pain. 'Nathaniel! It hur--'

Her vision went dim and her body felt weightless. All she could feel was the searing pain in her arm accompanied by the ear-splitting sound of her own screams. Her vision went dark. The world ceased to exist – there was nothing.

'Rarni, how are you this morning?'

'I am good, thank you, mistress Kirika.'

'Please, Rarni, you do not need to call me that – it sounds so official. You may be my student, but you are also my friend.'

'I like it.'

She smiled in return; given the child's awful curse, it was the least she could do to tolerate the formal address.

'Very well – if that is what you prefer.' she said. 'Shall we go for a walk before your lesson?'

'Yes please – I would like that very much.' said Rarni, eagerly.

Her morning walks with the child reminded her of the time she had spent with Aleska. When the distant cycle eventually came for her student to pass on the knowledge imparted to her, she wondered if Rarni would continue to honour the tradition, as she did.

'Let us walk alongside the river.'

Together, they slowly wandered down the slope leading to the old wooden bridge, away from the Tri-Spires. After crossing the river, they followed its northern bank east, skirting the edge of the woodland as they lazily walked towards the rising sun. She could see the child fidgeting, out of the corner of her eye, itching to unload with her usual barrage of questions.

351

'You are worse than Rayna – go on, out with it!'

'Is there any news of Krisis' recovery?'

'The last report that I received from Gaelin said that Krisis is doing well. Lothnar has returned to the farmstead to bring him back to the vale, now that his companion is well enough to travel.'

'What about your sister?'

'That wound will take far longer to heal. The mental trauma my sister has suffered will take many passes to abate, if indeed it ever truly does. I suspect that, in time at least, Darlia will learn to live with everything that she has endured, finding a way to either bury the past or make peace with it. However, in the meantime, she has Nathanar and us to lean on. We will help her to heal and adjust to her new situation. The important thing to focus on now is that, finally, my sister can begin her true recovery.'

'What happened to it?'

'Happened to what exactly?' she asked, confused by the child's strange question.

'Krashnar's claw.'

'Rarni, you are far too young to be concerning yourself with such awful things.' she replied, unnerved by Rarni's unexpected question. 'However, to answer your question, you will never see it again – I have made certain of it.'

'What did you do with it?' the child persisted.

'I sent it to the Ardent Gate. Heldran, the Knight Lord, has kindly agreed to dispose of it for us.' she explained, reluctantly. 'I do not want it in the vale, or indeed Freylar for that matter. Since I know of no shaper trustworthy enough to undo its construction, I have entrusted Heldran to see that it is lost to us.'

'I see.' said Rarni, in a curious tone of voice.

'Rarni, why do you ask?'

The child stared at her ominously, the glare from the morning sun reflecting off her black, glassy eyes.

'No reason. Mohraine and I were just curious, that is all. I should focus on my studies, so I guess the question is…irrelevant.'

– www.thechroniclesoffreylar.com –

If you enjoyed volume six of The Chronicles of Freylar, I would greatly appreciate an online review from you on the Amazon store. You can also 'Become a Blade Aspirant' on the website and join the ranks of The Blades.

DRAMATIS PERSONAE

Ruling Council of Freylar
Gaelin, Farmstead Leader
Kirika 'Fate Weaver', Valkyrie
Larissa, Dressmaker
Lothnar, Paladin
Thandor, Paladin

The Blades
Klein, Blade Adept, Scout
Lazrik, Blade Master, Scout – Squad Leader
Leyla, Blade Adept
Natalya, Valkyrie
Nathanar, Paladin – Captain of The Blades
Nathaniel 'The Teacher', Blade Master
Rayna 'The Guardian', Valkyrie
Saralia, Blade Mistress, Scout – Squad Leader
Yandar, Blade Master, Scout – Squad Leader
Zealia, Blade Adept

Knights Thranis
Heldran, Knight Lord
Xenia, Knight

Deceased Freylarkai
Alarielle, Blade Adept
Aleska, Retired Valkyrie
Caleth, Blade Lord
Krashnar
Lileah
Marcus 'The Blade Lord', Paladin –
Commander of The Blades
Ragnar, Paladin –
Captain of The Blades

Civilian Freylarkai
Darlia
Kayla, Administrative Aide
Lyra
Rarni

Exiled Freylarkai
Mirielle, Former Queen

Soulmancers
T'mohr

Dire Wolves
Krisis

Orders
Knights Thranis
The Blades

Races

Freylarkai

Louperdu

Narlakai

Septlari

Soulmancers

Humans

Anastacia, Practice Manager

Callum 'Fox'

Dylan

Ezra

Jacob

Kaitlin Delarouse

Kristen

Kyle

Ryan

Sebastian

The Director